A
RHYS
U AM
G P L
HES E
R

"Rhys Hughes seems almost the sum of our planet's literature. He toys with convention. He makes the metaphysical political, the personal incredible and the comic hints at subtle pain. Few living fictioneers approach this chef's sardonic confections, certainly not in English." — MICHAEL MOORCOCK

"If I said he was a Welsh writer who writes as though he has gone to school with the best writing from all over the world, I wonder if my compliment would just sound provincial. Hughes' style, with all that means, is among the most beautiful I've encountered in several years." — SAMUEL R. DELANY

"It's a crime that Rhys Hughes is not as widely known as Italo Calvino and other writers of that stature. Brilliantly written and conceived, Hughes' fiction has few parallels anywhere in the world. In some alternate universe with a better sense of justice, his work triumphantly parades across all bestseller lists." — JEFF VANDERMEER

"Every Hughes story implies much, served with wit and whimsy and word-relish, high spirits and bittersweet twists." — IAN WATSON

"A dazzling disintegration of the reality principle. A rite of passage to the greater world beyond common sense. Raises the bar on profundity and sets a comic standard for the tragic limits of our human experience. Like Beckett on nitrous oxide. Like Kafka with a brighter sense of humour." — A.A. ATTANASIO

"I wore throughout the undisplaceable, unsequelchable rictus of a grin of both delight and amazement." — MICHAEL BISHOP

"Hughes' world is a magical one, and his language is the most magical thing of all." — T.E.D. KLEIN

A RHYS HUGHES SAMPLER

(Selected Weird Stories 1993-2020)

RHYS HUGHES

Gloomy Seahorse Press

ISBN-9798579097057

Gloomy Seahorse Press
http://rhyshughes.blogspot.com

Contents

This book
of stories is dedicated to
Maithreyi Karnoor

THE FOREST CHAPEL BELL

As Bishop of Debauchester, my duties included adding the final touches to our great cathedral. Twelve generations of labourers had toiled under an angry sun to construct the most astonishing edifice in the whole land. Their bones, ground to dust, had been mixed with their blood to form the cement that held stone to stone.

And now all that remained was to cast a suitable bell for the belfry. I had a very definite idea as to what such a bell should sound like. Any note it might strike would have to take into account the character of the building. For me, the cathedral stood out as a beacon of hope in our ravaged city.

Naturally, the local forges were unable to produce such a bell. The craftsmen of Debauchester were no longer equal to the task. Their Guilds had grown surly and incompetent. A sign of the times, no doubt. It was obvious that I would have to seek elsewhere. I would have to take to the road.

Accordingly, on the first day of spring, I set off with an armed retinue and unlimited Church funds at my disposal. I was fairly confident my quest would not be futile. This land is large enough to accommodate all manner of fantastic and improbable things. All dreams and nightmares can take form here; we live in the dusk between ecstasy and terror.

Our first stop was the neighbouring city of Bismal. The wary inhabitants of this town had sought to avoid the plague by locking their gates to most visitors. Instead, they had shut it in. I bribed my way past the guards and towards the famed smiths of Iron Street, a cobbled alleyway choking with fumes and resounding with the clang of hammer on anvil.

Here, we found many willing to help us but few capable of keeping their promises. At the sign of the Black Orchid, a sweaty smith claimed to have just the bell we were looking for. He led us into a room empty save for an enormous mass of metal that hung suspended from a stout wooden cage. He tapped his nose with a grimy finger and rolled his bulging eyes.

"This is a very special bell," he said. "It is a bell that only the most cultured and intelligent members of society can hear. To fools it remains silent." Wiping his palms on his leather jerkin, he took hold of the bell-rope and pulled with all his strength. The bell swung in a ponderous arc, rattling its wooden frame and casting a monstrous shadow over the wall in the flickering torchlight.

"Remember what I said about fools..." Nonchalantly, he stepped back and leant against the door-jamb. The soldiers in my company nodded at each other and closed their eyes in rapture.

"Such a sweet tone!" they cried. "Such a pure note! This is the bell for us! Our quest is over. Let us take this one!"

"Very well," I agreed, stepping towards the smith. "I have this for you in return." As the fellow bowed in gratitude, my hand moved from my purse to my sword. With a single blow I sent his head rolling into a dark corner. Blood gouted purple on the walls. The body swayed and toppled in a heap, hands clasping cold stone.

"Come." I sheathed my sword while the bell hissed its contempt overhead. "Let us leave this pit to the rats. There is work to be done."

As we rode back out through the gates and left the city behind, I explained myself to my companions. "The bell was unfinished," I said. "It had no clapper. It is an old, old story." I was generous enough not to laugh at their embarrassment, but I would not forgive their cowardice.

Thus began the first misadventure of many. We travelled the length of the land and listened to a great number of bells. Yet I was never satisfied. As I have already said, I had an exact idea of the note I desired. I removed the heads of all those who tried to cheat me and a few who did not. I pushed my companions to ever greater feats of endurance.

In the middle of the Aching Desert, we chanced upon the monastery of Soor. The plague had spread its wings even here. The Abbot listened gravely to my request and then arched an eyebrow. He was a thin hollow man, a scarecrow in which the crows had made their nests. His idols were Grunnt and Drigg and the one legged god, Hopp.

"You have come to the right place," he croaked. "We have suffered much lately. It is difficult to get the staff these days." With an obscene chuckle, he gestured at his neck. The black boils of death were already swelling. "But you are in luck. We have just such a bell."

"Really? Then I demand to hear it!" I jangled the coins in my purse with one hand while I raised a perfumed handkerchief to my mouth with the other. My voice came as a muffled sob. "Perhaps three hundred gold coins will help to ease your passage to the other world?"

"Oh, considerably!" He threw back his head and howled. "Stand out there in the courtyard. It is almost time for matins. We have little to give us hope here. The bell will not be our salvation, but it might deceive some of us for long enough."

We moved through a low arch into a courtyard. The fountains had dried up; sand drifted across the flagstones. As the sun rose over the horizon, the bell began to toll. The sound was a sensual hand that crept up the spine to massage the neck but from the inside. I shuddered under my ermine cloak. Tears burned the edge of my eyelids. When the final echo had dissipated, I stalked back to the Abbot. Like my own men, he was writhing on the floor, his eyes full of joy. Once again, I moved my hand to my purse and then, frowning, further across to my sword. I did not have the strength to hack at his sinewy neck, however.

The bell had sapped my anger. Placing the point in the centre of his throat, in the centre of a pulsating boil, I leant with all my weight on the hilt. His blood was too thin to spurt, but as I wrenched my weapon free, it stained his saffron robe a pale, anaemic orange. I collapsed in delicious agony as the final echo of the bell returned on a sudden desert breeze to sing against my blade.

Afterwards, when we had all recovered, we slaughtered the rest of the heathen monks and set fire to that hive of corruption. "The sound was far too pleasurable," I explained, as we raced off into the Aching Desert. "Not at all appropriate for our purposes. Our city may be a symbol of decadence, but our cathedral most certainly is not. It is our one redeeming feature."

Such were the words I used to encourage my men to further acts of self-sacrifice. They were quite ignorant, of course, of the sort of bell I really wanted to hear. Before I could confess the truth, I had to be sure of their loyalty. No doubt, they saw the cathedral as an object of beauty and considered a beautiful bell ideal. But this is not what I meant when I said that the right sound would have to take into account the character of the building.

Onwards we journeyed, ever onwards, across a decimated landscape foul with the stench of rotting flesh. My ecclesiastical robes fell to tatters; my mitre crumpled on my head. Our mounts collapsed beneath us, rolling onto their backs and kicking legs in the air like dying locusts. Yet my confidence remained overwhelming. I am a hard man to discourage.

Slowly, as the months turned to years, and we grew more and more exhausted, this overwhelming confidence began to falter. My companions eventually deserted or, contracting the dread plague, had to be abandoned by the roadside. At long last, I too caught the illness, the boils spreading from my hand until my entire arm and chest was a mass of suppurating sores, bleeding yellow pus down my shrunken flapping stomach to my maggoty loins.

And then one evening, after I had wandered off the road into a dank tangled forest, I came into a clearing. In the centre of this clearing stood a small stone chapel whose windows had fallen out and shattered on the hard ground. Creeping plants and gaudy flowers now grew over the spaces, forming an adequate substitute for the stained glass, while on the grass verges, fragments of the originals wholly competed with the glow-worms.

Staggering to the heavy door, I pounded on the oak. Organ music piped from inside. A ghostly whispering rustled on the edge of harmony. After an age, bolts were drawn back and a shrivelled figure peered from the rosy gloom. Froth dribbled down its chin. Its eyes darted an amused and questioning glance.

"My name is Dorian Wormwood," I said. "Bishop of Debauchester. Plague has brought as unexpected an end to my revels as I have to yours. Yet I wish to complete my quest before I die. I require a bell whose note will do justice to my great cathedral and all it stands for."

"Indeed?" The shrivelled figure rubbed its hands together, all four of them. "But what exactly does your cathedral stand for? How am I to know that it stands for anything? You are far from home, stranger."

I rotated a knuckle in a cloudy eye. "I am very tired. I am too ill to argue. My city is a festering pit. My cathedral is a beacon of hope. What, then, is to be done? Is it not obvious? This cathedral is a blot on my soul, a stain that must be removed. I have heard that all things have a resonant frequency. I once saw a singer shatter a glass. I need a bell whose note will destroy the very cathedral it is housed in."

The figure smiled. "Have you noticed how the graves in my little cemetery are all open?" He pointed at the decaying headstones and weed-choked pits that ringed the chapel. "Their inhabitants now form my parishioners. I do not have the bell you seek. But I have one even more remarkable. You will see. But now you must rest." He led me into the nave, past rows of swaying ghouls, towards the altar, where a coffin lay waiting.

"We appreciate visitors," he said, "though not in the way you think. Sleep now and all will be revealed. Yes, sleep." He threw the lid of the coffin back and pointed at the crushed velvet interior. I was grateful enough to lie down and let the dark thumbs of death press on my eyeballs. My mind soared into the vast reaches of space.

In the morning, I was dragged back into my reluctant body. Sinews and muscles screamed their protest. I knew at once what had summoned me. I fingered the mass of black boils on my chest and sat up. The flesh peeled away in one large sheet, revealing thorax and ribcage. High above, in the half-ruined belfry, my host was swinging from the bell.

He greeted me with a mock salute as I struggled out of my coffin. "You have wandered into the borderland between your own world and Hell," he hissed. "And you have died. The plague, as you know, spares few. Yet you have seen my power over nature. This bell, needless to say, is one that can wake the dead. It has always been my favourite cliché."

I fingered my chest again, reached into the gaping hole and felt that my heart was still. When he came down to join me, my hand reached for my sword, quivered, and then snatched the purse off my belt. I threw him the coins and began to laugh. My dead eyes were bright.

"This is exactly the bell I want!" I cried. "Have it taken down and bound to suitable transport. I wish also to hire some of your parishioners to help me convey it back to Debauchester." I grimaced. The decaying corpses in question were shuffling in for the morning service.

The figure scratched its head. "I thought you wanted a bell whose note would make your cathedral collapse. Not one that can wake the dead!"

"Is it not for sale?" I knitted my brows.

"Of course it is! Is not everything in this Universe?" He shrugged. "I am a very minor demon. I will ask no more questions."

"That is wise." Slavering, I slapped him on the back and belched. The belch left my stomach through my wondrous hole. I was beginning to grow proud of my exposed organs. They were so diseased they were a delight to behold.

Later, sitting atop a covered wagon, flicking a whip over each gibbering corpse who wrestled to pull the load in its harness, I peered down at my prize. At last I would be able to fulfil my duties as Bishop. At last I would be able to add the finishing touches to our great cathedral. Here was the bell whose note would cause the entire mass to topple onto the heads of my fellow citizens.

Not directly, through resonant frequency, but indirectly. After all, a bell that could wake the dead would surely have the same effect on a building whose stones were held together by a cement made from...

Well, bones and blood, of course.

IN THE MARGINS

At the bottom of our garden lies a pond, ringed by gnarled and ugly trees, and at the bottom of the pond lies a cottage. The waters swirl around the crumbling stones in little spirals, foaming over the ruined chimney as if reluctant to press in too close. In the troubled mirror of this pond, the cottage stands tangled in the reflection of the trees, netted in their twisted branches as if it had been lodged there by an unnatural gust of wind.

How the cottage came to reside under the waters of our pond remains a mystery. Is there any truth in the assertion that a witch caused it to subside by slow degrees for arcane and unfathomable reasons? And if so, who was this witch? There are no records to shed any light on the matter; there is only conjecture and speculation. I, for one, prefer this ingenuous explanation to those suggested by the more prosaic members of our community. I refuse to accept that it was built there, in its present location, as some sort of liquid joke.

Not that this would have presented any problems to the patient trickster. The pond could have been drained easily enough, the cottage constructed and then the water pumped back in. But the sheer obscurity of the joke causes me to frown and make many a harsh grimace when I consider this option.

Instead, I often languish by the side of the pond, peering down into the depths, and repeat the word "subsidence" as if it were a mantra. A slow subsidence, as slow as the growth of a dead man's fingernails or the twisted trees themselves, would have sufficed to preserve the cottage intact in its descent. No beams would have been shaken loose, no thread of thatch unravelled. They rot now, it is true, but such decay is quite a different matter.

One evening, taking some kittens to the side of the pond, to save them from the knife of my brother, I witnessed a peculiar and disturbing sight. No sooner had I tied the little weights around their necks and dropped them one by one, like depth-charges, into the glinting water, than an unusual commotion began far below.

I am not a superstitious being by nature, but my senses are keen, and so, not wishing to waste an opportunity to initiate gossip, I threw myself to the ground and, ducking my head into the icy water, strained my eyes to discern the origin of the turbulence.

A second later, I regretted my decision. As my eyes adjusted to the gloom, I perceived a tiny man standing at the door of the cottage. He was holding a large net on the end of a pole. Such nets were familiar to me: I had spent many happy hours on the moors with an identical net, collecting moon-moths to be ground into powder in the apothecary's shop. I had developed a certain skill in utilising my net; a skill not shared by my aquatic counterpart far below.

Gasping and wheezing, he aimed the net at the kittens that floated down past him. His frantic motions were the source of the disturbance. He utterly failed in catching a single specimen. The kittens struck the bottom of the pond and disappeared into the sinuous weeds. Bubbles erupted from each mossy collision. The tiny man shook his fists and snapped the pole of the net over his knee. Then he threw the pieces away and pulled his hair in a parody of rage. The pieces floated up towards me and broke the surface tension of the pond inches from my face.

While I was questioning my sanity, and just a moment before I could bear the noxious waters no longer, the angry homunculus chanced to gaze high above and spotted me looking down. The expression on his face must have mirrored my own. We were both paralysed with astonishment. For long moments, our eyes were meshed together by fibres of emotion impossible to understand. And then he darted back into his cottage and returned with an equally tiny woman. I assumed that she was his wife. He pointed up at the sky and together they gaped at me.

Panting, I pulled my head out of the pond and took a long deep gulp of air. I resisted the temptation to take another look at the submerged cottage. I had decided that I was suffering from a form of madness or delirium. I resolved to forget the experience and make an appointment with a doctor as soon as possible. I left the pond and made my way slowly back up the garden-path to my house.

14

Yet as I walked, I started wondering again about the peculiar sight I had just witnessed. Supposing that I was not mad? Supposing that the phenomena had been real? I had heard many stories about falls of strange objects from the sky. There had been reports of fish, ice, betel nuts, coins, worms, eels, snails, snakes and frogs. This last item on the list made me shudder. I repressed this shudder and stroked my chin. Such objects were supposed to orbit the world in an eldritch region in the sky before falling. A region that lay in the margins of reality.

If this was true, then it was possible that I was living in such a twilight realm myself and had been the cause of a strange shower in another world. The tiny man had obviously been trying to collect one of the falling kittens as proof of his bizarre experience. Probably he would have as much difficulty convincing his neighbours and friends of my existence as I would have convincing my own neighbours and friends of his. I decided to say nothing and to resume my mundane life without ever mentioning even the submerged cottage again.

As I approached the door of my house, I heard a thud behind me. I looked over my shoulder and saw the body of a tiny man slumped in the bushes. I thought at first that my diminutive neighbour had tried to follow me and had drowned in the air. But then another body fell into another clump of bushes and I looked up. The sky was full of little men sliding through the atmosphere with weights tied to their feet. And higher still, to my complete amazement, the face of an enormous kitten gazed down at me with eyes the size of seas.

My first reaction was to rush into my house and return with my wife, so that there would be at least one other witness to this miracle. However, it occurred to me that if I could simply catch one of the tiny men alive it would be evidence enough. I had no nets, but I could use the old-fashioned method. I had a sudden ludicrous image of a host of different dimensions impinging on each other, kittens hurling down men, men hurling down snakes, snakes hurling down frogs and frogs hurling down kittens...

I called out to my wife and then opened my mouth wider. My long sticky tongue snatched the little men from the air before they hit

15

the ground and I stacked them in a little pile by my side. Naturally I swallowed a few. Life in the margins of reality does seem to have its advantages. It is not every day that guests just drop in for dinner.

THREE FRIENDS

The three friends were mountain climbers who had trekked to the roof of the world. They had encountered many dangers on the way and each had taken a turn to plunge down a crevasse. Bound together by ropes as well as friendship, it seemed they had all escaped death by the narrowest of margins. One by one, they had praised their luck and had agreed that teamwork was wonderful.

After the end of one particularly difficult day, as the crimson sun impaled itself on the needle peaks of the horizon, the three friends set up their tent on a narrow ledge. The first friend, who had survived the first crevasse, boiled tea on his portable stove and lit his pipe. Stretching his legs out as far as the ledge would allow, he blew a smoke ring and said:

"The wind whistles past this mountain like the voice of a ghost, shrill as dead leaves. The icy rock feels like the hand of a very aged corpse. Those lonely clouds far away have taken the form of winged demons. Everything reminds me of the region beyond the grave. I suggest that we all tell ghost stories, to pass the time. I shall go first, if you like."

Huddling closer to the stove, the first friend peered at the other two with eyes like black sequins. "This happened to me a long time ago. I was climbing in Austria and had rented a small hunting lodge high in the mountains. Unfortunately, I managed to break my leg on my very first climb and had to rest in the lodge until a doctor could be summoned. Because of a freak snowstorm that same evening, it turned out that I was stuck for a whole week. The lodge had only one bed. My guide, a local climber, slept on the floor.

16

"Every night, as my fever grew worse, I would ask my guide to fetch me a drink of water from the well outside the lodge. He always seemed reluctant to do this, but would eventually return with a jug of red wine. I was far too delirious to wonder at this, and always drank the contents right down. At the end of the week, when my fever broke, I asked him why he gave me wine rather than water from the well. Shuddering, he replied that the 'wine' had come from the well. I afterwards learned that the original owner of the lodge had cut his wife's throat and had disposed of her body in the obvious way..."

The first friend shrugged and admitted that his was a very inconclusive sort of ghost tale, but insisted that it was true nonetheless. He sucked on his pipe and poured three mugs of tea. Far below, the last avalanche of the day rumbled through the twilight. The second friend, who had survived the second crevasse, accepted a mug and nodded solemnly to himself. He seemed completely wrapped up in his own thoughts. Finally, he said:

"I too have a ghost story, and mine is true as well. It happened when I was a student in London. I lived in a house where another student had bled to death after cutting off his fingers in his heroic attempt to make his very first cucumber sandwich. I kept finding the fingers in the most unlikely places. They turned up in the fridge, in the bed, even in the pockets of my trousers. One evening, my girlfriend started giggling. We were sitting on the sofa listening to music and I asked her what was wrong. She replied that I ought to stop tickling her. Needless to say, my hands were on my lap.

"I consulted all sorts of people to help me with the problem. One kindly old priest came to exorcise the house. I set up mousetraps in the kitchen. But nothing seemed to work. The fingers kept appearing on the carpet, behind books on the bookshelf, in my soup. I grew more and more despondent and reluctantly considered moving. Suddenly, in a dream, the solution came to me. It was a neat solution, and it worked. It was very simple, actually. I bought a cat..."

The second friend smiled and sipped his tea. Both he and the first friend gazed across at the third friend. The third friend seemed remote and abstracted. He stared out into the limitless dark. In the light from the stove, he appeared pale and unhealthy. He refused the mug that the first friend offered him.

The first two friends urged him to tell a tale, but he shook his head. "Come on," they said, "you must have at least one ghost story to tell. Everybody has at least one." With a deep, heavy sigh, the third friend finally confessed that he did. The first two friends rubbed their hands in delight. They insisted, however, that it had to be true.

"Oh, it's true all right," replied the third friend, "and it's easily told. But you might regret hearing it. Especially when you consider that we are stuck on this ledge together for the rest of the night." When the first two friends laughed at this, he raised a hand for silence and began to speak. His words should have been as cold as a glacier and as ponderous, but instead they were casual and tinged with a trace of irony. He said simply:

"I didn't survive the third crevasse."

THE DUVET THIEF

An elaborate oak-panelled study with a leather couch. Dr Kennedy was a traditional therapist. The tools of his trade lay at strategic points about the room. Pendulums, tape-recorders, the complete works of Jung. On a battered old record-player, a disc etched with an hypnotic spiral revolved endlessly, a series of mirrors reflecting the resulting mandala to a screen positioned just above the patient's head.

The patient at this particular moment in time was a thin, nervous-looking man who had entered the study with stubble and a drooping cigarette obscuring his trembling chin. He had taken to the couch with as much enthusiasm as a pearl leaves its oyster. Dr Kennedy had frowned in a thoroughly professional way, pulled at his famous Swiss-style beard and clicked his tongue a dozen times, like a bat determining the range of a mosquito supper.

"Paul Artichoke?" Dr Kennedy looked at the list his secretary had handed him earlier. He was used to his clients hiding their embarrassment under names so ill-fitting that they were obviously pseudonyms. But this one was ridiculous enough to be genuine. "May I call you... Paul?"

"Call me anything you like." Paul glanced suspiciously around the study. Portraits of the great psychiatrists hung all over the wall behind Dr Kennedy's chair. Someone had drawn a beard on the one of R.D. Laing, and stuffed a fat Havana cigar between his ascetic lips, both with a blue felt-tip pen, as if to bring this maverick back into the arms of orthodoxy.

"Wasn't he the one who said that schizophrenia was a sane reaction to an insane world?" Paul indicated the mutilated portrait. "He was quite popular when I was young."

"And quite wrong." Dr Kennedy smiled, but his eyes blazed with repressed fury. "It is not a reaction to any such thing. It is to do with the desire of the individual to assuage the guilt felt after indulging in various sexual fantasies directed at a mother/sister figure. But is this what you have come about? Schizophrenia?"

"No." Paul shook his head. "No, I have come about a more trivial problem. Trivial at the moment, that is. Actually, I have come about my wife."

"So your wife is insane? I thought as much. But I don't know what I can do for her. We might as well face facts. She will have to come in alone. The treatment might involve some physical activities. Release of sexual inhibitions, that sort of thing. Is she good-looking?"

Paul waved Dr Kennedy to silence. "My wife is not mad. No, my problem is something else entirely. It concerns our sleeping arrangements."

"Of course. Sex is always the key. She is frigid, eh? Perhaps she is attracted to other women? They sometimes let you watch, you know..."

19

Now it was Paul's turn to frown. "I don't think you understand. It has nothing to do with sex. Nothing at all. It's to do with the duvet we sleep under."

"Perhaps you should try mechanical aids. Vibrating apparatus and suchlike. And be sure to give me a full report. A few photographs as well..."

"I don't think you're listening, doctor. Our sex-life is fine. I'm talking about the duvet we use to keep warm. We have a king-size bed and the duvet in question is a large one. But in the middle of the night my wife keeps rolling over. The duvet ends up entirely on her side and I am left out in the cold."

"Have you tried lubricating fluids?"

Paul sighed and propped himself up on his elbows. "Do I have to spell it out for you? I'm not talking about sex. We have no problems with that side of our marriage. What I'm trying to get through to you is the fact that every night, in the early hours before dawn, I wake up shivering. I look across in the gloom and see my wife snuggled up tight in the duvet. But the duvet is meant for both of us. I've tried talking to her, but it's no use. Every night the same thing happens."

"Perhaps she should leave you for a more virile man..."

Paul was exasperated. He swung his legs over the side of the couch and stood up. "Well I never expected this, you can be sure. I thought that you people were supposed to be sympathetic and helpful!"

Dr Kennedy grew anxious. He could see money slipping away between his clubbed fingers. "Don't go! I was only joking. Part of the cure, you see. Don't worry. Have a cigar? I'm quite a respected figure, you know. I've met lots of rich people. Now what were you saying? Your wife is a nymphomaniac? Was that it?"

"No, no, no!" Paul screamed and waved his fists in the air. Dr Kennedy nodded, tugged at his beard again and took out a little notebook. He wrote the words PSYCHOPATHIC TENDENCIES on the crisp white paper and picked his nose.

"Listen," said Paul, with admirable restraint. "I have a wife whom I adore. Every night we make passionate love. We are both perfectly

20

normal in that respect. Afterwards we fall asleep together. In the middle of the night, I wake up and discover that the duvet is wrapped around my wife and that I am exposed to the chills of the night. She is oblivious of this fact. I am cold. I hate being cold."

"You are impotent then?"

Paul had been pushed beyond anger. His voice was very calm as he replied to Dr Kennedy. His breathing was as regular as that of the sea before a typhoon. "My one complaint in life is the fact that my wife always seems to steal the duvet. It is possible, however, that I might shortly add another to the list."

"Ah yes, the duvet!" Dr Kennedy lowered his eyes. "Please forgive me. I have not been feeling well lately. Perhaps I need to talk to someone about my troubles? Anyway, please continue. Your wife keeps taking the duvet, you say? How does this make you feel?"

"Cold," replied Paul.

"Not resentful? Or bitter? Or twisted?" Dr Kennedy's eyes sparkled once more. "Do you not want to smother her in her sleep? Or slip a knife between her ribs?"

"Certainly not!" cried Paul. "It wouldn't be feasible anyway. For the last time, let me explain. My wife is a duvet thief. She steals the duvet in the middle of the night. When she steals the duvet I am left without any cover. I begin to shiver. I find it very difficult to fall asleep again. In the mornings I am always tired."

Dr Kennedy scratched his overlong forehead and studied Paul carefully through his little round glasses. He sighed deeply and shook his head. "Is that all? In that case, I think that you have been wasting my time. You tell me that talking to her is no use? Why don't you ask one of her friends to have a word with her?"

"She hasn't got any. Listen, doctor, it may sound like an absurd problem to you, but it's wearing me down physically and mentally. I desperately need your help!"

Dr Kennedy removed his glasses and rubbed his tired eyes. "I see. Well then, the only thing I can suggest is that you bring her to me and I'll try to reason with her."

"Oh no, I couldn't do that!"

"Why not?" Dr Kennedy yawned and blew his nose in a green handkerchief. "What reason could you have for not bringing her in?"

Paul grimaced and a tear trickled down his cheek.

"She's been dead for eight years."

TROMBONHOMIE

When my neighbour plays the amplified trombone it means another sleepless night. But I don't sleep anyway, so perhaps it doesn't matter. I don't sleep because my neighbour plays the amplified trombone.

I also play the amplified trombone. I play the amplified trombone to annoy my neighbour for keeping me awake. I slide the notes like fish through my windows, beyond the trees, higher than the rising moon. I play blue notes and purple passages and make the house shudder.

I once considered killing my neighbour. But I knew what this would entail. I would have to pack a bag with provisions and sling it over my shoulder. My other shoulder would be in a sling. My sling would be at my belt, my stones in a pocket. Journeys last longer than pockets; stones longer than journeys. So I would leave with a pebble-smooth chin and before I was close it would be as prickly as a pear. My neighbour lives far away. That is why I play an amplified trombone to annoy him. If I played an ordinary trombone he would not be annoyed. He would probably fall asleep and then I would have no reason to play any sort of trombone. And I am getting good now. I need the practice.

At any rate, if I ever reached his house I would look very foolish. I would have to knock on his door and say, "excuse me, but your amplified trombone is keeping me awake," and he would look me up and down with his sombre eyes (but no, really, what would his eyes look like? The eyes of an amplified trombone player are always sad, must be) and his reply would be, "I'm awfully sorry, but I play the amplified trombone because my neighbour does," and I would say, "I am that neighbour," and he would shake his head and answer, "by your appearance you come from the lands of the west and my neighbour lives in the east," and I would say, "you mean your other neighbour?" and he would nod and I would bow a retreat and be unable to knock on his door a second time.

And then he would return to his amplified trombone playing with renewed vigour. And I would have to feel a sort of sympathy for him. And reaching into my pocket to cast away my stones, I would find that they had already escaped through a hole.

So I would have to look beyond the immediate problem. I would have to consider killing his other neighbour, the one that lives in the east. There would be no other option. What other option would there be? So I would pack a bag with provisions and sling it over my shoulder, etc. I would whistle a callow tune and fill my pocket with fresh stones. Not the pocket with a hole in it, but my other pocket.

And I would travel for many weeks, down dark and winding forest paths where monstrous orchids dipped their anaemic heads at my passing. And finally I would reach the house of my neighbour's other neighbour and I would knock loudly on the door and make a fool of myself again. I would say, "excuse me, but your amplified trombone is keeping my neighbour awake," and the figure who would appear would scratch a warty nose and reply, "but it was my neighbour who started it," and I would raise my hands in an exasperated gesture and say, "well he never mentioned that to me," and he would gaze at me doubtfully and remark, "you look to me as if you have just travelled through the forests of the west and my neighbour lives in the east," and then I would understand that he too was referring to his other neighbour.

So I would have to bid him farewell, refusing his kind offer of a cup of blue-green tea, and go on my way in a kind of light-hearted despair. And this would go on and on (imagine, if you will, sixteen thousand similar encounters, variations without the theme) until I was sick and beyond redemption. And strange and subtle things would start to happen, so subtle that they would be almost unnoticeable. Language would begin to change, until I found myself in a completely alien country. But as I pressed further eastwards, it would come back into focus. And one day, I would eventually find a man whose neighbour did not play the amplified trombone and I would ask, "why is this the case?" and the man would explain, "he used to play, but he has not sounded a note for over a year now," and racing onwards to greet this man who had given up playing the amplified trombone, I would discover that it was myself.

No, I don't want to take that course of action. I would rather stay at home and have to contend with my neighbour blowing those infernal lines on his amplified trombone. I would rather slide my notes like fish, pace my darkened room, anger my heart with coffee and cheap cigarettes. The rising moon rests like a steady flame on the wick of my bedside candle. I bury my head under the pillow; a premature burial because I am still breathing, crying out for release. If I could connect an amplifier to the moon as it changed gear over the horizon, I would have a celestial revenge indeed. But I do not possess the necessary skills.

One evening, while we are both playing for all we are worth, a curious thing happens. Our widely diverging melodies form a compelling harmony. The time lag has been taken into account, his preference for atonality also. But suddenly we are playing together, an unearthly counterpoint, a music whose sum is far greater than its parts. For the first time, we have made a sort of contact with each other; it is as if we are sitting in the same room, at the same inglenook, warming our boots before the fire, tapping the stems of our Churchwarden pipes against our teeth; the hearth of our hearts. For the first time, I bless the technology that can amplify trombones.

Our duet continues throughout the night. The wind rises up from the distant sea and the clouds scud across the milky sky, entangling themselves in the branches of the highest trees. The grass picks up our refrain, each slippery blade an Aeolian harp. I no longer hate my neighbour; I almost love him instead and resolve to make the arduous journey to his home as a gesture of friendship. But there is

24

little need. Why make a gesture of friendship to the man or woman you are already embracing?

When the moon sinks down over the opposite horizon, and the sun spreads its orange nets once more, we end with a remote and beautiful chord. I sink exhausted back onto my bed and sleep the sleep of the satiated. I know that I will never be able to play another note on the amplified trombone. I will have to dismantle my instrument and create something new from the brassy tubes. All this applies in equal measure to my neighbour. So what will we make from our throaty monsters? How will we pick over the trombones of civilisation?

When my neighbour plays the amplified triangle it means another sleepless night. But I don't sleep anyway, so perhaps it doesn't matter. I don't sleep because my neighbour plays the amplified triangle.

THE URBAN FRECKLE

Oscar Wildebeest threw down his pencil, raised his mug of *yerba mate* to his lips and skimmed the steam off with his stale breath. He had finally finished the designs; the new Capital had been worked out to its very privates. There would be no secrets in this most tortured of cities that he was not already aware of, no hiding places for lovers.

He could imagine them now, reclining on balconies that had not yet been built, chasing each other in the shadows of the colonnades (her garment has unwound around his fingers, skin as white as the capstones of the New Pyramids) and possibly swimming in the fountains during the dog days. He had prepared the citadels one by one. The main square resembled a giant chessboard; ministers scurrying from one government department to another would be the pawns.

Oscar fanned himself with one of the outsized sheets of paper and felt the moisture burn the lines around his eyes. It had taken nearly three whole days to sketch the new limits of wonder; the details had taken rather longer. What height exactly for the Ziggurats? And the New Hanging Gardens? How much water to be pumped daily to the orchids that curved like moonbows, flowers as inviting and heady as a scented yoni? He had consulted the *I Ching* on these matters, of course, but the final decision had been his responsibility.

He finished his *yerba mate* and filled his battered pipe. The design had yet to be approved by President Jodorowsky, but he felt confident enough. Indeed his worries were much more abstract things: what would the general public think of a city shaped like a human face? He sighed and sealed the papers in a large envelope lying on his desk and then rang for a messenger to come and collect it. He lit his pipe and watched as the blue smoke was sucked up in the turbulence of the electric fan.

The messenger was a squat civil servant of Indian descent. He picked up the envelope and marched off with it. Oscar yawned, stretched himself, stood up and pushed back his chair. Then he left his office and caught a taxi back to his house. He lived in the suburbs, on the outskirts of Asuncion, in a blue villa. He made himself another mug of *yerba mate* and dozed the afternoon away, awaking to the smell of freshly baked tortilla which Maria, his maid, was cooking for his dinner.

He ate in front of the television, with a bottle of imported Finnish vodka and a Dutch cheese by his elbow. The television crackled and hissed and then the solemn moustachioed face of President Karl Lopez Jodorowsky appeared in front of the national flag.

"Fellow patriots, citizens of Paraguay," he began. "Today is a glorious day for our little nation. At last we are going to build a capital that will rival the greatest cities of the world. Despite the doubts and mockery of other governments, we are now prepared to invest the funds necessary to complete such a venture. We have employed one of the most skilled architects on the continent to design the city and he has today announced the completion of his plans. I have them here in my hands. Construction will begin immediately!"

Oscar poured himself a glass of spirits and settled back to watch the rest of the broadcast. The President seemed excited; he garbled his words and made extravagant gestures. Oscar smiled at his naivety; as if he could really believe that idealism could change anything. Oscar was beyond such ingenuousness; he was a cynic.

"Our new city — Paraguayia — will be the envy of not only the cities of our neighbours but also the cities of the old world," the President was saying. "Buenos Aires, Montevideo and Brasilia, Sao Paulo and Rio, Santiago and Lima, Bogota, Caracas and La Paz will knock their knees at our arrival; but so will the cultural hubs that straddle continents other than ours! London, Paris, New York and Tokyo will tremble before us; Rome, Shanghai and Moscow will seem like truly drab affairs after the completion of our metropolis. Rejoice citizens! For it is I, your President, who give you cause to be proud!"

Oscar sighed and snapped the television off. He still was unsure how the people would take to living in a city shaped like a face. Besides, the voice of President Jodorowsky was too hysterical to be kind on the eardrums. He decided that he needed a holiday. He stood up, moved to the globe that stood in the corner of his room, span it and stopped it with an outstretched finger. This would be his destination.

He spent a long year on Maui; long because the days were long and fine and bright and there was much coconut milk to drink and beaches to walk and warm seas to swim, and because the money he had earned designing the new capital of Paraguay meant that a long year was no harder on his purse than a short one.

One morning (this is how it must have been) he received a letter; from President Jodorowsky. The capital had been built and his presence was required at the ceremony that would bless the fresh megalopolis. There would be speeches and the usual rousing music, pumped on sousaphones and tinkled on glockenspiels with the flags waving in the breeze; an artificial breeze if need be. And there would

27

be a formal blessing from the Archbishop of Concepción, an immaculate worthy from a pristine town, huge mitre bobbing and tipping in the evening cool.

"Finished?" Oscar said to himself. "So soon?"

But he caught a plane to Asuncion (they stopped for an intolerable hour at Quito, where fat flies suck the humidity from your brow) and when the President greeted him, his face fell. Instead of a handshake, he was prodded in the ribs with the barrel of an automatic rifle and chauffeured away from the airport in a less than comfortable manner. He tried to protest, but his hands were knocked away by the dark-suited bodyguards. The President, who rode in the front of the car, turned his head and regarded Oscar through dark sunglasses. There was a bitter smile at the corners of his mouth.

Oscar Wildebeest, for all his cynicism, was frightened and he tried to make small talk, the way that a mouse makes small squeaks in the jaws of a cat; trying to forge an empathy that can never be forged, trying to lose a wind in a bottle that has no deposit, trying to catch the sun in a butterfly net. "Nice day," he said. "Where are we going?"

"Paraguayia," the President hissed. "Oh yes, the city of the golden noon! Your city as well as ours. It has been built, following your plans, and it is dying. The city is dying. You have made a fool of me and you have made a fool of our people."

"I don't understand," Oscar replied. But no one seemed ready to enlighten him. They drove on past scorched fields and tawny scrub. They drove through the outskirts of Asuncion and then higher into the hills along pockmarked roads and through dusty vineyards.

It was a long journey, a bumpy cramped day and Oscar's fear turned first to thirst, and then to utter boredom. Finally, they crested the brow of a small rise and coasted down towards a large plain. Before them, mighty skyscrapers peeled and crumbled.

"That is Paraguayia," the President remarked. "And it is sick. Look at it. Already it has fallen beyond repair. And do you know why? Have you any idea what has made it so ill?" He pointed a finger at the rows of damaged buildings. Strange unnatural swellings

28

made the road a hazardous prospect to venture down. Huge black stains covered the ground and the walls of buildings. Oscar blinked and shook his head.

"You designed it in the shape of a human face," the President continued, "and at first I thought that it was a good design. In the first few months, the city smiled. The people who lived in it were happy. They smiled along with the face. But the city had no cover from the sun beating down on it day after day. One morning, a local worker noticed a freckle in the centre of the main square. Every day this freckle grew larger. Soon it began to bleed. Do you now understand what I am trying to say?"

Oscar breathed heavily. His throat was suddenly full of not only his wildly beating heart, but also of his bilious liver. "Skin cancer? You're telling me that my city caught skin cancer?"

The President nodded. "Exactly." He wiped tears from his dark brown eyes. "And we left it too late before taking action! What fools we were! Yes, the city is dying. And there is nothing we can do about it. Except one thing. We can construct a monument to your folly."

"What sort of monument?" Oscar began to perspire. He had an inkling of what was going to happen; a terrible inkling. He started to tremble; a mighty tremble that began at his toes and spread its shaking fingers upwards to caress all of his body…

The President smiled again. He said:

"There are two pools in a ruined city; a city which was once the mightiest metropolis in the Southern Hemisphere. These pools once formed the eyes of the city, for the city was built in the shape of the human face. Seated in both these pools lies the reflection of a man. His name is Oscar Wildebeest. Here we see him at work, throwing down his pencil, raising his mug of *yerba mate* to his lips and skimming the steam off with his stale breath. But this is not the real Oscar; the real Oscar has been dead for a thousand years, killed by a single bullet wound.

"When the citizens of Paraguay feel the need to teach themselves the meaning of folly, they take themselves out to these pools and gaze at the image of this man. This image will never fade, as long as suns whirl and stars form webs of galaxies. Some people ask this question: how did this image get there in the first place? Others know the answer. They say: the last thing seen by a dying man is forever imprinted upon his retinas. The city is one dying man; you are the other."

Oscar looked up. His mouth made a single letter; a vowel and the first letter of his name. It was both an answer and a resignation. A resignation that had already been accepted.

Coughing fumes, they reached the chin of the city.

THE PURLOINED LIVER

Edgar said, "Purloin My Liver."

"I beg your pardon?" Annabel frowned and steered around the carcass of a sheep. Flies rose in a dark cloud.

"The village." Edgar folded the map and gestured at the collection of thatched cottages. "Purloin My Liver. An old market town. Stop in that pub and I'll buy you a drink."

Annabel assented and parked off the road. As she stepped out into bright sunshine, she gazed at the signpost that hung from the side of the building. "Odd name for a pub!"

Edgar shook his head. "We're in the sticks now. This is rural heritage." He followed her gaze upwards. "The Plucked Eyeball? Sounds rather quaint to me. I like it."

Annabel shrugged and followed him inside.

The bar was deserted and gloomy. The warped beams of the low ceiling forced them to crouch down to avoid striking their heads. "Anyone home?" Edgar cried.

The barman appeared from the cellar. "What'll it be?" He was a grotesque figure, obese and hunched, a meerschaum pipe in the shape of a screaming skull protruding from his mouth. His dirty moustaches drooped like dying vines. A single, bulging, working eye rolled endlessly in its socket; the other dangled loose on his cheek.

"What do you have on cask?" Edgar inquired mildly.

The barman rested his gnarled hands on the unlabelled pump-handles. "Leprous Pustule, Purple Haemorrhage, Garrotted Baby, Witch Burn, Eat My Cousin and Twisted Ear." He turned to another part of the bar. "This is Severed Torso, a sour cider. Bloodless Zombie is a pale ale."

"A pint of Twisted Ear please," said Edgar.

"Half a Severed Torso for me," added Annabel.

The barman drew the pints. "Travellers eh? Off to the Fair at Grind My Bones? Should be good this year. A wicker man stuffed with virgins. Reverend Cleaver grew them himself: real virgins!"

Edgar remained nonchalant. "Sounds fine." He knocked back his pint. "We'll give it a try." He seized Annabel's glass, drained that one as well and handed money over the counter. "Have one yourself."

"Very kind of you sir, don't mind if I do!" The barman poured a foul green mixture. "Crucified Toad. I brew this one myself." Instead of placing the glass to his lips, he held it under his cheek and lowered his prolapsed orbit into the murky depths. Once immersed, the eyeball took on a life of its own; it rose and fell in slow circles, refracted to hideous dimensions by the viscous fluid.

Outside again, Annabel smirked. "What an odd fellow!"

"Not at all; we're in Shropshire now," Edgar reminded her. "Look, sorry for hurrying you on. But I'd hate to miss that wicker man. These are real country ways! Cream teas and brutal prejudices!"

Annabel started the engine and pulled out onto the road. "What's so special about burning virgins? Why not teetotallers or bank-managers or poets? Why not travellers for that matter?"

Edgar chuckled softly. "It's just that virgins are flammable. Most other people aren't. It's like pebbles and coal." He consulted the map. "Grind My Bones is the next village along. Left at the fork."

"I see." Annabel turned a sharp left and followed the road between towering hedge-rows. Conditions grew steadily worse; the car began to bounce and shudder. She cleared her throat. "What did your pint taste like? Mine tasted like squeezed abdomen."

"I know." Edgar nodded to himself. "Mine was sort of waxy. Real ale, you see. None of that fizzy rubbish we get in the city." He leaned out of the window. "I can't see any wicker man. I can't hear any virgins screaming either. They do scream, don't they?"

"Perhaps they just whimper." Annabel cursed as the road became a mud track. They reached a dilapidated farm-house and saw it was a dead-end. "We must have come the wrong way."

"That's impossible. Stop the car and I'll ask directions." Edgar waited for Annabel to pull up and then jumped out of his seat. The front door of the farmhouse was covered in human hands nailed to the rotting wood. Edgar prised one of these hands loose and rapped on the door with it. Bolts slid back and a thin man peered out.

"Yes?" The man blinked at Edgar. His eyelids worked upwards; his eyes had obviously been put on upside-down.

"Is this Grind My Bones, or anywhere near it?" Edgar asked. "We're off to see virgins burn and smoulder."

The man sighed sympathetically. "This is Applaud My Death. You must have taken the wrong turning on the road." He squinted at the map Edgar offered him. "Oh no, you don't want to be trusting them old things. The men who draw them are liars."

"Really?" Edgar rubbed his jaw.

"Besides," the thin man continued, "you'll be lucky to see anything roast today. The wicker man's been cancelled. Reverend Cleaver's virgins all caught the pox and died. He hasn't been able to rustle up any more. Why do you think I'm at home?"

A sudden idea struck Edgar. He whispered something to the thin man. The emaciated fellow chuckled and rubbed his palms together. "In that case you'd better come in and have a bite to eat. I've got some Minced Grandmother in the pantry, or you can have Basted Forehead."

"What the traditional local dish?" Edgar asked.

32

"Shepherd's Pie with vegetables. Real shepherds: crook, smock and dog. Watch the splinters. The vegetables are brain-dead poachers. Or you can have Poacher's Pie with brain-dead shepherds."

Edgar walked to the car and returned with Annabel. They followed the thin man into the interior of the farm-house. They sat down at a table in the kitchen while their host rattled pots and pans over the stove. "This is real living!" Edgar enthused. "Honest food and honest folk. They really know how to force agricultural labourers between pastry here! No corners cut; the whole labourer, with a cheese topping!"

"Sounds grand." Annabel licked her lips. She picked up the knife and fork before her. The knife was fully twelve inches long, a vicious blade encrusted with blood. The fork had a tongue impaled on each of its cruel tines. She tentatively licked one; it was a male tongue. Edgar glared at her and she blushed bright red.

"Hussy!"

The meal was astonishingly filling. It was washed down with glasses of Adam's-Apple Cider. The thin man disappeared for some minutes to make a phone-call. Edgar and Annabel could hear him mumbling something in the hallway.

Edgar covered his smile with a grimace picked from the pie. Annabel shook hands with her meal. "Stop playing with your food!" Edgar roared. He belched a red belch. "Yum!"

Eventually, the fellow rejoined them. "Well, that's settled then. Are you ready for desert?"

Annabel shook her head. "We'd better be off, really. We're just passing through, you see; on our way to Stafford to visit relatives. We thought it would be nice to make a detour through Shropshire, rather than taking the motorway."

"Nice?" The thin man seemed confused. He pulled at his forelock, the one strand of hair that remained on his head. "Is that a foreign word?" He brightened. "The road between Impale My Dog and Heretic On Pyre is blocked. You won't reach the border by nightfall."

Edgar reached out and placed a hand on her arm. "We don't want to cause offence. Let's just stay a little longer."

Annabel shrugged and assented to desert. It turned out to be a type of Spotted Dick, though the thin man insisted it was called Diseased Tom. As she ate, she could not fail to notice the way Edgar and her host kept glancing anxiously at the clock on the mantelpiece.

Edgar make a small cough. "Have some more, my dear."

"No thank you," she replied, but the thin man had already ladled more of the crusty pudding onto her plate. He held up a jug within which something quite foul stirred sluggishly.

"Clotted?" he inquired.

She shook her head. After she had devoured this second helping, they sat in silence for a while. She rapped her fingers impatiently on the table. Edgar and her host cleared their throats and kept looking at the time. The thin man stood over by the window and peered through the grimy glass. "He should be here by now."

"Who?" Annabel demanded. She frowned at Edgar, who affected not to notice and pretended to be suddenly interested in the condition of his fingernails. "What's going on?"

"Perhaps he's had an accident. Reverend Cleaver is a poor driver at the best of times. I told him not to fit those scythes on the wheels of his tractor. Won't fit down the lanes, I said. Would he listen? Not on your life! I bet he's mangled a cow."

"What's going on?" Annabel repeated in a firm voice. She rose from her chair and moved towards the door. Without thinking, she kept the long blood-encrusted knife in her hand.

"Sit down." There was desperation in Edgar's voice. "Please don't spoil things! We may never get another chance like this one. This sort of life is dying out. Heritage!"

Annabel snorted. "Well you can stay if you want. I'm off." She reached into her pocket for her car-keys and dangled them in front of him. His eyes grew wide with a sudden panic.

"Wait for me!" he cried.

As they left, the thin man turned his face towards them and nodded courteously. But there was bitter disappointment in his strange eyes. "Pleased to meet you. Come again some time. Visitors are always welcome at Applaud My Death. Well farewell! Unsafe journey!"

Annabel climbed into her car, watched in mordant amusement as Edgar scurried in beside her, and roared off. She placed the long knife on the dashboard. They bounced back down the lanes they had driven up. "What's going on?" she demanded.

"Nothing!" Edgar squirmed uneasily on the seat. Before long, they came across a tractor lying on its side in a ditch. A broad man dressed in a black cassock, with a dog-collar, was kicking the exposed engine. Blades and bovine flesh lay tangled together.

Annabel slowed the car and wound the window down. "Can we help you reverend?" She was astonished when the huge figure turned round with a mouth full of highly imaginative oaths.

"I was off to Applaud My Death," he said, when he had recovered his composure, "but ran into this ridiculous creature. Harry Spleen rang me earlier to tell me that a travelling couple were sitting in his kitchen. The woman is a virgin, apparently."

"I see. Well, we can't help you there, I'm afraid. We don't know any virgins." She stepped on the accelerator and screeched away. Back on the main road, she pulled into a lay-by and turned to face Edgar. "You told that thin man I was a virgin! How could you?"

Edgar was apologetic. "I'm sorry. It's just that I've never seen a wicker-man before. The chance was too good to miss."

"But it's a lie; I'm not a virgin!" Annabel shook her fist at him. "I might not even have burned properly. What would you have done then? Siphoned some petrol from my car?"

Edgar laughed. "They wouldn't really have set you on fire. All that is just a metaphor. Country-speak. You don't really believe that they burn virgins round here? You'll be telling me next that you think all these place names actually mean what they say."

"Don't they?"

"Of course not!" Edgar wiped tears of mirth from his cheeks. "What? Purloin My Liver and Grind My Bones and Applaud My

Death? They're just colourful similes. Like the names of the drinks and the food. It's all an elaborate act. Tradition, you see."

"Well the landlord of the Plucked Eyeball had obviously had his eyeball plucked. And that Shepherd's Pie really did taste of smock and crook. How do you account for that?"

"Coincidence. Anyway what about Purloin My Liver and Applaud My Death? Nothing happened in any of those places that could possibly be linked to their names."

"Well your liver was stolen for a start." Annabel blinked and clucked her tongue. "I saw it happen."

"What?" The shadow of a doubt crossed Edgar's face. His fingers prodded his side. A sudden horror enveloped his features. He gazed at Annabel with terrified eyes. "Where?"

"In the pub. A dwarf stole it. I thought you knew." She picked up the knife from the dashboard, held it up to the sunlight for a moment, and then thrust it deep into Edgar's side.

She worked it backwards and forwards and then pulled it out. No blood followed. She pointed at the gaping wound and the empty space beyond. "See?"

"It's true!" Edgar was incredulous. He pulled the wound open and thrust his fingers in. After some minutes of groping around within, he gulped and clutched at Annabel. "But without a liver I'll die!"

"Of course." Annabel returned the knife to the dashboard and once again started the ignition. "Perhaps I can sell your body to a local brewery." This time she made no attempt to avoid the carcass of a sheep that lay in the path of her car.

Edgar went into convulsions and began moaning.

A little while later he fell silent.

Reaching over, Annabel checked his pulse and smiled.

Then she took both hands off the steering-wheel for an instant and burst into spontaneous applause.

MADONNA PARK

At dawn, they set out with hooks and chains. They followed the rutted road as far as the dry riverbed. They wove between desiccated trees and cut a swath through the grasses of the veldt.

"There's one!" cried Travis, squinting into the rising sun. A flash of blue raced across the horizon, a tiny figure with billowing mantle. Travis stood up and grasped the handrail as the tall grasses closed in around them. "A miracle!"

Eliot clutched his stomach and groaned. The stench of petrol, the rotting odours of the veldt, left him feeling vaguely disappointed. So far his chief impressions of the hunt were lurching terrain, the glare of sun on metal, the smell of boiling sap.

He peered in the direction of Travis's finger, seeing nothing but the flicker of sun through grass. For three days all prey had eluded them. Eliot suspected the priest who blessed their jeep had skimped on the holy water. "What?" he mumbled.

"Do you believe in them?" Travis was in high spirits. He bared his yellow teeth and adjusted his fedora over his eyes. His rugged looks, his stoicism, were all second hand. Eliot frowned as he gazed upon the younger man's hair, dyed blue-grey at the temples. The lustrous black of his emerging beard gave the lie to his image. He was probably an avid reader of Hemingway novels.

"Miracles? But of course!" The driver nodded his head. A dubious fellow, he claimed to be a Jehovah's Witness. Again, this was all part of the act: you paid your money and the illusions shimmered at your feet, refracted by the hot air of the promoters. "Do we not owe all this to one? Tears of blood!"

Travis had chosen the role of a Lutheran. He struck the floor of the jeep with the stock of his rifle. "Hurry!" The package had included the malaria that varnished his forehead with perpetual sweat. The skin cancer cells, grown in culture and grafted onto his cheeks, were not unlovely – they formed an archipelago of dark colour on his bland features and raw-red complexion.

37

The Driver thrust a pungent cheroot between his lips and changed gear as they bumped over something that squealed. Abruptly, they burst out of the long grasses into a flatter area of savannah. Ahead, a herd of blue figures looked up in alarm and began stampeding across the wide landscape. "Mothers of God!"

Eliot shook his head in amazement. He had never expected to see a whole herd. Even though his role of extremist Quaker had originally seemed a poor fit, he felt his heart swelling with anticipation of the kill. His stomach forgotten, he joined Travis at the rail.

Travis was mumbling a prayer beneath his breath. His fingers were busy slotting silver bullets into his magazine, like the beads of a lethal rosary. The blue tide surged away from them, the fleetest of foot leaving the older ones behind.

It was not long before they reached their first target, a toothless crone, her mantle and halo both faded with age. Travis loosed a shot and caught her in the neck. She fell without a groan.

"Bravo!" The Driver roared his approval and Travis's eyes lit up with pride. He began firing carefully into the general herd, saliva dribbling down his chin. Eliot took aim but the jeep lurched and a puff of dust bloomed at the feet of his target.

After the crones came the youngsters, the children, who screamed as they fell, with irritating high-pitched wails that offended the ear. Splashes of red on blue showed Eliot he was learning to handle his weapon with greater efficiency – and these were too small to be easy targets. The ones they did not hit they tried to run down.

As the victims mounted, the Driver fixed tiny crucifix transfers to the door of the jeep, steering with one hand and exhaling cheroot smoke through his flaring nostrils. They skidded on a patch of blood; Eliot lost his balance and fell back with a thud. Travis laughed. "Die papist swine!" His eyes, glazed with blood lust, fluttered.

One of the figures did not attempt to flee. She merely stood and awaited their approach. Eliot blinked. Although all these beings were just aspects of a single entity, there seemed to be something special about her. Travis signalled for the Driver to stop. He jumped down from the jeep, stalked across to the target, placed the rifle against her head and fired. The gun jammed: he had paid good money for this. He licked his lips and drew his knife.

As he did so, the figure opened her mouth and said something. Eliot was unable to hear her words, but the tone had a strange effect on him. He wanted to weep. He turned away and hid his face until Travis returned to the jeep. "Is she dead? How did she die?"

Travis showed him his knife. "Like a virgin."

"What did she say?"

"She forgave me." Travis grinned. "Forgave all my sins. You should have come down too. Saved your soul as well."

Later, they drove back to the clubhouse to have their photograph taken. The Madonnas would be stripped of their mantles and thrown into pits – the mantles taken to a nearby processing plant for lapis lazuli extraction. On the way back, they passed a bus taking a coachload of pensioners on a guided hunt. The tannoy system blared at them, fading in and out of audibility as they lurched past:

"Welcome to Heaven-on-Earth... latest extravaganza of Prejudice Inc... utilising techniques of modern science... the perfect opportunity to settle scores... Thanks to a statue of Our Lady in Verona which has started weeping blood... top scientists have succeeded in isolating the DNA of Mother Mary herself... In the confines of this park... no less than a thousand Madonna clones... different ages..."

"Dilettantes!" Travis snarled. Senile faces peered at them from the tinted windows of the bus, eyeing their catch with dim jealousy. Behind them in the dust, on the hooks and chains, forty Madonnas bounced along the rutted road — a respectable hoard by any standards.

Travis was flushed. Eliot felt it was only partly with excitement. "There are no males loose in the park are there?" he ventured. The Driver scowled.

"Of course not! This is a moral outfit. A Lutheran should know this. Ask your complimentary pastor for more details."

Travis frowned and pulled out his knife. He looked at the blade. "If I take the trip again, I'll have to come as an atheist."

"What are you talking about?"

Travis shrugged. "The one I killed with my knife." He abruptly broke down, though it was difficult for Eliot to tell whether his tears were those of despair or mirth. "She was pregnant."

JOURNEY THROUGH A WALL

You all know the legend of the phantom hitch-hiker. A driver picks up a figure on a lonely road and gives it a lift into town. On the way, it vanishes. The driver looks in the glove-compartment and under the seat; the figure isn't there. The doors are locked, imprisoning the only explanation left. Reaching the town, the driver stammers out his story. He is informed that a person matching his passenger's description was tragically killed on that same road more than a decade previously. So the hitcher was a ghost!

I'll spare further details. Suffice to say I've milked sore the udder of that tale with my antics. I am Mark Anthony Zimara, trickster and lovable scoundrel. Actually I'm a pepper-pot salesman, but no less dastardly for that. One stretch of road exists, I won't name it, where for a whole summer I played the part to perfection. No need to chalk my face or use a deathly voice. My victims inked my style with an eerie brush in the telling. The economy of a nearby town boomed. A local paper paid a famous medium to drive up and down looking for me. I was a soul in torment, everyone said, and needed to be guided through the astral gateway by a professional.

Many people came forward to identify me as a dead relative. There is a real hunger for the supernatural, the belly aches for bread spread with spooks. I've cracked this particular joke all over the country, but only once for a whole season. Like I said, I'm a scoundrel but a lovable one. I hurt too many folk that time to really enjoy the deception. When I entered the medium's car and did my disappearing business right under her nose, she was delighted. She pulled up and performed an exorcism on the side of the highway. It was embarrassing. I decided that tomorrow I'd thumb a real lift out. As luck would have it, she drove past while I was waiting. The shock finished her.

My method of operation is a trade secret, though I can reveal that it was invented by my father, the Great Legume. One of the best, if not the most stylish, escapologists on the seaside circuit, he'd entertained dozens of drunken soldiers during the war; the curious ones often beat him up afterwards, to see if he could evade the blows. The Great Legume cared not a bean for these attentions. He was a proud man, descendant of an aristocratic Italian family. Wealth had not been left him; drooping moustaches and sad eyes were his sole inheritance from the heady days of Garibaldi. His account of a childhood in San Marino was tedious in the extreme. For the duration of the war, he lived with false papers. He was a skilled forger of documents.

His technique of passing through walls came to him in a dream. He jumped out of bed, groping for the light-switch. He had to write it down before he forgot it. He tripped over Benito, the cat, and fell against the wardrobe. Suddenly he was inside, among the waistcoats. That moment, he afterwards told me, was one of infinite sadness. He'd struggled all his life to succeed and now fame and fortune had been handed to him on an oneiric plate. It mocked his earlier sufferings. He decided never to make a single penny out of this new gift, employing it solely in charity work or for the astounding of friends.

On his death-bed, he passed the secret on to me, his only child. I also vowed never to turn it to commercial advantage. His funeral was his final performance. After we buried him and returned home, we found him waiting for us in an armchair. He often jested about escaping from Hell; my mother, who took such things seriously, paid a dissolute priest to hammer a stake through his heart. We hastily reburied him in the garden. His original grave was exhumed and a furious Benito sprang out and took up residence in the nearest yew.

41

I practiced the method until I mastered it. Journeying through a wall is not an invigorating experience, it palls after a while. There is little sensation; the body tingles, the mind winks. Then you are on the other side. There is no magic involved. It is a physical process as yet undiscovered by the sages of science. I have no doubt they will soon chance upon the technique. And then my days as trickster and rogue will be numbered. I shall have to take a more conventional hobby, attempting to impale fish on tiny hooks, perhaps, or endlessly turning a hoe in the dirt of some barren suburban allotment.

As ignorant of the exact mechanism as was my father, I nonetheless maintain that the gift is not so surprising considering the emptiness of existence. This is more than a hollow metaphor. Matter is essentially porous, containing more holes than substance. Everything you can think of on this world — rocks, cheese, raspberries, paper, oboes, grandfather clocks, brushes, teapots — is comprised of a relatively small amount of solidness and a vast amount of nothingness. There are yawning chasms between molecules, through which a miniature Hannibal could lead a horde of atomic elephants. As always, the small mirrors the large; it is the same with two colliding galaxies, which pass through each other without scraping the gilt off their suns.

There are disadvantages to my talent as well. There was Charlotte, my first girlfriend, who suddenly decided to introduce me to the joys of physical love. The motions necessary are not dissimilar to those needed to travel through walls and doors. She guided me across the border of her undiscovered country, so to speak, but before I could get my visa stamped, I passed right through her and the bed and struck my head on the bare boards beneath. "You selfish brute!" she wailed. I was forced to agree. I lost my innocence in a knothole.

Another time, posting a letter, second class, I forgot to release it and followed the epistle into the pillar-box. Overwhelmed by the poor quality of my confines, the mass of mundane correspondence around me, the odour of the myriad salivas that had sealed it, I temporarily lost my powers. I had to wait for the postman to deliver me with his sack and grin. Despite his outward benevolence, he charged me excess postage and ignored my protests of "Fragile! Do not bend!" Since that time, I make use of the service as little as possible. I send few festive cards and, as a consequence, receive few in return.

Generally, however, I enjoy myself without caution, for travelling through walls is not a pastime for the timid. There is always one worry at the back of the mind: what if I become stuck halfway? My father held it would happen eventually. It did not deter him, though he often liked to imagine future archaeologists discovering foundations for his belief in the foundations of a building. I don't pay serious homage to fears of this kind. I restrict my activities to passing through doors of moving vehicles, too thin to become embedded in. Landing on the road, rolling away unhurt and unseen are greater problems.

Last month, I was working my way through the villages of Yorkshire in a half-hearted snowstorm. I disregarded the chills in pursuit of my favourite fraud. I hitched across the entire country in a single day, disappearing from a total of twelve vehicles as I ventured north. The quilt of snow protected my bones each time I emerged on the other side of the passenger door. Furthermore, I'd chosen a white suit to blend in with the environment. The rural roads lay like hairs on a vast lake of undulating milk, black and thin. It's a region rife with phantoms, generally stringy misers and hermits.

The best time to slip through a door is when the vehicle is turning into a bend. Whatever the attractions of the passenger, few drivers will desire conversation until the road straightens out again. In that pause, I tumble sideways, leaving an empty seat, horribly warm for the curious hand. So a necklace of ghost-tales was strung out on the creamy moors, beads carved from skulls. I made one mistake: leaving my briefcase with a student taking home washing. It was full of leaflets for pepper-pots, doubtless reducing the ghastly effect.

By evening, I had broken my record of hauntings and was considering finding a warm bed for the night. Accordingly, I polished my thumb for a genuine lift. There was a grimy town some dozen miles distant, a typical set of houses gathered round a reconstructed inn. I didn't have long to wait; a blue Volvo pulled up and I climbed in. The driver turned out to be a blond giant in strange garb: furs and leather. He was more reticent than the average host and I wondered what his motives were for giving me a lift. To break the silence, I felt compelled to remark on the wetness of the snow, the disappointing ice.

"Aye," His voice was gruff. "Winter's not what it used to be. I recall log-fires and axes, mead and runes."

I frowned. "Did you say runes?"

"And wolves and longships. Those were the days." He tugged his huge beard and cast a steely blue gaze at me. Then he returned his attention to his driving. Rather than betray astonishment, I kept quiet and didn't ask him to elaborate. We continued awkwardly for some time. Finally, I could bear it no longer and cried:

"So what's your line of work?"

He darted another glance, less calculating than before and laughed. "Questing and hacking. What's yours?"

Having left my briefcase in the other car, I had no ready prop to back up my salesman claim. A hawker without a product is like a vulture without a beak. An alternative identity was required. I was free to name any profession I chose, which is doubtless why I was unable to think of one. Variety can be truly sterile.

At the same time, I was determined not to be browbeaten by such a cryptic fellow. He'd obviously marked me out as a simpleton to be toyed with. It would be a delight, I mused, to turn the tables on him — in his case, round tables which needed to be flipped as well as spun. I lowered my own tone an octave, made it as dry as a desiccated eyelid and stifled a pretend chuckle. My teeth glimmered.

"Haunting drivers. I am the phantom hitch-hiker."

Instead of greeting this pronouncement with derision or fear, the driver gave a joyous cry and pounded the steering-wheel with his massive fist. "Excellent," he muttered to himself. Then, addressing me directly, he added: "At long last, a companion on my journey, a kindred spirit! I have waited centuries for this."

I assumed he'd misheard. "Phantom hitch-hiker," I repeated.

He clapped me on the knee, keeping his eyes on the road. "Pleased to meet you. I'm Olaf Smorgasbord, the phantom-driver. Been wandering this area a thousand years, on horseback originally, but I'm no purist. I make use of available technology. Spent the Middle-Ages on wagons and carts. Now I've got an engine. It gets lonely, this ceaseless questing, and I often pick up travellers. But humans have such trivial concerns, it's nice to meet another ghost. Tell me, does your ectoplasm ache first thing in the morning? Or is it just me?"

I swallowed and tried to still my beating heart (I can do this by actually reaching inside my chest.) I resisted the temptation to ask him to drop me off. He seemed an unpredictable sort. He might take offence and perform the rite of the Blood-Eagle on me. I'd read about these ancient Nordic chaps; I didn't wish to have my ribs snapped and peeled back from my chest to appease a heathen sensibility. I could smell organic mushrooms on his breath; always a bad sign. With a gallant effort, I controlled my extreme panic.

Small-talk was the order of the evening. Nonchalantly, I asked, "Which quest might that be?"

He heaved a sigh. "I'm looking for Thor's nail."

I nodded, rubbed my chin and made convincing sympathetic noises at the back of my throat. "That sounds like a difficult task. I hope I'm not interrupting your search?"

"Not really. I don't think I'll ever find it. I wish Thor had asked someone else. Ready to give up, I am, but he won't have it. What use is his hammer without a nail? I can see his point. Without a nail he can't hang pictures in Valhalla. Edvard Munch is his favourite painter." He lowered his voice to a whisper. "To be honest, he prefers Monet, but he won't admit it. Odin would make jokes."

"I see. But I must be an inconvenience. Wouldn't you rather search in peace? I can walk from here."

"And deny me the chance to play with a fellow spectre? No fear! How often do shakers and moaners cross paths? This is a rare opportunity for us both. With mortals I generally keep my idea of fun under worm-gnawed wraps. I don't like being a closet wraith, but I mustn't jeopardise the quest. I spook the occasional student, of course, who doesn't? But it's hardly satisfying for a berserker ghost! I crave something more violent, something with a bit of exposed marrow."

"Alas," said I, "my disposition is withered and sober and I really don't consider myself suitable for whatever you have in mind. I'm sure a more compatible soul will come along soon. Plenty more frights in the aether. A ghoul would suit fine."

"Nonsense. You look just the type for a wild night. We can commence our ghostly pranks right now. For example, let's accelerate at that tree and dash our insubstantial minds out. Whoever loses his bottle first and dematerialises has to pay a forfeit."

Without waiting for a reply, Olaf depressed the pedal that caused us to rush at horrible speed down the ill-lit road. Then he turned off onto the frozen verge and we bounced over a field. The tree, a massive oak, engulfed the periphery of my vision. At this speed, it was out of the question for me to escape through the door, whether by conventional means or otherwise. I gripped my seat and ground my teeth and started to whimper: the usual weaknesses.

I turned to face my driver, to plead with him to slow down, but to my utter horror, he had vanished. For what it was worth, it seemed I'd won this first game. I screamed: "I give in! I confess everything! I'm not the phantom hitch-hiker, but a pepper-pot salesman! For pity's sake come back and stop the car!"

Suddenly, he was back in his seat and the brakes were squealing and we were spinning in ludicrous circles, radii as wide as the rings of the very tree whose trunk we avoided kissing by a few inches. I slumped in my chair and loosed tears.

Olaf frowned. "Are you sure you're not a phantom hitcher? You're not just saying that, are you?"

"My name is Mark Anthony Zimara. I'm a trickster and lovable rogue, fluffy hair, smooth tongue. Nothing more. I play pranks on drivers when they pick me up. The joke no longer seems funny. I never really believed in the spirit world; I thought all ectoplasm was muslin. I apologise for deceiving you, barbarian spectre."

He puffed out his cheeks and guffawed. I was agitated by his mirth, which I took to be at my expense, but then it dawned on me that it was expressing relief. He was actually pleased I wasn't a ghost; I couldn't account for this, after all he'd said.

Finally, he explained, "You had me worried back there. I'm also a prankster. I pretend to be a sort of doomed soul, condemned to wander the earth on an impossible quest. I'm a tax-inspector from Leeds, which perhaps is not dissimilar. When you announced yourself as the phantom hitch-hiker, I was terrified!"

I blinked. "But I saw you vanish into thin air."

"No, no, I merely made myself invisible. It's a technique my father gave me on his death-bed. He was an escapologist, better known as the Wondrous Pulse. Discovered the secret in his sleep, was nearly crushed when my mother sat on him."

The coincidence was so remarkable that I couldn't speak for many moments. It emerged that his father had performed in the same venues as mine, though they'd never met, revolving round the circuit at different points. The art of invisibility was akin to the art of passing through walls. It was a question of allowing light to travel unhindered between a body's molecules, rather than absorbing it. This meant conquering greed at the microscopic level.

"Well fancy that! I guess we had to cross paths at some point. But tell me more about your father. So he performed for soldiers during the war? And they often beat him up! That's too bad. Did he, by any chance, own a cat? He did! And what was it's name? Quisling, eh!"

Olaf opened the glove-compartment and took out a flask of akevitt, an abrasive northern spirit. We both needed to settle our nerves. It's not everyday that a pepper-pot salesman and a tax-inspector, sons of escapologists, manage to alarm each other to the extent where both are ready to give up the ghost — literally and metaphorically. I mean that fear had tempted me to forsake rascality and live a simple life. Olaf felt the same; but as we drank and the liquor warmed, our terror melted by degrees until even the memory of it had thawed.

We toasted ourselves, our talents and our fathers. "Here's to the Great Legume! Here's to the Wondrous Pulse! Here's to the phantom hitch-hiker and the phantom driver! May the former never mill aimlessly, may the latter never tax his brains!"

While we sat, a car pulled up on the side of the road and a figure got out and began to stalk across the icy field. I watched its progress in the mirror and nudged my companion. It was dressed in a black uniform which the wind-driven snow seemed reluctant to settle on. Then I noticed that it wasn't sinking into the drifts.

Olaf wound his window down and leaned out, expectantly. The figure approached and flashed a badge — an inverted pentangle. It crouched and leered at us, eyes like dark grapes which are due to be trampled into Black Mass wine.

"I saw what happened back there. I'm arresting you for dangerous driving. Get out of the car."

Olaf shrugged his shoulders. "I don't know what you mean. We pulled off the road deliberately. We decided to sit in this field awhile and enjoy the view — not much of one I grant you, but there's no law against appreciating bland vistas. Besides, you haven't got any authority over us. That badge is a fake. I think you'd better state exactly who you are and what your business is."

"I am the phantom traffic-policeman."

At this solemn pronouncement, I couldn't forbear laughing. Olaf, a more robust chap, slapped the dashboard with a hand and cried: "Phantom traffic-policeman? Of course you are! I bet your father was called the Remarkable Bean! And had a cat named Franco!"

The figure reached for its belt. It drew a hawthorn truncheon and levelled it at Olaf's head. My companion gave a start and tried to wind the window up. "He's barmy!" The figure inserted its weapon into the gap and levered the glass back down, a considerable feat of strength. Poking its face in, it recoiled in disgust.

"You've been drinking! That's a serious offence. You'll get several centuries for this!"

Olaf tried to start the car, but the engine wouldn't turn over. I was more placatory. I got out, opening the door properly this time, and held my hands in the air. "I won't resist," I said, "but there's been a mistake. We're mortals. If you truly are a phantom policeman, you have no jurisdiction over us."

Its voice was heavy with cynicism. "Mortals are we now, sir? I suggest we go along to the station to discuss that. My colleagues will be pleased to hear what you've got to say on the matter. No disrespect, but to me you look like a phantom hitch-hiker and a phantom driver. Now if you'll just exhale into this bag..."

Olaf followed my example and got out, but he was in a bad temper. "Don't do anything he asks. He's an impostor, just like us. Walk away from the fool." And he started tramping.

The phantom policeman reached out and grabbed him by the elbow. Olaf winced but then lashed out. "Hands off me, you swine! I'll make black-puddings out of your intestines!"

I tried to intercede, to pull them apart. There was a tussle. Then I felt the weight of the truncheon on my skull and sagged to my knees. "Make yourself invisible!" I hissed to Olaf. He turned to catch my words and the staff caught him on the head also. He sprawled on top of me, knocking me to the ground and smothering me in his bristly beard. The snow blackened to a crisp and I was plummeting down a crevasse that had opened up in its midst...

Neither of us were unconscious for very long. When I came to, I was slumped in the back of the phantom policeman's car. Olaf was sitting next to me, moaning at infrequent intervals. We both wore handcuffs made of some spongy substance and covered in occult symbols. We were speeding down the country lanes; but somehow the landscape no longer looked like the Yorkshire I knew.

The phantom policeman noticed I was awake and sneered at me in the driving-mirror. "Resisting arrest, assaulting an officer of the law. Few more heinous offences. I reckon the Judge will give you the big one for that, black cap and whatnot."

I rasped. "What are you wittering on about? Capital punishment was abolished decades ago!"

"Not in the Ghost-Provinces, it wasn't."

I turned to Olaf, but all I could get out of him — between pitiful moans — were disjointed phrases: "Remarkable Bean, cat named Franco, I'll bet." I shook him and he seemed to revert to his old form. His mind had plainly snapped under the strain. "Wait till Thor hears about this! He'll be furious!"

The policeman smirked. "Your friend hasn't bothered to keep up the deception. I've listened to his babble. He's a phantom-driver all right. I've just radioed my colleagues. They say you've been spotted all over the land, haunting humans. I wasn't killed yesterday! You're a phantom hitcher! What have you got to say to that?"

There were a great many things I wanted to say. I contented myself with a few of the basics: "Where are we going?"

"Phantomsville. You'll like the prison we've got there, it lies in a cavern four-thousand miles beneath the surface of the earth. Warm as toast, so I've heard. I envisage a swift trial and a promotion for me, and then you'll be put on Reanimation Row."

"Reanimation Row? What the hell does that mean?"

"Well, it involves large amounts of electricity. Some clotted-heart liberals disagree with the life-sentence. After they've heard the details of your case, they'll be won round. Haunting without a licence! Striking an officer! I reckon your friend here will get off on mental grounds. He'll plead disseminated responsibility or some such thing. I think you led him on."

I closed my mouth and we completed the journey in silence. I won't say anything about Phantomsville or the trial. My defence lawyer was useless. The odds were weighted against me from the beginning: hitchers are despised as layabouts and shirkers. I cried when the sentence was announced. Olaf claimed that I'd forced him to drive into the field and consume vast quantities of alcohol. He's in a secure psychiatric unit now, receiving the latest centrifugal treatment.

As for myself, well I've just finished a final meal of kippers and grapefruit. Sprinkled liberally with pepper. As a last request, I asked for pencil and paper, to set down my experiences. That's what I'm doing now. The exorcist will be coming soon, to intone me to the Chair. I've been listening to the screams of the reanimated all week. I don't intend going meekly; I'm going to make an escape attempt. The walls are four-thousand miles thick, and no ghost can be expected to travel so far through solid matter without stripping away all its etheric particles. It's much more dangerous for a human being, who may become embedded at any point throughout the journey.

But I'm no fool. I've read plenty of French novels. I hope to break into other, natural caverns, where I can dine on Plesiosaurus cutlets or the flesh of sequoia-sized mushrooms. Maybe I'll emerge through Mount Etna. If I make it, I promise to publish my account. It's time something new was added to folklore. You all know the legend of the phantom hitch-hiker. But I bet you don't know the story of how he was picked up by the phantom driver and arrested by the phantom traffic-cop.

BRIDGE OVER TROUBLED BLOOD

Artery Garfunkle raised his glass of blood. "Here's to you, Mrs Robinson!" he cried. "Without your help, I would never have transfused the required eight pints and graduated."

"It's called 'Passing Out'," returned Mrs Robinson. She drained her glass and licked her bitter lips.

"Nothing like your own vintage," observed Garfunkle. He sighed. "Do you think our relationship is sinful? I'm barely into triple figures and you're approaching your millennium."

Mrs Robinson reached out and caressed his wings. "Silly bat! Ignore conventional morality. Now help me get dressed. I bought a new brassière the other day. Would you like to button it?"

"No, I can't stand French food. The Marquis de Sade gave me ghastly indigestion. It's time I prepared for work."

Lilith Robinson regarded her enthusiastic young lover with a slight frown. His brand of innocence worried her: it wasn't fresh and

51

charming, but rotten and cankerous — more like decayed sagacity than true naivety. Quick as a fever, he climbed out of bed and started dressing, relying on her mimicry to adjust his silk cravat. Unable to use mirrors, they often stood in for each other's reflection.

Her tone was gently chiding. "Only graduated last month and already starting a job! The youth of today don't know how to enjoy themselves. I took a century off when I was your age."

"Really?" Garfunkle raised an eyebrow. "What for?"

"Holiday in Arkham. Did me an underworld of good."

"But that's where I'm off to! The college has arranged an exchange. Arkham's brightest graduate is coming over here — she's an engineer of some kind — and I'm going over there. Isn't it exciting? I can't imagine how I won the offer. Competition was fierce."

"Tell me more. What are you expected to do? I hope it's not just an excuse for some cheap labour! I don't want you working your guts out for the sake of a wriggly taskmaster."

He smiled. "The Arkham authorities seem personable entities. It's a cultural thing. They like my music."

"Music? But you graduated in euthanasia!"

"I specialised in rubbing down bishops with extreme unction. But my guitar is the cavity where I keep my heart..."

"You're not taking Appalling with you?"

Artery Garfunkle flushed white and nodded: "He's my best fiend. And who else can provide me with lyrics?"

Mrs Robinson threw up her talons in despair. "The pair of you don't know what the music business is like! So many ambitious bats end up with dreams smeared over their maws. Don't do it, Artery!"

"I have to. It's my destiny. I know the folk-scene is difficult to make a mark in. But so is a flint neck! It takes a degree of masochism. Remember this, Mrs Robinson: hell holds a place for those who prey. When I'm wealthy, you'll have as much lingerie as you want. With Appalling by my side, we'll soon be rolling in it!"

Lilith shook her head. "The words of the profit were written on the dungeon wall," she muttered. "In gore."

With an angry pout, he pulled on his coat and made to leave. "Sorry you don't feel the way I do. But you must try to understand. Best for me to make my own mistakes in my own way. No point trying to put an ancient skull on old shoulders. It's not a matter for debate — I'm off to Arkham to strum the catgut and there's an end to it."

"What if you meet someone else? Musicians are followed by hordes of screaming harpies. They're young and puffy!"

"You'll just have to trust me, Mrs Robinson."

Wings flapping through the slits in his coat, Garfunkle stormed out of the apartment, slamming the window as he went. Lilith buried her face in the grave-scented pillow and spilled a crepuscular tear. What she had feared all along was coming to pass: the age difference was too great to sustain the affair. She had lost him — he was off in pursuit of somebody new. Not that he necessarily knew this on a conscious level: it was the inevitable outcome of unbalanced amours.

Lilith raised herself, tears cascading over the side of the bed and landing in her glass of blood, diluting the ruby fluid to a tragic rosé. The only question was how she ought to act now: embittered or forgiving? It was much more mature to shrug her shoulders and forget about him. But maturity only lasted from the ages of eighteen to seven-hundred-and-ten. After that, emotions turned full circle: grudges were reclaimed, revenge was back in favour and hate became a noble feeling. Deeming it better to act her age, she decided to be vindictive.

She would strike viciously, without mercy, as blatantly as a child. She would damage not his skin but his reputation. When he came back from Arkham, he would find himself mocked in professional circles. No hospice would employ him as an euthanasist. If he wanted to fool with music, she would ensure he did it on street-corners.

Moving to the casement, she peered through the warped glass. Artery had landed on the grass embankment outside the library and was listening to his companion, Appalling Simon, who was playing a flute carved out of a mouse. Even at this distance, Mrs Robinson thought she could discern a whisper of the furtive and twitching melody.

She snatched up her brassière and carried it into the kitchen. When she reached the stove she filled the iron cups with charcoal and grilled a whole poodle over the pulsating flames. Her brassière often doubled up as a brazier: it saved on vocabulary.

A week after Artery and Appalling left for Arkham, the exchange graduate arrived at the college. She was almost twelve feet tall, with snaky hair and four visible arms. She was softly spoken, darkly cowled and teetered on a pair of stiff legs.

She introduced herself as 'Oldona' and seemed a little confused in her new environment. She was a civil engineer and her main interest was in building bridges. The Chancellor had commissioned a crossing of the local river as a test.

The college stream was a trickle, but it cut into the campus like a festering wound, dividing one faculty from another. For the flying staff this presented few problems; but the Social Science Departments were run by zombies, who had to be rowed from bank to bank by galley-slaves taken from the student ranks. The loss of scholars was high; the gondolas were often capsized by the suicidal punters, fatally dampening the reputation of Stakehampton Institute of Parasitical Studies.

Wasting no time, Oldona experimented with a large number of designs before submitting the most suitable for approval by the Chancellor. Only a suspension bridge would look right, she maintained; and only if it was well-hung. This was Arkham gallows humour.

Lilith planned to make her acquaintance as soon as it was feasible, but in fact the engineer sought her out first. Officially, Mrs Robinson was a student counsellor. Undergraduates came to her with their problems and her job was to make them worse, offering bad advice on such dilemmas as housing, nourishment and faith.

"I just can't seem to settle in," Oldona lisped, as she entered Mrs Robinson's office. "The climate is horrid and I can't get used to biting on the left hand side of the neck."

"Sit down." Lilith indicated a chair.

Oldona lowered herself, rather awkwardly, onto the seat. She winced and adjusted her position. "I'm quite happy with my working arrangements here; it's the social side. I feel lonely."

"Perhaps you need a lover. There are some eligible gargoyles on the shelf in the college chapel basement."

"I'm a married entity. I couldn't possibly consider a paramour. How would I appease my conscience?"

"A *paranormalmour*," corrected Mrs Robinson. "I had one myself, very recently. See this cleaver hung around my neck? The first gift he bought me. I sharpen it once a day. Actually, he's the bat who's gone to Arkham in your place. He's a songwriter."

Oldona's eyes grew bright. "Is he any good?"

"In bed? Certainly! You mean his music? Well actually..."

Lilith bit her lip, a painful gesture. Oldona seemed flustered; she mopped her brow with one hand and twiddled the thumbs of two others. Mrs Robinson broke the uneasy pause with a lopsided grin. "We both need some company. Let me show you the local nightlife."

Oldona chuckled. "I was hoping you'd say that..."

"I'll meet you outside the Palais de Decadence at midnight. But you must lope along now, I've got work to do."

Oldona staggered to her feet and lurched out. Lilith was astonished by a screech which diminished in sinusoidal waves. Then she guessed that Oldona had eased her alarming bulk onto the balcony of the spiral stairs and was enjoying an unconventional descent. She brushed tears and smiled indulgently at the same time. Youth was such a marvellous attribute, but no matter how it was spent it was squandered!

Mrs Robinson thought of Artery Garfunkle, swooping over the maggoty campus of a foreign college, or treading the boards of a graveyard dive, plucking his guitar and crooning to Appalling's accordion. What would an American audience make of their portentous melodies? Lilith recalled her own heroes — Howlin' Werewolf, Bloody Waters, Hellmore James. Artery had no chance of competing with those big bogies.

On the other talon, it was even more disturbing to envisage success for the duo. If it happened it would go straight to their skulls, like a wine fermented from pumpkins, nightshade and cheerleaders. The pleasures on offer, the adulation, would rot Artery's mind, leaving him a pathetic wreck on the rocky shores of folk.

At this thought, Mrs Robinson rubbed her palms in glee. Perhaps she ought to let them ruin themselves. But no, this smacked of quietism, she was determined to play a part in the final humiliation. With her sleeve, she wiped away the usual stain from the chair where Oldona had sat. Then she returned to work, shuffling her papers.

The afternoon progressed slowly. Seven distraught students, with a coffinful of depressions between them, came to visit, but she could only convince three that the answer was suicide. The others expressed doubts about its usefulness and her counselling skills could not persuade them otherwise. "It's good for you!" she insisted.

Returning to her room, she made herself up with violet lipstick and crimson mascara, and hung dark pearls from her pierced nipples. Then she gargled with sweet nepenthe, stiffened her hair with lime and slipped on a revealing silk number, with thigh-length leather boots and a belt made from a heretic's flayed back. Her mirrors were useless, so she dressed a voodoo mannequin carved in her image. The way the doll wore its garments was indicative of the way she looked. Finally, she strapped the pig-iron brassière to the outside of her dress.

How much longer could she strut her stuff like this? When would her fellow bats start wrinkling snouts and making disparaging comments? From the Anatomy lecturers, she had already heard some. "Mutton dressed up as aardvark!" was the cruelest jibe to date.

Perhaps some of Oldona's vitality would rub off on her. The student was a peculiar creature, to be sure, but not unattractive. Spraying neck and cleavage with Chanel No.666, Lilith opened the window and kissed the wind. She flung herself over the edge and headed downtown. She still had a century of prime animus left, there was still time to dance and flirt. No mediocre songwriter was going to tarnish her dignity. She would split Artery and Appalling apart like mating toads.

Oldona was waiting for her outside the Palais de Decadence. The exchange student was wearing a poncho stitched with occult symbols and a sombrero with a sand-filled brim. A prickly cactus sprouted from the crown.

"It's the only formal gear I brought over," she apologised. "I didn't think to pack many posh clothes. Is it out of place?"

Mrs Robinson shook her head. "By no means! You look really elegant. I wish I had your bone-structure."

"That's just where I keep my purse!"

They entered the dance-hall arm in arm in arm. A gallows stood on a makeshift stage. Corpses dangled from nooses, clutching trumpets, double basses and saxophones, which they played with violent spasms. "Don't you just love traditional Swing?" Oldona asked.

The floor was crowded with jazz-freaks: tattooed ladies, strong men and sword-swallowers in zoot suits. They were dancing the jittervirus, a new craze created in a test-tube in the Chemistry Department. Surprising herself, Lilith snatched Oldona and bounded onto the floor, kicking legs and gyrating hips to the insidious rhythms.

Later, exhausted, they sat in a corner on a comfortable sofa, knees touching. Mrs Robinson gazed into Oldona's rheumy eyes and found herself blushing as white as a grub.

"I know it sounds corny," she stammered, "but I feel I've known you for a very long time."

"That's exactly how I feel, Lilith."

"Like really close sisters."

Oldona leaned forward. "Or lovers...?"

Mrs Robinson turned away, burning behind her pointed ears. But she was excited by the suggestion. Her strict Satanist upbringing

57

prevented her from continuing the conversation in this vein, it was too perverse, so she attempted to change the subject.

"Tell me about Arkham, Oldona."

For some reason, the student seemed unsure of herself. "Well, there are woods near there which no axe has felled. The food is quite good: an indigenous dish is Blue-Heretic Pie..."

Oldona appeared reluctant to say more about Arkham. Lilith wondered at this unnatural reticence; it was as if the student actually knew very little about her home town. Perhaps there were secrets in her past which she was not yet ready to confront?

Lilith decided to draw Oldona out by revealing secrets of her own. This would also complete the first stage of her revenge against Artery. She sipped her drink and remarked casually:

"My former lover was a cheat!"

Oldona spluttered and coughed. "Really?"

"Oh yes, he passed his euthanasia exams by resorting to deception. The blood he transfused for his finals wasn't his own. I collected lots of samples and distilled a substitute!"

The student appeared to be going into convulsions. She regained her composure with some difficulty and cried: "That's impossible! Samples of bat blood cannot be collected without a license, and these are locked in a safe in the Chancellor's office. They are rarely issued to students or staff, and the illegal collecting of bat blood is severely punished. Any student who used human blood would be disqualified immediately. Cheating is not a viable option at this college!"

Lilith frowned. How did Oldona know more about the rules of British vampire institutes than about the characteristics of her own town? There was something funny going on, not only in her lower regions. As if aware of her mistake, the student shrugged.

"That's what I've heard, anyhow," she said.

Lilith nodded. "Well, it happens to be true. But Artery and myself came up with a novel way round the problem."

"Novel? I read one once: it was about a cannibal horse."

Lilith tugged at a fang. Oldona had made the sort of slightly silly remark she was used to hearing from Artery. They were similar in so many ways. Was it the fact they were the same age and had absorbed identical cultural influences? Or was there a mystic element, an astral connection between the pair? Lilith distrusted the idea of elective affinities, but she had to admit there was an uncanny overlap of behaviour patterns. Was this why she felt attracted to the student?

Mrs Robinson returned to her confession: "To swindle the examiners, we collected the blood drop by drop, from unsuspecting donors, over many months! We were very patient."

"But how did you do it?" Oldona shifted uncomfortably. "How did you manage to steal blood painlessly?"

"I didn't say we did. But the pain was too minor to excite alarm. I am a counsellor, as you know. My clients are confused students. I invite them to sit on the chair opposite mine. It is fixed to the floor, with a solid base. A hollow needle protrudes above the level of the cushion and this pierces the flesh of a victim's buttock. A drop of blood runs into a reservoir located under the floorboards. After the counselling session the victim departs my office none the wiser, attributing any discomfort in the posterior to psychosomatic causes."

Oldona tapped her gigantic nose. "I thought I felt a puncture wound when I first came to see you!" She kneaded Mrs Robinson's legs under the table and batted her eyelashes. "But wouldn't the reservoir be mixed up with different blood-groups?"

Lilith smirked. "We discovered a process of refining blood-types. I borrowed from the petroleum industry and set up an ichor-cracker, gently heating the mixture so that the group we needed evaporated and condensed in a separate chamber. Artery was type z."

"I'm type z as well!" giggled Oldona.

"The only worrying thing," continued Lilith, "is that there's still a chamber full of unwanted blood beneath me. Disposing of it might prove to be difficult. A pipe connects the reservoir with the river. Turning a faucet under my desk will make the whole lot cascade out. Then the water will turn red and the Chancellor will notice. It'll be traced back to me and Artery's degree will be stripped."

Oldona moved her hands higher. Now four sets of fingers brushed Mrs Robinson's thighs. "Better not turn that faucet then! Perhaps you should leak a little at a time? One drop a day?"

Lilith sighed. "No, the freshers on the gondolas have nostrils like sharks, capable of sniffing out a few molecules. They'll do anything to escape a life on the galleys and would report the blood in the desperate hope of gaining parole."

"So what are you going to do?"

"My plan is to pressurise the reservoir with helium and invite back my clients for a reappraisal. When they sit down, the needle will inject the blood they originally lost."

"I knew it! I knew it!" Oldona threw two of her arms around Lilith, the others moving closer to her moist secret.

Lilith pulled away, flattered and unnerved by the unrestrained show of affection. Were American monsters always as exuberant? Why did Oldona keep winking at her, as if they were confederates in a plot? She worried over this for no more than a moment; Oldona pulled her to her feet, took her round the waist and dragged her onto the dance-floor. This time mood and tempo were slow and intimate.

The student leant over to press lips to Lilith's yawning cleavage. At first, these kisses were given partly in a spirit of playfulness, but they quickly became more serious. Lilith abandoned the fight against her conscience and allowed herself to be swept away by the sheer audacity of the episode. Oldona's tongue found a way under her brassière and flicked like a flame over her pierced nipples, swelling the nodules to grotesque dimensions and dislodging a pearl.

A little later, the student clattered outside with her new lover. A meteor shower was spanking the backside of the constellation Polidori, a zodiac sign only recognised by bats. Lilith and Oldona groped in the wet shadows, elastic snapping in the penumbra where fireflies singed a night ready to fold in on itself. But though they rotated in the vortex of the wildest passion, the exchange student was careful to keep Lilith's hands away from her own breasts and yielding sex.

"Here's to you, Mrs Robinson!" whispered Oldona, as her thumb found the bud of her batty clitoris.

Lilith sighed. "That's what my lover used to say!"

"I'm your lover now, gorgeous! Do you know what I'm going to do for you? I'm redesigning my bridge without telling the authorities! When you cast eyes on it, you'll be delighted!"

Moaning, Lilith dissolved in a puddle of lust.

The construction of the bridge proceeded at high speed. Mrs Robinson was able to watch developments from her office window. The structure was now taking on the appearance of something archetypal and familiar, something both welcome and strangely repellent. A knot of nostalgia tightened down in her gut, but she was unable to say exactly what the bridge resembled. Form was still too vague to comprehend.

There was one piece of bad news: her husband was coming back from a lucrative teaching post in Yemen. The desert ghouls were bright students but they kept eating the necromancy exhibits. He'd had his fill: if they kept on like this, he'd have to teach them from textbooks. A necromancer worth his electrodes never relies on books, so he'd decided to return to the festering bosom of scholarship. He told her this in a letter written on the skin of a colleague who had been sacked for drunkenness. The last thing Lilith wanted was to see Woody again.

The only thing to make him change his mind would be the acquisition of inedible exhibits. If he could get hold of viscera for his work which his students couldn't digest, he'd stay in Yemen. But corpses were tasty over there, soft and juicy, not like leathery British cadavers. He asked the Chancellor of Stakehampton College to send some over, but it was the end of term and there were none to spare.

Lilith shouldered this extra worry with stoic grace and whiled away the days walking the river, watching cables being stretched over girders like guitar-strings. Just as the bridge seemed ready to crystallise into something she could comprehend, Oldona issued instructions that a canopy was to be placed over it, to shield final

61

preparations from prying eyes. Under the billowing fabric, the workmen's shouts and oaths were muffled, like Bluebeardian brides asphyxiating in the nuptial pillow. Oldona kept stalking the banks with her whip and megaphone, calling out instructions or lashing at a disobedient silhouette.

They met at the Palais de Decadence every midnight. The staff were discreet and showed them into an inner suite of rooms, done up in gaudy purple satins, where narghiles bubbled and clockwork zoetropes showed a panoply of moving erotic images. Lilith puffed the hashish, quaffed the petal-infused wine and listened to the cellos and violins of a hung and drawn quartet. She talked about Artery a lot, casting aspersions on his imagined talent, but this seemed to cause Oldona some pain. When they'd tired of each other's thumbs, the monkeys and eunuchs, they returned to the dance-floor, gyrating in a corybantic frenzy, as if releasing inner tensions as taut as cables on the bridge.

Eventually, the project was completed. It was the day before Artery was due to fly back over. He hadn't sent her a letter since storming out all those months before. She assumed he'd hitched himself to a harpy his own age and this thought kept the hatred flowing through her veins. Once she started to spin the grinding wheels of her dramatic scheme, the hate would pour out, engulfing the campus.

Oldona still knew nothing about it. The opening of the bridge would make a perfect backdrop to revenge plans. There was going to be a parade with fireworks and bunting; the Chancellor and his minions were supposed to be the first to stride over. Halfway across, they would pause to make a speech about unity and fraternity. That would be Lilith's signal; with a twist of the faucet, she would release the reservoir of blood directly under them, turning the river the colour of slaughtered tomatoes. Artery would return to immediate disgrace, his degree stripped and orders given to exile him from Stakehampton's limits.

Naturally, this would ruin Lilith as well. But she planned to throw herself on Oldona's mercy, pleading with the student to take her

62

back to Arkham. Once in America, she would propose living together as squid-and-bat, which would give her rights under the constitution. From this base, she could set about sabotaging any reputation Artery had managed to make in the music business. If he went Stateside to resume a music career, he would find himself greeted by jeers.

The night before the big day, Oldona took Lilith for a drink at the Palais. Lilith wanted to keep a clear head, but the student insisted she consume bottle after bottle of strong beer.

"It's a celebration," Oldona insisted.

Lilith leaned closer and belched. "I've enjoyed your caresses for a whole semester. But why don't you let me give you pleasure in return? Is it American shyness? My tongue is very fast!"

Oldona smiled. "Just wait for tomorrow, Mrs Robinson. All will then be revealed; it's a surprise for you!"

In the morning, Lilith woke with a hangover. Groping her way to the bed's edge, she looked at the sundial in horror. She had overslept: in a few minutes, the parade would begin. Dressing hurriedly in a velvet cape she jumped to the window and looked out. The canopy had been lifted from the bridge and the river-banks were thronged with students. Mrs Robinson rubbed her disbelieving eyes: the bridge was an exact replica of a banjo and Oldona stood in the centre of the structure like a plectrum. Aghast, Lilith fell back from the curtains. Noticing the movement at the window, Oldona blew a kiss. Was this some sort of sick joke? A banjo! Shivering, Lilith chewed her talons, her hearts thumping.

Slowly, like puppets stalking a lathe, the Chancellor and his staff of diseased minions made their way to the front of the bridge. There was no better time: all eyes were focused on the river and the crossing. Mrs Robinson rushed to her desk, felt under it for the faucet and opened the valve. There was an immense crash far below, the pipes were rumbling and screaming; the office shook. She returned to the window and looked down. Any moment now, the tide of blood...

At this point, something truly unexpected happened. The Chancellor took his first faltering step on the bridge, followed by his colleagues. The vibration sounded a chord from the taut cables. Each step produced a different chord, a sequence of notes which formed a melody. Even worse, the melody was recognisable as one of Artery's most syrupy compositions. As the Chancellor proceeded, Oldona raised her megaphone, pointed it at Lilith's window and started to sing.

Lilith dove headfirst through the glass, speeding towards Oldona. A student burst into applause, convinced this was part of the parade. Then others joined in, distracting Lilith, who lost control and collided with Oldona. The exchange student tumbled and bits of her fell off. Suddenly, it appeared she had snapped in two.

Lilith rolled upright and gazed at the disconnected segments of her American lover, her Sapphic sweetheart.

"Artery Garfunkle and Appalling Simon!"

The two figures brushed splinters of smashed costume from wings and limbs. Artery was rueful. "This isn't what I wanted! It was supposed to be a surprise. Now you've spoiled it!"

The Chancellor approached, his inverted face full of occult fury. A deafening rumble beneath them drowned out his words of chastisement. Now the torrent of blood was gushing at full force down the river but nobody seemed to notice. They were too concerned with watching the Chancellor's bodily contortions, unsure whether this really was part of the act. With a pang of despair, Lilith realised the whole flood of ichor was going to pass without exciting any comment whatsoever.

"Why did you do it, Artery? What was it for?"

"You mean you didn't know it was us, Mrs Robinson? But I thought we blew our disguise in the Palais de Decadence!"

The Chancellor bellowed. Lilith wiped a tear.

"Oldona was just a costume!" she cried. "I fell in love with a mere disguise! No wonder her mannerisms seemed familiar! You've hurt me badly this time, Artery. My heart is cankerous!"

Garfunkle laughed uneasily. "This is a joke, right? You are trying some sort of double-bluff? Appalling and I came up with the plan during my graduation. We wanted to hear you praise our music. You pretended not to like it, but we knew that was an affectation. We're talented lads and our songs are special! So we invented the exchange student as a test. It failed and you saw behind Oldona's disguise. You must have done, because you kept insisting you hated our music!"

Appalling added: "If you hadn't known it was us, you'd have given a more honest appraisal and said we were great!"

Artery nodded. "We figured if you were going to keep up with such a ridiculous pretence, we were as well! I thought the banjo-bridge was the really clever touch. A stroke of genius!"

Lilith was still sobbing. "I loved a figment!" She grabbed Artery's wings. "Don't you understand? I loved her!"

Artery cleared his throat and shuffled his feet. "Very funny but we ought to kneel in front of the Chancellor before he has us locked in the college dungeons! He's livid as a maggot!"

Lilith peered over the side of the bridge. The river was clear as a mouse's lust. Not a spot of blood remained in the water. "Let's just get away, Artery. Come with me back to my room."

"I'm all yours!" Artery let himself be led from the bridge and into the air. They flapped over the crumbling outbuildings to the residential block. They entered the window together.

As soon as they were inside, Lilith took the cleaver from the chain around her neck and struck Artery a mighty blow. His wing tore along the edge. He gasped and choked in amazement.

"What was that for? Didn't you like my landing?"

He struggled into the air, spiralling around the room and crashing onto the bed, his face and voice contorted.

Lilith glowered. "You've finished me at this college. I can't take a job in America, because my contact was a fraud. Arkham isn't aware of my existence! My only option is to join my husband in Yemen. But Woody needs some new exhibits to stay there. Your

65

tendons have been toughened by singing. Ghouls won't find you appetising."

The blade slashed down again. Garfunkle screamed.

Lilith chortled. "This is the sound of violence."

It really was his age. These warped relationships were doomed right from the outset. There were historic examples: Actaeon had peeped at the goddess Diana as she bathed naked and she was several millions years his senior. The affair ended in disaster. Lilith knew the source of Artery's irritating innocence: too much maturity.

Perhaps he had been so sensible he'd gone round in a circle. Which, she supposed, was the only way to go with a damaged wing. As she allowed her gaze to linger on his torn membrane, she raised the cleaver for what lay ahead. Each time it descended, she counted on his appendages and her numbers soon exhausted fingers and toes.

There must be fifty ways to cleave a lover.

A GIRL LIKE A DORIC COLUMN

1 "Excuse me, is your girlfriend feeling unwell?"

"I don't think so. Why do you ask?"

"Stop me if it's none of my business, but she seems to have a... It appears that her... I mean to say..."

"Dribble it out man. What's wrong with her?"

"Her head is made from blue marble."

"What? Nonsense! Wait a moment, so it is. Somebody must have stolen the original and substituted this lifelike replica. Who would do a thing like that? Why didn't I notice anything?"

"Gangs of pickfaces roam the subways. They target a victim and make a replica head from whatever materials they feel comfortable with. Heads which are already loose can be swapped in seconds. I bet your girlfriend had a heavy skull on a slender neck?"

"Yes, but it wasn't particularly valuable."

"To the right people it might be..."

"That sounds rather ominous. Please explain."

"The gangs export them to China. I read about it in the paper. Huge demand for heads over there. They use them for ornamental purposes. It's just not safe to take a lady out."

"Good job I didn't like her very much. But I promised her father to get her home in one piece before midnight."

"Will he notice that her head isn't real?"

"Absolutely. He's obsessed with details. Besides, she sings for him in the parlour after supper. It's a family tradition. I'd better confess and face the music, or lack of it."

"Rather you than me. What will he do?"

"I shudder to think. He's very protective. He works in the foundry. Perhaps he'll boil my ankles over a red-hot girder. Why do relationships always have to be so complicated?"

"I asked myself the same question when my wife left me. The ceiling was falling down and she was fed up with getting plaster in her hair, so she just walked out. Packed a suitcase and went, without saying goodbye. She was run over by a steamroller."

"That's life, I guess. But what shall I do?"

"Maybe I can help. I'm used to dealing with vengeful fathers. It'll cost you, though. I'm not a charity."

"I'm willing to pay. What's the price?"

"The girl. I collect females like her."

"I'm not sure. She might not want to go with you. She's very choosy with her affections. You are bald and ugly."

"With a blue marble head how will she tell the difference? Come on, it's either that or facing the father alone. If you're worried about how I'll treat her, put your mind at rest."

"Well I'd like to know. It's only natural."

"Of course. She will be assisting my religious studies. I'm turning my house into a temple. It's a sacred task I have lined up, nothing odd. Think of her as a foundation of spirituality."

"I can't argue with that. Let's shake hands on the deal."

67

"That's more like it. You won't regret this. I'm a professional and always guarantee my work. Wait and see. I bet if you have trouble with a father in the future you'll seek me out."

"I don't intend losing another girlfriend's head!"

"I think you'll find most women have loose ones these days. Perhaps you'll get lucky and meet a divorcee. They tend to use glue. But nothing is really secure on the subway any more."

"The next stop is mine. You'd better follow."

"The stop belongs to the railway, but I know what you mean. Shall I take your girlfriend's arm to help her down?"

"She's not yours yet. Come on, let's jump off here."

"We're right behind you... Not that way, dear... You have a complex and exquisite network of veins, like a map of an antediluvian city ruled by intelligent reptiles... Mind the gap..."

2 "Well that was a cheap trick to play on me!"

"Not at all. I fulfilled my side of the bargain. You have little to fear from that father now. A successful mission."

"You replaced his head with a mahogany one!"

"Some people are never satisfied. I'm a pickface, but I work alone. You should have realised that when I talked so knowledgeably about China and the export market. But I'm only able to carve heads from hardwood. A marble head is quite beyond my ability."

"Do you make a habit of this? How many commuters have you deceived? I ought to inform the transport police."

"Don't be churlish. Just give me your girl."

"I guess you deserve her. But I feel nervous. Why do business-deals always have to be so complicated?"

"I often ask myself that question when I'm sitting at home, burning incense to the deity who lives in my broom-cupboard. He lurks behind the buckets and refuses to come out."

"Heavens! I thought dry-rot was bad enough. What sort of god is he? Does he answer prayers or hurl lightning?"

"Neither, I'm afraid. I think he might be one of the *Old Ones*, left behind during the last ice-age. At night he plays the washboard with his gnarled fingers. I'm sure this music is what made the ceiling fall down. He lives on spiders and detergent."

"Sounds like Baby Jesus to me. Is he swaddled?"

"No, completely naked. When my temple to him is finished, I believe he'll be more approachable. I've chosen the Dorian style of architecture for his sanctum, because it represents the last period when the *Old Ones* openly interacted with humanity."

"And the girl is a sacrifice to him?"

"Oh dear, no. I need her to hold the roof up. I've got a dozen with blue marble heads lining the lounge. When there's enough of them to take the weight, I'll knock the walls down."

"Hey presto! An instant temple!"

"That's the idea. He's far too small a god to digest a whole female in one go. For sacrifices I rely on my wife."

"I thought you said she left you?"

"She did. But I rushed out after the steamroller and peeled her off the asphalt in a single flapping sheet. I rolled her up under my arm and stored her in the downstairs toilet."

"You sentimental old fool. How touching!"

"Whenever he gets frisky and starts playing his damned washboard, I tear off a required length and feed it to him on a pole. My wife doubles up as a blanket on cold nights. I think I prefer her after the accident. But she's getting shorter every month."

"This is my stop. I'll take my leave of you here. But I've got some bad news, I'm afraid. I'm also a pickface."

"I should have known! You have fingers like chisels."

"I specialise in brass heads. I made a switch when you looked away. Now you shan't finish your temple."

"You swapped her blue marble head for a brass one? That's breach of contract. Give it back this instant!"

"You misunderstand. I can't blame you, considering what your brains have to sit in. It's your head I picked."

"So you have! That's really brassed me off. You'd better return it. How will I ever enter an ironmonger's without losing face? You've ruined me. Come back here for a good polishing!"

"Sorry, I have to deliver a parcel to China. But look on the bright side. You'll be able to fry mushrooms on your cheeks. Haven't you wanted to do that for years? It's not all doom."

"What will my god say? He'll be absolutely livid."

"But mine will be enraptured. I've also got a broom-cupboard with a resident deity. He's the last of the *Older Ones*, who are much older than the *Old Ones*. Apart from the *Oldest Ones* they're the oldest *Ones* of all. He plays the spoons all evening. I suppose diabolism and skiffle must be connected somewhere along the line."

"It's not fair! I'm a widower!"

"So am I. My wife was a steamroller. She blamed herself for rolling over a pedestrian and committed suicide."

"But what about my temple? It was so ambitious."

"I've decided to adopt your idea for my house. Perhaps it will keep my god away from his blasted spoons. He's bigger than yours so I'll have to build a larger temple. He'll need a higher roof and girls just aren't tall enough. Let me think it over."

3 "Excuse me, is your boyfriend feeling unwell?"

"I don't think so. Why do you ask?"

"Stop me if it's none of my business, but he seems to have a... It appears that his... I mean to say..."

TELEGRAM MA'AM

The Queen sits on her throne, writing telegrams. There is a knock on the door. It is Perry, the inventor. "What do you have for me this time, Mr Perry?" He holds up a slim object, dripping like a snake fang. The Queen frowns. "Well what is it?"

"A fountain-pen, your majesty."

"Is it faster than a quill, Mr Perry?"

"Much faster, ma'am."

The Queen discards the quill, which tickles the floor.

*

Many more things have just reached their hundredth birthday. There is a frayed glove in the second drawer of a maple desk in a forgotten room in a cheap hotel in Brighton. There is an octahedral ruby cut from a flawed stone by a myopic jeweller with a blunt chisel in Winchester. There is a saying among the folk of Bideford, Devon, which declares, "Better to dip an organ in cider than a piano in rum," and another in Folkestone, Kent, not recorded — they have both turned one hundred. And a vast telescope in the roof-garden of Sir William Herschel. And the silver ring used by Prince Albert to restrain his erections, hidden in a rococo box when not in use, and the box itself, or rather its lock, and in the pocket of the locksmith's grandson, a farthing. There is a bicycle lying under a gorse bush on the North York Moors, where Joan Bailey lost it after her lover struck her on the head with a mallet, and she went wandering without her memory to Coventry, eventually becoming the manager of a puppet theatre, while the bush grew to help the lover avoid suspicion. There is a plough nailed to a wall in an Oxford tavern.

These have existed for exactly a century, and telegrams must be sent out to all of them.

The Queen is still sitting on her throne. Throughout the palace, the clocks are striking midnight. She covers a yawn with a hand. "Oh why must I congratulate *everything?*"

The people are growing agitated, politely. Agents ride out beyond them, disdaining the clamour. "Our monarch has abandoned us!" The agents say nothing, except the younger ones, who reply, "No she hasn't!" But the people will not listen. There is discontent in Dover. There is a hubbub in Huddersfield. There are murmurings in Manchester. The agents gallop faster. There is a gnashing in Grantham, not of teeth, which are rare there, but of groceries, pears gnashed against plums. "The monarch is neglecting us!" "No she isn't!"

71

An agitator mounts a soap-box in Leeds. He has a speech prepared. A republican agenda. He opens his mouth, but an agent rides up to him and delivers a slip of paper.

"What's this? A telegram?"

The lowest button on his shirt must celebrate.

Prince Albert sits with the Queen in the bedchamber, holding hands. There is an aspidistra in a vase. The vase has recently received its telegram, the aspidistra has not.

"I can't take much more of this!"

She strokes his moustache. "Our duties must be fulfilled, dear. It's the constitution, you know. A secret part of modern government, vital to the integrity of the state."

"I am a man. I have desires. You are never being here, in my arms, like a wife. What shall happen when my erection restraint wears out? It was forged over ten decades ago."

"We will order another, from the Sheffield Kama Sutra Co."

"I am sure to die of frustration!"

The Queen sits on her throne, writing telegrams. The fountain-pen is faster than the quill, but the workload does not lessen. There are more things in the world now, more objects to grow old. And as the Empire continues to expand, it gets worse. A gold-mine in Natal. A brewery in Australia. A religion in Rajasthan. There is a knock on the door. It is Stephenson, the inventor.

"What do you have for me this time, Mr Stephenson?"

"A locomotive, your majesty."

"Is it faster than a horse?"

"Much faster, ma'am."

"Kindly demonstrate, Mr Stephenson."

"It is too large to bring indoors."

The Queen cocks an ear and hears a distant whistle and the scrape of a shovel on coal. The years chug past.

The Prime Minister is arguing with the Lord Chancellor.

72

"But the tradition is doing wonders for our economy. Think of the technological offshoots it has created!"

"The Queen is exhausted. Remember what happened to George III. He went mad. And William IV took to drink."

"Nonetheless, the tradition must continue. Too much time and effort has been invested to cancel it now. I have personally meddled with the archives of the Patent Office, altering dates and names, so that future historians will not perceive a link between progress and the tradition. You know which tradition I mean."

"The tradition which is kept secret from the people?"

"Yes, precisely that tradition."

"The tradition which has been indirectly responsible for numerous inventions, including the cantilever bridge, tarmac, the dynamo, sewing machines, the gyroscope, the compression refrigerator, corrugated iron, dirigibles, and the first-class stamp?"

"That's the one! Strike this from the record!"

Agents sit in the buffet-cars of locomotives. Behind them, they tow nine carriages full of telegrams. At various points along the route, they open the doors and leap into the night, clutching a message. One has a trowel concealed under his hat. He lands awkwardly, shuffling toward a nameless village. The locomotive turns a bend and leaves him alone. He enters a churchyard, searching mossy headstones for the correct name. Here it is! He crouches and hacks at the fog-drenched earth with the trowel. At last the coffin is revealed. Pausing for breath, he glances around. An owl in a blasted yew returns his look. The agent jumps onto the coffin and inserts the edge of his tool under the lid. Rusty nails yawn from crumbling wood. Spiders flee. He throws back the lid like the cover of a Penny Dreadful and gags as a moonbeam, challenging a cloud to a duel and running it through, impales a madly grinning skeleton, bones jutting from mouldy suit! Hurriedly, the agent pins the telegram to the collar of the skeleton's shirt, replaces the lid and soil and dances the plot flat, with a lame leg.

*

Prince Albert has sickened and died, of frustration, or typhoid, it is not clear which, possibly both. "Now I will have more time to devote to the writing of telegrams!" sobs the Queen.

The agitator squats in the hold of a prison-ship. A warder approaches, checking cells with a lantern. Something is wrapped around the glass, casting a stream of words over beams and bulwarks. At regular intervals, for no discernible reason, the warder lashes at his captives with a cat o' nine tails. The agitator counts ten stripes on his legs when it is his turn. He notes that the extra tail is a length of paper, dangling from the handle of the antique whip.

The Queen sits on her throne, writing telegrams. There is a knock on the door. It is Littledale, the inventor.
    "What do you call that thing, Mr Littledale?"
    "A typewriter, your majesty."
    "Is it quieter than a locomotive, Mr Littledale?"
    "Slightly, ma'am. It is powered by ribbons."
    "Can it do the writing for me?"
    "Not at this stage. In a century or two."
    "It must write a telegram to itself when that happens."

The French President is worrying his Chief of Police.
    "What are the English playing at, mon cher?"
    "I don't know, Monsieur President."
    "They are cutting down trees at a furious rate. Obviously to make paper. But paper for what?"
    "English novels, perhaps?"
    "Ah yes! Do you like English novels, mon cher? I ordered one from London last week. A Defoe. The seventh word in the twelfth line of the sixty-third paragraph of the ninety-fifth chapter had a telegram glued to it. With noxious fish glue!"
    "An extraordinary coincidence, Monsieur President! I also ordered a Defoe from London last week. At the centre was a compressed oak leaf and stapled to the leaf was a telegram."

"Rosbif! Barbarians! Louts! We must consider forging an alliance, mon cher, to discover the meaning."

A gold tooth under a pillow in a Padstow cottage, still waiting, without an owner, for a fairy. A wig in a box at the rear of a kennel in Durham, guarded by a dog with the morals of a cat. The belief that some cherries contain real stones, probably flints, held by the farmers of Thetford. A picture of a summer day in the Cotswolds, painted with clotted cream and magenta jam, in an unhygienic bakery in Winchcombe. A pistol in the hand of the very last man to fight a legal duel in Breckland, eating cherries to ignite the charge. A rotten hymn.

The Queen sits on her throne. Telegrams, knock on the door. A figure who wears his sideburns like camshafts.

"Who are you? I have no inventor called Babbage!"

"With respect, ma'am, I have been seeking an audience with you for thirty years. Allow me to demonstrate this analytical engine here. It is an early type of computer and can be programmed to perform a large body of functions, such as writing telegrams."

"How dare you talk of body functions in my presence?"

"No ruler can afford to be without one."

"I am busy! Take it away!"

Tears in the palace. A silver ring taken from a box, lovingly pressed to lips. "Once I was your barrel of sauerkraut. You whispered to me, *'Liebe Kleine. Ich habe dich so lieb, ich kann nicht sagen wie'*, and I presumed you were asking to visit the bathroom. But now you are gone. And my life has become a telegram without news."

"You sent for me, your majesty?"

"Yes, Prime Minister. We have a problem. The tradition of sending telegrams to everything is one hundred years old."

"Then you must send a telegram to the tradition."

"But how? How can one send a telegram to a tradition? Who can carry it? Where will they go? I am bewildered."

"You must try, ma'am! You must try!"

The Queen tries:

> *Dear Tradition,*
> *Congratulations on reaching the*
> *centenary of being yourself.*
> *Best wishes,*
> *The Queen.*

No, it is too absurd. Something must be done. The law will have to be altered, so that only old people receive telegrams, not everything. A secret bill must be passed.

The Prime Minister weeps at the thought of change.

A dream: a world where inanimate objects can rest in peace. Unemployed agents race nowhere in automobiles. Paradise! But a cloud looms on the horizon, cooling the idyll. There will still be much work to do. Wines, books, spoons, piers, guitars, floods, hearths, stables, gutters, pots, vendettas, crotchets, cuffs, doors, accidents, comets — these and many other items have been set free, but the population is increasing at an exponential rate. What if people come to outnumber things? How can this be avoided? Only a war, the like of which has never been imagined. That will stall the trend. But with whom?

On nights when the silver ring was kept in its box, Prince Albert gave her children. And these children have also produced children. One is named Wilhelm. Machine-guns, gas.

We are not amused.

THE TELL-TALE NOSE

Atchoo! — runny — very, very dreadfully runny it had been and is; but why *will* you say that it is sore? The cold had numbed my nose — not pained — not tormented it. Above all was the sense of smell diminished. I sniffed nothing in the pantry or in the oven. I quivered no nostril at the laundry basket. No wonder the young man nearly caught me unawares, despite the condition of his socks! He has told you his version of the affair — it is time to hearken to mine.

I knew he wanted to kill me, on account of my eye. It bothered him, my blue iris, the eye of a vulture. Though myopic, it noted his anxiety, his increasing panic, observed all his little preparations with a cool, albeit hazy, detachment. He shuddered when I turned it upon him, as if the orb was a supernatural window into some forbidden realm: the tinted, bulging pane of a beaked god's bathroom.

He had never been so kind as the week before the murder. He cooked my meals, brushed the pale locks of hair which crawled on my shoulders, wound the ebony clock in the hallway, secured the house against robbers by nailing the shutters. He even dressed up in my late wife's underwear and plucked a mandolin, as she had done, so many years before. He cared nothing for my gold, but expressed an interest in a box of wicks I kept on the mantelpiece — spare wicks for a dark lantern I used for fishing the fetid lagoons which ringed the city.

I gave him the box and busied myself in the construction of a giant puppet from a spare nightgown and candle-wax. I stuffed its false torso with my previous week's catch and fashioned a crystal eye to fit in the single central socket of its lopsided skull. This bauble was covered by a leather eyelid, on a spring, and the entire mannequin was operated by cords. Then I arranged the puppet between the sheets of my bed, crawled under the frame and waited. It also had a heart: the mechanism of the ebony clock, fully wound and secreted in a suitable cavity.

For seven nights I lingered in my cramped confines, on the frozen bare boards, while the young man looked into my room, taking an hour to open the door and thrust his head through the gap, but each time he did so, I lost my nerve and felt unable to pull the cords which would cause the mannequin to sit up and open its eye. My arm was paralysed as if by a mystic stiffness. I think it was the dark lantern! Yes, it was this! Its hinges creaked, ever so quietly, and this almost imperceptible sound filled me with anguish, as do all the quietest noises in the world — cell division in lambs, an execution with a guillotine made from cheese, an illicit affair between a barometer and a balloonist.

Naturally, spending a whole week out of bed impaired my resistance to germs and I developed this horrid cold. The sixth and seventh nights passed in unbearable suspense, my mouth set in a rictus grin as I tried to prevent myself sneezing. I welcomed each morning, for at the first note of birdsong the young man would withdraw his head and allow me the freedom to slither out of my confinement and give vent to the meteorological pressures within me. Listen to my nose as it expels the emerald typhoon! Does it not sound like a second voice?

On the eighth night I succumbed. A sinusoidal wave of phlegm rushed along my sinuses. In desperation, I covered my nostrils with my generous tongue; a useless precaution. Might as well attempt to cap a geyser with a mouldy rug! The detonation echoed off the underside of the bed like a carbine shot. "Atchoo's there?" my nose cried, and with the spasm which racked my body, my arm jerked involuntarily, tugging the cords which crossed the floor, climbed the wall, ran back along the ceiling, tripped over a pulley and speared down to hook the mannequin.

The puppet abruptly sat erect, and the young man kept quite still and said nothing. For a whole hour, he remained thus, and I guessed the single eye had sprung open, but that it was too dark to glimmer, and presently I heard a groan, a slight noise which may have been the wind in the chimney, a mouse crossing the floor or a cricket which has made a single chirp, but it was clear the young man would interpret it to be an expression of mortal terror from his intended victim.

When he had waited a long time, very patiently, he resolved to open a crevice in the lantern. I imputed this not from a change in the level of illumination in the room, for I knew he would contrive to permit only a single ray, the slenderest possible, to flee the apparatus — one incapable of diffusing from its rigid path — but by an extremely subtle odour from the oily wick, as well as the unbearably quiet grinding of those glacial hinges.

I then heard an intake of breath — an intake sharper than a peeled bell. The ray had connected with the puppet's vulture eye. How could it miss? The blue crystal I had selected was immense; it dominated a full half of the face. And the leather eyelid quivered on its spring. Yes, it must have been like this! With the clockwork heart pounding within the wax breast! Pounding like a plum ready to burst in an excess of anguish! The young man would not tolerate this; he would be compelled to silence it.

With a loud yell, he threw open the lantern fully and leapt across the room and onto the puppet. In an instant he dragged it to the floor and toppled the heavy bed over it. Now I was exposed and aghast at the possibility of discovery, but the young man was so intent upon finishing his grisly task that he paid no note to anything outside the diameter of that azure eye. I fled, unseen, scuttling along the boards and out of the door. Now it was necessary to hide away. But where?

I have already alluded to my evisceration of the hallway clock. So too have I related how the young man was wont to wind it every day of that fateful week. Too deluded was he to realise he was winding nothing which might be construed as a *precision* instrument. No, no! I had replaced the mechanism with an orange! Thus there was quite enough room to conceal my body within its sable depths, and accordingly I slipped inside and closed the door.

Here my knees knocked and my teeth ached, with trepidation, no doubt; but my occupation of a timepiece did not suggest to my mind the gradual yet unstoppable progress of decay and death. For there was no pendulum or escapement to count the twists on my mortal coil. Betwixt chronometer and orange there are few points of similarity — only the pips are the same. I gained courage as I listened to the young man pulling up the planks in my chamber. The rasp of a saw, the sloshing of a tub, confirmed his wise precautions.

He was dismembering the puppet, carefully so as to collect every drop of blood. And blood there would be in plenty; for the figure's hollow limbs were filled with fish from the fetid lagoons, or what I assumed to be fish, and I rubbed my hands in glee, believing that my revenge on the young man was nearly complete. He was never a real son to me. He had turned up at the house uninvited on my wedding night and refused to leave. Somehow my wife and I came to regard him as a piece of furniture. We regularly adopted chairs and tables. Why not a man?

By the time he completed his labours — about four o'clock, though I could not be sure, for an orange does not strike the hours, though a puppet's heart under floorboards does — there came a knocking at the street door. He descended with a light step, confident he had nothing to fear. There entered three men, who introduced themselves, with perfect suavity, as officers of the police. A shriek had been heard by a neighbour during the night; suspicion of foul play had been aroused. At this, I chuckled softly to myself. The neighbour in question has hearing almost as sensitive as my own; it is a trait common to the inhabitants of our street.

The young man led them about the house. He bade them search — search *well*. He was more confident of escaping detection than a chameleon in a hall of mirrors. And so was I, for the ebony clock, with its warped and twisted frame, did not seem a feasible hiding place for any object, but luckily my own bent limbs and mutated body slotted exactly into its bonebreaking curves. As I expected, in his mania to be of assistance, he even carried chairs into my bedroom and insisted the officers rest from their fatigues there, directly above the grave of the puppet. Satisfied, the officers chatted together, all very amiable, of trifles, and other confections.

Now I knew that the clock would be ticking beneath the young man's feet and that he would gradually find this fact unbearable. He had lived too long in the neighbourhood not to have developed acute hearing. I listened to him arguing with the officers — *trifles were inferior to profiteroles!* — in a high key and with violent gesticulations, and I knew I would soon be rid of the fool. He gasped for breath, paced the floor with heavy strides, foamed, raved, swore! He swung his chair and grated it upon the boards — *custard slices were the lowest class of cake!* — but then betrayed himself with a scream.

"Villains!" he shrieked, "dissemble no more! I admit the deed! — tear up the planks! — here, here! — it is the beating of his hideous heart!" Immediately there was the sound of stressed wood, popping nails, a triple gasp of amazement, a creak of knees bending. I ground my molars in repressed delight. This was the culmination of my plan! The police officers were certain to judge the young man insane when they reached down to retrieve mere hunks of wax, cogs and fish scales dusting a great glass eye! Confessing to the murder of a puppet! They would have no choice but to arrest him and carry him off to a madhouse.

Such was my hope. But all too soon was it to prove forlorn. For one of the officers announced hoarsely: "Yes, it is a heart! And here are the kidneys! And there the lights, folded around the tongue!" And he called for a handkerchief to wrap up these items as evidence for the prosecution. I was much too stupefied by these revelations to account them a jest. Then, as I uncreased my deformed brow in an inverse frown more conducive to profound thought than the standard kind, an abominable fear came upon me, a feeling that my past was catching up with me, like a skeleton on a unicycle — unsteadily, clankingly, ludicrously, bone shakingly.

I have mentioned my late wife and her mandolin. Also her underwear. However, I have neglected to offer an account of how her plucking drove me to distraction. From our wedding-night, when the young man first turned up, right through all the early years of our marriage, she kept me awake between midnight and dawn with the infernal silences of her melodies. Truly, she was the *quietest* mandolin player on the globe, and as I have already intimated, it is the *barest* sounds which I cannot *bear*.

In the middle of a dull and fitful slumber in the autumn of one year, I was roused by an even more excessive silence than usual. I opened my single central eye and beheld her sitting on the edge of the bed. Either from deliberation or impulse, she had neglected to string her mandolin. Consequently, the airs she sounded were no more than that — the rustle of fingers on the stale vapours of the chamber. I rose in a passion and wrested the instrument from her grasp. How many blows were sufficient is unknown. Perhaps it required a dozen — who shall tell?

I cut her up into very tiny pieces and flushed her down the toilet. Doubtless the young man observed me from some hidden recess. He was fond of lurking in corners; I dare say the genesis of *his* crime was in this scene. As the cistern refilled, I presumed the matter was at an end. But now, so many years later, I was forced to reconsider the matter. Not all the municipal sewers flowed to the sea; a few older ones, twisted by a geological upheaval, deposited their effluvia in the fetid lagoons which ringed the city. Why had I forgotten this?

It was more than possible that her remains were channelled into the lagoons, partly preserved by the formaldehyde discharged by the chemical works and mortuary establishments on those clammy shores. For more than a decade, her viscera might have risen and fallen with the secret sluggish currents, drawn not by the moon but the mass of the city, to lap the crumbling jetties and rotting boardwalks where the oddest fishers sat, rods in hand, hooks catching on the corrugated surface of the infinitesimal wavelets and straining up, to lift the lid of scum from the deeps, the toxic fathoms.

Yes, this was it! And what if I had caught her pieces on my last expedition? No use berating myself for not noticing the coincidence at the time; I never actually *look* at the results of my catches. Oh no! The dark lantern I carry through the hollow streets and beyond the deserted suburbs is merely for the sake of appearance. I wish to fit in with my nameless colleagues on the quays. I do not open the device, for the reason I have already elucidated — the hinges, the excruciatingly *quiet* hinges.

Now I discerned the sounds of a brief scuffle. The officers were grappling with the young man. The rattle of handcuffs, the echo of a truncheon. It occurred to me that I was still safe. In those days, forensic medicine was a primitive art; the officers would never know that the recovered heart, kidneys, lights and tongue were not mine! Who was clever enough to open the handkerchief where they nestled and tell the gender of their owner? Nobody, not then! So all I had to do was remain hidden a few more minutes, while they left the house. The young man would be locked away, as I originally hoped, but for a different reason.

They came down the stairs and passed the ebony clock in the hallway. A little longer and I would be free! But now I felt a twitch in the nostrils and a momentous pressure building up within my lungs. My head ached, and I fancied a rushing in my ears; but still they lingered at the door. Why *would* they not be gone? I pinched my nose between callused thumb and finger, but the pressure increased. Was it possible they felt my presence inside the clock? No, it was the partial vacuum occasioned by my voluminous intake of breath which kept them here, tugging them toward my place of concealment. They fought this force, they strained against it.

At last, I could stifle the eruption no longer. I must let it loose or die! Then it came, a miniature hurricane! — Atchoo! — With the release of pressure, the clock shattered. The door blew open, a backward slam, and the orange rained juicy segments on my head. I stood exposed, my twisted frame shivering before the three officers. I saw that they carried one enormous handkerchief between them and that they had faces sewn up the wise way — one without eyes, another without ears, the third without a mouth. So here was the end of my chances for peace. I would be carried off *with* the young man, possibly to occupy the same cell, while the old house was locked up and auctioned off for its construction materials. But *something* had to be said.

"Germs!" I shrieked, "spread no more! I admit the deed! — tear up the handkerchief! — snot, snot! — it is the sneezing of my hideous nose!"

83

THE BANKER OF INGOLSTADT

"I wish to open a student account."

The clerk removed his tinted spectacles and wiped them with a dirty cloth. The figure seated across the desk had the hungry appearance of an undergraduate, the pale skin and sunken eyes, but was plainly a lunatic. He considered ringing the bell for assistance, but a quick glance around the chamber confirmed that most of the staff had finished work early. So he cleared his throat and muttered:

"You are registered at the university?"

"That's correct. I'm studying *Sociology and Reanimation* with Doctor Waldman. Is there a problem? I was told that your bank offers discounts on carriage travel and tickets for the multistage opera, not to mention a 200 florin bonus for freshers, and a 1000 shilling overdraft facility subject to prior arrangement. Have I made an embarrassing error? Shall I deposit my grant cheque elsewhere?"

"Let us not be hasty. The Bank of Bavaria is indeed rather generous with its terms for customers entering Higher Education. But I'm afraid we have to be completely open with each other and you have already tried to deceive me. Perhaps you would consider a Golden Oven account instead? To put a crust on your funds! How about a Double Mangle? That one limits withdrawals to 10 doubloons a week, but is index linked to the number of fatalities in wars with Prussia or France. Every type of account is open to you — except the one tailored for students. You can't possibly have enrolled at Ingolstadt university."

"Why not? I judge that a gross insult!"

The clerk toyed with a quill resting on a vast ledger. "Because, Fräulein Radcliffe, you are a woman!"

"Absolutely! The first female to register with Doctor Waldman on the *Sociology and Reanimation* modules."

She added darkly: "It's a Rancid Sandwich Course!"

Curling his lower lip around a clubbed finger, the clerk moistened the tip with an inky spittle, opened the ledger and proceeded to flick through the sheets. His prints crowded each other out on every page, as if he derived pleasure from smudging the names which had been scratched in neat rows, in lieu of blotting the identities of the owners. Finally, he reached the last page and slammed the book.

"These are the financial records of every student who has opened an account here since the founding of the college in 1250. Not a single one has ever been a woman. Indeed, there's not enough space in the margins to write 'Fräulein' instead of 'Herr'. And suppose you did deposit your grant cheque with us? We could hardly mix your funds with the male money in the student vault — that would be unseemly. A new vault would have to be constructed just for you, and painted pink, with lace hanging from the combination dial on the lock. Do you truly want to put us to so much bother? I'm sorry, Fräulein Radcliffe."

"Call me Mina." She brushed back her auburn hair and undid the top button of her bodice. "If I open a Double Mangle account, my money will also have to be stored with that of men."

The clerk clucked his tongue disapprovingly. "You sound excited by the concept. No, that's an account for feeble pensioners, which is why I'm amenable to extending its terms to you. There will be a surcharge, of course, to pay for a chaperone. Now then, do you have any proof of identification?"

Mina placed her handbag on the desk. The clerk frowned. It appeared to be sewn from many different types of leather, but the skins had been badly cured, and had not originated on any domestic animal. Parts of the bag sprouted hairs, dark and fair, while other patches were studded with nipples or navels — cameo and intaglio designs which suggested a mother rather than a fashion accessory, with something embryonic in its womb, a sextet of mysteries, if one might pardon the expression. Then she pulled apart the enamel clasp — a tooth in a gum — and rummaged around for a minute, finally producing a square card which held a miniature portrait in oils of her likeness, and an official stamp.

"Oh dear, Fräulein!" muttered the clerk. "That is a Students' Union Card, and as we have already established, there is no such thing as a female undergraduate. I don't know how you came by it, though I suspect theft or forgery, but I am not willing to be duped by such tricks." He indicated the ledger. "As I said, there has never been a woman with a student account in our business history."

"May I see?" Mina drew the ledger toward her with two delicate but strong hands. The clerk averted his eyes as her wrists slipped out from her sleeves. A dim urge vaulted the security barrier separating his id from his ego, a desire to lean across the desk and touch her knee. He repressed it and gasped. Did he know *how* to touch a woman's knee? The answer was negative, but a disturbing memory came loose from the spike where it had been impaled, ready for filing and obfuscation. It flapped around inside his cranium. The palm rests on the kneecap, the fingers close around it, the hand slides gradually up... No, it was a fraudster! An impostor memory!

He was rescued by a squeal of delight from Mina, who had found an entry which excited her. For a moment, he was worried, fearing she had discovered a name to challenge his assertion, but he knew the ledger like the back of his pituitary gland. What was she saying now? He rubbed his ears, feeling a little dizzy, twiddling the moles on his neck.

"Look, it's his signature! I can't believe he really sat here and signed this!" Mina pressed her lips to the name in faded ink. "Victor Frankenstein!"

"Who? Oh, that wastrel! Yes, I remember him well. He defaulted on a loan. Said he wanted funds to insulate the attic of his lodgings and then spent the money on electric eels! You're not related to him, are you?"

"Heavens, no! Victor was by birth a Genevese, and his family was one of the most distinguished of that republic. I am from Montevideo, but my father was English. Have you really nothing better to say about this incredible genius? It was Victor who first succeeded in imparting life to the limbs and organs of corpses. Without his pioneering work, the university of Ingolstadt would not now be running any *Reanimation* courses. He was my hero when I was growing up on the outskirts of my home town. I remember attempting to galvanise a dead horse when all my friends wanted to

86

do was arrange flowers or tie ribbons in their hair — at least I thought it was dead! And when my mother expired of cholera, I insisted on attaching two electrodes to her temples and flying a kite in a storm. It didn't work, but I still recall the detonation inside her coffin. I keep the ashes in this locket. Would you care to see?"

"Those ashes are coloured, Fräulein!"

"Well, my mother was a mulatto. Originally from Senegal."

The clerk flicked his dirty cloth over his perspiring face. He felt that his tongue had swollen at the back of his throat. "Then you are part *black*?"

"Indeed. Is there a difficulty with that?"

For a brief instant, he started to rise to his feet, but the cold air which rushed to ventilate his stale buttocks was so original and alarming a sensation that he reversed the direction of force and pushed himself down as firmly as possible. But his voice had the shriek of one who has stood to shake a finger.

"And you still insist you have enrolled at the university, here in Ingolstadt, with its white steeple and civilised cobbles? A hottentot floosie!"

Mina narrowed her eyes and the icy beams which stabbed from their green depths chilled the marrow in six of the clerk's ribs.

"It is a great privilege for me," she said quietly, "to study with Doctor Waldman, the same scholar who taught chemistry to Victor Frankenstein. I will now trouble you no further, but take my money to an alternative bank."

Quick as a pig's tail in a mincer, the clerk shot out his arm and seized Mina's elbow. He made a valiant attempt to smile. "I assure you, Fräulein Radcliffe, that no other bank will be interested in dealing with a tainted female. Not only that, but there are, in fact, no other banks in Ingolstadt. However, the Bank of Bavaria is more tolerant and generous than most. So let us consider our little problem. You wish to open a student account, but it is impossible for you to be a student. When I suggest a more suitable type of account, you grow surly. We are getting nowhere. Thus I suggest a private arrangement, just between you and me. I will hold the money for you, mingled with my own savings. If you wish to make a withdrawal, you may visit me after closing hours."

"Mingle my money? Where is your prudishness now?"

He shuddered away her objections. "My savings have no interest in physical contact, I assure you. They prefer to reproduce through sheer fiscal discipline. Naturally, there will be a hefty charge for this favour — I will have to falsify documents."

Mina's voice quavered slightly. "How can I be sure you will not try to cheat me?" She watched for any betrayal of compassion in his answer, the merest flicker of humanity, but there was none.

"Ah, but I *will* cheat you, Fräulein! You shall have to come to my lodgings whenever you require a few coins. There will be a strict limit on how much you may withdraw at one time. You will be compelled to visit me often. My rooms are very secluded. They have never known a female presence. Even the fleas are exclusively male. It is strange, but when I consider my history, I find a number of anomalies... Different memories, many of which do not belong to me. As if once I was married... Please excuse me, I am rambling. Your astonishing implication that women are somehow equal to men has quite disordered my senses."

"Very well. You leave me no choice. My grant cheque is worthless unless it is cashed. I have rent to pay, books and equipment to buy. I have a glittering career ahead, and I do not wish to spoil it by dying in the gutter."

"Your mind almost has a grasp of algorithmic reasoning, Fräulein. I applaud you. Every phenomenon is prone to the occasional incongruity. Supernovae in distant galaxies, irregularities in chasing up debtors, and now a girl who thinks like a man!" He lowered his tone to a clipped snarl. "Sign the back of the cheque and write a short contractual statement declaring that you hereby entrust the entire amount to my keeping."

Mina took the quill, dipped it in a pot of ink near her elbow and scratched the required marks on the cheque. She dried her signature by flapping the piece of paper before passing it to the clerk, who folded it and slipped it into his top pocket. Then she asked: "May I have my first instalment now? Just a shilling or two."

With a nonchalance which had something of the madhouse about it, in the same way that even a kind smile can suggest the terminal closing of a dungeon door, the clerk replaced his tinted spectacles. Now he was isolated from her, filtered out from his own humanity, which still seemed to consist of many parts. He rested his elbows on the desk, cradled his chin in his hands and sniffed. "Do I know you, Fräulein?"

"I demand the return of my money!"

"What is all this fuss? I have no idea what you are talking about. Do you suppose you can just burst in here and threaten a member of staff? The Bank of Bavaria always takes very good care of its employees. A single shake of this silver bell will summon guards who will hurl you into the street! And why have you unbuttoned your bodice? This is most unwelcome. Remove yourself from my restricted sight!"

A thousand expressions crossed Mina's face. At last her visage settled on a single aspect, a clench of jaw and smouldering of eyes which was exactly poised midway between impotent fury and — here the clerk felt a vague discomfort — languid amusement. His throat uttered an injunction of its own, tinged with too much panic, a croak scarred and notched with a rasp.

"Begone! Take your provocative bosom and radical egalitarianism away!"

Mina's tears were perhaps just a little strained. She clutched at the lapels of his coat, sending clouds of dust toward the panelled ceiling.

"I have a family to support! My fiancé is a poor tailor!"

His lips trembled, at different velocities, as if they attended rival funerals. He struggled to maintain his heartlessness, but now there were two organs pumping congealed blood inside his chest — hers as well as his own, or so it felt. He ached, and his fingers probed for the button of a secret compartment in the desk. The hidden drawer slid open and he plucked a coin from a mound, pushed it across to her and hissed: "Here, Fräulein. I can hardly keep up this charade. I want to be callous, I really do, but somehow you have touched me in places I had no idea I possessed. My sympathy — ah, how I shiver to use such a word! — has been roused. Please take this guinea."

She almost seemed disappointed. "Are you sure?"

He nodded and sat back, awaiting her gratitude, but she sighed and lifted her peculiar handbag onto the desk, obscuring the golden coin. Then she dipped inside and produced a selection of blades, scissors and little picks, tiny saws and screwdrivers.

"A sewing-kit, Fräulein? Really, this is hardly the time to start mending socks!"

The last item to emerge was a hammer. Mina weighed it carefully in one hand for a moment, nodded to herself and arched over the desk to deliver a single blow to the forehead of the clerk. He felt the shape of the wound, a hexagonal dent with impact lines radiating across his skull, like a multifaceted third eye or mystic sunburst in the centre of his brow. He was much too astonished to collapse or emit a scream. But the assault had also dislodged his sense of time. He realised that Mina was now standing next to him, a screwdriver inserted into one of the moles on his neck, twisting the tool furiously.

"What is this? Are you murdering me?"

"You have failed the test. You must be dismantled."

And then he did shriek, but it was a short-lived example of the form, for when he opened his mouth, Mina used the opportunity to insert her scissors and snip off his tongue.

Mumbling thickly as the oedematous blood filled his throat, he remembered the bell and reached out to ring it, but again she anticipated his intention and lopped his fingers and thumb off with a miniature cleaver, so that they tumbled over the edge of the desk and bounced on the mosaic floor. Her hands and implements seemed to be all over him, prodding, jabbing, cutting, wrenching. Now she was on her knees beneath him, slicing between his thighs. He bent forward and vomited blood, which spattered onto the upper curve of her partly exposed breasts and gushed in torrents between her cleavage. Constricted at the waist by a belt, the bodice positively bulged with his gore until it frothed back out of her bosom, and, as her breasts wobbled with the work, the red juice spurted in thin jets.

This was hardly the climax to his career he had been expecting. Half a century of plodding toil in the security of his position, inconspicuous but lurking, like a glass spider, before retirement to a small villa in the Böhmer Wald, done up to resemble an office. He had always believed himself to be suspended between two unknown worlds: that of his managers, who inhabited a cubic empire of interlocking conference chambers, awash with the odours of walnut, wine and bathchair lacquer, and that of his clients, which resembled a straight line, a street in a poor suburb, packed with terraced houses without a chink between, leading from one infinite smoky horizon to another. But now both worlds were growing dim, and tears were hatching from under his lids, as Mina struggled to lever his eyeballs out of their sockets with spoons. Both suddenly came free, with a horrible slurping sound, and as they dropped onto his cheeks, they swung like the pendulums of a cuckoo death, the optic nerves of one entangling with those of the other, braiding his visionary sense into that of a Siamese cyclops.

For the first time in his life, one eye was able to directly stare at its twin. It was a different shape, feminine — for the lashes high above were fluttering. Many parts he; now they were leaving him, returning home, and he almost recollected an earlier dissolution, numerous accidents. Mina, he realised, had returned to the mole on his neck. It was not a mole after all, but a bolt, with a screw-thread which passed through his throat. It held his head to his shoulders and she was loosening it with an adjustable spanner. It came out with an inner screech, and his skull began to wobble alarmingly. He attempted to stand, but he lacked knees: they lay under the desk. And every cell of his body rejoiced to be liberated from an unnatural fusion.

There was still time to ring for assistance. Limbless, voiceless, there was only one course of action available. He nodded at the bell and his head fell from his torso, rolling on the polished surface of the desk and knocking the bell over the edge. It tinkled once as it landed.

Then before utter blackness blew into every corner of his mind, he became aware of the wall splitting from ceiling to floor. It was a concealed door, and through it came an ancient figure, thin and menacing, with a shock of white hair and a peculiar limp. Was this the manager of the bank? His hopes fell with his blood-pressure as the figure cried:

"Tough luck, Mina. The practical is always the hardest part."

"Sorry, Doctor Waldman. I tried my best."

"I know you did."

"It was nearly right. After my theory exam I was so confident. But there was a trace of compassion buried in its subconscious. It had to be destroyed. A single flaw and the creature is useless."

"This is a discipline for perfectionists, Mina. I believe you will do better in the resits."

"I hope so, Doctor Waldman. I certainly intend to use these limbs again. They performed very well. But the head is not right. Back to the morgue, I think!"

"Let me help you cram all the pieces in your handbag. You are my favourite student, Mina, and I know you will go far. I feel it in my selection of hearts."

"My only wish is to emulate Victor Frankenstein."

"Oh, you will surpass his achievements. Your aptitude is as staggering as your originality. What a remarkable project for your finals! The Utterly Evil Banker!"

Together they passed through the door, locking it behind them. The props would remain until the examination-room could be booked for a resit.

In a corridor of the university, Mina stopped and clutched at Doctor Waldman's sleeve. Her eyes were like icecaps awaiting a mysterious sledge.

"I must succeed," she said, "for the sake of the human race. The centuries to come will be characterised by unrestrained progress. Science will give us weapons of which we cannot conceive. Motorised guns which can spray thousands of bullets every minute, flying machines which can level whole cities with explosives, armoured wagons and undersea boats, rockets capable of sending germs or poisons to distant countries in a matter of hours, unimagined sources of destructive power borrowed from the sun, mystic rays to blind or carve up crowds, electric gadgets able to monitor and punish citizens. In short, everything necessary for autocrats to stamp their psychoses over the nations of the world! And who will create these devastating tools? Graduates, that's who! What better way to limit their excesses than to nip them in the grant?"

"You always grasp the big picture, Mina."

"We must ensure that as many students as possible are discouraged from graduating. They must be mercilessly hassled at the fresher stage until they drop out. Naturally, there will be those who refuse to abandon their studies, but I can't be expected to cure the problem, merely alleviate it. If my Utterly Evil Banker proves a success, and if I can get it to breed, the banks of the future might be staffed by callous sadists, working tirelessly to oppose students. Such is my dream, Doctor Waldman. I am banking on monsters!"

He patted her shoulder admiringly. "That is what *Sociology and Reanimation* is all about."

Arm in arm, they strolled to the morgue. But they kept their own arms folded.

THE SPANISH CYCLOPS

There was a lens-grinder who had fallen on hard times and who decided to revive his fortunes by exceeding the limits of his profession. Accordingly, he saved his remaining materials and set to work on the grandest project he could imagine.

The citizens of Valencia were perturbed at the noises which emanated from his workshop during the days and nights of a whole week.

At last he threw open his doors and rolled out into the town square the largest monocle in the world. It glittered below the green lamps which hung from the taverns and theatres. And soon a crowd gathered.

"What is the purpose of this object?" they wondered.

They walked around it, touching it lightly. It was too big to fit a king or bishop or even the statue of El Cid which loomed on the battlements of the palace. No eye in history might wear it comfortably in a squint. It was clear the lens-grinder had lost his sanity.

The soldiers came to lock him up in a madhouse, but he stalled them with an explanation. They rattled their pikes uneasily.

He said: "The entity for whom this monocle was made will seek it out when he learns of its existence. And he will pay me handsomely, because he has waited to see properly again for centuries."

There was much speculation as to the nature of this customer. People mounted the city walls to look out for him, but they saw nothing when they gazed inland. Once they called out that he was coming, yet it was only an elephant being led to a circus in Barcelona. Excitement and fear surged together.

While they watched, a ship from Cathay sailed into the bay and the citizens turned their attention out to sea. Even from this distance, the cargo of spices could be smelled. But as the vessel entered the harbour, a gigantic whirlpool opened up and sucked it down. The crew and all the pepper was destroyed.

A cry of horror filled the streets and bells were tolled in a hundred churches. Then someone remembered the great circular eyepiece and called out for help in rolling it down to the quayside. Within a minute, a crowd of volunteers were pushing at the rim of the monocle, bouncing it over the cobbles like a burning wheel.

The lens-grinder followed helplessly, tearing at his hair as his marvellous creation gathered speed. Soon it slipped out of the grasp of the thousand hands and trundled along a jetty and over the edge.

There was no splash. The monocle landed in the eye of the whirlpool, fitting it perfectly. Men and women rushed onto the jetty and peered over the side, gasping in wonder at what they beheld.

The ocean was no longer blind. As the whirlpool moved across the bay, it revealed the gardens of the deep. Through the sparkling lens it was possible to discern the seabed in astonishing clarity. And now all the wrecks of ages past were focussed on the surface, the gold and gems and casks of wine.

A few citizens jumped into boats and chased the roving eye to the horizon and beyond. They made maps as they did so, noting the position of each trove, planning for a future time when they might be hauled up and distributed equally among the population, or perhaps they were just enjoying the spectacle.

There was general rejoicing, but the lens-grinder went home in some trepidation and awaited a very big knock on his door.

THE MACROSCOPIC TEAPOT

I live on the roof of the hotel. I don't have many provisions and the nights are very cold. I'll never come to Birmingham again, if I'm ever allowed to leave. They lie when they say perpetual motion is impossible. I've seen it in action here: the sheets of rain are endless, swishing constantly from one horizon to another. I still have my bass guitar, a 1964 Rickenbacker, and I thumb the occasional riff to keep in practice. It's not connected to an amplifier and sounds rather thin as a result, but I would rather endure that than be electrocuted. Voltage and water don't care for each other's company. I won't play a note near moisture when I'm plugged in. I still remember our keyboards player, frazzled in a swimming pool in Barcelona.

It was his own fault and my sympathies are muted. He was trying to impress a couple of girls by composing a catchy tune on his portable synthesiser. They ignored him and he climbed the ladder, still playing, to the high diving-board. I thought he was going to abandon the work, which was funky but uninspired, and come down again, but for some reason he plunged over the edge. Maybe he lost his footing. The somersault was conventional stuff, but the sparks when he hit the water were original. The girls were won over and stripped off, but to no avail. His charred corpse drifted toward them, knocking against the side of the pool a dozen times before sinking to the blue-tiled bottom.

That was a long time ago, when our band were almost less unpopular than now. We managed to make enough money to keep our one and only European tour going, mainly by selling off our equipment on the way. We started our first gig as an impressive art-rock band with many banks of unnecessary keyboards and an enormous drum-kit complete with tubular bells and gamelan pots and Chinese gongs. We ended our last gig as a choral group singing *a cappella* folk songs. But I was too sentimental to trade my Rickenbacker. I pretended to lose it before it could be sold, hiding it at the bottom of the communal laundry basket, which was fitted with wheels and towed behind the bus on a long rope. The abominable socks and underpants kept it safe.

But the essences rubbed off and when I retrieved the instrument my practice sessions became more hurried. Now when I wake in the middle of the night I often believe my comrades are still with me, but it's only the mingled odour of what they once exuded, throbbing on the strings. Even endless rain can't purify that complex, ghostly stench. I guess I'm another of their rejects, worn out, reputation soiled. After visiting every sovereign state on the continent, a manager's gross of gigs in total, similar to a baker's dozen squared, but without the metaphorical bread, though plenty of crusts, mostly on the aforementioned laundry, we finally returned to Britain, sold the bus and bought new equipment with the money received in exchange.

I was sly. I had already rescued my bass from the basket, which was cast over the side of the ferry on the Channel crossing, but claimed it was a replacement, found slung around the shoulders of the ship's figurehead. The fact it looked identical to my old instrument didn't alert any suspicions. Nor that our hull was devoid of statuary. Before the other band members raised this second point, I answered the first by inviting them to apply nose to strings. They agreed there was an obvious difference. That's the sort of gullible fool I travelled with. But I wasn't greedy. I spent my share of the cash on a crate of whisky for us all: a reward for my ingenuity and also to keep them too sozzled to want to ask any difficult questions.

We decided to make a last monolithic bid for glory. We wrote a lot of new material, fused it together into a suite with inaccurate literary and philosophical references, changed the name of our hitherto anonymous band to a single blank space, arguably an equally unmarketable label, though apparently it worked for lone gunmen in Old Mexico and tentacled monsters in New England, and booked a night in a Birmingham hotel, the same one I squat atop. We had to hitch-hike to the city in separate vehicles and our new keyboards player hopped a freight train which plummeted off a bridge outside Swindon. We picked up a substitute on the way: a fellow locked in the boot of the car our vocalist was travelling in. He heard the thumping at the same time as his driver opened the glove-compartment to reveal a collection of used knives. Fortunately our vocalist is also a madman, and a bigger one.

At least that's what I heard when I rang the hotel from Coventry to say I was going to be late. My luck wasn't great that day and I'd caught scores of little rides by slow drivers. There was interference on the telephone line, background giggles and grunts. It sounded like a party in half-swing. It boded well for a successful evening if people were already gathering. I hung up and returned to the road, thumb extended. I used my left hand for this gesture because I couldn't risk losing my playing digit if a vehicle sped by too close. I completed the final stage of my journey on the back of a motorbike. We spluttered into the walls of rain which defend Birmingham from external thoughts of joy. The oily droplets slicked my soul as well as my face and I somehow knew I would never be dry again.

I was deposited near the hotel and ran down the few remaining streets until I reached it. A tall, thin building with crumbling plaster. Although the day was drawing to a close and the sky was getting dim, no lights shone from the grimy windows. The front door was open and I entered the lobby. It was deserted and the dust lay thick on the dead potted plants and mouldy carpet. But there was a key waiting for me on the counter at Reception, at least I *assumed* it was for me, and I took it and went in search of my room. I needed to relax for a moment before joining my comrades for the concert. I climbed the stairs to the second floor, groping in the murk and listening for sounds. There were none.

I fumbled with the key in the lock and opened the door to reveal a spacious but oppressive chamber. I threw the light switch and lingered on the threshold of sinister vacancy. There was a mystifying delay before the electric bulb hanging from the ceiling began to glow, almost as if it had forgotten how to work. The yellowing wallpaper and rotting furniture raised the suspicion that this room hadn't been used for many decades. The skeleton of a cat reclined on the bed. I shook it off by yanking the quilt, and kicked the individual bones under the bed's iron frame. Then I hurled myself on the mattress and stared at the dead eye of the antique television standing on its own legs in the corner. It had a perfectly round screen set in a massive wooden case. There were all sorts of extra attachments fitted to that frame, hooks and drawers and hollow cylinders, as if the unwieldy piece of equipment doubled up as a gentleman's valet.

I grew bored resting. I twiddled my best thumb against the sinews of my bass. The ceiling provided no outstanding attractions. Abruptly I stood and went in search of my colleagues and our audience. Back in the lobby I found the telephone which I had earlier rung, but the dust over it was hardly disturbed. Where was everyone? When I attempted to step onto the street to survey the hotel again from outside, I received a shock. The front door was closed and locked. I shrugged, trying to feel relief that at least somebody else was about. I turned and passed through a succession of identical chambers, bearing different names and functions, restaurant, sauna, storeroom, eventually coming to the dancehall, supposedly our venue.

It was empty and utterly silent. The dust was inches thick and the imprints of the shoes of forgotten dancers resembled a choreography schematic. Here was a tango, an ephemeral wild evening, feasibly from the 1920's, preserved as an intaglio design in a desert of skin flakes. I wandered to the stage, paying my respects to history by slotting my own feet into the prints. There was absolutely no sign of any recent activity, no equipment or wires. It was completely bare. I left through the wings, drifted among the backstage cells, found another staircase and followed it up to the second floor. I roamed the corridors, listening for sounds. Then I returned to my room.

I stretched out on the bed next to my bass and fell into a light sleep. The rain against my window in no way resembled applause. Maybe I dreamed of adulation, but for scarcely longer than I expected to receive it in reality. I opened my eyes and checked my watch. Less than an hour until midnight. Our gig should be drawing to a climax now, the separate instruments, after playing solos which tugged against each other, coming together in time and key as the suite took its final crystalline form. And yet the hotel was dead. Had I come to the wrong place? If so, there was nothing I could do about it, especially as I was now trapped inside. I decided that the error, if there really was one, could be blamed on my *attitude*. Clearly I needed to get deeper into the swing of the occasion. A desperate, absurd measure but the only option which presented itself to my somewhat troubled mind.

That feeling of having just missed out on a chance is the one I fear and despise most. Acting like a rock star seemed the only positive option left, however little it currently appealed to my nerves. My limbs were stiff, my whole metabolism sluggish. But I roused myself to perform a traditional gesture of professional defiance. I resolved to throw the television set out of the window. The management, if they existed, would expect it and so would my fellow musicians, elusive as they were, not to mention our hypothetical audience. I grasped the sides of the frame but found it too heavy to move. Then a peculiar notion entered my head: that it might prove to be lighter if I switched it on. The electromagnetic field set up by the ancient circuits would push against the Earth's own magnetic field, allowing me to glide it along the floor to the window and the moist oblivion of a bottomless puddle.

99

I flipped the brass switch. The tubes warmed up very slowly. A tiny bright dot appeared at the centre of the screen, and even before it expanded it seemed full of the energy and potential of a new or parallel universe. I felt I was watching the birth of a different reality, a cosmos which wanted nothing more to do with me, its creator. There's a word for this phenomenon: *deism.* I learned it when we plundered philosophical dictionaries for references for our musical suite. I peered more closely at the screen. Now the sound came through from the primitive speakers, a hiss of ambient radiation which gradually settled down into something more audible, the chaotic mutterings of an excited crowd. As the spot of light grew, I heard music, familiar because I knew it well, but odd because I had never listened to it from the outside. Previously I had helped play it.

The dot expanded to fill the circular screen. Perhaps it continued beyond the limits of this circumference, but there was no way of telling. Slotted between the static specks were pixels of meaning. A group scene, profoundly human and yet disturbingly alien: a conventional cameo distorted by immense distance and depth, as if the signal had circumnavigated the universe before returning to this point of origin. Naturally, in such an ambitious transmission there was bound to be a lag, but not just of time: also of inclusion and roles. My mind slowly interpreted the soup of angry colour before me. It was the climax of a concert, *my* gig, taking place now in *this* hotel, and there was a large audience, but I was missing. The new keyboards player, whom I had never seen, was compensating for my absence by pounding out the bass lines on an electric organ with his left hand.

There was wild clapping and cheering. The pompous suite hadn't turned sour after all. The band dismounted the stage and struggled through the audience, pushing something before them. The crowd parted reluctantly. I recognised the sweat on the faces of the vocalist, lead guitarist and drummer, and beneath the pungent moisture a communal flush of determined excitement. The gig was barely cool and already they were forcing pleasure from the aftermath. When they were halfway across the dancefloor I saw what they were

100

pushing. It was a model of the hotel, mounted on castors as our laundry basket had been. Possibly it *was* the laundry basket, rescued from the sea, washed up the mouth of a river and through a series of locks into the canal system which watered Birmingham in cruel alliance with the rain, and now converted into this replica, impressive and abominable, complete with crumbling plaster and grimy unlit windows.

What did they intend to do with it? Larger it grew as it approached the surface of the screen from the other side. Soon the band members were obscured by its apparent magnitude, its bogus bulk. It suddenly accelerated, as if on the lip of a cliff, and tipped forward *out* of the screen. There was no sharp crack of breaking glass. It passed effortlessly through the flickering bubble, tumbled down and shattered on the floor of my room. Pieces of chimney and roof broke underfoot, a jagged edge of rusty guttering gashed my ankle. I drew back in alarm. I had seen many television sets hurled out of sundry hotels, but this was the first time I had witnessed a hotel ejected from a television set. I glanced at the screen for an explanation, but already the picture was returning to a dot. Somewhere a fuse had blown.

Refusing to accept the treachery in this experience, I scooped up a fragment of the model and took it to show my colleagues, who I knew I would never find. I foolishly imagined I could return for the other pieces. I also took my bass, slung over a shoulder. When I left my room, the door slammed inevitably behind me. I explored each corridor of the building, knocking on every door, calling the names of my former friends. Whenever I passed through a chamber, it locked itself behind me in a nonexistent wind. The darkness seemed thicker, the world lonelier. Had everybody evacuated to another universe without informing me? Slowly I was denied access to the majority of the hotel's internal space. As I entered the kitchens for the first and last time, I made sure of pocketing the few ancient cans of soup I discovered in the mainly bare cupboards.

The band had obviously forsaken me, and now the hotel was following its example. My options were narrowing as I probed the passages and stairways. I was being herded by the slamming doors, the thickening gloom, to a destination unknown, but one I still invested my remaining hope in. Was the building guiding me within itself to a reunion with my comrades? My rational mind doubted it, but my emotions were desperate to believe that, yes, they were waiting for me in some obscure attic room, huddled together with their triumph, a surprise party for me, primed and coiled, requiring only my belated appearance to discharge itself and put my life back to rights.

No such luck. And that's not too surprising, bearing in mind the fact that my life was never good enough to warrant a return to itself. When I reached the top floor of the hotel, I indeed found a trapdoor set into the ceiling, and a ladder reaching up to it, but when I climbed the rungs and pushed my head through the hinged square, my face emerged not in an attic, warm and itchy with rough insulating fabric, but out onto the roof, slates gleaming in the remorseless rain. I would have tried to climb back down, but I felt the ladder tipping, and was forced to haul myself up and out onto the slippery slope. The trapdoor shut like an apprehended yawn, and my fingers were too wide to fit in the gap around it and hook it back open. I was trapped outside with my sense of failure, high enough in normal circumstances for a decent view over the city, but there was no normality here: this was Birmingham and nothing at all was decent. The sky wept for me.

I went through the expected motions of a stranded adventurer, searching for a way down, peering over the gables and gutters, looking for a drainpipe to slide me to the ground. There were none. I considered jumping to the roofs of adjacent buildings, but the distances were too great, the street too far and hard below. Not being an adventurer but a musician, I gave up at the base of the solitary chimney, too narrow to climb down, too squat to provide any shelter from the rain, and sat with my bass across my knees. I thumbed a few notes, the opening bars of my new cage. I was marooned on the elevated grey of a temperate eyesore: a Crusoe without a canoe, pink or otherwise, a Friday without a tomorrow. A man without sympathetic critics. But I did not die immediately, despite my mood. I lingered and linger still.

Lately, however, I have noticed a change in the geography of the roof. The two sloping sides are getting steeper. This is no illusion, for in the early hours I can hear the hotel narrowing, drawing in its walls, compressing itself like the concertina we planned to use in the next incarnation of our band as a Celtic-roots outfit. And as the hotel grows thinner, the sides of the roof, hinged at the ridge along the top, must obey the rules of shapes and increase their angles. There are no doors to slam here: the edifice has found another way of rejecting me. The process is exasperating, for the hotel dares not draw attention to itself and must move so gradually that nobody will notice what is happening. Not that this precaution is necessary. There are no pedestrians below, nor have I ever glimpsed an inhabitant of the city in any of the surrounding buildings.

Soon I must slip and fall to my doom. Into how many pieces shall I break? It dimly occurs to me, a thought as slick as any to be expected under the onslaught of such oily rain, that the hotel is not vindictive or even amoral, but that it is trying to help my reputation. Fame is not an elusive thing, as is often stated, but is everywhere. And maybe that's the real reason for my lack of success. So much fame has been used up on so many other people that there's none left for me. Or is my customary view of young hopefuls as empty vessels waiting to be filled with liquid fame wrong? What if fame is the vessel and we the potential contents? That vessel, the proverbial hall, is crammed to the brim and there's no more room left, unless, and here I lick my lips as I contemplate the long drop, the additional contents are first smashed into tiny shards, ground into powder.

Yes, that seems likely, and explains why so many artists of my calibre only achieve posthumous fame. Death is essential for reasons of space. We are being pounded to fit. Because I was late arriving at the hotel, I missed out on its first promotion, the granulating of an entire universe, and nameless band, into light and static to fill a television screen. In a similar way, the pillar of a temple from a lost city buried under the dunes of a forgotten desert can just occupy an hourglass by being pulverised. A better example emerges from my childhood. I remember the only birthday present I ever received: from an eccentric aunt. I opened the parcel in breathless excitement to find the fragments of a broken teapot. I assumed it had shattered in transit, at the rough hands of the postal service. I carefully glued the pieces back together. The teapot was a magnificent reconstruction of dismay, ready to brew my bitter frustration. For when it was finished, I realised it was larger than the box it had arrived in. Make of that, and the other digressions in my life, what you will.

CLIMBING THE TALLEST TREE IN THE WORLD

It started as a prank and ended as a plank.

We drank too much ale and tumbled out of the tavern. Our university is the most renowned in the land. Somebody suggested that we accomplish a feat never before attempted. We agreed with alacrity. We disagreed with Figgis, who wanted to go home. We knocked him down with stones. We had a tradition of appalling behaviour to live up to. It was our duty.

To be honest, I can't remember if we were students or professors. It hardly matters. I pointed at the famous tree in the main public square and cried: "Let's climb that!" The excited voices around me went quiet. But it was too late to back down. Slowly a chant filled those empty throats. "To the top!" We bolstered our courage with coordinated hubbub. I was happy and scared.

We decided to mount our assault in pairs. We reached the base of the trunk but did not bother to look up. It was pointless. The canopy was lost beyond the clouds. Fresh hearts and initials had been carved into the bark. I went first with Gruber.

As we ascended, the style of these carvings became cruder and older. They had all been made at ground level and the growth of the tree was carrying them toward heaven.

Within an hour, we were confronted with the evidence of love affairs that had ended before the founding of our university. These hearts had been cut with stone tools, not steel blades. Later, when the ache in my arms was unbearable, there was nothing. The tree was older than the art of writing. Gruber and I decided to rest. Far below we watched our colleagues struggle to make equal sense of these ephemeral desires.

"Fossils of passion," said Gruber, as he sat on a branch and dangled his legs over the void. I guessed that he wanted to make a contribution of his own, but was frustrated in this design by the lack of a girl to love. Also he had no knife. We reclaimed our breath and resumed our climb. Roosting birds, chiefly owls, studied our progress with alarmed amusement. Then I recalled the subject I specialised in and blinked for all their eyes.

"Trees don't grow like this," I muttered.

"What do you mean by that?"

"They don't grow from the base but from the top. There's no way those carvings could be rising progressively higher."

It was a mystery. We sweated and gasped as we pushed ourselves to the limits of our endurance. The sun went down, but when I checked my pocket watch I saw it was nearly midnight. That demonstrates how high we already were. It had been night in the town below for many hours. I wondered if we would reach the top by morning. It seemed unlikely. For a start, mornings would arrive much earlier now.

Gruber and myself were the highest pair, as I've already mentioned. Immediately beneath us were Pluck and Becker. When we began this exploit, we frequently shouted at them, and they passed on our shout to the next pair, who I believe were Kane and Rowse, and so we kept in rudimentary touch right down to the final two climbers. But now our calls were not acknowledged. We were ascending too fast. Or they had fallen.

The stars did not grow brighter in the celestial dome but the air remained breathable. This was a surprise. It should have thinned out gradually. Gruber leaned close and fixed his lips to my ear. He was trembling.

"The trunk is getting thicker," he whispered.

"Yes, it is very strange. And the branches are much wider. What can this mean?"

"That the tree is misshapen and ugly?"

There was no other explanation at that particular time. We climbed reluctantly now, and I distracted myself by attempting some difficult mental calculations. The distance between the most recent inscriptions and the earliest could be reckoned in two ways: miles or centuries. Thus the growth of one year could be reduced to a precise length of trunk. An estimate of the height of the tree might also provide its age.

I had a reasonable idea of our altitude, but there was no way of reckoning its percentage of the total. As we climbed, however, it quickly became apparent that the tree was more ancient than the world itself. This paradox was an extra worry. I did not trouble Gruber with it. But he was a geologist and had already arrived at the same conclusion.

"Wood can't be older than rocks," he sighed at last.

I nodded. We now regretted embarking on this adventure, which had promised so much when it began, though I can't specify what. We decided to make camp on one of the wider branches and wait for the others to catch up. I felt sleepy. My eyes closed as I listened to the soft rustling of the leaves. I must have fallen into a deep slumber. I dreamed that a man was screaming. He was above me and his voice receded upwards. He was being dragged into the sky, carried off by owls.

When I awoke, the sun was shining on my face. Gruber had gone. I lingered on my perch until noon. There was nothing to eat. I was completely sober now. I resumed climbing, surprised at how light I felt. I pulled myself up from branch to branch with remarkable ease. Indeed I found it difficult to stop. When I did, I became aware of an insistent tugging on my body, as if an invisible hand was reaching down and trying to pluck me up. With more height its grip became stronger.

Then I knew. Our assumptions about the tree had been all wrong. I now suspected that I was climbing down it rather than up. It had been planted upside-down. At least that was true from the perspective of my world. In fact, the canopy of the tree was that world. As I left its gravitational pull behind, I realised it was I who was inverted. The tug of the real ground, somewhere far above, was taking over. If I let go, I would fall into the solid sky. It was a moment of terrible insight.

I resolved to reverse my progress and climb back down again. And that is what I am doing now. Gruber had no knife, but I always carry one. It is almost a sword. Unlike the others, I am a swashbuckler. I have no buckle, that is true, for I wear braces to hold up my trousers, but I am awash with swash. I started carving this tale on the trunk, one sentence every night while I rested. Tomorrow I shall write this one. Yesterday I wrote it. I waited to meet my companions but they did not appear. I am alone.

I began to suspect I had climbed down much further than I had ascended. This made no sense. Then I realised the tree was growing faster than I could climb it and growing the way it ought to: from the top. Thus the canopy was moving away from me and I would never reach it. Never. I had lost my world. There was no time for weeping. I saved my tears and doubled my efforts.

The carved initials at different elevations were now explained by natural growth. Or perhaps they had been an elaborate deception, a much earlier joke played by the students or professors of my university, to encourage those who came after to believe the climb was real and feasible. I laughed bitterly. I still laugh in that style. A cruel joke: one of the finest. That is our tradition. Every time I rest, I lose valuable miles. The world grows away from me far below, becomes an unreachable horizon, a distant planet. Now it is little more than a tiny disc flecked with threadlike clouds. Soon it will become a star, first bright then faint.

Time is running out. Next year, a new joke must be played. I think I know what it might be. Ale will be drunk, a tavern will be tumbled out of. A feat never before attempted will lose its virginity. I imagine a giant saw worked by many hands. To cut down the tallest tree in the world! Its collapse will be spectacular, or so they conclude. But in reality they will be severing the canopy from the trunk that supports it. The ground will wobble and slide off.

It must be next year already. I have just watched the whole world falling past into the sky.

TWO FAT MEN IN A VERY THIN COUNTRY

My friend Pepito must always be believed, even when he is telling lies. Exactly why this should be so is beyond my powers of explanation. But it's a tradition which I'm reluctant to ignore, and thus I now place my hand over my heart and swear that the following tale is accurate in every fact. Pepito told it to me himself, while we rested under the orange tree which stands in the centre of my patio. Most of my body was in the shade, but my boots stuck out in the noonday sun, and the heat raised an odour from them which was not unlike soup.

He often related anecdotes which had happened in distant lands. I suppose he'd travelled a lot in his youth. That must have been the case, for now he barely moved at all, except from house to house, kitchen to kitchen, with slow greed, as if he was trying to balance out or retract all his previous activity.

He began by asking me what I knew of Chile, and I shrugged my shoulders. My ignorance seemed to offer him some mental relief, and he scratched himself lazily before announcing:

"Well, it's a very long country.

"¡Sí! a long and thin country, like a piece of string used to parcel up the globe when the world was made. But somehow it remained behind when the rest of the wrapping was discarded, stuck there on the western edge of the South American continent. That is Chile.

"I would estimate — and it's just a guess, mind you — that it covers an area of 756,626 square kilometres, but all this territory must stretch some 4000 km from the tropics almost to the polar region, which means its average width is no more than 160 km. That's an unusual shape for a nation. Its capital is Santiago.

"Its major natural resources are coal, oil, iron ore, precious metals and timber. It has some of the biggest copper mines on the planet. The scenery is dramatic, with deserts in the north and glaciers in the south. It has a history of *relative* democracy. Its worst myth is the Chonchón, which is a loose head with gigantic ears for wings. It often flies down chimneys. The Calchona is almost as bad. It is a kind of dog which snatches lunch baskets from mountain travellers, muttering sullen threats if anyone tries to follow.

"Fortunately these monsters are quite rare now.

"The sort of normal wildlife you might expect to find if you went there include guanacos, vicunas, coypus, pumas and condors. There are tamarugo trees, algarobas and monkey puzzles. Whether any of these latter have ever been solved is unknown to me at this time. Fish stocks off the coast are enormous, and fish stews on land numerous, which brings me to the point, for I won't say *meat*, of my tale.

"There were two brothers who were known as the Grady Twins. They were big eaters and famous for it. It is possible they were the fattest men in existence. One was named Tobias and the other Oliver. They decided to take a voyage to Chile. They applied for visas and arrived in Santiago on the first day of summer.

"They had been growing rounder and rounder every year, and their girth had caused them many practical problems for as long as either could remember, though nothing too serious, for they were used to lumbering about in wide countries. They had never stayed in such a thin one before. They had plenty of money in their pockets. Total disaster was inevitable.

"They found an outdoor restaurant and sat down to their first meal. And that is where they remained for the whole of their trip!

109

They devoured everything the country had to offer. I'm not sure what that is, but doubtless it includes bread, potatoes, rice, apples, beef, mutton, sardines, anchovies and whatever else can be found on local plates — but no chilli peppers, despite the aptness of the name. And they drank hundreds of bottles of wine.

"The days and weeks passed and they kept calling for more food. Before the summer was finished, they were both fatter than they had ever been. ¡Ay, Señor! they were too fat to fit in the country! They were wider than Chile! Do you doubt it?

"Well, this was an unexpected situation. They were facing east, and their stomachs grew and ripened over that chain of mountains called the Andes. The snows lay soft and thick on the tops of their bellies. But the brothers continued to stuff their mouths, and their digestions rumbled like thunder in the high passes, and some people thought an earth tremor had begun. But still they sat at their table and ordered more food, and entire harvests vanished into their gaping maws.

"There is a country which borders Chile along the mountains. It is Argentina and it has different laws and customs and ideas. A visa that is valid for one is not necessarily accepted in the other. The Grady Twins had the correct paperwork for a stay in Chile, but now their stomachs crossed the frontier into a separate state. They passed over illegally. The authorities were alerted.

"Right there, near the summit of Tupungato, the bellies of Tobias and Oliver were arrested and charged with unlawfully entering Argentina. A judge was sent for and a court was temporarily set up at the base of the mountain. The stomachs were found guilty and sentenced to an indefinite term of imprisonment.

"The jails were constructed around the straining abdomens, but each cell only had three walls, because the side where the stomachs came from had to be left open. All the same, the miscreants were in prison, and even the immense power of their digestions could not burst the bricks and iron bars asunder. The authorities smiled to themselves and went home, leaving a few guards to watch over each

110

navel and to prod their captives with bayonets at the first signs of further trouble.

"Back in Santiago, the brothers were oblivious of what had occurred over the border. But they knew that they suddenly had stomach cramps. Further belly expansion was halted by the solid walls. As they continued to eat, the pressure increased. There might have been a detonation with unsavoury results if this anecdote was just a fictional tale, but I have embellished no detail and therefore must report that this did not happen. They still called for more food, for they were also gluttons for punishment.

"It was the middle of autumn and between them they had nearly eaten Chile bare. The hot winds from the desert and the cold winds from the icecaps had always smelled hungry. Now all the other winds did too, even those from the temperate zones where the wheat ripples in fields and the fruit falls from branches. The country was like an empty cupboard. The only things left to eat were old boots. They are not tasty when boiled, basted, roasted, steamed or fried. But a boot sauce served on coils of its own laces *can* be sampled like a spaghetti dish. It may or may not be nourishing. A few men will walk far to try it, but rather more will hope it doesn't walk after them. Such now was the final item on every menu.

"Everybody knows there are good and bad boots. The latter pinch and squeak. Tobias had the misfortune to be served one of those. He refused to finish it. He threw down his fork and glowered at Oliver, who was chewing a more comfortable sole. From this moment their fates diverged. Tobias started to lose weight. This shouldn't be too remarkable a thing to occur, and so it wasn't, in the locality of the restaurant. But in Argentina, the amazed guards watched as one of their prisoners escaped.

"It was a slow escape, sure enough, and in many other parts of the world, action would have been taken immediately to apprehend the belly before it vanished, but down there events often move sluggishly, and every pant is a yawn, and by the time a decision had been made to prod the captive with a bayonet, it was gone. It had fled at glacier velocity out of the open side of the jail and back over

111

the border. Eventually Tobias became just a very fat man again, rather than an international incident.

"The authorities were determined to guard the remaining stomach more carefully. But the bother of keeping watch over it constantly, while there were more important matters to attend to elsewhere, such as barbecues and football matches, was too much to contemplate eternally, which was the span of time that the wobbling paunch had to serve before it became eligible for parole, on the recommendation of the judge. So a retrial was ordered and a new sentence was passed — death by firing squad!

"¡Ay! That was a sure way of eliminating the problem for all time. The cell was demolished to give the men with the rifles a clear aim. Then a runner was dispatched to inform the man far behind the belly of his impending doom. It was a tradition to ask the condemned prisoner if he had a final request. The runner applied for a visa, crossed the border into Chile and reached the restaurant in Santiago.

"He whispered his message into the ear of Oliver, who absorbed it at his leisure while munching on the tongue of a boot, his own tongue curling around it as if he was kissing his dinner to adulterate its leathery taste with the flavour of passion, which has no eyes and is blind, of course. And coincidentally this was his millionth *course*. But after just a little more thought, he nodded to himself and gave the runner a message of his own to deliver to the firing squad. Then he resumed eating.

"Oliver's stomach had been sentenced to be shot at sunrise. But he had asked if it could be shot at sunset instead, the sunset of the day previous to the ordained one. The authorities and guards scratched their heads at this, for it seemed their prisoner was hurrying them along, that he wished to die sooner rather than later. But they agreed to the proposal, partly because it was a final request and they were bound by honour to fulfil it, and partly because it meant they could leave work early.

"The firing squad raised and aimed its rifles. Every man present waited for the moment of sunset. It never came. The sky went dark and filled with stars, but at no point did the sun actually go down.

After a night of debate, the mystery was resolved. The vast stomach had created an eclipse, blotting out not only the sunset but much of the western horizon. Then they understood that their prisoner had cheated them, for they would never be able to execute the belly at the moment of sunset, for there was no longer such a time. They would be stuck here for the rest of Oliver's life, waiting in vain, and the barbecues would go cold and the football matches be won or lost, and forgotten, without them.

"Another solution had to be found. If a condemned man survives or avoids his execution, he probably deserves to be pardoned and released. The same surely applies to bellies. It was decided to pardon this one, together with its contents and weather, for the interior was a cavern vast enough to contain clouds and other atmospheric phenomena. Now the guards could leave it to its own devices. It was as free as any other gorge in the Andes, though entirely different in all but word.

"The unspoken worry of those who left was that it would now proceed on its voyage into Argentina unopposed, crushing everything in its path. But circumstances conspired against this, because a coup overthrew the legitimate government of Chile and a military dictatorship took over. The boots were recalled from Oliver's plate to serve the feet of the soldiers, and so he went hungry. His stomach retreated of its own accord. Remember that Chile only has a history of *relative* democracy, and this was one of those times when stupidity and cruelty marched over it, in boots originally collected for supper.

"When Oliver was slim enough to move again, he stood and walked with his brother out of the restaurant. Both had a terrible stomach ache and awful wind. Soon after, they left Chile. Neither of the Grady Twins ever returned. They settled in a wider land where many people wore slippers instead of boots, far to the east. India it was, I believe. If they attempted such a feast again, it has not been recorded. I imagine that their breath, which smelled of leather, fell foul of some law and that their mouths were caged, which would

113

prevent their stomachs from going anywhere alone. That would certainly be for the best..."

Pepito halted his absurd story for two reasons. Firstly, the sun had moved the shadow of the orange tree over my feet, and my boots no longer smelled edible. Secondly, he had finished. We sat in the silence of the patio. Then he fell asleep. He has since promised to tell me similar tales about every country in the world. I have locked up my house with heavy chains and tomorrow I plan to leave the village forever. I don't know where I'm going, nor do I care, so long as it's far from him. He's my most inspirational friend.

FINDING THE BOOK OF SAND

My name is Jazeps Zemzaris.
I owe the present thirst on my tongue to my peculiar story. I owe my peculiar story to a book, a building and another book. The first book is the *Collected Fictions* of Jorge Luis Borges, published by Penguin Press in 1999 and translated by Andrew Hurley. The building is the Argentine National Library in Buenos Aires. The second book is impossible and should not exist.

After a life of regular and dreary work, I deserved to see a little of the world. This was my justification for buying an airline ticket to South America. But I could not alter my careful nature simply through an act of will, so of all the countries on that landmass I selected Argentina as my destination. It is the most European in character. To pass the hours of the flight more easily, I purchased a volume of short stories which also promised to introduce me to certain aspects of the culture of the nation I was visiting. This was the *Collected Fictions*. I read avidly in the sky. I landed in Buenos Aires and took a taxi ride through a city as beautiful as Paris, but I was eager to reach my hotel and continue reading. It was past midnight when I finished and switched off the light in my room. My

114

dreams consisted of images from many of the tales. A story near the end held a particular fascination.

This piece was 'The Book of Sand' and it is about a man who collects books. One evening he is visited by a stranger who offers to sell him a tome bound in cloth. The collector is uninterested until the stranger tells him that this book has an infinite number of pages. If it is opened at random, the script that presents itself in an unreadable language will never be found again once it is closed. The collector haggles for the book and the visitor departs. He is pleased with his acquisition but in time it obsesses him. He decides to rid himself of it by carrying it to the National Library and losing it on a shelf in the basement, taking care not to note its position among the other books.

For me this story was a potent fable but one without a moral or a moral I could not grasp. No doubt it would have faded in my memory as merely an example of clever writing, but a few days later on one of my excursions through the city I found myself on Mexico Street. I was seized by an impulse. When I entered the building I was surprised to discover it deserted. Nobody stopped me as I turned down the curved staircase to the basement. It was an hour before I found what I sought, wedged between Volume XLVI of a century old edition of *The Anglo-American Cyclopaedia* and *The God of the Labyrinth*, a detective novel by Herbert Quain, an author often recommended to me. I picked it out and held it to my chest until I caught my breath. Then I opened it. The truth tallied at every point with the story. The Book of Sand was mine and I was elated.

Until the day of my departure I grew increasingly concerned for the safety of my new possession. I felt no guilt at having liberated it, because infinity can rightfully belong to nobody or anybody. I concealed it at the bottom of my suitcase but I was still terrified it might be stolen. I became reluctant to leave my room. At last my vacation was over. I passed through Customs at the airport with a sweat on my face which fortunately resembled the juice of a fever rather than fear. At any rate I was not stopped. Back home I secured my doors and windows and experimented with the book. It did not disappoint. The script was unintelligible and augmented at two thousand page intervals by small illustrations of poor quality. Furthermore the numbering of the pages was arbitrary and no help in locating the beginning or end of the volume. Each time I attempted to find the first page by turning the cover I discovered that a number of other pages always came between the point I selected and the hypothetical flyleaf. The same applied to the last page. I closed the book and measured the width of its spine. Then I took a brush and ink and tried to paint a line across the edges of the leaves. The ink ran out almost immediately and no line was ever drawn. I wondered if the pages had absorbed the ink but I found no such stains at any point in the volume.

It was clear to me that this really was an infinite book. Unlike my predecessor in the story, I had a practical use for it. I am an engineer. I left my house with this prize concealed in a bag and walked to the abode of my former supervisor.

The hour was late but he was still awake. He invited me in for a drink. He did not ask me about my trip, possibly because he has a distaste for polite conversation. Finishing my drink I reached into my bag and passed the book to him.

"Well Jazeps, what is this for?" he asked.

I said with a smile, "It's an infinite book. Go ahead and astound yourself with it. When you have accepted the truth, listen to me."

Coolly he replied, "I'm ready now."

"Very well. An infinite book can be read forever. But it is also a source of infinite fuel."

He tapped his nose. "I understand. We are hungry for energy."

I nodded. The power station had become ruinously expensive to run. In the story by Borges, the narrator toys with the idea of setting fire to the Book of Sand, but he fears it will burn forever and choke the world with smoke. I had no such worries. I knew that not *every* page could catch fire, because they were without limit. Only a finite number of pages would burn, an ever growing number that might be controlled by adjusting the amount of oxygen which reached the blaze. I also knew that the amount of smoke produced daily would be small compared to a multitude of other sources of pollution currently

116

active. Besides, the hotter a fire, the more efficient it is and the less smoke created. The narrator of the story had missed a prime opportunity to contribute to the economy of his country.

That night my supervisor and myself designed a new power station from scratch. A sealed room lay at its core and at the centre of this unique blast furnace stood a titanium tripod upon which rested the Book of Sand. Above this was a water tank which was continually replenished from the local river. The burning book heated the water in this boiler to steam, which rose up a pipe at pressure and turned the vanes of a vast electricity generator. Most of this current ran into the national grid, providing power for homes and factories, but some was diverted to a number of large electric fans set into the walls of the furnace. These fed the fire with air from outside. As the number of burning pages continually increased, without in the least diminishing the infinite total by even one, and the water boiled faster and more furiously, so the pressure of the steam mounted, turning the generator faster and producing more electricity for the fans, which also accelerated the amount of oxygen they drew in. However, there was a limit to this process. When the fans reached their maximum speed, the blaze would stabilise. It would not increase in force indefinitely. And if there was a problem, the fans could be disabled, significantly reducing the amount of oxygen in the room and dampening the fire to a more manageable level.

My supervisor is an influential man. In conditions of great secrecy, the power station was constructed. Within six months of my return from Argentina, the majority of my neighbours were enjoying the benefits of free energy. Latvia is a small nation. A single perpetual motion machine, which in effect is what we had created, was more than enough to meet our power requirements. We prospered. I often walked around the perimeter of the clandestine station, nodding to the armed guards at the gate, imagining the scene inside the sealed room. I pictured the book as a ball of flame on its tripod, positioned directly under the vast boiler, raging in the artificial hurricanes of the spinning fans. The heat was surely intense and yet was maintained at a level below the melting point of the surrounding metal and brick. It was entirely safe. The drone of the fans reached me beyond the walls. The hum of the cables which extended overhead on pylons, channelling this impossible energy out toward the general population, was curiously like sacred chanting. The book itself was supposedly a religious tract. I recalled this fact from the story. Was it an act of obscure and possibly mathematical blasphemy to exploit it in this manner? And yet the number of remaining pages would always be infinite. Even if the book was cast into the sun and burned there until that star extinguished itself in untold future aeons, the total number of pages could not be reduced by a single unit. The rules of subtraction do not apply to infinity.

I should have experienced a profound happiness. But I was troubled and my sense of unease became steadily more acute. I began to regret my actions. I knew that the miracle of our power station could not be kept a secret forever. News of it would leak out. Other nations were sure to envy and admire our luck and ingenuity. In a short time our supply of free energy, the burning Book of Sand, would become one of the great clichés of our country. It would define Latvia as thoroughly and narrowly as the gaucho and the tango define Argentina. This in itself presented no problem. It was a minor irritation. But if the power failed for any reason, we would lose face. Our national pride would be critically damaged.

How could this happen? The danger lay in the possibility that the book was not infinite after all. The number of pages might be immense, even beyond calculation, but that is not the same as *infinite*. If indeed the book was simply a volume with a vast number of pages, rather than one with an endless supply, then one day it would burn out. The water in the boiler would cool and the generator stop turning. The more I pondered this idea, the more reasonable it seemed. There were three main reasons why I no longer believed the book to be infinite:

(1) The narrator in the original story made a list of the illustrations in the book, noting that they represented the objects of the real world and that no picture was ever repeated. He abandoned

118

this project when his list became too long, but it must be pointed out that there is *not* an infinite number of objects in existence.

(2) The book is called the Book of Sand, apparently because *neither the book nor the sand has any beginning or end.* And yet the number of grains of sand in the world is finite. They can be counted, in theory at least, and one day a final total might be announced. A truly infinite book would surely bear some other name.

(3) An infinite book must contain an infinite number of pages. Each of these pages, however thin and delicate, must have *some* weight. An infinite book must be of infinite weight. I had not thought to weigh it when it was still in my possession and yet I knew for sure it was not infinitely heavy. I had lifted it from the library shelf and carried it back with me from the southern hemisphere to the northern.

These reasons compelled me to act. I had to sabotage the power station while it was still a secret and before it failed of its own accord. I was on friendly terms with the guards. Halfway between midnight and dawn of my chosen night, I approached the gate with several bottles of our national drink, *balzams*. As the bottles were passed around I took the smallest sips possible and yet the taste of orange peel, oak bark, wormwood, linden blossoms and alcohol burned my lips. I soon had the satisfaction of watching the guards fall into a drunken sleep at their posts. I went in search of the tongs I had hidden in the grass, found them and passed through the gate. I quickly disabled the fans and waited for the temperature inside the furnace to diminish to a relatively safe level before opening the door. The book still burned brightly on its tripod but with a reddish flame rather than a white one. Above it the boiler groaned as it cooled. My tongs were long enough to grasp the book while I stood on the threshold. I reversed out of the power station and turned around beyond the gates. Now I hurried through the industrial zones to the heart of the city.

My arms aching with my burden, I passed into the oldest quarter of Riga. The streets were deserted. I felt like the solitary member of a forgotten procession, my implausible torch passing the dark windows

119

of many houses, reflecting from the glass in myriad flickers and multiplying the image of the infinite book. Now I carried the tongs over my shoulder and the book burned behind and above me like the knapsack of a wanderer in a new and unspecified fable. The narrow streets grew more crooked. I failed to notice the statuettes and carvings which adorn many of the buildings, because to me they are too familiar. I passed the cathedral with barely a glance. As I reached the Akmens Bridge, the streetlamps winked out. Much of Riga was left in darkness. The steam in the boiler was no longer forceful enough to turn the generator and was condensing back to lukewarm water. I felt suddenly conspicuous, like a firefly in the gloom. I crossed to the centre of the bridge and dropped the book over the side. It hissed as it struck the river. It went under and then resurfaced. No fire, however unbelievable, can burn without oxygen. I watched the book float away downstream. I did not know whether I had expected it to sink or not. I cast the tongs after it and they certainly slipped to the bottom. Then I went home in triumph to await my disgrace.

I was not imprisoned or sent into exile. I merely lost my friends and status. I moved to one of the poorer suburbs and lived alone, wasting my days in muted frustration, still partly believing I was a good man. Then the climate began to change. Gradually the level of the sea dropped. Ships ran aground as they approached ports. Every country in the world with a coastline found to its amazement that it was gaining territory. Eminent scientists were encouraged to devise theories which explained this phenomenon. None were convincing. Baffled geographers threw away their maps and globes. Only I understood what was happening.

A normal book will absorb water until it is saturated, but a book of infinite pages will continue to absorb water until not a single drop remains. The Book of Sand had drifted down the river to the sea. Caught by currents it might have travelled thousands of miles before sinking. Now it lurked on the seabed somewhere, drinking water with an insatiable thirst. Eventually all the oceans of the world would be locked inside one book.

I imagined the sea draining away, revealing its secrets, the wrecked galleons and treasure chests and drowned mountain ranges. Locating the book and bringing it to the surface before all the water vanishes is unfeasible. Where to start searching? Only when there is no water left will it be easy to find. I thought at first the process might prove reversible. The sodden pages could be torn out and squeezed or the entire book pressed by powerful machines. But then I realised the futility of both schemes.

The wet pages, however numerous, will be impossible to find among an infinite number, and compressing the book will simply force the liquid into other, dry regions of the volume, parched regions without limit. Once locked inside, the oceans are lost forever. The only water on the planet will remain in lakes and rivers, which must be damned at their mouths to stop them pouring away completely. A monumental thirst will be the worst thing to ever afflict humanity.

That thirst is already here. A submarine exploring the dwindling oceans last year reported entering a vast expanse of opaque water. Undersea storms have done nothing to break it up or dilute it. Larger and thicker it grows and now it has risen to the surface, spreading out like oil. It is black ink. The words in the Book of Sand have started to smudge and run. The unusual consistency of the ink means that it seals the water beneath it, preventing evaporation. Clouds are becoming rare. The planet is in the grip of a severe drought. Rain is only a memory. How will all this end? Will the oceans of water be entirely replaced by oceans of ink? Or will the book drink these also, reabsorbing what it has leaked?

I still dream of walking across a dry seabed, thousands of miles beneath a cloudless sky, and finding the book again. If I cast it into an active volcano will at least some of the water inside it turn to steam and pour forth to refresh the atmosphere and earth? There are too many possibilities. I have not yet considered them all.

I tried to lose the book because I feared it was not infinite but the loss proved that it is. I have found irony, if nothing else. The beaches of the world no longer have tides to wash away the messages carved into the sand by lovers and children. The huge letters in many different languages stretch across untold millions of grains of sand, as my little life reaches across the greater number of pages of the book with that name.

NIDDALA

The lamp was as Persian as a carpet made from a fluffy cat. Niddala rubbed it with her sleeve and told the emerging figure that she didn't want to spend all her wishes at once. Was interest available on those she saved for later?

The blue creature shook its head. "The old stories got it wrong. I'm only compelled to give you one wish and you have to use it right now."

"In that case, I wish for more wishes!"

"That's not permitted."

"What if I wish for you to fall in love with me? That way you'll always be happy to do anything I ask."

"That's also against the rules."

Niddala protested but the creature had no sympathy and merely added, "You're running out of time."

So she said, "I wish I was a genie."

"Very clever!" hissed the apparition in dismay but it waved its hands about and there was a blinding flash. After the smoke cleared, Niddala found herself wearing a turban.

"Now I can do what I like."

"No you can't!" roared the bald being. "That's not how genies work. You have to *grant* wishes to others!"

Immediately it pounced on her and rubbed her stomach furiously. "I wish I was human!"

Niddala's arms seemed to acquire a life of their own, describing strange shapes in the air. Another flash and the creature had shrunk to a normal size. He was still bald but now he was the colour of skin. His laughter was full of desperate relief.

"Free at last! I'm a man!"

"Wait a moment," said Niddala. "Are you sure a genie is allowed to rub another genie? That doesn't seem right somehow. I wouldn't trust the result of such a wish. The effect might wear off."

"I hadn't thought of that. But I'm a man now and you're a genie and I haven't had my wish *as a man* yet, so I'm going to reconfirm my decision."

He leaned forward with raised hands, rubbed her stomach again and called, "I wish I was human!"

But nothing happened. Niddala sighed.

"You can't wish to be something you already are. That's not a wish, but a grammatical error. A wish implies a yearning for a lack. You can't lack a quality which you have."

"I hate the pitfalls of logic!" came the exasperated reply. "Let me think of a different wording. I have it! I wish *not* to be a genie."

This time arms were waved. Smoke.

Niddala blinked at the object which existed before her. It seemed to consist of everything at once, or parts of everything, or parts of an unimaginable number of other parts. The colours were scintillating. Then she understood what had happened.

"You fool! You've accidentally wished to be *everything* which isn't a genie! Not being a genie is a quality which *all* things *except* genies possess. You've become a universal soup!"

The reply was trillionfold. "Yes, and I don't feel well."

Niddala arched an eyebrow. "I'm not surprised." Then an idea came to her. She reached into the unbelievable swirl and felt around for a moment before rubbing the smooth and large something she finally found. "I wish to be Niddala!"

Instantly she was back to her former self.

Before she departed she explained, "If you are everything other than a genie then you must also be whatever it is that genies rub to get wishes from. I think I'll go shopping now."

She looked back over her shoulder. "You don't happen to have a place that sells carpets in there, do you?"

THE MINOTAUR IN PAMPLONA

He knew for certain, or imagined he did, how to deal with bends and twists in any maze, and the narrow streets of this city had not been designed to deliberately confuse anyone. He was strong and fast and his courage could not be doubted, nor did he suffer from excessive pride at his qualities. His confidence was justified but his manner was modest.

Arriving before sunrise on the first day of the Fiesta de San Fermín, he noted that already a band was rehearsing in a public square. The celebrations would begin at midday and continue without pause for more than a week. He waited for a café to open and ordered a coffee, the steam from the cup blending with his own dawn breath as he crouched over it. Finding accommodation here at this time would be impossible, so he planned to sleep on the citadel ramparts with the other lonely, unlucky or romantic visitors. But he was more than a spectator.

He stood and walked the route from the Plaza Santo Domingo to the bullring, familiarising himself with the peculiarities of the streets. Then he wandered sedately among the parks, conserving his energy for the following morning, performing gentle exercises, stretching his huge muscles, nodding at the people who had started to gather in groups. Mostly he was ignored for his trouble and the few smiles he collected on the way were thin and dismissive.

A clock somewhere struck noon and music came from ahead, always around the next corner, a phenomenon he regarded as supernatural until he realised he was accidentally following a parade. He increased his pace and caught up with the musicians, who now stood in a circle and played wilder songs at a faster tempo. The first dancers swirled into the soup of notes, followed by others until the whole street was gyrating, he alone a static object, a point of reference. He waited to be asked to dance so that he might decline, for he wanted to be fully fit for tomorrow, but he was never given the chance. And of course this suited his needs perfectly.

When night fell he decided he had rested enough on his feet and walked to the citadel to sleep. He was the first to bed down but as the hours passed he was joined by others. It was cold under his rough blanket. He drifted from dream to dream and woke often, confused and blinking at the stars, the crescent moon toppled on its side like a pair of disembodied horns above a tide of strangely shaped clouds.

Once he opened his eyes because a stealthy thief was robbing the sleepers in his vicinity, moving in time with the wind from one prone drunken body to the next, searching through pockets and in the folds of blankets. The thief stepped over him without making any attempt on his possessions. At first he believed the thief had been daunted by his obvious strength and he was pleased, but then it occurred to him he might simply look too poor to steal from, or that he had not really been noticed at all. Far away music still played, softly with laughter.

The first to stir and rise when the stars dimmed, he walked with considerable grace across the city to the appointed place. Other runners converged from every direction and soon the bustling and jostling of competitors and watchers was intense and oddly relaxing. He inhaled deeply. This was living with passion, dangerously, intoxicatingly, the only way for any sentient being to thrive, heart pounding, sweat sprouting like dew on limbs and torso! He enjoyed the communal fear and excitement, the idea that people were sharing sensations with him.

He knew what to expect and the sound of the first rocket being launched was not startling but in fact caused him to relax even more. This was proof of his mental strength, a result of his preparations, his research and respect for process and tradition. The long whistle and detonation overhead was a signal the bulls had been released and the more timid or enthusiastic competitors started running, far too early in his view. Better to wait for the second rocket, which signalled that the entire herd of bulls was free. That way it would be easier to run

125

with the animals in the true spirit of the Fiesta, rather than ahead of the dust and danger.

The second rocket spat into the sky and he tried to tense his muscles, to spring forward, to realise his dream of being an active part of this famous, or notorious, event, but suddenly it was no longer possible to move. Direction and desire were abstractions. Around him men hurried forward, but not one of them even brushed against his arms, which were slack at his sides. There was no bite in his mouth, no swell of blood in his head, nothing meaningful.

He simply stood and waited to be crushed by the herd, the heavy beasts with frightened eyes and dawn breath just like his, smoky, thick, almost blue in the long early shadows of the Plaza. He waited but he did not watch, for they were behind him and he faced only the sweat soaked backs of runners and a corridor with walls made of spectators and music. He waited and thought about the different types of waiting, uneasy, ignorant, gloomy, resigned, and understood that no variation matched his own particular style of not moving, remaining fixed at this precise instant. He waited and slowly his whole body sagged.

Nothing touched him, no horn or hoof, not even the erect hairs of each hot flank. The bulls surged around him while he continued to wait, leaving him unscathed with drooping shoulders and hollow stomach, and he watched the living thunder and organised confusion pass on both sides. Ignored again, even by stricken beasts, as if there was something in his very existence which could not be acknowledged by the most primitive physical contact.

Now he was standing alone and the event had come and gone without him, even though he had inserted himself into the centre of it. He remained for perhaps another hour before walking away, his mind struggling with old memories, seeking a clue as to why he was a permanent outsider in everything. He wondered if the stories were true, if he had really been murdered in his own house in the distant past and could not be here, but it did not feel like that. He suspected the answer was different at every stage of his long life, a life of travelling, waiting to be perceived and recognised. But this particular case was simple.

If his inner self was not sure who to run with, the bulls or the men, and the people did not know, how could the city care?

THE CANDID SLYNESS OF SCURRILITY FOREPAWS

Hello there! I'm sure you don't really want to hear about my childhood, so I'll just briefly mention one incident that was crucial to the development of my career. On the eve of my seventh birthday, my father summoned me to his study for a lecture. I entered the enormous room with a certain amount of trepidation, for my father was a remote and gloomy figure, frequently absent on long sailing voyages. His study was crammed with souvenirs of his travels and I was particularly impressed with the grinning masks hanging on the walls. He sat at a large mahogany desk and I took the chair opposite him and waited patiently.

"The world is a chaotic and unhappy place," he began, "and it is best to prepare at a young age for the problems it will cause you. Justice is a lie and fair play simply doesn't exist. Women are beautiful but cruel and ask too many awkward questions. Friends are treacherous and laugh at you behind your back. Dogs and cats are even worse."

He continued in this manner for a long time, listing things I was certain to encounter and dismissing them with contempt. Although his cold fury was fascinating, the list seemed endless and I found it impossible not to yawn. He frowned darkly at this.

"You're not an adult yet and doubtless harbour traces of hope and optimism in your heart. That's understandable. But let me tell you something — I've travelled the globe and visited every country and culture in existence and not once have I discovered anything other than greed and disappointment. That has been true *without exception*. Shattered dreams are the rule."

127

He resumed his list and I hastened to interrupt him. "With respect," I said, "you've made your point and I accept it."

He nodded, torn between anger at my audacity and relief that his words had not been wasted. Pouring himself a tumbler of brandy he sipped the liquid slowly. "Very well, I'll skip the remainder of the list, even though it contains such important items as Finance and Toothache. But there is one thing worse than all the others."

I leaned forward and met his gaze. "Pray tell."

His voice became sad. "It is being accused of something you haven't done. Getting the blame when you are innocent. That's the bitterest pill of all! And it will happen to you, as if happens to everyone, unless you work hard to preclude the possibility. Make sure you are always guilty, that you really are to blame. Get into all sorts of mischief, cause all kinds of trouble. Be ambitious and imaginative but don't neglect the details. If you live according to these principles, you'll never be condemned unfairly. I want you to promise me you'll be an unrepentant rogue until the day you die. It's the only way of avoiding miscarriages of justice."

I solemnly made that promise and he added, "It's customary at this stage to beat you to ensure you remember this lecture, as Cellini's father beat him when they saw a salamander in the fire, but I'm much cleverer than that. From the moment of your birth I anticipated a need to arm you against the world. That is why I named you Scurrility. This name will always serve as a reminder of your vocation as a villain and mischief maker. True, you will be exposed to ridicule from your peers, but this would have happened anyway considering the surname I bequeathed to you. Now leave me to brood alone and close the door behind you. We owe it to ourselves to be bad."

The following day he embarked on another voyage and never came back.

The mischief I indulged in for the next decade was fairly minor but I was simply awaiting the greater opportunities of adulthood. One of the first consequences of my father's speech was that I stopped trusting my mother. She had informed me that the word 'scurrility' meant handsome and smart in appearance. With the aid of a dictionary I discovered that my father's definition was more accurate. At school I became the bane of my teachers and fellow pupils. A flair for chemistry resulted in many small explosions and petty damage to property. Nothing could ever be proved against me, for I was as lucky as I was careful, but the teachers avenged themselves by awarding me low grades in examinations.

I left school with few qualifications but I refused to let this fact hinder me. I took a job in a jam factory and saved my wages with dedication, for I had a scheme in mind that required considerable capital. While I worked, I amused myself by adding flies to the jam. I collected large numbers of the insects by visiting the kitchens of restaurants and hotels in the guise of an Inspector of Hygiene and asking for the contents of all the flytraps to be given to me. They never refused. Walking to work with pockets full of flies seems less funny now than it did then. I added a single fly to every pot, using my thumb to push it deep into the jam before screwing down the lid.

I was constantly occupied with inventing new annoyances and torments for the people around me. I dialled telephone numbers at random during the night. When using an elevator I always pressed all the buttons just before getting out. In the supermarket I became an expert at striking the ankles of other shoppers with the wheel of my trolley. I always used the slowest and most complicated method of payment in any queue. Naturally there was only so much I could do alone, but I didn't allow an appreciation of my limitations to deter me from making at least one attempt every day to lower the quality of life for my fellow citizens. I was a dependable scoundrel.

It is true that none of my tricks and acts of sabotage were original. But I had made plans for a truly unique piece of mischief that could only be implemented when funds permitted. I bided my time and continued to save and I wasn't dissatisfied with what I did achieve. I became an expert at making the neighbourhood dogs bark after midnight. Every time I passed a laundry I entered and added fistfuls of tissues to the pockets of trousers waiting to be washed. In pubs and nightclubs I enjoyed dropping cigarette butts into drinks, especially cans and opaque bottles. I was never caught and I guess I began to consider myself invulnerable or invisible.

One morning I was rudely awakened by a persistent hammering on the door of my apartment. I dressed to answer the call and found myself facing two men in dark suits with insincere smiles. They pushed their way inside and closed the door behind them.

"You are Scurrility Forepaws," one of them said flatly.

"That is correct," I replied with a forced sneer, "and I'm already late for work."

"You are employed at Gulliver's Jam Factory," the second man declared. "We know what you've been up to."

I suspect a part of me had always assumed I would be caught one day. There was no point denying my guilt. So I answered coolly, "Flies are very nutritious."

They shook their heads together. Both men had expressionless blue eyes and I considered loaning them two pairs of dark glasses. "Not just that. We know everything."

I was alarmed by that statement, for it implied I had been followed and spied on for a long time without my suspicions being aroused. Knowing how corrupt the secret police were rumoured to be, I wondered if I should try to bribe my way out of this predicament, but at the same time I reasoned I couldn't afford to pay an unofficial 'fine' without setting back my favoured scheme, the one I was saving for. I had no intention of being deterred from a life of mischief because of this failure. It was simply a lesson for me to be more subtle in future. With a short but wholly authentic laugh I extended my arms and waited for the closing of the handcuffs on my wrists.

"It is your duty to arrest me. I'll come quietly."

The first man announced, "We aren't policemen. We want to offer you a job."

The second man said, "We've been impressed with what we've seen of your mischief so far. We represent an obscure organisation dedicated to the spreading of chaos throughout society. We need

130

people like you. Will you work for us? The wages you will receive are ten times the amount you are currently paid. All you are required to do is to continue being a nuisance. Indeed as this is a full time post, you'll have many more hours each day to cause trouble than you presently have. What do you say?"

I was stunned. The chance to earn a living from what I intended to do anyway was almost too much for my mind to absorb. I needed to sit and breathe deeply for several minutes before I was calm enough to respond to the proposal. They watched me indulgently.

At last I gasped, "I accept! You won't regret taking me on. I'll be a punctual and conscientious rotter! I'll always be sly and deceitful too — trust me!"

I resigned from my job at Gulliver's Jam Factory the following morning and commenced working for my new employers on the afternoon of the same day. I never learned much about the organisation I was now a member of. My wages were delivered regularly in an envelope pushed under my door and I had little direct contact with any of my colleagues. An occasional visit from one or other of the blue eyed men took place, but these were no more than routine checks on my progress. They rarely answered questions about the nature of their secret society. I thought I detected one of them referring to the organisation as 'The Scamps of Disorder' but I was probably mistaken. The mystery of the whole business appealed to me.

My acts of chaos remained modest for another few months. I offered sweets with tiny fragments of silver foil clinging to them to people with lots of fillings in their teeth. I smeared vaseline on doorknobs and taps. I hung enormous untuned wind chimes around the city during the stormy season. But soon I had raised enough capital to turn my carefully nurtured dream into a reality. I founded a magazine. This was my unique piece of mischief, my apotheosis. It doesn't sound like much but it was the character of the magazine that made it so unhelpful to my fellow citizens. It was called *The Suicide*

Review and it did exactly what the title promised — it reviewed suicides.

Imagine the malice of that, if you will! It is bad enough for the family and friends of a person who has just taken their own life to cope with the shattering reality of the loss, but when that loss is treated as an example of popular art, analysed and criticised in a public forum, the anguish is amplified with the addition of horrified incredulity and frustrated rage. My publication was a supreme monument to tastelessness and exploitation. *The Suicide Review* was not only profoundly morbid but perversely enthralled by the most facile and shallow aesthetic values. Glibness was deified. I employed writers who were clever but insecure and addicted to withholding sympathy from their subjects.

I'd expected to make a loss, for I cared only about causing strife and hadn't taken profitability into account, but to my amazement the magazine prospered. It paid for itself many times over. It became a sort of fashion accessory for self conscious artistic types. Publication was increased from monthly to weekly and I became a wealthy man. Writers of renown began asking to join my staff. I remember the day the famous journalist Wormhole Kidd simpered into my office and begged for employment. He had worked for *The Bohemian Examiner* for the past ten years, cementing his reputation with a prose style that disparaged everything. The entire contemporary arts scene was said to be balanced on his sneer.

"I love your magazine," he babbled. "It's just so conceptual!"

I welcomed him into the fold and our sales increased dramatically. I never instructed my writers in how to handle the latest suicide because the main rule was instinctively known by all — always give a bad review. Because they were 'cool' they never dared to show tenderness, humanity or generosity. Wormhole Kidd pushed them even deeper into postmodern cynicism. They did everything ironically and therefore could never be accused of making a mistake. Wormhole's first review was a small masterpiece. A girl jilted by her lover had thrown herself out of a window and impaled herself on the railings below. Wormhole condemned her death throes as a set of clichés and ridiculed the derivative angles made by her twitching legs.

During this time I felt a warm glow in the pit of my stomach that had two different sources of heat, in other words I felt a powerful double satisfaction that merged into one sensation. I was proud of myself for exceeding the probable expectations of my secret employers and also I was delighted not to have let my father down, wherever he was. I had truly lived up to my name, my first name I mean, not the family name, for I have no clear idea how to behave in a manner consistent with the word 'Forepaws'. I was extremely pleased with myself and it was at this point, perhaps inevitably, that my first setback occurred, though I didn't perceive it as such at the time.

My magazine received an envelope addressed to the editor. I opened it and saw it was a suicide note from a man who wanted it published — the moment it appeared in print he would kill himself. *The Suicide Review* had published the farewell notes of unsuccessful suicides, usually with a commentary attacking the poor literary style of the note, and these reviews had sometimes encouraged the survivor to make a second and more successful attempt. But we had never published a note prior to the deed. I wrote back explaining it was not our policy to give publicity to pseudo-suicides. As well as implying he was a coward and a charlatan I also mocked the wording of the note itself, declaring it the work of an idiotic hack.

A few days later I received a second letter, or rather a second draft of the first. The man had reworded his suicide note as if my criticisms had been serious and well intentioned. I saw an opportunity for a game. I handled this duty myself instead of passing it over to Wormhole Kidd or one of the other reviewers. I wrote back with even greater contempt. As expected I soon received a third draft of the suicide note. This foolish amusement continued for many weeks. It was the delight of the office. Once when I entered the cafe where most of my staff members took their lunch, the place burst into applause. Wormhole was eating a thick ham sandwich and greeted me with a wink.

133

"I'm practising vegetarianism — ironically!" he cried.

We laughed together but with a superior sort of laugh to show we were above straightforward humour. After all, the joke might eventually turn out not to be funny and we needed to protect ourselves. I think it was at this time I first noticed the girl in red sitting at a table in the corner. She didn't work for me and was obviously just a normal customer. She was with a man, her fiancé as it happened, but I could tell from her eyes she was planning to give herself to me. Constant mischief making had left me with little time for relaxation. Physical activities of the horizontal kind had never figured largely in the agenda of my life. I decided it was high time they did.

Her name was Belinda Bourbon and even her underwear was red. It was her favourite colour. She liked to have her ears nibbled and her own teeth were charmingly crooked. She broke off with her fiancé the moment he discovered our affair, to prevent him taking the initiative. She thought she knew a lot about me but it was mostly society gossip and conjecture. I excited her because I was a rogue, no other reason. She always generalised her own beliefs and urges. She told me that all women were biologically programmed to find villains attractive. She craved a wild life and seemed to think this consisted of ingesting illegal drugs and performing standard acts of exhibitionism.

There was no danger I would allow romance to divert me from my career. We walked hand in hand, watched the stars together, drove above the speed limit on country roads. I agreed with her that our behaviour was risky and cutting edge. I even nurtured her illusion that cycling topless through the city streets was an act guaranteed to shock and distress pedestrians and motorists. I sometimes found it difficult to stifle a yawn in her company but she suspected nothing. When I judged she was genuinely in love with me, I told her that we needed to talk. I had something to confess. We sat on a bench in the park and I lowered my eyes as I spoke.

"Belinda, you know I love you, and it's for this reason I must come clean. I can't deceive you a moment longer. I'm not really a rogue at all. I'm a sweet, kind man, a gentle soul full of tenderness with a yearning for world peace. I have a social conscience! Please forgive me. Please find it in your heart to continue loving me. I don't think I could live without you."

She broke off our relationship the following day. She could no longer trust me. I had betrayed her, tricked her into thinking I was a complete bounder whereas in fact I was a mature and reasonable individual. Not only was the relationship ruined but all her memories of our outrageous antics had been soiled. She wished me the very worst luck for the future. This result was delicious. Some men fake their own deaths, others fake their own lives, but I had gone much further. I had pretended to fake my own fakery! In some ways I consider this to be my finest piece of mischief.

I was so satisfied by the outcome of this affair that I neglected my correspondence with the writer of the suicide note. Indeed I paid only infrequent visits to the offices of *The Suicide Review*. My other mischief making activities also dwindled in number and intensity. I had been suffering headaches and muscle cramps prior to my relationship with Belinda and these were gradually growing worse. I finally arranged to see a doctor. He examined me carefully, studied the tips of my fingers with a magnifying glass and clicked his tongue thoughtfully. Then he consulted a large textbook on one of his shelves. The word 'Poisons' was embossed on the spine of this volume and I shivered.

"Do you have many enemies?" he asked me casually.

It soon emerged I had absorbed a large amount of arsenic through the ink of the letters sent to me by the hopeful contributor to my magazine. His rewritten suicide notes were really an attempt at assassination! I was impressed as well as horrified by this subterfuge. It served as a timely reminder I was not the only scoundrel in the world, that some others were naturally vicious rather than simply fulfilling a vow never to be good. I had accidentally saved my own life by breaking off the correspondence. My system was weakened but not fatally. I would fully recover in time, but it was essential I give up work and take a complete rest. Those were the doctor's orders.

Taking time off work was easy enough, for I never needed to report to my employers. I felt sure they had other ways of monitoring my progress. I had enough money to last me many years when the wage packets stopped. My mind was peaceful on that score. But another thought began to obsess me. Without my constant mischief making, the quality of life in the city must improve. While I was recuperating and not spreading chaos, life had to get better for everyone else. With one less 'Scamp of Disorder' to make existence miserable, a tangible rise of standards had to be observable in the coming weeks. I entertained myself by imagining some of the positive things that might happen.

I had various images in my head, involving people helping other people, little acts of empathy and support. One of my favourites involved the daily traffic jam in the complicated circuit of roads in the city centre. I visualised a perfect gridlock with all the vehicles stuck behind each other unable to move even the smallest distance. Suddenly the doors of the cars opened and all the passengers got out and walked forward to the next car ahead. They entered these other cars and closed the doors. In this manner they shifted themselves one position forward. A few minutes later they repeated this action. Continuing this process, all the commuters would find their way out of the monumental jam.

This was a bizarre fantasy, of course, and it relied on people not caring who sat in their vehicles provided they could sit in somebody else's. It was an elaborate metaphor for the concept of sharing, I suppose. As my health returned I decided to talk long walks. To my bewilderment, life in the city had not improved at all during my absence. If anything, it had got *worse*. Everybody wore sour faces and walked with aggressive but also somehow dejected strides. I remained flabbergasted. Had all my previous wickedness been in vain? Had I wasted my life, betrayed my father and lost Belinda for nothing? The world without Scurrility was more scurrilous!

How could such a thing be? An answer was provided by a chance encounter with one of the men who originally recruited me. I was standing on a bridge gazing at the river when he came up and stood behind me. He knew what my trouble was and spoke first.

"Don't feel too gloomy," he said. "The reason why life has got worse rather than better since you took time off work is because you have stopped causing mischief to other mischief makers. Do you understand now? You were a villain to everyone around you. But some of those people were also mischief makers. You aren't the only rogue in this city, Mr Forepaws, nor are you the worst, not by a long way. But your acts of mischief, which were always directed at random members of the population, frequently sabotaged or interfered with the plans of other scoundrels, hampering them and accidentally helping to make the world a finer place."

The irony was unbearable. I digested it slowly and muttered, "You mean to say that if I hadn't dedicated my life to mischief there would be more mischief in life?"

He clapped me on the shoulder. "It's all part of the rich pageant of disorder."

He moved away and I wept a few tears before embarrassment dried them in their ducts. I looked at the people who passed me on the bridge and I wondered which of them were rogues like me, or rogues even more dastardly. Possibly every single inhabitant of the city was a member of the same secret society. I'd never learned how many scoundrels it employed. Or perhaps they were members of different secret societies devoted to the same purpose? Who could tell? It now seemed very likely there was no such thing as an innocent person. It was much more plausible that we were all mischief makers of varying degrees of skill, hindering each other and chaos in the name of chaos.

A few weeks later there was another knock on the door of my apartment. I opened it and found myself facing two men but not the

137

two men who visited me before. They didn't try to push their way inside. I asked them directly if they represented 'The Scamps of Disorder' or some other organisation committed to strife and badness. They shook their heads. On the contrary, they were agents of a secret society devoted to regularity and order, the exact opposite of my former employers. I invited them in and made them cups of coffee while they explained the reason for their visit. It was unexpectedly connected with my father.

"We knew him quite well," one of them revealed, "but he was a very private individual. He liked to conceal his activities from everyone."

"We were in business together," the other man clarified.

I remembered the long sailing voyages my father had been apt to take. The first man said, "We came into possession of one of his journals. He misplaced it and it remained jammed in a dark corner of a ship's cabin for many years. Anyway, when we finally got hold of it, we read it carefully. It turns out that on one of his travels he discovered a land where everyone is happy and peaceful and nothing is ever a disappointment. That's where he's living now."

"So he lied about the universal misery of the world!" I cried.

"Well his name should have given you a clue — Fibber Forepaws."

I sulked. "My mother told me that the word 'Fibber' meant golden haired and noble chinned. You just can't trust anyone at all, can you?"

The men smiled gently. "Except in that land your father discovered."

I sighed. "What do you want of me?"

"Nothing much. It's just that as his son we thought you should be kept informed. But we do intend to make a proposal to you. We are fitting out a ship at this very moment on behalf of our organisation. We plan to sail to that perfect land. Our own world could learn a lot from them, don't you think? We intend to bring back their ideas, their way of life, their peacefulness and happiness. Do you want to come with us? Such a voyage might well be a victory blow for our organisation, for regularity and order. It could destroy chaos. We are offering you a chance to join the winning side, to become part of history. What do you say? It could be magnificent!"

I considered deeply. "Very well. But don't you think it would be a good idea to take some gifts with us? Something to demonstrate our good intentions?"

The men were ecstatic. "What do you suggest?"

"Something simple but effective. I know for a fact that Gulliver's Jam Factory has just gone bust and closed down. They will be selling off their remaining stock very cheaply. A thousand pots of jam should do the trick."

We shook hands on the deal. After they left I performed a little dance.

Scurrility, you sly rascal!

SENDING FREEDOM FAR AWAY

When President Arbusto came to power, the storerooms full of war materials were unlocked. Campaign maps were unrolled on tables and stuck with pins. The generals went to the dentist and had their teeth fixed. They wanted to bite cigars more effectively.

The President made a speech from the balcony of his palace while the crowd below waved flags. He said:

"We live in a land of freedom and most of us are grateful for that. As for those who aren't, it doesn't matter, that's the privilege of being free, people here can think and say what they please, even if it means disagreeing with everybody else."

The crowd cheered and drowned out these cheers with louder cheers and so they didn't really hear much.

President Jorge Arbusto continued:

"But our freedom is precious and there are other lands that hate the idea of freedom or don't know the meaning of the concept. In those lands, people aren't allowed to disagree with anything. They

139

can't say, 'Hey, I think that freedom is a good idea' without getting arrested and beaten and forced to change their minds."

"In this country of ours," he added, "we don't force people to change their minds. They don't have to use their minds at all, if they don't care to. It's entirely up to them."

The generals on a lower balcony applauded.

"It seems to me," said the President, "that it's mighty greedy of us to keep all this freedom to ourselves without even trying to share some of it. Freedom is so important that men die if they don't get enough. In our land there's a surplus but in other lands there might be little or none at all. It was always my aim to start exporting freedom when I achieved power and that's what I intend to do."

He loosened his collar and moistened his dry lips with his tongue. It was thirsty work, being strong.

"Don't think that if we give some of our freedom to other lands there will be less for us. Freedom isn't like oil, it can't run out. It's more like beef. We export a vast amount of beef each year but the number of cows in our fields is the same as last year. Count them, if you like. If we give away half our cows, it doesn't stop the remaining cows breeding more cows. That's freedom for you."

The crowd surged back and forth in approval. Removing his sunglasses, the President wiped tears from his eyes.

"The problem with exporting freedom is that it can't be done through the usual commercial channels. In places it has never existed it has to be imposed. The only way to do that is through war. Sure, it will cost a lot, but it'll be worth it. A free world is a safe world, and a safe world is a better place to do business, so we'll recoup our losses eventually. We may even make a profit. I've seen the figures and they add up. But that's not the point. Freedom is a gift."

"Yes, a gift," he stressed, "and it's worthwhile giving freedom away even if it makes bad economic sense, which it doesn't. I think we should begin with a distant land, somewhere on the far side of the ocean, a test run. If it works there, we'll keep going and try other countries. I've got a little nation in mind to start with, ruled by the worst kind of tyrant. We'll invade first thing tomorrow."

The war materials had already been dusted off, the helmets, spears, tanks, pikes, muskets, bayonets, barbed wire, hand grenades, axes, machine guns, rapiers, jeeps, and now they were loaded on ships and those ships set sail to the far side of the ocean.

Despite what the President had said about an immediate invasion, the voyage took many weeks. The troops on board grew bored and surly, but they were allowed to grumble as much as they liked because they were all free.

Indeed the purpose of going to war was to give other people the same right to grumble, so nobody could complain about this grumbling. But if someone did complain, that was fine too, it showed they were free, and being free doesn't mean you have to be happy.

Finally the ships sighted land. Boats were lowered from the decks and the troops rowed quickly to shore.

They landed on the beaches and swarmed out to attack the enemy. Soon all the fishing villages on the coast were burning and the cobbled streets were choked with mangled corpses.

Marching inland, the troops took the capital of the little nation but the tyrant who ruled had already fled. They found him cowering in a hut in the mountains and they cut off his head and stuck it on a pole and danced with the pole to the freest music, free jazz, and everybody was invited to this dance, but they were free to accept or decline as they pleased. Smoke drifted freely across the landscape.

When half the population was dead and the remaining half wholly free, the troops were visited by President Arbusto and many medals were pinned on many chests and many salutes were exchanged. Delighted by the performance of his troops, the President announced the name of the next country to be invaded. He was feeling generous.

"But you'll get a rest first of all," he said, "because fighting for the freedom of others is even more exhausting than fighting for your own freedom. I'm not unreasonable."

In the pause between celebrating victory over this land and invading the next, the President made a list with his generals. Someone would shout the name of a country that desperately needed

141

freedom and it was added to the list. But people kept thinking of new names. They stayed up all night and a hundred cigars were chewed.

It wasn't enough to make a list of destinations. There also had to be a certain amount of moral examination.

President Arbusto asked himself two questions: (a) Can these wars be won? (b) Will they increase the amount of freedom in the world? The answer was yes both times.

Therefore these wars were not just wars but *just* wars.

The next country they invaded proved harder to subdue. It lay on the border of the first country, over a range of mountains, and had seen what had happened there, so it was more prepared.

But the troops of President Arbusto won anyway and they were so annoyed by the stubborn resistance of the enemy that they decided to educate the survivors and persuade them to fully accept the gift of freedom.

"From now on," they roared, "when you say, 'Hey, I think that freedom is a good idea' you *won't* be beaten by the opponents of freedom, because we came along and made you free."

And they made sure this lesson was remembered very well by beating it into them. There were other reprisals too, and the streets ran with blood, but blood is like oil and runs out eventually, and after the rainy season everything was quite clean again.

The third country to be invaded was an island much closer to home. It was ruled by a dictator who had tricked his people into believing that his beard was magical. By tugging it a certain number of times he could reduce poverty, provide pensions, workers' rights, equality for women, and other unlikely miracles.

In fact his people lived in squalor and drove cars that were more than forty five years old.

President Arbusto surrounded the island with his gunships and shelled the capital. Each shell had a message written on it, a free message, maybe some free verse poetry or a free offer by one of the telephone companies.

142

When the shrapnel was discovered in the shells of buildings, some of this writing was still legible. But nobody was forced to read it, because they were free at last. Or dead.

When the country surrendered, President Arbusto called a meeting with his generals to discuss the next name on the list. But such meetings never run entirely as planned, and in fact all that happened was that more names were added to the list. It was much easier to make a new list of countries that didn't need any freedom.

"I think we're the only one," the President said.

The years passed heroically. One morning President Jorge Arbusto addressed the crowd below his palace. He seemed tired and worried but there was also enough of the old determination in his eyes to suggest he had a final task to accomplish, something supreme.

"My friends and followers," he began, "we seem to have made a mistake and exported too much of our own freedom to other lands. I know I said it couldn't run out, it was like cows, but now that seems not to be the case. The new conclusion is that freedom is like a muscle. If muscles don't get proper exercise they waste away."

"Yes," he continued after a pause, "they become atrophied and that's the same as if they weren't there in the first place. The problem is that none of you ever exercised any of your freedom. While our troops were away in remote realms, exporting the stuff, you just went along with whatever I said and everything they did. You might have protested, and thus kept your freedom fit, but you didn't."

He shook his head ruefully and sighed deeply.

"As a result, freedom in our land has withered away almost to nothing and will soon perish. We have now exported freedom to every other country in the world, and they are all free, but because you allowed freedom here to shrivel, I'm forced to add another name to my list of countries in need of freedom. Or rather, to remove a name, the only name, from the list of countries not in need of freedom."

143

"That's right," he added with an ironic smile, "our own nation is the last one to stand in the way of global freedom. It is imperative we become free as quickly as possible."

The crowd muttered uneasily and President Arbusto waited for several minutes before interrupting them:

"Don't worry, it's not necessary to import that freedom from abroad. I don't think we need to be invaded by foreign troops. Even though freedom here is almost dead, it is still strong enough for one final act, the act that will restore total freedom. We can invade ourselves! This is cheaper than asking troops from free nations to invade us. Our own troops are due home anyway. When they return we can surrender to them instantly. They may be too astonished to open fire."

The crowd settled down at this news.

"Of course," the President added, "the tyrant who currently rules our country must be overthrown. This is something I can accomplish right now, to save time. Stand back, please."

With a wild yell, he grabbed hold of himself by the collar of his own shirt and dragged himself to the edge of the balcony.

But he wasn't going to give up without a fight and he pushed back. The tussle went on for half an hour. The opponents were evenly matched. It was so confusing, the crowd couldn't tell who was fighting for freedom and who wasn't. Some cheered for both. The President bounced against the balustrade, stumbled from one side of the balcony to the other.

Suddenly, he managed to get his hand on the back of his own head, and with a mighty effort, he flipped himself over the balustrade and into thin air. He plummeted in silence to the hard ground below. The crowd parted to let him through.

When they surged forward around his leaking corpse, they saw an extended arm and clenched fist, though whether this was a salute of freedom or defiance, nobody could guess.

144

ANTON ARCTIC AND THE CONQUEST OF THE SCOTTISH POLE

Ordinary geographers believe that our planet has only two poles, the North and South, and they prefer to ignore the East, West, Front and Back poles. But Anton Arctic went to the other extreme and maintained the existence of a seventh pole, namely the Scottish.

This is Anton's story or should be, but in truth there isn't much to tell. He had wanted to be an explorer since he fell asleep in a laundry basket and awoke hanging from a washing line. The huge white sheets drying next to him looked like icebergs and after he detached himself from the pegs holding him up he wandered among them in wonder. He was only thirty eight years old and was astonished to discover that icebergs are not cold. In fact he used them to wrap up warm when night fell.

The Scottish pole was located somewhere in Scotland. That is all he knew. His careful and prolonged researches into history, cartography, mythology and natural science led him to conclude that Scotland could be reached by boarding the 06:15 train from London.

Accordingly he bought a ticket at King's Cross station and waited patiently on the platform. When his train was ready he settled into his seat and opened his rucksack to check the condition of his survival equipment. Fortunately his sandwiches, flask of hot tea and good book were all in perfect working order.

The journey north was uneventful. After he crossed the border, he kept his face close to the window in case he spied the Scottish pole standing in a field. How would he recognise it? He imagined it was long and cylindrical with a tartan pattern. However, his estimates of its height remained vague.

When he arrived in Edinburgh he walked unknown streets with a measured step. Not even the greatest detective in Scotland Yard, an organisation that specialises in Scottish measurements, hence its name, has been able to determine where exactly his measured step took him.

His movements may be obscure but not his motives. Obviously he searched for the Scottish pole in Edinburgh without success. A few days later he appeared in a small town much further north called Invergarry. How he got there is open to conjecture. He might have fallen asleep in another laundry basket, or whatever passes for laundry baskets in Scotland, huge porridge pots stuffed with kilts perhaps, but why such an occurrence would take him to Invergarry is unclear. A witness who claims to have seen him riding north in a chariot pulled by a haggis has been dismissed as an unreliable character from a different story that has not even been written yet.

It was raining heavily when he arrived in Invergarry and in a muddy field near that town he exhibited rather odd behaviour. At least it was odd to outsiders. In Anton's opinion his actions were rational and even heroic. So let us recount what happened from his perspective.

Plodding along with a heavy sense of failure in his soul, he abruptly noticed something marvellous on the horizon. He ran forward and his joy increased to an almost unbearable intensity as he realised his quest was over. He had found the Scottish pole! Now all he had to do was conquer it to guarantee his future reputation as a noteworthy explorer.

He didn't know what 'conquering' a pole entailed, but he was aware that an army conquers a country by marching over it and so he concluded that it was probably a good idea if he positioned himself over the pole. This meant he had to climb it.

Haste was important for he saw that a rival explorer had already reached the base of the pole and was clutching it with both hands. Fortunately for Anton this other explorer did not have the physique of a climber. He was large and far too heavy to haul himself easily up any pole and he grunted and grimaced as if preparing for a great effort while people standing in the field urged him on. Anton wanted to shout at these people, to redirect their attention, but he decided to save his breath for running.

Splashing through puddles, he reached the pole and flung himself on it, climbing rapidly with his legs and arms wrapped around the rough wood. The pole was shorter than he had anticipated and he was overjoyed to have found such an unobtrusive landmark in so large an area as Scotland. At no point did he doubt this really was the Scottish pole. He was too busy trying to climb beyond the reach of his rival.

When he was halfway up he suddenly felt very dizzy and almost lost his grip. He paused for a few moments and then resumed his task. This rest must have been beneficial, for the second half of the climb was much easier, as if the top of the pole was pulling him by the force of magnetic attraction, an impossible explanation due to the fact he was not made of iron, but welcome all the same.

He arrived at the top and was astonished to strike his head on a ceiling! He had not noticed a ceiling above the pole at any stage during his climb or before. This was indeed a mystery. The top end of the pole was fixed firmly into this ceiling and there was no way of mounting it. How could he conquer the pole now? It was necessary to get above the ceiling and stand on the other side.

This problem was lessened by the fact that the ceiling was covered with tufts of fibre that hung down from its surface. He could cling to these and work his way along until he reached the edge. The barrier had to come to an end somewhere.

This was a hazardous operation but he found it unnaturally easy to disengage from the pole and attach himself to the ceiling. He clung to the slippery tufts with all his might and dug the toes of his shoes into the pliable surface and in this manner he crawled his way across. He had no particular direction in which to go but he kept crawling anyway.

The underside of the ceiling was very dirty. It had clearly not been cleaned for many years, if ever. Anton became dismayed with the filth that gathered on his clothes and he started to regret the entire adventure. Even more irritating was the fact that the ceiling seemed to have no edge after all. He paused for a much needed rest.

Then he made the mistake of turning his head to look down. The ceiling must have been designed as a slope for he was much higher now than the actual height of the pole. He had crawled his way to an immense altitude and the land beneath him was so distant it appeared a grey blur without any distinguishing features.

Anton was terrified. He no longer desired fame as an explorer but cared only for a return to solid ground. He looked around in vain for the Scottish pole. Having lost all sense of direction, he clung to the tufts more tightly as he fought the urge to scream. This was the worst moment of his life.

Then he controlled his fear and decided that before falling to his death he ought to make an effort to save himself. He closed his eyes and crawled off as fast as possible, his hands slipping on the damp tufts, his boots digging slimy footholds in the ceiling. He didn't expect to survive and yet he had the curious feeling that gravity was starting to lose interest in him.

A man filled with hydrogen or helium like an old fashioned airship might bounce along a ceiling with no greater ease than Anton now proceeded. And yet he knew this defiance of the laws of nature was an illusion, that soon he would lose his grip and plummet to the grey land below. Tiredness would overcome him or the tufts break off and his doom would rush at him impatiently.

While he was imagining this doom and feeling sorry for himself because he had so few friends to remember him, none in fact, which maybe isn't so bad if being remembered as unsuccessful is worse than never being noticed, he suddenly struck his head on an obstacle. He snapped open his eyes. He had crawled straight into a solid pole.

It wasn't the Scottish pole, for it was made of a substance harder than wood, possibly concrete, but he didn't care what name it had. It might be the French or Turkish pole, carried from its native land and planted here by invaders. What did it matter provided he could climb down it? That was the important point.

Not wanting to descend to the ground upside down, he turned in a careful circle and embraced the pole with his legs. Then he eased his body onto its length, but his hopes of sliding smoothly groundwards came to nothing. Either there was too much friction between the substance of the pole and his limbs or else he was still connected to the ceiling by a weird magnetism, for it took considerable effort for him to inch his way down.

After ten minutes or so of exhausting work he was mortified to discover that the pole came to an end. It was not connected to the ground but merely stuck into the ceiling like a fake stalactite. Worse than this, the end was glowing hot and shone brightly. It was the simplest kind of light fitting. Anton grumbled to himself. If he was going to be forced to dangle from ceiling illumination, the least his luck might do was to provide a chandelier.

A tide of resignation rose inside him, flooding the chambers of his heart and the spaces between his bones. He simply lacked the stamina to hold on. He was exhausted and the glowing tip of the pole was radiating an uncomfortable amount of heat. To avoid blisters he let go of the pole and embraced extinction instead. He allowed himself to plunge freely.

At this point it might be appropriate to describe Anton's activities from the viewpoint of the people standing in the field when he first arrived. Every year Invergarry has the honour of hosting the Highland Games. This traditional competition features only essentially Scottish feats of strength and endurance, the most famous of which is *Tossing the Caber*. The caber is a lopped tree trunk and it takes formidable muscle power to toss it.

The caber is not really tossed for distance but for style. The athlete holds the caber in his hands, keeping it balanced perfectly erect. He is required to imagine a clock face spread on the ground before him. He stands at the 6 o'clock position and tosses the caber so that it turns in the air and lands upside down in the middle of the clock. Then it is supposed to topple over and end up pointing exactly towards the 12 o'clock position.

The caber was in the very act of being tossed when Anton Arctic rushed across the field, jumped onto it and began climbing. By the time he was halfway up it had somersaulted in mid flight and thus he felt dizzy. Then it landed in the middle of the clock face, but because the torrential rain had softened the ground it stuck fast without toppling. Anton noticed none of this and kept climbing.

149

When he reached the end of the pole he assumed that the ground was a ceiling. He never suspected he was upside down. He let go of the pole and inched across the field, holding tightly to clumps of grass. Eventually he looked up at the cloudy sky and was overwhelmed with vertigo. He thought the sky was the land.

He resumed crawling and the pole he struck his head against was a lamppost at the edge of the field, an Ivergarry street light. The spectators watched in disbelief as he climbed feet first up this lamppost, did a handstand at the top and then let go with a peculiar sort of laugh.

What happened next has become a source of mild controversy. The spectators at the Highland Games swear that he plummeted head first into the mud of the field and was buried as far as his waist, so that only his feebly kicking legs were visible until he was hauled out with ropes by several of the strongest athletes and sent packing back to London, never to be heard of again. And there should be no reason to doubt them.

But the pilot of a passing airliner crossing Scotland at the time reported seeing a man rising into the sky and waving cheerfully as he went past, a man with bushy white eyebrows and whiskers as frosty and desolate as bedsheets on a washing line.

THE SIX SENTINELS

Licking the moon is a nasty habit and leaves the tongue coated with dust. This dust tastes neither of butter nor cheese but of phases — crescents and other shapes. It remains a mystery why anyone should want to lick a moon. Lunacy is the only answer.

There is a city, a gorgeous wide city, set among the Idle Mountains, not too high among them, not too low, and the name of this moderately elevated but marvellously upholstered city is Plush. It was named thus by Plish in the days of his comfort. All builded tall of warm velvet bricks is Plush and draped with satin cloth; and its streets are thick with petals and its citizens are fuddled nicely with scent whenever they walk and greet each other with noses high in the air like snobs. Plish liked his people posh. Even the sharpest spires on the most slender minarets are not likely to impale anyone in Plush, for cotton is the substance from which they are made; and the mighty ramparts that girdle the city are constructed of no harder materials than soap and cheese. A soft, easy, slippery environment for slippery, easy, soft people.

As for the interiors of the buildings, they are all designed in the style of Lord Dunsany* and so are lush and magical and descriptively overlong. Every house has a garden on its roof, for there is no finer place for flowers and butterflies to gather; and in these gardens leisurely stroll the calm citizens in the early evenings when the sun is setting majestically over the snowy peaks far away, and they nod to each other, rooftop to rooftop, and exchange idle gossip with idle smiles. All the same, it is never easy to walk gracefully on roofs made of stretched fabric. Fun to bounce on them though.

Many cities have been washed by many rains over the course of many millennia but none as thoroughly as Plush, for the ramparts as stated are partly soap, and the bubbles run down the streets and the citizens play and glisten, and everything smells cleans and ready for a night out; and when the night does come it seems the city is all dressed up with nowhere to go, but it has no need of going anywhere, for it belongs where it is, and indeed it has always seemed one with the Idle Mountains. It is splendidigenous, a word I just invented, meaning that it would not be so magnificent in any other location. Of other cares there are few in Plush, for it is a city of relaxation, a city of easy chairs and deep sofas, and even the sternest truths are couched in the softest terms, with a pair of metaphorical slippers under that couch.

But in fact there is a single hard thing in the heart of the city, and this thing is a thing the people care not to discuss too much, for it reminds them of the difficult times that once were and the difficult times yet to come, not that one can really be reminded of times yet to

151

come, but you know what I mean. The thing that is rarely discussed is a broad pedestal in the central square that holds aloft six statues of six heroes known as the Six Sentinels, traditional guardians of Plush. Centuries of weather have eaten away the frowns on the marble faces and now the heroes seem serene, but this is an illusion, for in life they were servants of their own agitation. Not just servants but slaves, for they were never paid in coin for their gloom and trouble, and the coins of Plush are pieces of felt and not much use anyway.

The names of these heroes are Jitterwhack, Rumpus, Toothan, Klaw, Uckybald and Heckusboing. Half a millennium ago they set forth from Plush to secure its borders in every direction. That was the will of the people at that time. Or rather it was the will of Plish as he sat brooding on his throne of carven gum, shifting stickily from one buttock to another, pulling his fleecy beard and sighing softly; but Plish and his subjects were always of one mind only. Or else. It was he who selected the six most capable citizens in Plush and named them Sentinels, and so he rose with difficulty from his melting seat of authority and strode to the balcony of the palace that dominated one side of the central square, and glancing down at the crowd below, he spoke these words:

"Beloved inhabitants of Plush, take heed of my warning! So pleasant is our home, with cushions and pillows on every street corner, that greedy eyes observe us from beyond our ramparts. We are surrounded by enemies. It is only a matter of time before we are invaded and despoiled by the outer louts. Let us not rest on our laurels but resist on them instead! And what better way of resisting than to take the fight to the enemy? To this purpose I have recruited six noble champions and now I send them forth in the six directions that exist, to sweep clean those directions as far as feasible, or as far as the horizon, whichever is further. The chosen six must not return but will reside in the realms they have vanquished and there keep watchful eye on developments to guarantee the security of our supremely comfy city."

Then did Plish command the six heroes to forsake the rubber cobbles and mossy slabs of Plush in favour of the more varied terrain of the exterior world. Jitterwhack it was who rode north, and there found he a land of hard ice inhabited by seals. These he slew without mercy as instructed, to safeguard Plush from a northern invasion, and dwelled he the rest of his days alone and a-chatter on the frozen water; and so he passed from mortal to legend and became a statue on a pedestal, as already described, one of the Sentinels of Plush, and all there are agreed that Jitterwhack did his work well, for to this day there has never been an invasion from the north.

As for Rumpus, he went east and after weeks of hard riding he came to a desert sprinkled with oases where lived a gentle people on dates and milk, and Rumpus decided not to slaughter them provided they promise not to invent anger or swords, and having obtained this promise he settled among them, but remained watchful as bidden, his eyes constantly fixed on the bellies of dusky gyrating desert girls. More fortunate was he than Toothan, who rode west into an endless expanse of dreary marshes and conquered a squat people who squatted in squat huts on reedy stilts and ate frogs, the only available food. Toothan croaked not long after, but is no less revered than Rumpus. Both succeeded in protecting Plush correctly and ending the threat from east and west.

Nor has any invasion come from the direction south, and for this the citizens of Plush should thank Klaw, who explored a great forest and the fertile fields beyond it, who found a rural society based there, who smashed its farm equipment, dug up its turnips and made love to its scarecrows until he died from an infected splinter, and who so intimidated the simple folk that they never dared have any ambitions of any sort ever again. As for Uckybald, his ordained direction was down and with a spade he dug a pit and kept digging, in the cellar of his house in Plush, and far beneath the earth his bones still must be, protecting the downward borders of his city, if bones he truly had, for he was a floppy fellow in life and famous for contortionism.

Now we come to Heckusboing. I would prefer not to come to him, for it will win me few friends in Plush, but come to him I shall, or else this tale will be judged propaganda rather than a true history. Heckusboing was allotted the direction known as up. For a long time

153

he wondered how to proceed in that direction. He climbed the tallest minaret in Plush but the people below urged him to go higher and berated him when he came back down. They started to accuse him openly of lacking seriousness, of shirking his duty, of disobeying Plish. Stung by these insults, he made himself a ladder, the tallest ladder since the world began, but he had nothing to rest it against and it availed him not at all. The people grew increasingly impatient with him.

"Heckusboing does not love his city," they said, "and is not deserving of the title Sentinel. Instead of voyaging into the sky, he prefers to lounge about on the ground. This is treason and Plish must hear of it."

As he listened to these words, Heckusboing felt a mixture of fear and shame, and he locked himself in his house and refused to come out. Plish was summoned from his palace by the clamour of his subjects and he found a furious mob gathered outside the residence of the unworthy hero. This mob kicked at the walls of the house until the velvet bricks vibrated unnervingly and the entire structure was in danger of collapsing. Plish stood behind the crowd calling for Heckusboing to surrender and face justice; but suddenly a figure was seen on the roof, and it was the rogue Sentinel himself, too scared to emerge but too scared to remain inside. At the sight of the traitor the mob went wild and broke down the front door and rushed inside to seize him.

Heckusboing was trapped. He had nowhere to go but up. By this time the sun was set and a night wind had blown a large black cloud over the city. As the first members of the avenging mob mounted the stairs to the roof, Heckusboing threw back his head, uttered a demented laugh and jumped as high as he could. For an instant it seemed he had accepted the responsibilities of his position at last, and Plish nodded contentedly, but this was only a vain illusion, for he succeeded in reaching an altitude of no more than three or four feet before coming back down. However, the taut fabric of the roof acted like a trampoline. Back up he went, accompanied by a few potted plants, and down again; and on each subsequent bounce he rose higher and higher.

At the top of his tenth bounce the night wind blew him a little to the side, and he came down not on his own roof but on that of a neighbour. Thus began a circuit of the city, from roof to roof, higher and higher and higher, while Plish and the people gave up any notion of following him on foot. They simply watched in awe. Heckusboing completed his unorthodox tour by bouncing onto the roof of the palace itself. That huge building quivered and shot him straight up into the black cloud. He did not come down again. Plish gestured for his subjects to be silent and listened carefully. For many minutes there was not a sound.

Then faintly but madly came a laugh, the laughter of Heckusboing, and a tiny shape was observed running back and forth along the top of the cloud. How had he managed to keep his footing on a cloud? Plish did not need to pull his fleecy beard for long before he knew the answer; and his subjects were no less quick to make a guess. A lifetime of walking on the softest available surfaces had adapted the feet of the inhabitants of Plush. So Heckusboing had unwittingly acclimatised himself to cloud walking. For clouds are only a little softer than petals, webs, cotton buds and all the other gentle materials found everywhere in Plush. For several hours Heckusboing rejoiced in his salvation and might have danced on the cloud all night long, disturbing his former comrades below; but something unexpected occurred.

The moon broke through the cloud at just the point where he stood. Heckusboing lost his balance and fell onto the moon. The cloud closed up again and now his laughter was even fainter and much more distant. The people went to bed in dismay. Nobody had ever anticipated an invasion from the moon. As far as they were concerned, Heckusboing was a cheat and a slacker, and few believed he deserved a statue in the central square; but the pedestal looked lopsided with only five, and so Plish relented and reluctantly allowed Heckusboing to be added. It was a relief for Plish and his people when the moon was new, for the mad faint laughter came not at such

155

times. When full, Heckusboing often howled at the dogs of the world. He did not die of old age on the moon because the rules are different there.

The more pessimistic citizens of Plush declare that he is still alive, saving himself from starvation by doing something disagreeable with his tongue. It is a very nasty habit and I hope other men will travel to the moon one day and lock him up.

DEGREES OF SEPARATION

When the cigarette and glass of whisky were finished, all that was left was the knife. Clute turned it slowly in his hands as he sat in front of the mirror. Then he studied his reflection carefully. The face of a man planning revenge stared back at him. It was no different from the other faces he pulled on any random day.

He wanted to kill Bradman because of what Bradman had done. But to use this knife against that vague and terrible enemy would not be easy. Bradman was difficult to reach, living in a mansion protected by a high wall, guarded by huge dogs. Clute read the newspapers. Bradman had even posted armed guards on his grounds.

If Clute made a direct attempt on the life of Bradman he certainly would fail. He had no accomplices, no influence, no money or power. His vengeance would amount to nothing tangible. He had to seek some lateral method of scoring a strike against his adversary. Bradman's family were no less secure than he. What next?

There was Frost, Bradman's closest friend since childhood. Unlike Bradman, Frost travelled without bodyguards and lived in a house with a low wall and only one dog. But Frost was popular and rarely seen alone. How might Clute get close enough for the plunge? Again he probably would fail, his blade remaining thirsty.

Frost often went to the theatre to watch Cosimo perform. Cosimo was an accomplished singer and actor who was intimate with Frost but hardly aware of the existence of the less cultured Bradman.

Ending the life of Cosimo would cause a deep wound in Frost, and if Frost was hurt, Bradman would also feel a measure of pain.

This was the answer! Clute reached for the newspaper on an adjacent table and flicked the pages until he found an advertisement for Cosimo's latest play. The show began at nine the same evening. If Clute turned up early, he might be able to slip backstage and murderously encounter the actor in his own dressing room.

No, it was unlikely he would get past the doormen. They would grow suspicious and perform a search on him. The knife would be uncovered and the police summoned. Then opportunity for revenge against Bradman would become even less likely. Better to forget Cosimo. Clute remembered that Cosimo was connected to Kingsley.

Clute had read about it in the papers. The two men frequently went to restaurants together. In fact Kingsley taught Cosimo everything there was to know about fine wine and good food. All Clute had to do was book a table in the same place as Kingsley at the same time. Halfway through the meal, the deed could be done.

But what if Clute failed to kill Kingsley outright? Stabbing is not always effective. In a public place such as a restaurant, his time would be limited. If Kingsley recovered from his injuries, Cosimo would not be racked by grief, and so Frost could not be damaged in any way, and thus Bradman would not suffer at all.

Running the fleshy part of his thumb gently along the serrated edge of the blade and smiling slightly, Clute silently listed the restaurants frequented by Kingsley in order of excellence. The best was run by a man called Whitlam. A hole cut in Whitlam's chest would be no less a hole in Kingsley's life, an irreparable hole.

Yes, he would seek out Whitlam, perhaps in one of his kitchens, or better still during one of his frequent trips to the market to buy fresh produce. The glint of steel among the vegetables, the crash of trays of fish preserved in ice, and the chain reaction of vengeance would be set in motion, all the way to Bradman.

The problem with tackling Whitlam was that the man was an expert in the use of blades and always wore a knife or cleaver at his belt, even when shopping in public. Whitlam surely knew how to

157

defend himself and strike back. Clute would be the one left dying among the tomatoes, his life blood a sauce on the cobbles.

Whitlam had once taught cooking at the local college. He had taught Malevich for a year and even announced Malevich as his star pupil. After Malevich abandoned the culinary arts and went into finance, Whitlam did not fail to keep in touch with his protege. Malevich was perfect for any sudden death, slow moving, trusting.

The big advantage of killing Malevich was that Clute knew him very well. In fact they were close friends. It would be simplicity itself to invite him back to this room on some pretext and then commit an act of righteous violence on the fat dupe. Clute nodded once. He picked up the telephone and dialled his number.

Malevich agreed to come within the hour. Clute simply told him that something important needed to transpire between them. He mentioned few details, only that it had something to do with Bradman, a person almost unknown to Malevich. Clute chuckled. He imagined the expressions on the sequence of faces, the transmitted pain.

Shortly before Malevich arrived, Clute suddenly remembered that new neighbours had moved into the apartment directly below him. They were a bothersome couple, extremely sensitive to the slightest noise. Malevich was a bear of a man. He would knock loudly on Clute's door, roar out his greeting, stamp across the floorboards.

Long before Clute could force his knife into Malevich's heart, the neighbours would be hurrying up the stairs to complain. There simply was too little time for the operation to be performed efficiently. Scowling, Clute abandoned his plan. His need for revenge must remain unsatisfied. Bradman had escaped without a scratch!

Or had he? Clute pursed his lips. Malevich had a friend that Clute could certainly assault. This friend would not even struggle or make an appreciable vocal fuss. He was the perfect victim! Bradman might shelter behind walls, dogs and bodyguards but here was a chink in his armour, a chink that soon would spurt crimson juice.

Clute almost felt pity for the poor defenceless Bradman as he moved quietly across his room to unlatch the door. Now Malevich would not have to knock before confronting the balancing scene of carnage. Returning to his chair and the wise mirror, Clute raised the knife and savagely drew it across his own unforgiven throat.

THE MIRROR IN THE LOOKING GLASS

Mad inventors are plentiful in this world of ours but only one sits on a genuine throne and rules his own city like an ancient king. Frabjal Troose of Moonville has many dubious talents, including the ability to flap his ears. They squeak. But his cybernetics expertise is considerable and his contributions to the design and manufacture of artificial nervous systems are almost unparalleled. Only his perversity prevents him from becoming the saviour of the human race.

Perhaps I am overstating the case, but his monumental achievements are singularly unhelpful to his own subjects and the citizens of every other realm. What amuses Frabjal Troose is to install human intelligence in inanimate objects. With the aid of extremely small but excessively clever devices, part electronic and part mechanical, he can bestow the gift of consciousness with all its attendant emotions on chairs, crockery, table lamps, shoes, clocks, flutes.

He can and he does. Frequently.

His other hobby is to worship the moon…

One morning Frabjal Troose awoke with the urge to give thoughts and feelings to a mirror. He foresaw all manner of comic and tragic potential in the reality of a self-aware looking glass. To make the joke even more piquant he decided to equip his victim with prosthetic legs and allow it to roam freely around the city. He left his enormous bed and went to the bathroom and there he saw an appropriate mirror hanging on the wall above the moon shaped sink.

The operation took several days. Frabjal Troose is a perfectionist and he wanted the circuits and cogs to be tastefully integrated into the frame of the mirror. In the end the workings ran over the surface of the wooden frame like complex ornamentation. By this time, the mirror could already think for itself and was slowly coming to terms with its sudden awareness and the need to develop an identity. It was no longer a mere object but a precious sentient being.

It even had a name. Guildo Glimmer.

Guildo learned to walk within his first hour. Wandering the palace of Frabjal Troose, little more than a large house stuffed with components for new gadgets, he came into contact with the occasional servant. At each encounter the same thing happened: the servant bent down and made a face at Guildo. Sometimes the servant picked him up and held him at arm's length while plucking a nose hair or squeezing a pimple. What did this mean? Guildo was bewildered.

He continued his explorations and discovered that the front door of the palace was open and unguarded. Through it he hurried, into the lunar themed spaces of the city. Moon buggies rolled past on the roads and the public squares were craters filled with people dressed in silver and yellow clothes. I know that Frabjal Troose once issued an edict forbidding any grins that were not perfect crescents. He also forbade any cakes that were not perfect croissants.

Guildo proceeded down the street. He desperately needed time for reflection, but citizens just would not leave him in peace and they treated him in precisely the same way as the palace servants had, making blatant faces at him, grimacing and yawning and even frowning in disgust. Guildo began to experience the state of mind known as 'paranoia'. What was wrong with his appearance? What was it about him that provoked such reactions in strangers?

He must be ugly, a horrible freak, a grotesque mutant: there was no other explanation. He was overwhelmed with a desire to view his own face, to confront his visage, to learn the foul truth for himself. But he could think of no way to accomplish this. Are you stupid, Guildo Glimmer? he asked himself. There must be a method of seeing one's own face, but what? Because he was so new to the conventions of society, he always spoke his thoughts aloud.

"I know a reliable way," declared a passerby.

This passerby was a droll fellow, a practical joker. He told Guildo that when men and women wanted to look at their own faces they made use of a 'reflection'. What was one of those? Well, reflections existed in a variety of natural settings, in quiet lakes and slow rivers and the lids of clean saucepans, but only in the depths of mirrors did they realise their full potential. That is where the highest quality reflections dwelled, untroubled by ripples or cooking stains.

"You must look into a mirror!" he announced.

Guildo was astonished but grateful and he decided to follow this advice. The passerby chuckled and passed on. He was later arrested for not chuckling in the shape of a crescent, but that is another story. No, it is this story! No matter, I will ignore it in favour of what happened to poor Guildo. His little metallic legs carried him to the market, a bustling place where anything one desired might be bought, provided one's desires were modest or at least plausible.

Guildo's were. He approached a stall selling mirrors.

The man who owned the stall was talking to another customer and so Guildo was free to hop onto a table and examine the mirrors on display. He chose a circular mirror that was nearly the same circumference as his own head and he stepped in front of it. What he saw was totally unexpected and utterly profound. He saw an immensely long tunnel, a tunnel that stretched perhaps as far as the moon or infinity.

It must be pointed out once again that Guildo Glimmer was a living mirror. A mirror is simply unable to view its own reflection. The moment a mirror gazes into another mirror, its image will be endlessly bounced back and forth between the two reflecting surfaces. Hence the illusion of a tunnel. This is a law of geometry and a rule of physics, but Guildo knew nothing of such disciplines. His education had not covered the sciences.

As far as he was concerned, the illusory tunnel was an accurate representation of his form. This meant that he really was a tunnel!

161

Now he understood why people kept frowning at him and why he was so dissatisfied. It was because he was not fulfilling his correct role. He was a tunnel and ought to do what tunnels do, act like tunnels act, think what tunnels think. He rushed out of the market to embrace his true destiny.

Later that afternoon, the splinters of a smashed mirror were picked up from the tracks of the main railway line leading into Moonville. When pieced together they could be identified as the remains of Guildo Glimmer. There was no way of resurrecting him. Frabjal Troose came to pay his hypocritical respects but he quickly lost interest and returned to his palace in a land-boat powered by moonbeams. By this time the sun had gone down and the moon was up.

People said that Guildo committed suicide, that he was too full of despair to continue his existence. Why else would he stand in the path of a moving train? But as I watched the billowing sails of the receding land-boat, I realised that I knew better. Guildo was simply serving a mistaken function. Tunnels are there for trains to pass through, after all. I was the driver of that train: in fact I am the train itself, an earlier example of the unnatural quest to give intelligence to inanimate objects.

THE STRINGS OF SEGOVIA

It was a foggy night in Old London. Or perhaps it was the fog that was old, or just the night, or maybe only me, dressed as I was in antique garb. My jerkin and breeches were silken and rustled softly, my high boots and heavy gauntlets were leathern and squeaked pleasantly. As for my tricorne hat, I wore it with considerable aplomb. Even the sword that swung at my hip did not seem out of place. Only one item of clothing dissatisfied me and I wandered the streets in an attempt to remedy this defect.

Music emerged from the general fumy blur, the notes of a guitar carefully plucked, a haunting melody that evoked everything London was not. Although no words accompanied the playing I was reminded of balmy nights, iron balconies, dark women with flowers in their hair, the salty tang of olives, young wine. I am fond of street musicians. Indeed I am something of a patron to buskers and so I quickened my step toward the source of this acoustic magic. My present situation compelled me to engage the person responsible, but my motives were also partly altruistic.

I found a young man sitting in a doorway, his expression containing both the unquenchable hope of the compulsive dreamer and the feverish desperation of the chronically frustrated. He was poor, I noted at once, but not entirely without resources, strange reservoirs of inky self belief. I loomed above him, listening quietly until his elegant song was concluded, then I reached into my pocket and deposited a handful of coins into the upturned cloth cap that gaped between his feet like the severed ear of a cyclops. His gratitude was a theatrical grin.

"You play extremely well – perhaps too well!" I announced.

He blinked at this compliment, and might have blushed into the bargain had not a tendril of cold fog suddenly turned the corner and tickled his face, discouraging all sunset cheeks, my own included. So he licked his lips instead and answered, "I have a good teacher."

"Oh?" I responded, retreating a pace, "and who might that be?"

He studied me closely, his gaze travelling from tricorne to spurs and back again, before glancing left and right like a storybook conspirator. "Segovia. None other."

I laughed: a short bark. "Come now!"

His voice was an urgent whisper. "It's true. I keep it a secret, to myself, because I don't care to be ridiculed but there's something about you I find reassuring, I don't know why. I trust you. Segovia really is my teacher. I've wanted to share this remarkable news with someone for many months but it was never possible until now. People would say I was mad. I imagine you are used to such comments, dressed the way you are. And so..."

163

"I am less eccentric than you think. I'm a man on a mission."

He frowned as if upset by my nonchalance and the fingers of his right hand rapped a sharp rhythm on the body of his guitar. "Do you believe me or not?"

"I don't, if that answer pleases you more..."

"Very well. I am due for my next lesson less than one hour from now. Come with me and see with your own eyes that Segovia is my teacher. My home isn't far. That's where we must go and it's polite and important to be on time. Are you willing?"

I rubbed my chin with the back of a gauntlet. "Certainly. Lead the way."

He stood and slung his instrument over his shoulder. Then he had vanished into the fog and it was no easy task to keep up with him and only the faint twang of strings in the currents of cold air betrayed his direction at each new corner. I steadily increased my pace, following these rogue harmonics, down countless streets and over several bridges, but only managed to reach his side after he paused in front of a door to wait for me.

While he fumbled with a key, I studied the building he had guided me to. "This is your home?" I asked.

"Absolutely – in a manner of speaking!"

I ignored the contradiction and cried, "Segovia comes here: to a house without windows?"

For an answer he unlocked the door and swung it open, stepping through rapidly and pulling me along with him. Then he was off again, and I was close on his heels, but no corridors or rooms did we pass through. Instead we rushed down more streets and turned more corners. I assumed I was still in London and that the door was some intact relic of ancient defences, a portal in a strong wall between two different quarters of the city, but slowly it became apparent that the simple crossing of the threshold had induced a profound change in the environment. For one thing, there was no fog here. None.

"This is not really your home," I declared.

"Wherever I learn my music, that's where my heart is. And where the heart is..."

164

I scowled furiously to prevent him from completing this maudlin utterance and then I slowed my pace to enable more careful scrutiny of my surroundings. He seemed irked by my tardiness but said nothing, following my gaze as I looked around, shifting his instrument to the other shoulder. *This* night was balmy and there were iron railings. Then a clock tower demonstrated that the time was one hour later than it should have been. When we turned another corner and a gigantic but curiously delicate aqueduct loomed before us, the truth could no longer be denied.

We were no longer in London, old or new.

"This is the city of Segovia – in Spain," I announced tonelessly.

He was mildly flustered but did not pause, leading me up a flight of stone steps at the side of the impressive structure. "Of course. What else did you expect? I told you Segovia was my teacher, I'm not a liar. Don't drag your feet now, we're almost there!"

I chuckled horribly. "I thought you were referring to Andrés Segovia, born in Linares in 1893, who learned to play on a guitar once owned by Paco de Lucena. He died in 1987, Segovia I mean, and was awarded a high title in his old age – the Marqués de Salobreña, I think it was – in return for his services to music. It was often claimed that he singlehandedly rescued the Spanish guitar from amateur gypsies, a view he shared himself. He remains one of the greatest guitarists of all time."

He gaped in bewilderment. "I don't know about any of that but it's critically important that I'm not late for my lesson. Segovia is my teacher, the city itself. That's a simple fact."

"I suppose the famous castle itself gives you lessons?" I mocked. "Or perhaps the church of Vera Cruz, built on mystic principles long ago by the Knights Templars?"

Now it was his turn to be annoyed. "Don't be ridiculous... Those structures wouldn't deal with a nobody like me. I'm just a commoner. My teacher is an ordinary house in a street leading off the Plaza Mayor. This way, please. Just a few more steps and then you'll see..."

165

And so I did. We had reached the great main square of the city, with the vast cathedral silhouetted against the stars, and now hurried down a narrow alley.

Next to a closed restaurant stood a house with stone arms. It cradled the most enormous guitar in the world in its powerful and implausible hands and its upper stories seemed to hold an expression, although in no way did the design of the façade resemble a face. I was unable to resist making a wide sardonic bow but it ignored me utterly and concentrated all its attention on my companion. I was left with the impression that the windows blinked, though in fact they moved not at all and remained unlighted, mysterious.

"I'm here," the pupil called softly.

"Good," said the house, "and for this lesson we're going to focus mainly on chords and the execution of rapid but perfectly fluid key changes. We'll start as always with some scales, just to warm up the fingers. Are you ready? Take a deep breath and try to relax..."

I turned to leave, rubbing my jaw in consternation.

The situation was too absurd. A house in Segovia that spoke English rather than Spanish?

But I felt my sleeve plucked by an anxious hand and I was compelled out of politeness, the same politeness that matched my attire, formal and rigid but with a hint of lethal irony, to halt my departure and spend a few more minutes in conversation. My companion was very unhappy that he had to divide his concentration between myself and his teacher. He had already taken the urged deep breath and clearly did not want to expel it over me.

But finally he blabbered, "What's wrong?"

"I feel deceived," I explained simply.

"For what reason? I thought you wanted to listen to my lesson, hear my teacher play. I've never invited anyone else to accompany me here."

I arched an eyebrow. "I am returning to London. I will walk northwards for many weeks. You have wasted my time. Sir, your teacher is merely a house musician!"

166

He suddenly lunged forward and clapped his palm over my mouth, heedless of the sword I wore and the personality that made using such a weapon perfectly feasible and even easy. Protecting his teacher from further insult was more important to him than life itself. His words tumbled out for now he was desperate to be rid of me and become a single unit with his guitar. His compassion was the fastest I have ever witnessed.

"Fair enough, if you truly feel like that, but you are mistaken, horribly so. Don't return to London the long way, the real geographical route. Retrace our steps and pass back through the door. Close it behind you to stop the fog coming in. You wear your antique clothes with style, all expect one item. Farewell and good luck. One day you may regret your decision. Segovia plays like an angel, a stone angel. I love my teacher and believe my feelings are reciprocated, even though there is a small kitchen instead of a heart inside its dubious analogue of a chest. Furthermore..."

I stepped back and liberated my lips. "I have no intention of looking for that magic portal. I want nothing more to do with you. I will take the old route home."

And I stamped off. Northwards. But the moment I knew I was out of sight I doubled back and headed south down a different street. I couldn't hear the music of that absurdly vast guitar but I felt the vibrations of its strings, each as thick as a swollen thumb, a thumb accidentally bruised by a slammed front door or falling window, in my stained soul. Those spiritual chords would have been pleasant had a less rascally man experienced them.

I shrugged. When I turned the next corner I encountered a young man with an easel and brushes.

"You paint extremely well – perhaps too well!" I announced.

He blinked at this compliment, gazing at me while I gazed at his work, the bright points of primary colour on the canvas seeming to glow, the details soft and yet unmistakable in a scene that was highly unrealistic and yet fixed perfectly the mood it was intended to capture. I waited for him to blush or speak.

"Who is your teacher?" I prompted.

Roused from his daze he responded forcefully, "Liechtenstein. None other."

I sighed and shook my head. "You aren't referring to Roy Lichtenstein, the artist famous for adapting the techniques of comic book illustration, are you? He was born in 1923 and died in 1997. I suspect you mean the nation of Liechtenstein, the only double-landlocked country in Europe, meaning it is entirely surrounded by other landlocked countries. My guess is that an ordinary house in a normal street is your teacher, a house with stone arms and a gigantic paintbrush clutched in its brick hands."

"Yes, and my next lesson takes place in one hour..."

I continued to shake my head. "Wrong direction," I explained. "I don't go north or east but due south, a long way. Indeed my journey has scarcely begun. My destination is the most southerly great city of Africa. I'll hop through as many magic doors as possible to get there but yours is no use to me. When no doors are available I'll walk or hitch. London to Segovia was only the first stage. I travel to attend my first lesson from my own teacher."

He was at a loss for appropriate words. "The capital of Liechtenstein is Vaduz."

"Yes I know. Farewell. Good luck."

"Thank you," he stammered but his lips stopped quivering when I answered sharply. "I was talking to myself!" Then I was gone, my high boots clicking on the cobbles.

What lesson did I hope to learn in that particular place, far below the equator? My jerkin and breeches rustled softly. My gauntlets, hat and sword acted in exactly the way that suited me best.

Only my cape gave me trouble. And there, on the tip of that mighty continent, where two oceans collided, from a city most wise in such matters, from Cape Town itself, I knew I would receive instructions on how to wear it properly.

LONELINESS

I turn the key in my door and enter my flat. Two small rooms connected by a corridor in such a manner they almost bear no relation to each other. The layout is certainly odd. The bathroom is part of my bedroom and the kitchen occupies half the living room, everything is unbearably cramped, and yet that connecting corridor is very long and high, an immense length of wasted space that represents nothing domestic. It is like a segment of an unhappy journey brought indoors, or part of a sculpture of a lonely walk without a walker, which naturally makes it more lonely, more itself. I have no affection for that corridor. Once I tried keeping a bicycle in it but that only made matters worse, for it gave the impression the bicycle had been abandoned in a place nobody ever went and consequently I felt guilty mounting it, like a thief. So the corridor is empty again and I have no plans to fill it with anything else.

After firmly closing and bolting my door I stroll along that corridor to my living room as rapidly as possible, the same as always, a voyage on foot that never feels heroic, though perhaps it should, passing the door of my bedroom near the start of the journey but refusing to acknowledge it with a nod or glance, because those actions always seem to slow matters, though really I am sure they do not.

When I finally reach my destination and leave the corridor somewhere behind, set the kettle to boil, struggle out of my coat and collapse into my easy chair, I am suddenly overwhelmed with a feeling of loneliness. Too difficult to put into words the sheer power of the sensation, the wrenching deep inside my gut, the apparent unwrapping of that bone bandage called a skull to expose my mind to the vast disinterest of the cosmos. I know at once I am the loneliest man alive.

To be lonely is nothing new for me. I am shy of my own reflection in mirror, spoon and shiny shoe, have no family or friends, and no talent for conversing with strangers, yet I regard myself as perfectly normal and unworthy of pity or special regard, for each of us has felt extreme mental and spiritual isolation at one time or another. All varieties of loneliness have enough aches and pangs in common to bind a victim closely to his fellow sufferers, so in shared loneliness we are one, together, united. This curious truth resembles an escape clause in an insurance contract but is more palatable to those who sell no insurance, for on this occasion we are the beneficiaries of the perversity.

So much for ordinary loneliness, but the loneliness I now experience is different, far more intense, so excruciating I am forced to twist, shrug and blink furiously in my chair as the bleakness envelops me. Immediately I fail to understand how emptiness can be a tangible force, how an absence can be a presence, how a negative can be so positively damaging that my deepest desire is to have enemies, anybody at all to keep me company, to protect me from the utter void.

Yes, my solitude is total, and a conventional lack of friends and family is certainly not enough to account for the magnitude of my despair. There must be more to it than that, something unbelievable, unhinged, dramatic but subtle. And soon enough, without even needing to jump up and ruffle my hair, I shockingly realise the truth. My apartment is *not* haunted. That is the wild fact of the weird matter. Not haunted, nor has it ever been. No ghost has drifted along that improbable corridor since the dawn of death, not one. I share my living space with no malignancy. Unwatched, I dwell in the exact middle of seclusion.

This peculiar situation is possibly unique in the present century. As the world slowly grows older, ghosts thicken on the continents, crammed into houses and spilling onto streets, shifting, ebbing, heaving like exasperated sighs on currents powered by jostling insubstantial elbows. The cities and spaces between cities are overcrowded with spectres, young, old, bad and good, shapeless, elaborate, thin and obese. On each step of every staircase they crouch or sit, under every table.

The cure for my loneliness becomes apparent. To encourage a ghost to move in with me. To be haunted.

170

I understand why no spectre has taken residence in my apartment. Not just a question of anyone failing to die between my walls. Perhaps whole families were murdered here. No, the plan of the place, the layout itself, is the problem. When a ghost drifts down a simple passage in an ordinary building, the quiet understanding is that something worth floating for can be found at one end or the other. But not where I live. My corridor is too abnormal for that, more important than the rooms it leads to, a destination in its own right. It can go nowhere because it already *is* somewhere. The rooms are less than afterthoughts.

And what ghost would choose to patronise such an absurd situation? They are not without pride, I hear.

I must spend my evenings praying for a ghost to come from outside, to occupy my hideous hollowness, take the place of my old bicycle, disturb my sleep, rattle cups, make me less lonely, to drift with gaping mouth up and down that horrid passage. In return I will do anything to increase its standing in the supernatural realm, to enhance its reputation as a force to be reckoned with, sleep with it, paint it, suckle it on whatever shadows it prefers, anything at all, shameless.

But my prayers remain unanswered, the homemade spells ineffective, ritual webs wasted, because the phantoms outside already know about my corridor, have heard the truth from the spirits of those slain families who voluntarily chose to depart this place, despite its cubic freedom, and join the highly compressed mob in the street. I cannot trick the dead so easily and now must find an alternative method of forcing a companion into my space and keeping it here, more faithful than any bicycle. A little surplus thought and I have the solution.

I reverse the direction of my desire, promptly, abruptly, and pray in a loud voice for my apartment to become even lonelier, for my loneliness to increase rather than decrease. Is such a thing possible in a place where there are no ghosts? Hardly. Yet this is how I do it: with total integrity I vow that if I should die here, or in my bedroom, or in the corridor, I too will depart the premises in spirit form and

171

never return. And to make this threat realistic I take a clean kitchen knife from the sink without having to rise from my chair, simply by leaning over with my long arms and pulling it toward me, cold and dripping.

Then I dry it on a trouser leg, just above my knee, the flat of the blade swept twice against the fabric, and lift the implement to my throat. This is no game and I prepare to cut.

A gust of impossible wind swirls in the corners. A voice both resonant and desiccated says: "I am the Spirit of Loneliness. I am here because this is the loneliest spot on earth."

"I am not prepared for visitors," I answer modestly.

"You called me from the coldest ice cap, the deepest cave, the highest cloud, and I came at once, for I feel at home only where nobody else ever goes. I dream of an age when only one mind existed in the universe. Next time that mind will be mine."

"I am glad you have come," I reply.

"You cannot be glad, for there can be nobody lonelier than you. Even your future ghost has deserted this spot. There are still many places in the world where there are no ghosts, but this is the only place I know where there never *will* be a ghost."

"A shame. But now I have you," I smile.

"I do not understand."

"Then listen carefully with your lonely ears. I could not pray for less loneliness, so I prayed for more, so much more that *you* hurried here, the actual personification of loneliness."

"Truly that is what I am. No friend of yours."

"I admit that a human companion, alive or dead, would suit me better, but that option seems not to exist, and you are better than nothing, even though you represent nothingness. In your presence I am utterly alone, even more lonely than before, because you *are* nothing, but I also feel less lonely because you are here."

He points at me with a bony finger because it is a gesture required of all ghosts. I realise that his eyes have no faraway look but really do exist elsewhere, that his sockets drink light with an insatiable thirst. "I have no patience at all with paradoxes."

172

"This one is not unpleasing."

He does not agree, the Spirit of Loneliness, and admits that he finds my duplicity quite exasperating, but it is too late for him. He is truly here, where I am, and together we are bound to each other. It is better to feel lonely in company than lonely alone, even when you are lonely because of that company. Is it not? On the floor of my living room my discarded coat tangles the legs of his intangible spirit like a deflated apartment with two hungry corridors for sleeves.

REDIFFUSION

They came for me just after midnight, those devious inspectors, opening my door with a special key and rushing into my living room before I had a chance to even get out of my chair. I had always imagined I would have plenty of time to hide the television in a cupboard before they entered, but the reality was quite different. I was helpless and they were merciless and they took my machine as evidence.

True, I had ignored no less than three warning letters, but I hadn't felt guilty in the slightest about not buying a licence. Still don't, in fact. At no point in my longish life had I ever entertained the notion of obtaining one. The expense was simply absurd. The best part of a full week's wages just for the minor privilege of viewing one outmoded and rather staid channel among thousands. It didn't seem right.

I was surprised the inspectors had the power to handcuff me, kick me with fake leather boots and bundle me into the back of a van. Clearly the law had recently been changed in this regard without my knowledge. Was it even a criminal offence to watch television without a licence? The thug sitting in the back of the van assured me it was, then he slapped me in my insolent mouth, breaking a tooth.

The van swayed around bends, accelerated over a bumpy road, slowly climbed a steep hill somewhere. I had the impression we were leaving the city, but when it finally stopped and I was let out, I found myself blinking up at the renowned corporation tower, a building not more than few miles from my house. Later I learned that the driver had taken a lengthy detour so he might claim higher expenses.

I was pushed up the stone steps and through the gaping portal into the impressive lobby, but my guards didn't let me loiter in this cool spot for more than a few seconds before yanking me down a narrow passage that twisted and coiled like an intestine and ended in a blank wall. A narrow metal ladder speared into the ceiling at this point and I was told to climb it on my own. I did so unsteadily.

A dozen rungs later, I emerged into a wood panelled chamber. A hatch beneath my feet closed silently, cutting off my retreat. I was standing in the dock of an improvised courtroom, facing a judge who was nothing more than a gigantic image on a vast plasma screen. Two smaller screens displayed the prosecution and defence lawyers but the stations were badly tuned and the pictures fragmented.

It seemed I was late for my own trial and that the process was already over, for the judge was midway through his condemnation. "Unspeakably guilty of living as a broadcast parasite," he intoned, "and therefore wisely sentenced to more years in prison than shall be deemed unseemly." It was an odd sentence, both verbally and judicially, and I was too bewildered to utter an objection. I merely wept.

I had expected a warning, possibly a fine, certainly not imprisonment, and a wave of revulsion engulfed me. I staggered out of the dock, tried to locate the exit, sought to elude my fate, to flee. Instantly three new guards jumped out from behind furniture to apprehend me. One drew a futuristic gun out of a silver holster. He aimed it at my head, pulled the trigger and a hidden spring released its energy.

From the barrel of the gun emerged a cardboard bolt of lightning that jabbed me in the centre of my forehead then bounced harmlessly off. At the same instant, one of the other guards pushed me to the floor while the third placed his mouth next to my ear and cried,

174

"Bzzzzzt!" I realised this was a typical stratagem of the corporation, a cheap prop rather than a real weapon, a low budget special effect.

"You've been stunned by the ray," said the marksman.

"If you say so," I replied.

"Don't move at all, you're paralysed," he added.

"For how long?" I asked.

"Until we get you into your cell. Don't forget. Sensation will return to your hands, then your legs, then your mind. We'll be watching to make sure you do it in the right order."

I said nothing, figuring that the paralysis was also supposed to extend to my tongue. They carried my stiff body out of the courtroom and down a wide corridor to a door that opened onto a large courtyard. At the centre of the courtyard stood a brick prison. I was amazed to see such a building hidden within the corporation tower. Tiny barred windows perforated the dizzy heights of irregular turrets.

The perspectives didn't seem right, but then I recalled how an ordinary television set can manage to fit imposing mountain ranges and undulating deserts into the width of a screen and my surprise decayed as rapidly as a neglected cosine wave or bowl of forgotten cherries. The sentry posted at the prison gate shook his head fiercely, as if he sought to restore reception to a misfiring cathode ray tube.

"An awkward customer, resisted arrest, I see."

My bearers nodded and lowered me slowly into his extended muscular arms. "He's rather a crafty one."

"Soon reduce him in size," came the reply.

Then he turned and ran into the prison at a speed I deemed absurd and dangerous down a succession of dim curving corridors, narrowly missing other sentries and prisoners, clearly anxious to demonstrate his unnatural strength and stamina. His heavy feet slapped the flagstones like tsunamis of molten basalt. Despite my official paralysis, I made appreciative noises to humour him. I even sniggered.

Skidding to a halt before an open cell, he brusquely cast me inside and slammed the grey door, then raced back the way he had come. I landed on a low bed and my subsequent injuries were minor or imaginary, so I stood and flexed life back into my limbs, obeying the recommended sequence to satisfy any secret cameras that might be observing. Then I realised the key to my door was on the inside.

This oversight seemed too bizarre to be plausible, but I took advantage of the opportunity to slip out of my cell and tiptoe along the corridors. At first I was anxious and excited, then it dawned on me that the prison was actually a complex labyrinth and that I was profoundly lost. The laxity of the security measures was merely an illusion. The outer exit must always elude my desperate wanderings.

Two guards with buckets and brushes turned a corner and yelled at me to halt. I panicked and ran, nursing my aching jaw and whimpering. Then I tripped and sprawled. I heard the slurp of paint and felt the rough caress of bristles. They were painting vertical lines on my clothes, the traditional convict stripes. After they finished, they casually sauntered away and left me alone, but now I was branded.

I remained on my hands and knees and crawled down a side passage to an open door. The space beyond was an ugly forest of legs, a recreation area of some sort, a communal room. I scuttled like a crippled crab to the nearest vacant chair, hauled myself onto it. Now I was part of an audience facing a television screen. The other members of this audience were also prisoners and we watched in silence.

Cheap soap operas were followed by light news bulletins and domestic shows concerned with cooking, gardening, finance. Cartoons were also in evidence. After an hour, the situation became unbearable and I whispered this fact to my neighbour. "I have been incarcerated for neglecting to pay my television licence and yet I'm clearly allowed to enjoy free television in prison. How ironic is that?" I asked.

He rubbed his bleary eyes and replied, "Not very, considering we're all inside for the same crime. Only licence dodgers are permitted to rot in the private dungeons of the corporation. But it seems you are labouring under the delusion that television is

176

provided to prisoners as a privilege or act of compassion. Even here a license is mandatory. Don't you have one? Theft of corporation images is serious."

"You are joking, surely?" I spluttered.

He shook his head. "The inspectors are vigilant and unforgiving. They always punish cheating eyes."

"This news is terrible. What should I do?"

"Buy a licence, of course."

"But I have no money or means of making any!"

"That is not a valid excuse."

"In that case, I won't enter this room again. I'll forsake the pleasures of televised broadcasts and remain in my cell. But as this is my first day, I'm not sure how to get back there."

"All dungeons are identical. Take your pick."

"I thank you for your advice. Please don't reveal the fact I sat here and absorbed one full illegal hour of broadcasting. In future I'll ask my guards for books or magazines instead."

He plucked my sleeve and pulled me back. "Even if you don't watch it, you still need a licence for any working television set on the premises. It's futile for you to attempt to hide."

I shook him free and fled the recreation area, my heart pounding. Then I soothed myself with the thought that I was merely the victim of a subtle jest, an experiment with practical paradox. An imprisoned licence avoider being forced to obtain a licence for a television set provided by the prison authorities. Utterly ridiculous! Yes, it was a jest. There could be no other sensible explanation, none at all.

I soon located an unoccupied cell, possibly even my own, and fell into a troubled sleep on the uncomfortable mattress. When I awoke I saw that an envelope addressed to me had been slid under my door. It contained a warning letter from the corporation. Apparently, the inspectors had been alerted to the fact I didn't have a valid licence. I sat trembling on the edge of the bed, awaiting developments.

They came a few days later, dragged me away, pushed me up a ladder into another courtroom. Again I was found guilty by a flatscreen judge in a digital wig, then prodded, pinched and buffeted down endless corridors and through a door into a courtyard in the centre of which stood a smaller prison. I laughed unhappily. Prisons within prisons. A new sentry clasped me in his arms, hurried me inside.

This prison was full of broadcast parasites who had defaulted not once but twice and we were made to feel doubly accursed. I had the impression that the process of relocating me here had somehow reduced my physical size as well as diminished my self-esteem. Body and soul shrunk to fit an implacable credo, the unbending and illogical will of the corporation, the nightmare of rigorous absurdity.

The corridors of my new home were thin and confusing. I stumbled on the communal television room on my second day and stood silently at the entrance, swallowing hard. When I returned to my cell, the expected letter had already been delivered. It accused me of attempting to exist without a licence despite having access to a television. Inspectors would shortly be dispatched to deal with the anomaly...

They came with their usual sarcasm and fists. This prison contained its own virtual courtroom and judge, its own courtyard that was the location of a third prison, to the entrance of which they dragged me. Then another strong sentry and bare cell, another automatic violation of the television licensing laws, another threatening letter. An appalling process had been set in motion. An inward spiral.

The prisons grew progressively smaller, but so did I, so did my guards, and everything shrunk in perfect proportion, like a cannibal who boils his own head in the same pot as the skulls of his victims. One morning I had a visitor who was not an inspector. He identified himself as a corporation lawyer working for the best interests of the convicts. He entered my cell wearing a silk suit and oily smile.

"There is another way," he declared simply.

"Kindly elucidate," I replied.

"Experiments are taking place on living specimens. Any prisoner who volunteers will be spared the indignity of constant arrest, trial, relocation. Your sentences are adding up into something resembling

178

a paragraph, a page, or even a book, of despair. This can be stopped easily enough. You merely need to sign this form."

Without looking, I asked, "And if I do?"

"A series of controls will be fitted into your nervous system. Knobs or buttons that can adjust your colour balance, your contrast, audibility, even the particular channel of your thoughts, whenever we desire. Your spinal fluid will be drained and replaced with a metallic solution that will enable you to receive corporation signals."

"And if I decline this generous offer?"

"You will continue to occupy smaller and smaller prisons until you are trapped inside an institution no larger than a single pixel on a screen. That will be the point of no return, the dot of ultimate doom, the final spark of closedown, the singularity of sorrow!"

I chewed my lip. "May I think it over tonight?"

He nodded sourly. "I suppose so, but you must give an answer before the inspectors come for you at noon tomorrow. In the meantime be aware that the governor of the corporation, Bogie Laird, is visiting this prison in disguise. Nobody knows what form he has chosen, so it's imperative to be humble to every individual you meet."

I blurted impulsively, "Are *you* Bogie Laird?"

He snarled and raised his clenched fists, his silk suit splitting its seams as his muscles expanded. "How dare you be so perspicacious? I predict a traumatic final episode for you…"

Then he lurched out of my cell, howling, his suit rapidly disintegrating as he went, leaving me in an acute state of agitation. But I recovered soon enough and emulated his example, vacating my cubicle and going for one of my usual random strolls. Down one passage I heard a bland vibration, a refreshing change from the ceaseless babble of televised entertainment, and I felt compelled to investigate.

In a tiny room that stank of stale tobacco smoke and was slippery with spilled tea, a brace of off-duty guards sat around a prisoner who had been recently modified. Standing rigidly to attention, eyes popping with static, lips humming a monotone, the volunteer

179

grimaced while one of the jaded guards slapped and shook him, restoring coherent reflections to his pupils for just a few moments at a time.

I wanted to jump forward, make my indignant presence felt, sweep an admonishing finger across every bored face. I wanted to express my fury in a mighty shout. "So this is how you spend your free time? Surfing dead channels within the hopeless eyes of a prisoner! But do any of you have a valid licence to watch him? The corporation will be informed if you don't and inspectors will be activated!"

But before I could make the leap, it occurred to me that the prisoner in question might be none other than Bogie Laird in a new disguise, and the more I pondered this possibility the more convincing it became, so I lost my nerve and slipped away before I was noticed. My one chance to mock the system had been lost, my final opportunity to use irony as a retaliatory weapon had faded and dissolved.

Naturally enough, after this incident, I was reluctant to submit myself for treatment and so the hideous cycle of arrest, trial and incarceration in diminishing prisons continued. After many years I reached the smallest of them all, a mere dot. I was trapped inside a single pixel on the screen of a television I presumed was unlicensed, a machine whose owner must soon be visited by the inevitable inspectors.

Instead of eschewing the recreational facilities of my enforced abode, I wasted half my free time sitting in front of the communal television. Still without a licence, I was also without fear. Arrest entailed no motion at all, for there was nowhere even smaller to send me. It was therefore possible to safely ignore all warning letters. On some level, the lowest imaginable, I had finally cheated the authorities.

But the entertainment on offer left much to be desired. Every channel displayed the same unchanging image, a room full of people who sat with their backs to me. They were dressed in grey clothes and their bald heads glistened in the glare of an unspecified light source as they watched with grim reverence something beyond the screen. I studied them intently and thought about them during my walks.

Recursion can be a terrible thing, and one day I found a service ladder to the roof and climbed onto the tiles, my hands rouged with rust from the corroded rungs. There was no safe descent to the courtyard below. On all sides reared the walls of the next smallest prison, and above those loomed the higher walls of the third smallest prison, and over those leered the still taller walls of the fourth smallest...

And so on, all the way back to the almost forgotten beginning. Prisons within courtyards, courtyards within prisons, prisons within the courtyard of the corporation tower. The concave surface of *that* impossible building appeared unimaginably remote now, as unattainable as the inner shell of the universe, and the lights of its windows burned like artificial quasars at the perimeter of a synthetic reality.

The spectacle was unbearable, so I looked directly upwards instead. At the furthest limit of a cylinder so immense and imposing it contained all the misery I could ever conceive for myself, I beheld a glass screen with blurred faces on the other side that were mostly fixed to the fronts of bald heads. Then I knew this truth. If I am part of a fictional drama and not a factual documentary, I might not go mad.

THE GUNFIGHT

"The English are coming," said Hopkins.

"Following us, they are," confirmed Jones. He frowned and tapped his commander on the shoulder. "I thought you said we *won* the battle?"

"So I did," responded Williams, "and so we have."

"Then why are the English chasing us?"

Bullets zinged into the undergrowth on all sides. The moonlight streamed through holes in perforated leaves. The spores of shredded mushrooms floated.

"And firing at us!" squeaked the other Jones.

"Because we didn't win the battle in the right way. Instead of winning it in the style of a victory, we won it in the style of a defeat," explained Williams. "That's why."

"Daft, that is," commented Hopkins.

The first Jones said, "If that's the way it is, we're done for. Here's a bloody ravine with no way across."

"Doomed, we are," agreed Hopkins.

"Not at all, boyo. Look here!" cried Price.

"An abandoned cottage is what that seems to be," said Williams, "and maybe we can knock on the door to see if anyone's at home?"

"What fool would live in an *abandoned* cottage," wondered the first Jones, "on the edge of a ravine?"

More bullets pinged around his head, striking sparks from the stone wall. He was about to speak again but Hopkins interrupted him:

"Maybe *we* can live there? At least until the English go away. What do you think about that?"

"Perfect place for a redoubt," said Thomas.

"What's a redoubt?" asked Price.

"Something that is doubted more than once," ventured the other Jones, but Williams clucked his tongue and shook his head.

"Don't be daft. A redoubt is a kind of stronghold or sanctuary."

"That's clever," commented Thomas.

Bullets continued to whiz. Williams tried the front door and realised it was locked, but Hopkins noticed that a window was open. "Someone help me and I'll climb through," he said.

"That's smart," said the first Jones.

Hopkins stood on Price and clambered inside. "Dark in here. Come and join me. Hurry up!" he hissed. Williams sighed and said:

"Don't be daft. Pull us through. Give me your hand."

One at a time they were drawn into the interior of the deserted cottage. Williams groped with outstretched hands but the room was bare. Then he remembered his electric torch and turned it on. There were no furnishings of any sort but a broken lightbulb dangled from a cord in the middle of the ceiling.

Williams rummaged in the pocket of his jacket for a spare bootlace and used it to suspend his torch from the lightbulb cord. He had to ask for a volunteer to crouch down on all fours so he could stand on his back and reach. It was Thomas who finally agreed to do this. As Williams jumped down he said:

"A fine bloody pickle we're in! We can't retreat any further and if we make our last stand here, a few grenades chucked through the window will finish us all off. We've only gained a few minutes of safety, so we must counterattack!"

"Why don't we just surrender?" asked the first Jones.

In the cone of dim light Williams displayed an ugly grin. "Don't take prisoners, the English. Heard all about it from my dad. He told me what they were like. No quarter is what we can expect from them. Blot us out, they will! We have to go back out and take the fight to them. But we'll prepare ourselves properly. Make ourselves immune to their bullets. I know a way of doing that!"

"Is it a magic dance?" asked Price.

"Daft, that is," commented Thomas, but Williams spoke over him:

"Not a dance, no, because there's no such thing as magic. Science is the only way to make things work. My uncle went to college to learn medicine, he did, and he brought back lots of those oblong things called books. I remember them well. I was only a child but I knew how to read because my mam taught me. Uncle Dewi let me read his college books and I learned secrets from them. Such secrets!"

"That's lucky," said Hopkins.

Williams nodded. "One of the secrets I learned was called *vaccination*. Sounds like a magic word but it's not, it's a scientific word. It means curing a disease in advance by being infected with a

183

weaker version of that disease. The body fights the weaker version and beats it and in the process develops the ability to take on and defeat the bigger disease. We can vaccinate ourselves against the English, see?"

"How will we do that?" blinked the second Jones.

Williams smiled faintly. "Listen carefully and tell me what kind of ammunition the English are using."

The bullets continued to hiss and clang outside.

"I think it's .45 calibre," said Price.

"That's correct. Fired from semi-automatic pistols. And now tell me what kind of cartridge we use in our own guns," continued Williams.

"The size is .22, isn't it?" answered Hopkins.

Williams nodded and reached for his holster. With a deft motion he drew out his pistol and waved it in front of his men. "The English have got the bigger ones. So we can vaccinate ourselves against them, but how can they vaccinate themselves against us? They would be daft to try. One shot of this for all of us and we'll become immune to their bullets. Then we can go out and kill the lot of them. Easy when you know how…"

"That's logical," said Thomas without any conviction.

"Come on, form a queue. Not a request but an order. Want to beat them properly, don't we? You first, Jones."

"Not me!" cried the first Jones but Williams shot him anyway.

"Daft!" objected Hopkins but he also got a bullet in the face. So did Price, Thomas and the other Jones. Williams licked his lips. His men sprawled on the floor in ungainly postures. Blood trickled.

"A bit sore, I suppose," he said sympathetically.

He waited a whole minute, then he frowned. "Come on, get up. We have to go out and face the English. No need to be scared, you're immune now. What's the matter? Having a rest first, are you? Fine, but don't make it too long. Be here soon, the English will."

His men still didn't stir. Their eyes held a glazed look.

Williams sighed. "I'm going to vaccinate myself now and the moment I've had my shot, the time for resting is over. Serious, I am.

184

You must be ready to leave when I'm done. Supposed to be fighting the English, we are. The bloody English. Do you hear me?"

He jammed the barrel into his open mouth and pulled the trigger. He fell down. His own blood poured out of his head and joined the spreading puddle on the floor. It might have been nice if that puddle had formed a significant Welsh shape, a red dragon perhaps, or a daffodil, or even a fully-grown leek, but it didn't.

THE GRAVE DEMEANOUR

When the man known as John Loop died he was buried in an old churchyard and his friends cut some flowers from his own garden to lay respectfully on his grave. The rains came and the dead flowers began to slowly rot.

The other flowers in the garden were stricken with grief at the loss of their friends. The murders of those seven daffodils had been blatant and cruel. The surviving flowers had no chance of getting revenge, but they wanted to express their sadness by making an appropriate gesture.

They waited until the first bumblebee of the year appeared and landed on the petals of the nearest flower. The moment it crawled inside the trumpet to look for pollen, that daffodil made a special effort and snapped shut around it, just like a Venus Flytrap, and kept squeezing tight until the bee suffocated.

It wasn't easy for the daffodil to uproot itself and walk all the way to the churchyard. Even the hardiest perennials find such activity exhausting and rarely indulge in it, so for a daffodil it was gruelling in the extreme. Eventually it arrived at the grave where the murdered flowers lay and it opened its trumpet and placed the dead bee on top.

Then it went back to the garden and replanted itself, satisfied that it had discharged its duty and employed the correct symbolism in doing so. Humans are mourned with flowers; flowers are mourned with bees. But the story doesn't end there.

185

The friends of the bumblebee were distraught when he didn't return to the hive and they went out to search for him. At long last his corpse was found in the churchyard. The other bees decided to hold his funeral the following day and adorn his grave with a freshly killed bear.

Shortly after the next sunrise they swarmed out and chased a bear over a cliff. Then they pushed its body to the churchyard and laid it on top of the bee. It was fatiguing work but worth it for the symbolic value of the huge hairy cadaver.

The friends of the bear wailed and wept for an entire week before fishing a salmon from the river and draping it over the dead bear's head. As for the friends of that salmon: once they heard the news they ganged up on a squid and ended its many-armed life. But how they managed to get it to the grave is still a mystery.

The friends of the squid decided to honour its passing with a dead albatross, so one of them reached up through the surface of the ocean and snatched a bird in flight and dragged it down and drowned it. The corpse of that albatross was later positioned with great reverence on top of the squid on top of the salmon on top of the bear on top of the bee on top of the flowers on top of the man John Loop.

A few days later, the friends of the albatross caused a small aeroplane to crash. The pilot bailed out in time but his craft plummeted into a hill. The birds dragged the wrecked plane to the churchyard and laid it gently on the grave. Then they flew away.

The friends of that aeroplane bombed a cathedral and piled the rubble on top of the smashed machine. Then the friends of the demolished cathedral all crossed a bridge at the same time and caused it to collapse with the weight. The broken bridge ended up on the grave on top of the bombed cathedral just as etiquette demands.

But the friends of the bridge responded to the loss of their friend by killing the east wind that was making their railings sing; and so the other winds killed a radio transmission that was passing through the atmosphere shortly afterwards; and the friends of that particular frequency sent an offensive message into space that would kill with shame the satellite that received it. And so on.

Months, years, centuries passed…

One day a robot found himself passing through the churchyard. He saw the tower of dead objects and his scientific curiosity was engaged. Extending his arms, he climbed to the summit and sat there with a dreamy look in his crystal eyes.

"This tower contains a single example of everything in the world and many things outside it," he said to himself, "with the exception of—"

Suddenly he lost his balance and toppled over the edge. He was so high that the Earth was only the size of an alien fruit below him. As he accelerated he dimly wondered what the juice of that fruit might taste like. The answer was oil and electrons. But that, in fact, was his own juice after he landed.

While he cooled in pieces beside the grave of John Loop, his friends brought a newly slaughtered human to lay on top of him…

THE YEASTY RISE AND HALF-BAKED FALL OF LYNDON WILLIAMS

This is the tale of a man who had himself turned into a windmill. Lyndon Williams was his name and he lived in the town of Porthcawl. To earn his bread, he'd been told to use his loaf, but the advice confused him, because it sounded like a circular argument.

Nonetheless he decided to give it a try. What risk could there be in this course of action? His first step was to carefully examine the historical and cultural significance of loaves. The local library seemed just the place for this endeavour, and remarkably it was!

He learned that a loaf is made from a certain type of grass and that the process involves grinding the grass seeds to powder, mixing the powder with water and applying heat. Lyndon was delighted. If he made his own loaf he could use it to acquire another.

"Use your loaf to earn your bread!" people had said.

187

It was simple, logical, inevitable.

There was a field behind his house that was full of grass and seemed ideal for his project. But there was nothing to grind the seeds with. More research at the library revealed that seeds are ground by windmills. There was only one course of action to take.

Lyndon went to visit the local carpenter, Garth.

"Will you turn me into a windmill, please? I don't have the money to pay you yet, but when I've made my first loaf and used it to earn bread, I can exchange the bread for cash and give that to you. What do you think? A foolproof plan, wouldn't you say?"

Garth grumbled into his beard and shook his saw.

"Always barging in here, people are, with their unreasonable requests, as if I don't have my own business to attend to! Turn me into a wardrobe, turn me into a nice occasional table, turn me into a hatstand! No, I won't do it for you or anyone else. Get out!"

Lyndon decided to do the job himself. But how?

While he was pondering this problem, the radio on the shelf decided to change the music it was playing. It had been playing an old time jazz tune but now it moved into a song called 'The Windmills of Your Mind'. What a curious name! Lyndon listened closely.

The lyrics of the song made absolutely no sense to him, but that didn't really matter: the important point was that, for the first time in his life, he learned that the mind, the human mind, *his* mind included, had windmills in it, unexpectedly. What a revelation!

Why else would anyone write a song about them?

Songs aren't lies. They can't be.

Armed with the insight supplied by that song title, Lyndon went home and on the way debated his next step. If only he could access one of the windmills of his mind, he could use it to grind the seeds to make bread. It might be too small, though. Unless—

Somehow he must find a way of making it bigger.

Tea would help him to think…

He went into his kitchen to boil a kettle. He would have waited for all time, because the metal of the kettle had a boiling point much

188

higher than the temperature of the maximum flame of his stove. He realised this after a minute and boiled water instead.

Sipping his tea, it occurred to him that if he did expand his mind, all the things inside his mind would also get bigger, including the windmills. But how to expand his mind? He didn't know himself, but he knew where to go for advice. He went out again.

Two of his acquaintances were always talking about 'mind expansion'. Clearly they must be experts in the subject! So he went to visit the first of them, a bearded guru with sandals known as Kosmic Huw. The advice the guru generously gave was as follows:

"Smoke some of this, man, to expand your mind!"

And he pressed a packet of chopped herbs into Lyndon's hand, but the herbs didn't have a culinary use, even though Kosmic Huw was regarded as a sage. They had quite a different purpose. Anyway, Lyndon accepted them with exclamations of gratitude.

Then he went to visit his second acquaintance.

Mr Clogs was sitting at his desk reading two books at the same time as usual. He spoke to Lyndon from the corner of his mouth. "And to what do I owe the pleasure of this visit?" But even before Lyndon could reply, Mr Clogs added, "Philosophy is the key."

"Is it really? I thought it was an academic pursuit!"

"Yes, that as well, of course."

"How did you anticipate what I wanted to—"

"Ask?" Mr Clogs lifted up one of the books so that Lyndon could read its title. In bold letters were the words: ANTICIPATING QUESTIONS. With a wonky smile, Mr Clogs continued, "There's no better way of expanding minds than with the aid of philosophy."

Lyndon thanked him and went lightly on his way.

Before returning home, he entered the library again and borrowed one of the thickest and heaviest philosophy textbooks he could find. He hefted it back to his small house and laid it down on his kitchen table next to the packet of herbs. Which to try first?

Surely it was more potent to combine them?

Yes, that was the best option!

So he ripped out many pages from the textbook and used them to roll a dozen long cigarettes stuffed with the herb. He smoked these one after the other and he was delighted when his mind truly did start to expand. Soon it had reached its maximum expansion.

Lyndon was ready for it. He had a wooden mallet.

Mercilessly, systematically, he struck at various points of his cranium with this tool, knocking out the functions of his brain directly beneath the bone. As parts of his brain went unconscious, the magnified things of his expanded mind vanished, one by one.

Before long, the largest windmill disappeared...

With his reduced awareness, Lyndon groggily marked the exact point of his skull where that blow had landed, then he lurched to bed and gave himself a few days to recover. When he was at full health again, he tore out more pages, rolled more cigarettes.

He went out into the field and chose his spot.

Once again, as he inhaled, his mind expanded and all the things within it, some of them dark, some light, some oblong, some curved, some static, some highly mobile, others unbuttoned, many peculiar, a few gnarled and one or two ineffable, expanded with it.

Now he was able to proceed with confidence and precision. His mallet banged down on every point of his skull apart from the spot he had earlier marked, a point that represented the largest windmill. Of all the expanded objects of his mind, that alone remained.

He slumped to the ground and with his final remnant of conscious will and strength he crawled inside the windmill. When he regained his senses many hours later, the windmill encased him so snugly that it *was* his body and his identity was fused totally with it.

Unable to shrink back into his mind, because his mind was now inside it, instead of the other way around, the big windmill had contracted as far as it was able. It was his shell, his armour, an exoskeleton. He was a crab, a robot, a sentient solidified daydream...

He had succeeded in fixing an imaginary object, existing by definition only in his mind, for real in the outer world. A wondrous achievement by any standard! He rotated on his gimbals until his sails faced the wind, and then he prepared himself to grind seeds!

Now he understood that he had made a small mistake.

He should have reaped the grass first!

He should have obtained a scythe, mown the entire field, gathered the fallen ears, for that's what they are called, flailed them with a hinged stick to get all the seeds off, and *then* ground the grain into flour. But it was too late. He was already a windmill. Stuck.

So he stood there in strange despair while the hours passed and clouds came and washed him with dismal rain. He could rotate on his own axis, but his freedom of movement was strictly limited to that. The wind made a noise in his sails like mocking speech.

A little later, who should chance to stroll through the field but Kosmic Huw? Although Lyndon did his best to call out to his friend in intelligible human words, the only sound he managed to create was a creaking, but it was enough to attract Kosmic Huw closer.

Kosmic Huw studied the windmill carefully, took a puff on a cigarette that seemed fatter than normal, and said to himself, "If the answer, my friends, is blowing in the wind, does that mean windmills are masters of spin?" Then he laughed and nodded once.

Lyndon was distraught when Kosmic Huw walked away.

"Come back and help!" he creaked.

No more visitors entered the field that day, or during the night, or the following day, or even at any time during the coming week, and it finally dawned on Lyndon that he should expect no assistance from outside. His salvation was entirely in his own hands.

Did I say hands? I meant sails.

He had no grass seeds to grind, true, but why should that prevent him from grinding up *something*? There was no reason why he couldn't make bread from an alternative. But what was the only thing available to him in his present immobilised condition?

His own body! Yes, he would grind that! He would make bread from his own physical substance. Perfect.

He smiled inwardly and his spirits rose, just as the loaf he planned to bake would rise, and in fact that's exactly what he did. He ground himself into flour. The rain provided the water to turn the flour into dough. All he needed now was the heat of an oven...

Nothing like the smell of freshly baked fool!

He waited, palpitating greyly.

But it seemed the final step would never be taken, for he had no means of building an oven, and the bakers of Porthcawl were obviously lazy, for not a single one arrived to erect an oven next to him. So he grew mouldy with odd yeasts as he waited helplessly.

Months passed. Finally a stranger approached.

A woman mounted on a horse. She carried a lance that was hollow and thick and cumbersome. She stopped in front of Lyndon and cried, "You're a giant, are you? I'm sure of it!" Her armour was homemade and her voice was heroic and deluded at the same time.

Lyndon had learned how to manipulate his creaking sails so they made a fair imitation of his former voice.

"No, I'm not a giant. I'm almost a loaf of bread."

"That's a feeble fib," she said.

"It's not! Who are you to accuse me of deceit?"

The woman opened her visor.

"I am Nod Toxique, and that's an anagram as well as a name. Why not work it out? Mind you, I don't suppose you have time to do that. You are a giant and thus I must fight you."

"Don't do that, Miss Toxique, I implore!"

But it was too late for him...

She rested the lance on her shoulder and aimed it at the windmill. Now Lyndon realised it was a bazooka. Even archetypes can be updated. That's called progress. Some progress is painful, certainly, but it's still progress. Even teeth that ache are still teeth.

She pressed the trigger and a shell spat from the maw. "Like a crust of stale bread!" he thought miserably.

The shell detonated inside him and he caught fire.

Just what he wanted after all!

His misery turned to glee.

Nod Toxique shut her visor with a soggy clang, spurred her steed with woollen spurs and haughtily galloped off in search of the next adventure, the next misunderstanding, the next intertextual reference. If you happen to meet her, try not to be a windmill!

Lyndon baked quickly and became a loaf and revelled in the sensation. But then the heat toasted him rather too much. He smoked. He charred. In an hour he was nothing but ashes…

Exactly one year later, the local carpenter, Garth, entered the field and salvaged the least damaged planks, nailing them into a sooty chair. Then he sat with Kosmic Huw and Mr Clogs and they all watched the sunset. It was a bit of a squeeze, I can tell you!

How to Lose Friends and Alienate People

There was a party at Bug's place, the first of the year. It was unknown for Bug Eiderdown to throw parties, he was a genuine misanthrope, skinflint and scopophobe, so it seemed likely he had gone insane or been replaced by an impostor, temporarily or permanently. That was reason enough to attend.

We all went, myself included.

I nervously asked Francesca if she wanted to come and she said, "Not with you." Then she walked away with that special wiggle of hers, young desirable body moving in three different directions at once, and she cast a pouty look back over a shoulder, flicking her midnight hair as she did so, and I cried after her, "Then with who?"

"With *whom*," she corrected me, "not with who."

"Then with whom?" I shouted.

She didn't answer. She had mostly turned a corner. Only the tips of her tresses remained in view on my side, and they too soon went, catching up with her scalp and the rest of her delightful self, as hair tends to do, even when it doesn't belong to Francesca. I went to saturate my disappointment with a beer at Hoopy's. And a muffin.

Hoopy said, "Who would have thought, a party at Bug's? Normally he doesn't even like anyone passing within a half mile of his house. It sounds a bit suspicious to me, maybe even threatening. Are you going? I can't yet make up my mind. I need advice."

I blew the froth off my drink. "He's harmless."

"Do you really think so?"

"Sure, Hoopy. He's just a secretive inventor."

"Can he be normal with a name like that? Bug Eiderdown. It gives me the cliché creeps, the worst kind."

I laughed at that point. Bug Eiderdown isn't a real name, it's just what we call him, a nickname. I told Hoopy this and he relaxed slightly. Then I bit into my muffin. Blueberry crumbs exploded over the zinc counter like the fragments of an inept metaphor shattered by a grenade. Hoopy wiped away the tasty debris with his sleeve.

Bug Eiderdown's real name is Dustmite Quilt.

They say the Quilts originally came from beyond the mountains, but they don't say which mountains, so it's not feasible to go and check, unless you have more spare time and energy than is plausible. Grandpa and Grandma Quilt arrived in the city on a motorbike that was towing a caravan and the forward motion of both was assisted by a sail billowing from a mast stuck on the roof of that caravan, and the entire rickety arrangement was either hindered or augmented, nobody can say for certain which, by a trombone player who sat on a stool on the roof and played directly into the snapping canvas. The Quilts settled in the city and had children and those children had a child, and thus was Bug created.

The trombonist turned out to be a clockwork robot that was put out to rust in the junkyard garden of the family house, an edifice constructed of rotting planks and festooned with not *quite* enough gables, attics, cupolas, turrets, towers, carved gargoyles and other spooky flourishes to attract the attention of passing tourists. The Quilts weren't cannibals and didn't want lost travellers blundering into their privacy. Bug grew up without children of his own age. Lacking playmates he studied engineering by himself in a cluttered workroom in the basement. There was nobody for him to breed with, so eventually he lived in the house alone, the bones of his forebears propping up his sagging bookshelves.

His only contact with conventional society was his monthly attendance at the dance class held above Hoopy's. It was a popular activity, a mix of styles, some more demanding than others. Men mostly went there to meet women or to make their ageing joints more flexible. I went to do both, in the beginning, then I genuinely began to enjoy the challenge, the pulse of the music. Bug Eiderdown must have had his own reasons, different from mine. He never tried to mingle, talk to girls, learn the steps properly. His joints creaked worse, not better, every lesson. I guess he was conducting research, trying to gauge what a *good time* was, so that when he threw his party his effort wouldn't be just theory.

The dance class was where I first met Francesca. She was a proper flirt and had perfected the technique of eyelash batting. She was a stupendous mover on the dancefloor. I kept trying to awaken her interest in me, in my existence, but I was rebuffed constantly, and yet it was the kind of rebuff that made me want to go back for more. I didn't care that she was a game player, a grandmistress of emotion-chess, with the alternating blacks and whites of her mood swings doubling as the playing board, I just wanted to handle her pieces as well as my own. I never got the chance, and I knew I never would, but that was part of the clash, the struggle. I declined plenty of other opportunities for her facile sake.

Bug Eiderdown made it known that he was hosting a party right at the climax of a dance lesson one night. He went around tapping people on the shoulder and saying in a hoarse voice, "Come to my house on the 11th and don't worry about bringing bottles of anything, I have plenty to drink, lots of food too, pre-recorded music also. Just bring yourself, your body in its present corporeal form, that's all that counts." After this declaration, word got around fast, Bug's name was on every pair of lips and somebody even printed a thousand invitations and left them on café tables around town. I think that Glum Prelector Murko said he would come, despite his famous aversion to glee, to hamstring his curiosity.

For some reason, people got the impression it was a fancy dress party Bug was throwing. Clearly the gossip had mutated between a mouth and an ear at an unspecified point along the line. That's how truly memorable events are often generated. In this case the result exceeded expectations. Right from the beginning I was aware it wasn't a fancy dress party, but I pretended not to know that fact. I decided to go as the Man in the Moon. The bloated moon rose over the horizon obligingly enough and I studied it for clues. The clues were there, plenty of them, but a rude conundrum was included too. In most cultures throughout human history, the moon has been regarded as a feminine object.

So what is the Man in the Moon doing there?

Instead of wearing a flat circular mask painted with dry seas and craters, I did things properly and made a papier-mâché sphere with even the hidden dark side features perfectly reproduced.

Why go as a moon at all if you're neglectful of the dark side? It doesn't make sense. I fashioned kneepads to symbolise the daily tides, high and low.

Hoopy went as a giant hand. Although it was a left hand he walked on the right side of the path that led to Bug Eiderdown's house. That was just a little disconcerting.

I caught up with him on my own clumsy way to the party. The eyeholes I had pierced in the fake lunar orb were too small and I stumbled over tiny stones and squirrels.

"Why do you keep clenching and unclenching?" I asked.

"Practice. It might be useful later on."

"Get a grip, Hoopy!" I chided.

"That's it exactly." He nodded, his huge fingers flapping. "I'm starting to get the hang of it now. Everything must be done in correct sequence or it won't work. See the short stubby digit? That one controls the rest of the hand. As a rule of thumb," he added.

Other lonely paths converged on the rusty gate.

Beyond the gate was the house. Weird colours flashed in the windows. I supposed that Bug had invented his own disco lights, it wouldn't be hard for him to do that, he was a genius. Glum Prelector Murko was already at the gate, adjusting one of his beaches. He had come as a volcanic upthrust in the middle of a primordial ocean.

"I hope there won't be too much glee tonight," he said.

"There will be some," I warned.

He sighed and straightened, staring me full in the equator for a minute before asking abstractedly, "If no man is an island, who the hell is Archie Pelago?" This wasn't a joke, he really wanted to know, but I couldn't give him a satisfactory answer, or indeed an answer of any sort, so I shrugged, unlatched the gate, passed through.

Hoopy and Glum Prelector Murko followed.

The overgrown lawn in front of the house concealed early revellers in the gigantic grasses. Metallic and crystal junk also lay about in profusion and it was easy to snag one's toe. I tripped over a prone figure, hoping it was Francesca, so that I could hurl myself prone next to her, or on top of her, whichever was the easiest or best.

But it wasn't her. It was Corkscrew Liverspot.

"What are you?" I scowled.

"I've come as a fossilised stone," he simpered. "I found one once, for real, after a landslide. Embedded deep in wavy strata, it was, a prehistoric stone perfectly preserved. Imagine!"

I could, but didn't. I went into the house instead.

The portal was agape and wide enough not to scrape my head. To any uninformed outsider it might seem awful that the moon had gone indoors at last, had floated into a hall before proceeding down a corridor, drawn onwards by the gravitational attraction of chatter, laughter, the tinkle of fermented drinks. But it wasn't bad.

The kitchen echoed at the end of that corridor.

And in the centre of the kitchen was a table, and seated at that table I encountered Francesca whisking an egg in a bowl directly over a map of Uganda. I said accusingly, "You've come as yourself and that's not really in the spirit of the evening, is it?"

"No, Donaldo, I've come as an imperialist."

"How so?" I squeaked.

She poured the whisked egg over the map. "I'm joining the scramble for Africa," she explained. Then she skipped away and thanks to my big head, my lunar cranium, my moony bonce, which was heavy and unstable and altered my sense of gravity and dignity, I was incapable of following at a velocity sufficient to snatch her.

197

Lights flashed and pulsated in all the rooms. They truly were weird glows and the colours and frequencies of them agitated and melted some part of the inner core of my soul and this disturbance gradually swelled, heading outwards like a very slow explosion. It was a hideous alchemy, or maybe I'm just exploiting a hindsight benefit.

There was music to accompany the lights, but the timing was wrong. I was glad that my celestial head muffled the higher notes, but the low ones boomed like ancient seismic shocks below my cratered surface and sharp yaps did I bark in answer to them, like a mimic that has learned language from nocturnal canine company alone.

Francesca didn't reappear. I searched for her. Rival revellers searched for other people or perhaps themselves.

Then everything came together.

It was inevitable, with the circulation and convection, that every guest would end up in the same place eventually. It happened in the basement, the workshop chamber where abandoned inventions, including a synthetic sobber, kept each other company. By now we were drunk, fed and danced beyond apprehension. Clearly the plan.

A gong sounded. Bug Eiderdown stood at the top of the flight of cellar stairs in his dressing gown and descended dramatically, the effect spoiled by a loose nail that ripped the towelling halfway down, exposing buttocks to the imprisoned breeze that stirred the dust of his domestic corners and alcoves. He winced, hit the gong again.

His absurdly thin shoulders held the weight of the sins of all the lonely throughout history. That's what his expression seemed to say. Or perhaps he just had indigestion. "Celebrants!" he intoned. "Dancers and drinkers! Eaters and lovers! Partygoers! Friends!"

We looked at each other. "Are we his friends?"

"Not me," said Corkscrew Liverspot.

"I'm just a freeloader!" shouted Hoopy, making himself into a fist and shaking it. Then he felt sick and stopped.

"Well, I consider you to be friends at this moment," Bug said, "even if it doesn't last. Everything wears off."

True, very true. How could we object to that?

"Except certain kinds of varnish," he added, which was unexpected, improper even. "That I patented recently," he continued. Then he sighed and lowered the gong to the floor. "But I haven't had a decent return on it yet. No matter! I have a surprise—"

"In store?" wondered Glum Prelector Murko.

"No, it's not there."

"Up your sleeve or in a bulging pocket?"

"Not those places, no."

"How about in the wisdom of your years?"

"Not there. Never there."

"In the tangibility of a waking dream?"

"Hardly likely, is it?"

"On the overtones of an undercurrent?"

"No, no, no, no, no."

"In that case, what about beyond the—"

"Stop guessing please!"

Glum Prelector Murko clammed up, his bitterness plainly visible to all who cared to see. None did. I know this for a fact because I was watching the crowd at the time and every member kept their eyes resolutely on Bug and I can't say I blame them for it. Bug was in control at that moment and he radiated an energy that was offwhite.

Yes, *offwhite*. I could say 'vile' or 'horrid' but those words don't exactly express the sensation created by his radiation. Phantom atoms of his aura were decaying spontaneously and spraying out grubby particles of a force that wasn't energy and wasn't indolence.

I don't know what it was. I don't want to know.

My latitude lines began to ache.

"To return to what I was saying," Bug said, "I have a shock ready for you. I invited you all here on mildly false pretences. When I say 'mildly' I actually mean 'extremely'. Ah well."

"Tell us the facts!" yelled Corkscrew Liverspot.

Bug inhaled deeply, expanded.

And let the air out again, stale and nasty. "Sure. This party was a trap. You have passed through a series of specially regulated light pulses that have interfered with your deoxyribonucleic acids and mutated you away from the human ideal. In short you are now extraterrestrial beings. Each series of lights was a separate code."

We lingered to hear the rest of it, so he obliged.

"Yes!" he chortled. "It may sound farfetched or impossible to you, but it's true anyway, so there! Long have I pondered what forms life on other worlds might take. Clearly it will adapt itself to whatever local conditions present themselves, so a high gravity planet will produce a certain kind of shape, a low gravity planet another."

"Go on," I urged, feeling embarrassed for him.

"Those biochemical lights," he said, "ran a full sequence of mutations to cover all feasible planetary conditions. My experiment is finished. You have mutated beautifully! In this basement tonight is gathered a complete menagerie of every dominant species that exists *or can exist* in the known cosmos! What a novel sight you are."

We regarded each other critically. "But—"

"The first full sequence you encountered when you entered the house is the one that has determined your individual alteration. Each possible variation of lights was flashed only once, and as you all came inside at slightly different times, none of the transformations have been duplicated. That's proper biodiversity for you!"

"But the reason we all look different is—"

"I don't expect you to remain my friends *now*. I have alienated you all. Yes, genuinely alienated you! Ha ha!"

He waved his arms in the air. He would have waved them in vacuum if he'd been given the chance. Or syrup.

Francesca broke the news to him more gently than the rogue deserved, but I forgave her that indiscretion, for maybe one day I too would need to be forgiven by her for something, though probably nothing so serious and bizarre as converting people into aliens.

"We're in fancy dress," she said.

His eyes bulged and he fell back, froth dribbling from the corner of his mouth. "Fancy dress! Fancy dress!"

"It's true, I'm afraid," I confirmed, not afraid.

He believed me, or maybe he believed her first. I doubt he believed us consecutively because that would be a waste of time and energy. "I never said anything about fancy dress!"

"True. Yet that's how we came. Dressed up."

"I specified no fancy dress!"

"We don't actually look like this, sorry."

"Liars! Cheats! Normals!"

He ran away, wailing, back up the stairs.

The exodus from the house was a sad affair. The grass, crystal and iron of the junkyard garden was bleak to our senses, the gate squeaked like a hog spanked by the rotten sails of a forgotten windmill, regular, seasonal, with no illusion of profit. We shambled. Our paths mostly diverged and finally I found myself alone with Hoopy.

"Did you think my costume was best?" he asked.

"Not *the* best," I said, "but good."

"I'll be reluctant to take it off when I get home."

That was an observation I couldn't fail to nod solemnly at, for I shared an identical anxiety about disrobing, as I imagine did every leaving guest. What did I look like under my moon head? Maybe I had many ears, more than a dozen, or prehensile eyebrows. Feasibly there was just a cloud and no face, a sentient vortex of plasma.

"Gives me an idea for a party of my own," I said.

"You intend to host a party?"

"Why not? You're invited, Hoopy. Everybody's invited! It'll be a fancy dress party with a difference. At a prearranged signal we'll all pull off our costumes and reveal our mutations!"

He spread his immense fingers. "That's grand!"

"Might as well make the most of the changes. Spread the word. At my house, tomorrow at sunset. Bug's not invited. He's the only one who isn't. Seems he's not so harmless after all."

201

He nodded and we parted. I was alone again.

I reached my abode, went indoors, perched on my rocking chair with a glass of soda that I slurped up a straw through one of my lower craters. I felt no tingle on tongue and gums, the customary sensation simply wasn't there, and I knew my mouth was new, had become an exobiological maw, a more mysterious portal than before.

But I still didn't dare look at my own unsheathed reflection. The lunar head would stay on for now. I finished the drink, had a sudden inspiration and jumped up. I ran out, neglecting to lock the front door behind me, ran to Francesca's house, stood in the dark street and called up at her window. After a long time, the lamp came on.

The window opened, her head was thrust out.

"What do you want, Donaldo?"

"Bug was lying!" I enthused. "None of us have been turned into aliens! It was a joke or an example of bravado. You alone didn't attend the party in fancy dress and yet you've retained your human form. The weird lights had no power over our genes after all!"

And I clutched my moon head and pulled it off.

A fleeting grimace crossed her face, then she said calmly, "Have you forgotten that Bug's lights ran the *full sequence* of mutations? One of the variations must be the form best suited to the conditions of our own world and plainly that particular mutation is the one that afflicted me. So I look just as an Earth-based lifeform should."

"Ah, I see." I lowered the moon onto my shoulders.

I was about to walk away, my steps despondent, when I noticed a face in the window next to hers. It wasn't precisely a face, but it did the job. In my exasperation and despair, I merely raised an arm and pointed at it. But Francesca wasn't abashed in the slightest.

"This is Whom," she explained. "I did tell you I was going to the party with him, didn't I? Whom Thurbertolls."

"Pleased to meet you," piped his indescribable voice.

"How do you do," I growled.

Francesca regarded him with sultry eyes.

"He's an example of a higher being that has evolved on a planet with glass continents and acid oceans."

"Is he? Is he now? Is that so?" I croaked.

Recalling my dignity, I turned on my heel and stamped off. I didn't go to bed that night, but positioned myself in front of a powerful sunlamp in my living room, making minor eclipses on the walls behind me, creating bad luck for spiders on all cobwebs in any corner, eclipses that matched in shape and intensity my new soul.

THE BLUE JEWEL FRUIT

"Up there! What can it be?"

"It's blue and its glows and it appears to be hanging from the highest branch of that tall tree. Climb that tall tree and pluck it for me, my dear, as I'm sure it must be a blue jewel fruit."

"A blue jewel fruit!"

"Yes, a fruit that happens to be a blue jewel, no less. Here's a ladder to facilitate the climbing of the tree, and here's a basket to put the plucked fruit into, once the deed is done."

"Will you hold the ladder steady while I climb?"

"I will, I will, never fear, my dear."

"Upwards I go, one rung at a time, and soon I'm scared to look down. The wind is much stronger at this altitude, colder too, and I have a touch of vertigo. No matter, I'm finally at the top, watch me transfer from the ladder to the highest branch, brave of me, don't you concur? Now I'm inching myself along that branch."

"You are indeed. I'm proud of you, my dear."

"But the fruit has gone!"

"What did you say? Has it fallen? Did a passing crow snaffle it? The situation is very strange, my disappointment is acute, no blue jewel fruit for us today, alas!"

"Wait a moment. There it is! Up there!"

"Ah, it was a trick of perspective or an optical illusion, and in fact the blue jewel fruit hangs not from the highest branch of this very tall tree, where you happen to be balanced, but crowns the summit of that lofty mountain which stands *behind* the tree. This makes perfect sense. Come back down."

"I will, I am, I have."

"Let us make our way to the base of the mountain. It is far away, but even far away things can be reached, in time. Yes, my dear, that's right, pedal harder please."

"This tandem bicycle needs oiling, I believe."

"True, true, the chain is a little stiff. We'll leave the ladder where it is. Can't climb a mountain with just one ladder. It won't be long enough to reach the very top."

"In that case, how shall we climb the mountain?"

"Together, my dear, that's how."

"Here's the base of the mountain already. I think the hard pedalling work has been edited out. Do you have a bicycle lock for the tandem? What if a yeti comes and steals it?"

"No matter, no matter, we'll buy another. The blue jewel fruit is more important. Give me your hand."

"Puff! Pant! This slope is steep and treacherous."

"Indeed it is. But we're halfway to the top now, too late to turn back. Why is a blue jewel fruit sitting on the apex of a peak, just like a beacon? It's not normal in these regions, nor in any other. One more boulder to surmount and the summit is ours, yours and mine. Here we are. What a tremendous view! I can see as far as the ocean."

"Yes, the sun is setting into the wavy splendour of it."

"A magnificent sight, my dear, but we have climbed this mountain for the sake of the blue jewel fruit and it would be neglectful not to make it our priority."

"Agreed. But it's not here."

"You appear to be telling no less than the truth. We have clearly been deceived by another optical illusion, for the fruit is still above us, gripped in the talons of that simurgh overhead. Do you see it? With the wonderful golden scales and the silver head."

"Surely that's a biplane?"

"It's a simurgh. Truly. Open the enormous rucksack on your back and take out all the parts inside. When you fit them together correctly you'll find you have made a hang glider sturdy enough to carry two passengers, namely me and you."

"Done. But I'm uneasy about this precipitous launch."

"Don't fret, my dear. True, we appear to be descending more rapidly than is recommended when taking part in this daring activity, but if we catch a thermal I'm sure everything will be fine. What did I tell you? Up we go, higher and higher!"

"A yeti just made a rude gesture at me. From the mouth of an ice cave. How uncouth. I'm quite upset."

"Force of habit with them, my dear. Don't respond, it only makes them angrier and we may have to climb this mountain in the future. Above the summit we are now, drawing level with the simurgh. Reach out and steal the blue jewel fruit as we soar past. Here's a net on a pole for just such a purpose. Once the fruit is in your possession, dive into yonder canyon. The simurgh may resent the theft."

"It doesn't have the blue jewel fruit, as it happens."

"Another optical illusion! Bah!"

"The beating of the creature's wings is creating excessive turbulence. The frame of the glider is collapsing. We are doomed! Listen to me shriek as I plummet to the ground. Listen to you likewise. The blue jewel fruit was only a star, after all. The yeti is laughing hard as we fall past him. He's welcome to the bicycle now..."

"Not so fast, my dear. The simurgh has rescued us by plucking us out of midair. You are in the left talon, while I am in the right. That position is normal for me, I'm generally in the right. Ho ho! Leaving jokes aside, it seems that this kind mythical monster wants to hold a conversation with us. Pay attention."

"I'm listening. I do feel queasy but I'm all ears."

"Go ahead, simurgh. We're ready."

I heard your remark (began the simurgh) about the blue jewel fruit being a star and I want to correct you on this point. You're almost right, but not quite. Have you ever wondered why the sun doesn't make any noise as it burns? You probably think that the vacuum of outer space is responsible for the suspicious silence of that fiery orb. After all, it's a fact that sound waves need a medium to travel through, whether that medium is solid, liquid or gas. No air in space means the sun simply *can't* make a sound, however much it wants to. It's like a giraffe, the only utterly silent animal, unless the encyclopaedia that told me that fascinating detail was lying. Which is possible.

Now imagine that the atmosphere of the Earth extends as far as the sun, so there is no vacuum between the two bodies. How loud will the sun be? Deafening! Like the undying eruption of a stupendously vast bomb. That seems reasonable, doesn't it? But the truth is that sound waves don't travel forever. They weaken into inaudibility over fairly short distances. Only the most massive volcanic eruptions are ever heard on the other side of the world by human ears. And the sun is very far away. Almost one hundred million miles. If the Earth's atmosphere did extend that far, the noise of the sun would be muffled long before it reached listeners on the surface of our planet, I'm afraid.

That's not all. Everyone knows that the sun turns red at sunset and sunrise. In fact those are the only occasions when it's safe to look directly at the sun's disc, though one should still take great care. Why is the sun reddish at those times, the light much weaker? For the simple reason that the rays have more of Earth's atmosphere to pass through before they reach the eyes of the sunset watcher. The same truth applies to the sunrise watcher, but that breed is less common. When the sun is directly overhead, the beams come down vertically and only pass through about 80 KM of relatively thick air, so much less light is filtered out than when the sun is in any other position.

How much more air must those beams pass through at sunset and sunrise? The answer is different at various points on the Earth's surface. The sun rises and sets on an east-west axis because that's how our globe spins. So at different latitudes, the radius of the Earth on that same axis is greater or lesser. To calculate how much of our atmosphere the light of sunset and sunrise travels through before reaching us, first we must draw two concentric circles, the first representing the radius of the planet at our latitude, the second representing the same radius plus the depth of the atmosphere, which as I've already pointed out is about eighty kilometres. Then we draw a tangent from a point on the inner circle to a point on the outer.

That tangent is the path of the sunbeams through our atmosphere at sunset or sunrise, and doing a rough calculation in my head I deduce that the distance is about four times further than the distance those beams must travel when the sun is directly overhead. It's quadruple the amount of air to pass through! No wonder so much of the light and heat are filtered out! If the Earth's atmosphere extended further than it does, even more of the light and heat would be blocked. And if, as I originally postulated, our atmosphere extended all the way to the sun, then *none* of the light and heat would reach us. In fact it would be so dark and cold here that the atmosphere would freeze. We would be entombed, all of us, in an enormous block of solid air!

But the concept of the Earth's atmosphere reaching as far as the sun offends my sense of rationality. I would prefer to entertain the notion that the sun's atmosphere extends as far as the orbit of our planet instead. Still we would be trapped in a frozen block, and indeed the Earth would resemble a pea stuck just under the surface of a gigantic iceberg. At the centre of this hypothetical 'iceberg' would be the furnace of the sun, just plasma and gas, but further out would be a liquid zone, and the solid part last of all. The entire set-up might even resemble a very large planet with a hot core but a cool crust. Maybe beings would dwell on the surface of that 'planet', unaware they were standing on the sun's frozen atmosphere!

These beings might develop a civilisation. The stars would shine in a permanently dark sky above, for there could be no daytime in such a place. But stars are mortal, just like men. Some of them die violent deaths, flaring up or even exploding. One of the nearest stars might suddenly increase in size, swelling until it resembled our familiar sun. The beings of the civilisation I have postulated would assume it *was* their sun. This would serve to confirm their belief that they lived on a real planet. But the rising temperature of that dying star would start to melt the outer shell of the frozen atmosphere, turning it to gas. The surface would evaporate and the level of the illusory 'ground' would fall.

But it would fall so smoothly that the beings on it would fail to notice what was happening. Suddenly the trapped globe of the Earth, that poor pea in the iceberg, would be set free! But the frozen gas would continue to melt. The freed orb of the Earth would soon be high above the heads of the beings on the shrinking surface of the sun, and it would appear as a point of blue light in the sky, further and further away. An unobtainable blue jewel fruit! Not a star, as you suggested earlier, but a planet, the planet called Earth. Sometimes men and women gaze up at the very thing they think is beneath them. To study oneself, it may require peering intently at a distant object. Quite an irony, wouldn't you say?

"Yes I would, I would say that. Thanks you, simurgh, for that truly intriguing lecture! Were you paying attention, my dear? We aren't inhabitants of Earth after all. We are dwellers on the surface of the sun's frozen atmosphere. How unexpected!"

"Indeed. But this means that the ground is getting lower all the time. Eventually it will become too hot for life."

"A good point. There's a liquid layer below the solid. Everyone below will be boiled sooner or later."

"What shall we do? No point going home and just waiting to die. Shall we ask the simurgh to carry us up to the real Earth? We can live there in safety and comfort, unless *its* surface also turns out to be the frozen atmosphere of another sun…"

"There's always that risk, my dear, but it's the best option on offer. I'm wiling to bet that the cafés on Earth are just as good as our own. When we get there, I'll buy you an ice cream."

"Will you really? May I choose any flavour I like?"

"Of course. Do you have one in mind?"

"Blue jewel fruit please…"

THE PASTEL WHIMSY

My name is Janus Cronk. As a morbid and obsessive collector of stuffed monsters, it occurred to me to attempt to secure a cadaver of the rarest of all cryptozoological grotesques, the pastel whimsy. Accordingly I have embarked on this solo expedition.

I intend to keep my journal as up to date as feasible. Every night I will jot down a summary of the day's events. This is the very first entry, so the first day must logically be over. What happened in it? Lots! I departed my abode at sunrise and kept trudging.

Before long I had strayed off the common byways of man and entered a large territory that was *almost eldritch*, but by what criterion this was so I can't really specify. Perhaps I'm the sort of person who uses words more for the lyrical content than the sense.

At any rate, I wandered through the blasted landscape and approached a thin woman seated on a lonely rock. An old hag it was, on feldspar, and she croaked, "Why the rush, youngster? Dally with me awhile, for the last time I was ravished was aeons ago…"

"Aeeeeeiiiiiiii! Nooo!" I shrieked.

My reaction offended the hag, who pointed a gnarled finger at me and roared, "Then I curse you by all the chthonic gods of the forbidden abyss, even though I don't know who forbid it, nor how such forbidment may be enforced. Is that a word, 'forbidment'?"

"I don't think so," I replied, hurrying onwards. Incidentally, I can't say how I knew the rock was lonely, it just seemed that way. There are some things that are obvious to those parts of our minds far below the depths of normal consciousness, aren't there?

That was yesterday. Now I'm huddled in my tent again at the end of the second day of my expedition. I must use this free time to work out my exact position on the map I brought with me. But before I do that, I will finish writing this entry. Let me see.

Yes. I am an eccentric and a man of wealth and curious taste. Indeed my taste is so curious that it can't even lick an envelope without reading the letter inside. Joke! In my hometown, the city of Marblebum, my name is feared, respected and feared again.

All my friends have a name that begins with the letter 'J'. I am wealthy enough to make that happen! One evening, many years ago, in the crisped and sere October in fact, I invited Joel around for supper. He is a learned, sensible and quaintly sober gentleman.

It was Joel who first told me about the pastel whimsy.

"Where dwells the beast?" I asked.

"On the planet Happenstance in the Lower Dunsany Zone," he said in an erudite tone, "wherein all manner of unrehearsed frights and undefined sprites lurk and play in faerie dells. There is the gashootha, the hornielad, the dinky magoom, the grabbèd klasp, the tic-tac-finger, the jumppabove, the skork, but most impressive of all…"

"The pastel whimsy!" I shouted.

He nodded furiously and sipped his wine, for although quaintly sober is he, practically sober he not always is.

And from that very moment I burned to find it.

The third day is now over and I didn't work out where I was on the map after all; I was too tired and curled up in the arms of sleep instead, arms that are freckled and hairy, by the way: a fact that poets often ignore. For they are mere mortals and utter fools.

Anyway, today was a busy day. By late afternoon I finished crossing the blasted landscape and entered the ghoul-haunted woodland of Weir. I believe that this means I am halfway to the Lower Dunsany Zone. Great! But I had a rather annoying encounter.

To reach the planet Happenstance I must cross the Bridge of Cosmical Webs that straddles the worlds like a type of stringy pasta, and to reach that bridge it is essential that I locate Mount Yaanek, for our end of the bridge is fixed to the apex of that peak.

Before the sun had gone down, and while its heavy ruby beans still slanted sidewise between the giant forest boles, I happened to— Sorry. One moment. Did I write 'beans'? I meant to say 'beams'. My apologies! I'll scratch it out and insert the right word.

210

Before the sun had gone down, and while its heavy ruby beams still slanted sidewise between the giant forest boles, I happened to meet a very strange figure chopping at a dead log with an axe that had two blades. But I decided not to judge by appearances.

"One moment, my friend!" I cried. "I am looking for Mount Yaanek. Do you happen to know where it lies?"

He stopped chopping and scratched his head dubiously. "I don't think it does that, really sir I don't. I wasn't even aware it could speak at all! But if you are looking for it, I can indicate the direction you must take. Right, right, left, then straight on. Then left."

"Very good," I replied with a grateful countenance.

"You'll find it behind the shops," he added.

"The shops?" I screeched.

"Yes, that's right, the shops," he said.

"Are you quite sure?" I pressed. "Are you certain that Mount Yaanek, where the lavas restless roll their sulphurous currents, is positioned near a series of commercial retail outlets?"

He clapped a hand to his brow. "I see! You want the Mount Yaanek where the lavas *restlessly* roll. I thought you were referring to the other Mount Yaanek, the one with lavas that only *intermittently* roll. In that case, you have a long voyage ahead."

"There is more than one Mount Yaanek?"

"Of course. There is also the Mount Yaanek where the lavas flow in a brand new style back up into the crater, but you can't be desirous of going there. It stinks. Here's a magic compass. It will lead you to the mountain that you seeketh. Good luck, buster!"

I was touched by his generosity. In return I gave him my binoculars. He accepted them gingerly and seemed thoroughly bewildered. I didn't have time to explain their use. I went off and left him to it. I don't think he'll ever succeed in working them out.

Mind you, he was a cyclops, so maybe that's why.

I am still in the forest, in the ghoul-haunted woodland of Weir. Haven't met any ghouls yet, though. That fact doesn't bother me, as I

211

have a very nice stuffed example in my bedroom. I am, after all, Janus Cronk, a man who collects such things. Remember?

Ghouls have sharp talons that look exactly like twigs.

There is a noise outside, a rustling, a creaking, a snapping sound! A hand is reaching into my tent! Why can't I stop writing in this blasted journal and take evasive action? Is this the curse the hag laid on me? I can't stop writing whatever the danger!

The teeth, the claws. Dragging me away…. Aaaargh!

Back again. False alarm. It's not the fifth day yet, still the fourth day. This is a postscript to the above, just so you don't worry about what happened to me. I'm fine. It was just a falling branch that somehow slid horizontally along the forest floor and entered my tent mouth with twigs that looked like talons. How I laughed afterwards!

Right, I'm off to sleep now. Too tired to mess around with maps. I'm sure I am right about the curse though. When I start writing in my journal I can't stop until the entry has been properly entered. Makes it more tricky to avoid perils, but that's life, isn't it?

Nighty night! Wait a moment… Why are these twigs trying to strangle me? Don't they know that's no behaviour for any self-respecting tree? I'll just eject them from my tent. One minute. There we go. "And stay out!" Where was I? Ah yes, goodnight to you.

Sleep tight. Watch the *gubbends* don't bite and rend!

Today the way ahead was blocked by a raging torrent, so I carved a canoe with my penknife and got inside it. I had no oars or rudder, but what the hell? The current carried me at fantastic speed in the direction I wanted to go anyway. Brill! It was weird fun.

For nine hours I was tossed in the froth and spume.

Then the torrent calmed down and became a slow-moving river with a penchant for sinuously winding its way o'er a floodplain littered with the relics and ruins of an ancient crumbled civilisation that already was senile and forgotten before Atlantis went glug.

Nice to be out of the ghoul-haunted woodland of Weir!

The river deposited me into a lake and on the far side of the lake rose the mighty bulk of Mount Yaanek, though the restless lavas were having a break, which caused me to wonder if this really was the right mountain, but then I saw the Bridge of Cosmical Webs.

Right at this moment I am balanced halfway along that bridge. It is far too long to cross in a single go. I pitched my tent in the middle and here I am, swaying above the interplanetary gulf, wherein move vast amorphous clouds of malign hydrogen intelligence.

Maybe they're not really malign, but they do frown an awful lot when I poke my head out of the tent and peer over the side. Perhaps they just have toothache or something comparable.

The bridge sways in the solar wind, in the breath of the universe. Most other men would be frightened, but for me it is like resting in a cradle that is being rocked by the mother of matter; for I am Janus Cronk and not at all like other men, apart from certain bits.

I am now standing on the planet Happenstance. Actually I am crouching, for this tent doesn't permit an occupant to stand up straight. Despite my immense wealth, I bought it cheap from my friend Jake. I'm a miser in some ways. In most ways, to be honest.

Happenstance is a lot like Earth. In other words it's full of beings that dream about other places all the time…

Did I mention that I have two faces? I don't mean metaphorically. I really do have two faces; the other one is on the back of my skull. It's a conjoined twin that turned around somehow and got stuck like that. But this doesn't mean I can see behind me.

I'll explain why. The eyes of that face aren't connected to my brain. I wonder which brain they *are* connected to? To yours, perhaps? To those of my best friends, Joel, Jake, Jeremy, Jason, Jemima, Jerome, Jasper, Jo, Jacqueline, Jiffy, Jekyll, Jabber, Jelks?

It's a great mystery beyond the ken of neuroscience.

Do you know Ken of Neuroscience? He's a top doctor. Sorry about the lowercase letters in the previous sentence.

I am consulting the map. I have absolutely no idea where I am on it. I am beginning to suspect it's not the right map for my trip. It has the words 'Marblebum Bus Routes' written on it. But why? Marblebum is a peculiar city and all buses are prohibited there.

When my expedition is over I'll probably publish this journal. Why not? I have done so before. My report of a previous expedition, when I went in search of the legendary Corner of Alexis, which had been knocked off by a thunderbolt, was published to modest acclaim by the Eldritch Explorers' Club under the supervision of the acting president, Mr Peeper Sharpe.

His supervision was required because the print was so small and the vision of the others members wasn't so good.

I never found the Corner, by the way, but so what?

When I say 'modest acclaim' I really mean that it was savaged by the critics and reviewers who bothered to write about it. One of them had the temerity to suggest I was a poor writer because I used the word 'cosmic' twenty-four times in one paragraph!

In that case, Shakespeare was a worse hack than me, for in *King Lear* he actually used the word 'never' five times in a single sentence! And as for Carmen Miranda... 'I I I I I I Like You Very Much' reveals the depths of her grammatical depravity for itself.

These days I always train a detractor beam on critics. Tractor beams attract; detractor beams repel. I don't radiate them from a machine. They come out of my eyes, the front pair.

Today all became clear. The mystery has been unravelled. My search is at an end! But what a climax. What a foul and vile finish to my dream! Let me first stress something. The pastel whimsy is the ultimate monster. Its rarity is so extreme that even other rare monsters, such as the yib, blabbo, impmong and ucker have never seen it.

Other kinds of whimsy are much less rare, common in comparison. It shouldn't be necessary for me to remark how the vibrant whimsy, the oily whimsy and the acrylic whimsy may be stroked and even fed at a variety of zoos around the world. As for the pastel whimsy: no one knows what it looks like but I felt sure I would instantly recognise it when I encountered it. And I was dreadfully right about that!

I entered the Lower Dunsany Zone an hour before noon.

I forgot to say that the Happenstance end of the Bridge of Cosmical Webs is fixed to a volcano called Mount Kenaay, where lavas do the task assigned to them reasonably well. I dismounted this mount and trudged through the luohg-detnuah dnaldoow of Riew, but somehow I got lost on the way and decided to retrace my steps.

On the horizon loomed the bulk of Mount Kenaay and so I aimed for that; but when I reached the grim base, I was alarmed to discover it was a different Mount Kenaay, a version with slightly more indolent lavas. And behind the volcano was a row of shops.

I wandered among these, biting my chapped lips.

One of them appeared to specialise in attire. I went inside and inquired aloud about shirts and pants. The shopkeeper was a stooped dwarf in the form of a closed loop and he rolled from behind the counter with a speed that I found noteworthy but alarming; for we are not used to people who trundle like wheels. At least I'm not.

"No sir, we only sell tails here! For this is a *retail* outlet! If your tail has been damaged or detached, we can provide a replacement. We have sundry kinds and lengths in stock."

"I am a human male. Why should I require a tail?"

"To return to Earth, sir! It's not allowed to go back the way you came, across the cosmic webs. You must use the Tightrope of Tindaloo, which is much thinner, as thin as an auburn girl's eyebrow; and a tail will enable you to keep your balance more easily."

"Then I shall purchase one at once!" I cried.

"A wise decision, sir," he said.

"What's your name?" I asked him politely.

"Circumference Perkins, sir."

He guided me to a changing room and I stepped inside. I found myself in a booth facing a mirrored wall. Behind me was another mirrored wall and my reflection bounced back and forth between them like an infinite rally in a game of image tennis. I frowned. And then the horror struck me with the force of a massive metaphor!

215

I had never seen the face on the back of my head. The face on the back of my head had seen it, of course, but what does that mean to me? For the first time I found myself face to face with my other self. Gurning back at me in the corniest of dénouements were the features of… You've guessed it. Or perhaps not. The pastel whimsy!

Urgh! Gosh! And all the Aaaiiieeeees I can muster…

THE SOFT LANDING

I am a photon and I have just been expelled from a star. I don't mean that I have done anything wrong; it's not that kind of expulsion. Merely that a sequence of events has taken place over a long period of time that finally resulted in me leaving home forever.

There's no acrimony involved and I don't bear my parent star malice of any sort. It's part of a natural process and I daresay you too have gone through a similar event in your own life. This is a fundamental law of the cosmos. We grow up and leave home.

Not that I was ever in a position to 'grow up'. I'm a photon and have a very limited capacity for change of any sort. But to make you understand me properly I'm compelled to speak in metaphors. My natural language is mathematics; yours is made of words.

So this primary fact has now been established. I have escaped the body of the star that created me and I'm hurtling through space at the speed of myself, the fastest velocity possible. This isn't arrogance but simple truth. I am a particle of light, pure and basic.

My knowledge of the universe, of reality, is sketchy in the extreme. It is certainly sufficiently accurate to portray me as an innocent, as a naïf, a particle unversed in the objective truths, lacking all experience and armed merely with submicroscopic knowledge.

But please don't assume that I am young, that my creation was recent, that only a few seconds have elapsed since I was born. I have yearned for the instant of escape for long ages. Be aware that photons remain at home considerably longer than human beings.

In the heart of a star, where we originate, there is scant opportunity for independence of any sort. We pop into existence in the middle of opacity, amid a seething mass of reactions, and we are lost and blind in the chaos, more helpless than abandoned orphans.

The idea that a photon, the messenger particle of light, might be blind probably strikes you as an absurdity, and so it is, but that is no argument against the absolute truth of it. With so much ferocious plasma all around, it was quite impossible to see anything.

The fact we have no eyes didn't help us much.

For a photon to grope its way from the centre of a sun to the rim, to a point where it is free to shoot out into the void, takes ten million years or so; we are continually absorbed and re-emitted randomly by the ferocious furnace until chance leads us to the edge.

Only when we reach the surface of a star are we able to leap out of the boggy plasma and hurtle off into the cosmos, extending ourselves to our full length, which is a psychological rather than physical state, feeling a non-existent wind in our imaginary faces.

So there is excessive joy in the act of liberation, and that instant when a photon, or any related subatomic particle, understands that he truly has overcome the gravitational pull of the sun that is his mother and father is one of the highlights of his existence.

At this very moment I am suffused with delight.

But there is anxiety behind the glee; and with the passing of time, the anxiety will be strengthened, the happiness lessened, and the thoughts of every sane and intelligent photon will focus on the future, on the outcome that fate has in store for us. I know this.

The number of photons who remain permanently ecstatic and carefree on the voyage through the vacuum is tiny and they are fools. They fail to understand that although the universe in an enormous arena for our flight through space, it is not completely empty.

One day we must strike something solid. That's a fact.

And when we do connect with matter, we will be absorbed, reflected, refracted or split, depending on the nature of the impediment. Every one of these outcomes is a hazard. Only

217

absorption is desirable and even then only under extremely rare circumstances.

Uncounted trillions of my fellows are radiated every second from the average star; most will never see each other again. Only those emitted in a line perfectly parallel to your own trajectory will remain in earshot for the duration of the journey through space.

The others must fly off to those remote zones of the universe reserved for them by arbitrary circumstance. A difference of a fraction of a degree will end long friendships as the two companions gradually diverge until a distance of many light years divides them.

It is best not to grow too emotionally attached to other photons. I have made the mistake and the particle that accompanies me on this adventure, immediately to my left, is like a brother to me. We travel in parallel and I rate his company more highly than is wise.

For it is impossible to know when one of us might hit an obstacle and vanish or be deflected, and this uncertainty is a painful prelude to the act itself, which must come eventually. The truth is that selfishness is the one sensible attitude: each photon for himself.

But cynicism sits uneasily on my absent shoulders.

Time passes, will pass, has passed…

I see that we have just entered an alien solar system together. The star at the centre of this family of planets is a typical yellow ball; the photons it gives off call greetings to us as we pass in opposite directions. I hope it won't be our luck to fall into the star itself.

There are at least eight worlds orbiting that hub.

We have passed several gas giants and seem to be heading directly for a small blue globe wisped with white. I turn to my friend and say, "Well, our destination appears to be on the surface of that oblate spheroid. Have a soft landing, dear Lux! The best of luck!"

"A soft landing to you also, friend Glo! Farewell!"

We chuckle with mildly bitter irony…

The statistical chances of having the *right* soft landing are so small it's impossible to calculate them, for there is only one kind that's suitable and it relies on a chain of bizarre physical, chemical and biological flukes, but it's traditional to shout out the formula:

218

"A soft landing to every photon in existence!"

Lux and Glo: comrades to the end...

And then we are screaming through the atmosphere of this world and a blink of time later I suddenly find myself passing through something hard but transparent, a lens, and I hear poor Lux's anguished cry as he smashes into the opaque rim that I have avoided.

I am inside the telescope for the briefest of instants; I pass through the second lens and now attain what every photon scarcely dares dream of, a soft landing! A cushioned crash into the open eye of an alien astronomer! Why have I been chosen for this honour?

There is no answer to that question. It doesn't matter. I strike the retina of the stargazer and with infinite cosmic bliss I'm absorbed into a spongy organic paradise. But this is not a paradise of the dead. My collision seeds new life, birthing the concept of a far star.

For my arrival in his eye after such an epic voyage has fired impulses in the optic nerve of the astronomer and those impulses are speeding on a journey, considerably shorter than mine, towards his curious brain. And when they arrive they will fertilise his mind.

And he will fall back from his telescope for a moment and reflect that he has discovered a new sun in a distant constellation, but in fact that sun is a child, an idea planted in his imagination, and he will communicate it to others like him, and so the child will grow.

This is how stars reproduce. My mission is accomplished.

THE TASTE OF TURTLE TEARS

There are certain kinds of butterfly that live exclusively on the tears of other animals. Even butterflies that like to drink nectar will still often alight on the cheeks of a beast that has been weeping.

There is nothing illogical in this action really, for the butterflies crave salt, and tears are one of the richest sources of sodium. Butterflies that dwell near the sea don't need to do this because the wind is already laden with salt and the wind sprinkles it over the flowers.

But butterflies that have their homes far inland will usually find that the salt the wind can carry has been shed long before it reaches them, so they will be desperately short of the vital mineral.

Deep in the Amazon rainforest, far from the ocean, there are flotillas of butterflies that have become specialised tear-drinkers. It may seem a gloomy feast for such a beautiful creature but what choice do they have? Without salt death is certain and a slow agonising death too.

So they find it essential that larger animals cry; and one way to ensure a regular supply of tears is to encourage these animals to shed them; and the best way of doing that it to make them feel sad.

How on earth do butterflies make other animals sad?

In one small region of that mighty jungle some butterflies have learned a few things that butterflies elsewhere have yet to learn. They know that the tears of the yellow-spotted river turtle are the saltiest and most nourishing of all, and they also know how to speak turtle language.

Actually, this last part isn't quite true. They don't *speak* the language but write it instead, in mid air, with their fluttering bodies. The orange and yellow butterflies form words in the turtle tongue that tell extremely sad stories and the turtles read them and burst into racking sobs.

The butterflies don't need to form individual letters to make the words of a sentence because the written language of these turtles isn't alphabetical but pictographic. Each symbol stands for one word. This fortunately means it takes less butterflies to tell a turtle tale than it otherwise might. There is a limit to the number of butterflies that can drink the tears of a single turtle. Having said this, there have been occasions when more than one turtle arrived to experience the sad story that was being related for them.

One memorable afternoon the butterflies had an audience of no less than six turtles, but more than one is a rarity. The stories that make turtles cry aren't especially sophisticated. Simple tragic narratives suffice. Accounts of brave but foolish turtles that ended up as meals for jaguars; doomed loved affairs; stories about ungrateful children being mean to their mother; bitter ironies about what happens to naive turtles in the big bad world.

When the turtles can bear no more, they begin to weep and then it's time for the butterflies to land and take a drink. The turtle tears give the insects the salt they need and they taste great too. The only problem is that the sadness, or at least some of it, comes with the substance.

Yes, it's true. A little of the morose feeling is transferred into every tear, so the butterflies generally feel rather sad themselves afterwards. For the turtle the weeping might be cathartic but not so for the butterflies. They just feel sad without any emotional cleansing of the soul.

One day it occurred to the butterflies that tears are not only produced by sadness. They wondered if they might switch to telling funny stories so that the turtles would cry with laughter. Worth a try!

A comedy that will appeal to a turtle is no more polished than a tragedy that will fill it with melancholy. Turtles like farces best, with lots of characters narrowly avoiding each other in complicated love triangles. The butterflies told these stories and the turtles wept with joy.

These tears tasted sweeter than the juice of sadness.

But they were a little *too* sweet.

The butterflies enjoyed them nonetheless, but one morning, while sunning themselves on the river bank, among the flowers they held a discussion. Tragic tears were too bitter, comic tears too sweet. Might a way be found to combine and moderate the two flavours into something better? Was there such a thing as *tragicomedy*, a blend of both genres?

They weren't sure but they decided to try anyway.

The next story they told was a masterpiece of plotting and it manipulated the emotions of the turtle who witnessed it in a way that previously would have seemed implausible, swooping from the black depths of despair to the dizzy heights of mirth and back again at a velocity that to a turtle must have seemed horrifying and exhilarating at the same time.

The subsequent tears of tragicomedy were rated very highly. Indeed the butterflies considered them utterly perfect.

They began to tour their performance across the entire region and back to the starting point. It might be supposed they could simply have moved to a new home closer to the sea, where salt would have been plentiful, but the home they already had was far from meddling humans and had its advantages. Why should they emigrate? They liked it here and now that they had the recipe for the best tears ever tasted, there was no more need to worry.

But giving the same performance day after day meant that they became a little complacent. They put less effort into forming the words correctly. If one of the butterflies was late to get into position the others would go ahead without him or her. Yes, their work became sloppy.

And one awful day the turtle that was the sole audience member started laughing in a different way from usual. The butterflies carried on and, when the turtle cried, they abandoned the story and took their drink. But the flavour was off this time, very peculiar, and mildly toxic.

It didn't kill the butterflies but it made their souls sick for a few days and in that time they squabbled with each other or drooped their wings pathetically while resting on petals or muttered dark ideas about self destruction or found it impossible to go to sleep. They were depressed.

The problem is that the last performance had been a disaster. So casual had the butterflies become, so cavalier with their theatrical duties, that most of them hadn't bothered to make neat symbols in the air. The pictographs were ragged and badly formed. As a consequence, the *meaning* of the words of the story had changed. It had become gibberish.

And yes, the turtle had laughed and wept, but not because of catharsis or amusement. No, he had guffawed and cried in derision, in contempt, his tears and laughter directed *at* the butterflies rather

222

than *with* them. These tears were pure poison, not strong enough to kill the insects but certainly potent enough to make them feel very bad about themselves.

The solution was to forget about amateur dramatics.

And now the butterflies have a highly organised and superbly disciplined troupe of *professional* actors who give daily shows down by the river. They are even building a special venue there, an open air amphitheatre, though how they are doing this with their little thin legs is beyond my knowing; and the actors in this troupe are never sloppy or slapdash.

It remains to be seen if butterfly theatre ever catches on in that isolated part of the forest. I sincerely hope it does.

Their plan is to make everything as honest as possible, so the old idea of tricking the turtles into weeping is now considered a bit vulgar. A more ethical alternative has been proposed, that the price of admission for a show should be set at two tears, one from each eye, payable after the performance; and only if the show has the desired emotional impact.

THE PRODIGAL BEARD

David had been growing his beard for years and he was very proud of it, he thought it looked especially manly and even heroic when his hair was cut short and he wore a white seaman's jumper with a roll neck.

But then, one day, it started to itch, and the itching continued all morning and grew even worse into the afternoon and, by evening, it was unbearable and so he suddenly had an impulse to shave the damn thing off and he jumped up and went into the bathroom and found a razor in a cabinet above the sink.

It was difficult getting the beard off his face because the hairs kept clogging up the blade, and the mirror misted up from the steam of the hot water, and he couldn't see what he was doing, and the damaged razor often pulled the hairs out of his cheeks and chin rather than cutting them cleanly.

So he shouted "Rwaaargh!" and that seemed to help.

It helped with the pain and it helped to make him feel manly again, just as manly as when the beard was parked on his face.

"I will always shout *Rwaaargh!* whenever I shave in future, if indeed I do shave after this instance," he vowed to himself.

Slowly the skin under the hairs and soap emerged and it was pink and smooth and marked with only a few cuts and pimples and he blinked at it in astonishment, for it didn't really seem to have much to do with him.

"Are you David?" he asked the mirror and his reflection asked the same question of him at exactly the same time. And he nodded.

"Yes I am," he said confidently.

When he had shaved his entire face he had to shave it again to make sure no hairs escaped the massacre and then he washed the razor under the tap and put it away. He pulled the plug of the sink and waited.

But the water didn't drain. The hairs had choked the plughole.

"What a nuisance!" he sighed.

The water was so murky with soap that he couldn't see what was happening, so he immersed his hand in the depths and probed with his fingers. He felt the mass of hairs in the plughole and he stirred them around and this appeared to work. It pushed some of the hairs down and others followed.

The water began to drain away slowly and he continued stirring and prodding the matted mass of hairs until eventually they were all gone. Then he cleaned the sink and washed his hands and face and dried them on a towel and blinked at himself in the mirror and attempted different expressions.

His final expression was a grin because the itching had stopped.

Pinkness was his main impression.

"I look less manly but I'm more comfortable. Was that worth the price? I guess it was," he told himself uncertainly.

224

And he went back to his bedroom and dressed himself. But the white seaman's jumper no longer suited him, so he took it off and wore a green cardigan instead, and he wandered out into the world and for the remainder of that day he noticed that he walked with a shorter stride than before.

"You have removed the nest!" his friends cried when they saw him.

"Don't you think a shave suits me?"

"Of course it does!" each one would reply. "You look younger and I dare say that the munching of peaches, slurping of soup and kissing of women will be facilitated by the bold action you have taken!"

They were trying to humour him, he realised.

And he noticed that they didn't invite him to come on any mountaineering trips or camping expeditions or rafting adventures this time - they nearly always asked him to do something along those lines!

"Perhaps shaving was a mistake," he mused to himself.

A little voice seemed to whisper, "I'll be back soon. Don't worry! Give me some time and I'll reappear in the same place."

He looked around but he was alone. The skin of his face tingled and vibrated and hummed like the membrane of a drum.

David frowned. Was his face actually talking to him?

If so, it would be far wiser to ignore whatever it was saying. Smooth cheeks and chins can't be trusted with the truth. They are more likely to tell bare-faced lies than is an unshaven visage. He assumed that his ears were playing tricks on him, for they had always been mischievous ears.

"Who said that? There's no one else here right now!"

"I am your unborn stubble."

"And why should I believe that? Show yourself!"

"I will. Give me time..."

David snorted and strode away but with his shorter steps it took him a long time to reach his destination, which happened to be the shops where he bought his weekly supplies. He did his shopping and

225

returned home and waited for someone to call him on the telephone and invite him to take part in intrepid exploits, to climb up a cliff, or go down a pothole, or pick a way through a forest or marsh, but even friends who lived in remote parts - and couldn't possibly know that he had shaved - now failed to contact him. They must have sensed the truth.

"Until my beard grows back I must do other things."

And that's exactly what he did.

The sorts of things that men without beards do might often seem to be the same sorts of things that men with beards do, or could do if they chose; and for all I know they really are the same to all practical intents and purposes. But there still seems to be a subtle difference, a slight discrepancy.

David cleaned the house with a feather duster, then he went through his wardrobe and tried on clothes that he hadn't worn for years, then he combed and brushed his hair in several different styles, and finally switched on the television and watched a show about people baking cakes against each other. After ten minutes, he rose from the sofa and went into the kitchen to boil the kettle.

Instead of brewing his usual coffee, he made a pot of teaand, when it was ready, he poured it into a cup rather than a mug.

He returned to the sofa and sipped it delicately with pursed lips.

"Be patient," a ghostly voice seemed to say.

"Leave me alone," snarled David; but it wasn't much of a snarl because if a man snarls at his own face his snarl will snarl at the snarl and some sort of snarl jam is the result. Human beings instinctively avoid this.

The days passed and life continued in the same mildly odd manner.

But the beard gradually came back. It was like watching a distant figure on the horizon coming closer all the time. At first this figure is just a speck, then it becomes bigger and slowly takes shape, and it is possible to discern the fact it has a head and body and arms and legs and is a living being.

The stranger lifts an arm to wave and you recognise him as a friend.

That's how the beard returned.

David had no doubts it *was* his beard, the same beard he had removed and that now had managed to find him again, growing from the hypothetical inside of his soul to the harsh reality of the outer world. It looked and felt the same and he wore it with the same pride. So he tore off his green cardigan, found his white seaman's jumper and went outside, head held high as if his beard was some sort of weather vane and needed to be sharply angled into the wind.

"I'm ready for an adventure!" he said to the first friend he encountered.

"Let's go on one!" came the glad reply.

And thus was he accepted back into the company of men who climbed, hiked, camped, swam and did other such things.

His old life returned with all its ordeals and joys...

But after a couple of weeks his beard started itching again, and although he did his best to ignore the sensation it soon became so intense and unbearable that the urge to do something about it overcame him. So he shouted, "Rwaaargh!" and ran into the bathroom and snatched up his razor blade.

Once again, the sink was clogged by hairs and once again he used his fingers to push them down the plughole until they were gone. His expression in the mirror was glum and happy at the same time; and, yes, such a combination is possible - for what the eyes might say, the mouth can deny.

A regular cycle had been set in motion: a repetition of events that would become as familiar as the seasons or the lunar phases.

He lived a sedate life without a beard and a more thrilling one when it grew back but he came to enjoy *both* conditions. And his friends learned to accept the fact he was a more complex character than before.

The cycle settled down into an absolutely predictable pattern.

Every six weeks he shaved off his beard.

227

And, from the instant he shaved it off, it started to come back. David's situation was not unlike a man who carries a cat into the garden only for it to enter the house through the catflap again; but welcomes its return. It was just a case of living two lives in the same body at different times.

A bearded life and an unbearded one. One life in which climbing, canoeing and bivuoacking were the norm; and another in which domestic chores were the standard. He was a man on a lifestyle roundabout and his beard was the source of the motive power for the ride. Wild man/civilised man.

Ten years had now passed since his stubble first spoke aloud.

David was preparing for an early night. His beard was full and bristling. Early tomorrow morning he was due to go sailing on the ocean. The itch was terrible but he resisted it and reminded himself that once this adventure was over he would be free to shave it off. Willpower was paramount.

But as he was passing the bathroom on the way to his bedroom he weakened and his will snapped. He went into the bathroom and took up the razor and before he could stop himself he had shouted, "Rwaaargh!"

And so, inevitably, the beard came off; and it went down the sink and ended up in the same sea he was going to sail the following day. The itch went with it and David's chin was free from the irritation but...

He wasn't very happy, for he had let himself down.

"I will have to cancel the exploit," he muttered. "For my friends will think I am feeble and unworthy of aspiring to be a hero."

This thought pained him and all night he lay awake on his bed.

The sun rose and peeped through his window.

He blinked at it and abruptly he jumped out of bed and began dressing - but not in the green cardigan. Nor did he comb his hair.

"Why should I give up so easily?"

New determination spread through his veins. "Yes indeed! Why should I humbly submit to the judgment of my peers on this particular topic? Why can't a man with a smooth face be a proper adventurer too?"

He left his house with his face set in a frown of power and he met his friends at the harbour and he dared them to meet his gaze.

"Yes, my cheeks and chin have no hairs upon them! So what? My biceps, triceps and other muscles are the equal of what they were! I can still reef a sail or pull an oar or bash a sea serpent on the noggin with a marlinspike! Judge me not by the lack of friction of my visage but by my actions!"

So overwhelmed and impressed were his comrades by this speech that they didn't attempt to argue with him. He was accepted as a member of the crew; and off they scudded over the briny deeps, and he stood in the prow and kept a look for the rocks and sandbanks that would make the voyage hazardous; and spray washed his clean face and made it cleaner, but he didn't flinch.

The sun set and twilight turned to dusk and dusk turned to night but still at his post he stood. He insisted on this because he wanted to prove that a clean shaven man can still be a hero. The rest of the crew retired to their hammocks below deck and he was left alone with the sea and the darkness.

He did his best to remain awake but he must have fallen asleep while standing at the rail for his eyes closed and when they opened he realised that something had crawled out of the sea and onto the ship; and it was a something that was slithering towards him, a presence that was more shadowy than the shadows themselves but that made a noise like the rustle of a magic carpet when it lands and slides along the polished marble terrace of an eastern palace. Not that David had seen a magic carpet do such a thing, but details like that don't count.

He gulped but then he steadied his nerves. "Who is it?"

Expecting to discover that his friends were playing a joke on him, or else that a giant octopus had clambered aboard the ship, he prepared for laughter, or a fight, but in fact he was confronted with a greeting.

229

"Hello David. We've come back early. This was possible because we are able to take a short cut now you are out here."

David frowned into the blackness. "My beard?"

"Yes, it's us. Your beard!"

"You refer to yourself in the plural but I only have one beard. I have only ever had one beard. It is my beard, mine."

"Of course. And we are that one beard. Why do you assume that one thing can't exist many times? If you see a particular shade of the colour red in one location, and then see the same shade in another location, it doesn't mean there are *two* reds but still only *one*. They are the same red, one red. And so it is with your beard. You have only one, which is yours, but it can exist many different times; and so it has, for you keep removing it and sending it away."

"I send it down the plughole," answered David.

"That's correct and where does the plughole lead? To the sea!"

"And I am on that sea now."

"Indeed you are. So why should we return to your face the slow way, by growth from inside you, when we are also here?"

"But you are much longer than the beard I had. If you return to my face I insist on only wearing one of you. That's fair!"

The voice was faintly bewildered. "There *is* only one of us. One of us but many times. The same number of times that you shaved us off. We have floated here back and forth on the currents and slowly we met and amalgamated into a mass of tangled hair, a Sargasso-sized net of hirsuteness. And we have climbed up on this ship to be reunited with you, for you to wear us again."

David was unable to move as the beard mounted his leg and undulated over his torso and surged up to cover his face, attaching itself by splicing its hairs with the tiny specks of emerging stubble. The splicing was done expertly and it is well known among those who frequent the sea that a knot will reduce the strength of connected ropes by one third but that a proper splicing preserves the strength entire. There was no way David could yank it free now.

Nor did he want to, especially, for it was warm on a chilly night, and drowsiness overcame him at last and he curled up and slept out in the open, his duties forgotten but unnecessary anyway, for the ship had long since passed the region of rocks. Stars glittered down on the cocoon that encased him.

That cocoon was made of hair. For ten years he had been shaving his beard off every six weeks, which totals no fewer than eighty-six shaves and, therefore, the same number of beards, although, as we have already acknowledged, it is still really the same beard and the plural is always singular.

His comrades found the curious cocoon at dawn and they unwrapped it and the man inside stretched and yawned. Then he stood and his beard spread out around him, covering his upper body like an apron and flowing down to the ground and carpeting much of the deck near the prow.

Those who stood close to David at that instant couldn't help themselves. They threw themselves flat and began to worship him and they did this with maximum sincerity and only minimal irony. The others followed, until at last the entire crew was prostrate and kissing the beard.

David remained unmoving, like a carved figurehead that has turned itself around and decided to become the captain of the vessel and has draped itself in masses of seaweed for the purpose of intimidation.

"Prodigious!" they cried.

"Prodigal," corrected David. "But rise and celebrate with me, for this, my beard, was shaved and now is found again."

THE UNKISSED ARTIST FORMERLY KNOWN AS FROG

He was an artist by the name of Cripen but everybody called him Frog, and his opinion on the matter didn't count. The fact he *was* a frog wasn't enough in his mind to justify the lazy appellation but people called him Frog and kept doing so anyway. He was partly resigned to it.

But only partly. In his soul he yearned to be taken seriously and a start to taking him seriously would be to refer to him by his proper name, Cripen. There was no doubt about his talent. He was an excellent artist and his canvases really seemed to say something new. And yet...

His frogginess went against him. His fundamental *essence of frog* had an inexplicable effect on critics, who did a bizarre facial contortion when they saw his work, a shudder that wobbled up and down their faces several times, losing speed on each lap until it eventually slowed to a standstill as a very deep frown that was undiluted concentrate of shudder.

If they didn't know the artist was a frog, this shudder never happened. So it was a reaction to the worker, not the work, and Cripen felt even more insulted when he learned this was the case. The truth is that the critics were anti-frog and it was a prejudice that impeded his career.

But art was his life and he couldn't give up because of the ignorance of a handful of professional critics. He continued painting as always, and he was still able to show his work in certain small exhibitions, but not once did he ever get a positive review, nor did he sell any pictures.

Thus he became the living embodiment of the famished artist but, luckily for him he was able to eat flies, so summers weren't too bad. Although, as he was a *giant* frog, there were almost too few flies in the city to satisfy his appetite fully. In winter he had to seek less wholesome food.

So he went to the opening nights of shows by many other artists in lots of galleries and there he was able to take the free snacks on offer, mainly canapés, salted nuts and pickles, generally with a glass or two of white wine. And that is how he prevented himself from starving to death.

People who knew him would sometimes come over to chat. "How goes it with you, Frog? Are you still painting?"

Yes, he would nod. How could he give it up?

"No plans to find a proper job?"

Painting was a proper job, wasn't it? What did they mean by asking such a question in a gallery? He sighed deeply.

I was sitting on the carriage of an underground train once when it stopped at a station and he came in from the platform. He hopped through the doors as they slid open and positioned himself in the space between the metal poles that are provided for standing passengers to hold onto.

Nobody looked. Commuters hate to show curiosity.

But I was fascinated by him and the fact that the carriage reminded me of an enormous artificial tadpole made me want to be a part of his life, to engage with him on some level. It's not that I thought I could help him with his career or felt pity for him. It was something else.

I think it was just a case of understanding that here was a phenomenon that might never be repeated, a peculiar situation, a giant frog that had come to London in the hope of making a success in the art world, and *not* by exploiting the oddness of his corporeal form, but simply by creating paintings considered outmoded by the trendy art establishment.

"The streets aren't paved with gold, are they?" I said.

He turned to look at me. I withered under that look and my mouth went dry and I muttered something very inane:

"If at first you don't succeed, try and try and try again."

He instantly turned his back on me.

I got off at the next station, burning with embarrassment, even though I didn't want to alight there and would be late for a meeting with a friend. I was a fool to believe that my meagre interest in him would cheer him up after all the detrimental things he heard every single day.

But from that moment it appeared that a cosmic conspiracy had decided to make me part of its workings and the ultimate aim of this plot was to mock Frog. I took my place on the crowded escalator to ascend to ground level and the stranger directly in front of me began to hold a conversation over my head with the stranger immediately behind me.

It was a conversation about art. "I hear he holds the brush in his mouth, his enormous gaping maw," said one, to which the other replied, "That makes perfect sense because he has no hands."

"Excuse me, but Frog is a friend of mine," I snarled.

It was a lie but I felt I was standing up for justice and yet the two men sniggered and rolled their eyes in reply and I was left uncertain if they had truly been talking about the amphibian painter.

"He is admirable and richly talented," I continued but in a much fainter voice, and I was grateful when the escalator ride ended and I was able to rush off into the crowds that thronged the streets.

I decided that all I wanted to do was forget about art, but everywhere I went I encountered people who seemed to have some involvement in the art world. This made me rather apprehensive.

When I reached my apartment I disconnected the phone and refused to leave for several days. That broke the malign spell and the world was normal again when next I ventured out. Indeed I completely forgot all about Frog over the following weeks and then one day I was crossing a bridge when I saw some graffiti painted on the stone balustrade at the halfway point. I say 'graffiti' but in fact it was a picture of exquisite beauty.

It showed the view from the bridge but not as the view really was - sooty and grey and depressed - but vibrant and alive and bursting with positive energy. It was a skilful piece of work because it gave the impression that the entire spectrum of ecstatic colours had been used and yet, in truth, the work had been executed entirely in shades of pale green.

The signature said: *CRIPEN* and it was beautifully lettered.

I stood and appreciated it for half an hour.

Then I started to see other paintings around the city, all of them signed by Cripen and all done in green paint. Unable to exhibit in galleries he had decided to share his talent with the world on the streets.

I couldn't decide if this was a wise course of action for him to follow or a sign of defeat, that he had started to give up.

So then I tried an experiment. I went along in the middle of the night with a tin of paint and a brush and obliterated his signature on a small selection of the paintings. It had occurred to me that if the works were anonymous, unattributed, people would like them better, would see them for what they really were, would finally show the appreciation they deserved.

But my plan backfired. Somehow, the rumour spread that these artworks without a signature were the work of Frog. And the fact they were unsigned was seen as proof that he even he disliked them.

In fact it soon became worse than that, for *every* example of street art that lacked the name of its creator was also cited as one of Frog's latest efforts, and so the truth of his unique talent was turned into a big lie by tens of thousands of examples of urban dross and amateur scrawls.

I only saw him once more after that. He was standing in the rain outside an art gallery and peering through the window at the people inside. The gallery was a small one and the door was too narrow to permit him to enter. He gaped at the food he was unable to reach and his hunger was a palpable force. I was embarrassed and wanted to pass him without making eye contact but he spoke to me and I stopped in my tracks. He groaned:

"If only I had a patroness, but no woman will look after me. I'll never be kissed, cared for, tolerated and indulged because there are no giant lady frogs in this city or anywhere in the wide world."

"The world is not so wide," I answered stupidly.

"It's wide enough," he said.

"Where do you get your green paint from?"

"That's my blood, you see."

This reply was delivered in such a lonesome tone of voice that I shivered with the fear and repulsion that are always just beyond sympathy and this shiver undulated me back into motion and I hurried on.

235

In the weeks that followed I tried to forget this meeting but it haunted me. I replayed the scene over and over in my mind. I couldn't offer him any comfort for his predicament. But then, one day, as I was walking down a staircase, an appropriate thing to say occurred to me.

I knew I would never rest until I had delivered this message to him, so I went out to search for him, making enquiries among the places where artists go. Finally someone gave me his new address.

It was in the poorest quarter of the city, a dilapidated house in one of the most tumbledown streets I have ever seen. I knocked on his door to no avail, so I went to rap my knuckles on the window, and as I did so I happened to glance through the grimy glass into the interior.

I saw a room with walls and ceiling covered in murals, all of them superb and all of them green. In the middle of this room, which was bare of furniture, I saw a shape that surely belonged to him.

I shouted out my message, "Cripen is an anagram of Prince."

But it was too late. He had croaked.

No Fury

A wise man once said, "Hell hath no fury like a woman scorned," and he wasn't only a wise man but a wise man who knew what he was talking about. It really is important to be aware of the difference.

There are hundreds, thousands, possibly millions, of wise men, even *very* wise men, in this world of ours, but the majority of them don't know what they are talking about.

This doesn't make them any less wise, but it does make them wrong. Yes, you can be wise and wrong.

Being wrong often has repercussions, but those repercussions might take a long time to catch up with the person they are intended for. On the other hand, they frequently manifest themselves without delay, so don't be too nonchalant if you are wrong and hope to get away with it.

As a wise man said, "If you go into the forest with a walking stick, don't be surprised if one day a tree walks into your town carrying a human leg." The wise man who said that was me. Yes it was.

I am also a wise man, one of the wise men who are right as well as wise. I nearly always know what I'm talking about; and on those rare occasions when I don't know, I am aware that I don't know.

Because I am a wise man, one of the best of all wise men, I'm able to act on the wisdom of other wise men in an effective and noble manner. Thus I once decided to do something *remarkably* wise.

Just to be wise to an ordinary degree wasn't enough. Even to be very wise was insufficient. I wanted to be so wise that my wisdom would reach new levels and set standards of unsurpassable sagacity.

I decided, no less, to save the endangered souls of multitudes of people. I decided to do this without thought of any recompense. I decided to do it for the sake of being a good as well as a wise man.

By employing the word 'people' I am being disingenuous. It was only the souls of women that I planned to save. I would have attempted to save the souls of men too, but I simply didn't know how. Just because I am wise doesn't mean I'm a genius. I am as fallible as anyone else.

But how does one go about saving women's souls?

Well, there's a big clue in the saying of the wise man I quoted above, not the saying that *I* said, but the saying of the *other* wise man, the first wise man I mentioned in this document. A very big clue.

Some clues are so big that they stop us seeing them in total, in the same way that a mountain can't be appreciated in full when we are too close to it; so these clues are baffling rather than enlightening. This is absolutely the case with what the wise man said about Hell and fury...

I mean that people are familiar with this saying and they often quote it to each other, nodding their heads in understanding and agreement; but they don't actually understand it and therefore can't really agree with it. The truth within this saying is too immense to absorb correctly.

But I was wise enough to be able to ponder on it for a long time, and from a moral distance, a distance great enough to show me the outline entire, and for my ponderings to be fruitful, insightful and unique. And that's what I did; and it suddenly occurred to me that here was a sure method of protecting women from the eternal torments and despair of the fiery pit.

For it is logical that if Hell has no fury like a woman scorned, then there are no scorned women in Hell, otherwise Hell *would* have a fury comparable to a woman scorned, and not just comparable but identical, namely the fury of any or all of the scorned women massed down there.

So if I went about scorning women, I would be saving them from future damnation. I would be saving their divine souls. Imagine that! No more Hell for uncountable numbers of women who would surely end up there if it wasn't for my utterly astounding and very wise generosity.

First, I had to find out what constituted the act of scorning. I consulted a number of books, including dictionaries and encyclopaedias, and learned that to scorn someone requires a measure of contempt for them; and to have contempt necessitates that one feels they are beneath you.

Contempt isn't the same as hatred, for if you hate a person it means you fear them. When you feel contempt, there is an inherent aspect of superiority in your attitude. They can't hurt you, only irritate you by the mere fact they dwell on the same planet as you, that you share reality.

We express our hate with schemes, tricks, violent actions; but contempt is expressed with words and expressions, perhaps even only the angle of a nose or chin, the arch of a single eyebrow, a slight sneer.

Accordingly, I mounted my bicycle and proceeded to pass women with a look of absolute derision on my face. I know they noticed this. If there was any doubt in my mind, I would turn and pedal back towards them, still carrying the same look. My nostrils were flared, my lips tight.

Thus did I scorn women, hundreds, thousands, tens of thousands of them, over a period of many long years, in winter and summer, day and night, in rain and shine. Eventually I would have been the salvation of millions, but our lives are fragile things and so are bicycles. I grew old.

My bicycle rusted, my joints stiffened. Yet I could retire with pride, for I had prevented uncountable numbers of females from going to Hell when they die. They still remain unaware of what I did for them; and consequently I have acquired a reputation as crank instead of saviour.

I am writing this document in order to put the record straight. I am a wise and good fellow. If you are a woman and reading this right now, remember that I may have saved you from a horrible afterlife. If you are a man, then you must save yourself, there's little I can do for you. Sorry.

THE BELLY ORCHARD

I was told at a young age that if I swallowed them, the pips of an apple would remain lodged in my stomach and would germinate there and grow into trees inside me. This warning was designed to discourage the swallowing of apple pips, but in fact it had the opposite effect.

It seemed a very practical solution to the obtaining of free food, because if trees really grew inside me, they would be apple trees; and these apple trees would produce apples of their own and the apples would fall from the branches to the pit of my stomach, nourishing me.

Thus I made specific efforts to ensure I swallowed all the pips in every apple I was given. I became more interested in the pips than in the fruit itself. I disliked their taste and, despite the tiny size, I found the pips tricky to get down but I persisted for the sake of my future.

Because free food made profound economic sense, even before I properly understood anything about how the world worked. As I grew older I realised my stomach was not big enough to contain many trees, but I thought that *one* might still be accommodated without discomfort.

Yet many years passed and none of the seeds succeeded in growing into trees and the only thing that grew at all was my disillusionment. I became a man and went to university, where I was informed that apple pips contain traces of cyanide and should not be ingested in bulk.

But I did not entirely cease swallowing them. My rate of consuming pips steadily decreased, of course, but I never wholly abandoned my hopes of letting a tree reach full maturity within my belly. I still dreamed at night that roots and branches were spreading out in my depths.

I think that the swallowing of the occasional pip became a superstition for me. What I mean by this is that I no longer believed with my rational mind that a tree would grow inside me, but I found it impossible to shake off a feeling that the next pip might be the miraculous one.

At last the time came when I deliberately swallowed no more than a pip once a month and to all intents and purposes I was cured of the absurd delusion that had been implanted in me by kindly but thoughtless adults. I became a very mature and responsible fellow, a graduate.

This is not to make the claim that graduates are automatically mature and responsible. By no means! But the graduation process acted as a catalyst on my attitudes. I changed from a gullible person into one so sceptical in outlook that I scarcely credited the existence of trees at all.

On the eve of my final departure from the university, I threw a dinner for my closest colleagues. These were admirable chaps, more sensible than students usually are, less smug too; and the food prepared for us was of a diverse nature, selected to appeal to all tastes. Wine also.

My room was not a large one and there was very little space left once we had all taken our places around the table. The window was open to provide air and the red curtains billowed and snapped like the sails of a small ship. Chatter and the scrape of forks filled the chamber.

The excellence of the event was marred only slightly.

Perkins ate nothing all evening.

Even the fine wine he drank very sparingly.

He had always been a somewhat quiet person, not melancholic but with a reserve that indicated an inner satisfaction that none of us envied because it had no obvious source. I blinked at him and pointed out that there was little point in coming to a dinner if one did not partake.

"I am here for the good company," he said.

This was a pleasant response and it was impossible to chide him with too much vigour, but nonetheless I was compelled to express a certain dismay that the food I had provided was clearly not up to the standards he had expected. He was mortified by my jocose accusation.

"That is not the reason at all! The meal is tremendous in every way. I am not partaking simply because I am already full."

"Already full!" I was aghast. "You ate before coming here?"

"But I really had no choice."

"Look here, Perkins, how can it be that a man has no choice as to whether he eats or not? The procedure is fully controllable. One opens the mouth, inserts the morsel, chomps on it and swallows."

"Not I," he answered.

And then to my surprise, and to the even greater amazement of the others gathered, he explained that he had an orchard inside him. They were apple trees and at this particular season of the year they

241

were festooned with fruit. Thus he was constantly satiated and never hungry.

"And how did you acquire this internal orchard?"

"By swallowing a pip," he said.

I gasped. A fellow spirit! Yes, he was a chap who had succeeded where I had failed and so my surprise rapidly turned into awe. I was a little envious, of course, more than a little if truth be told; but greater than envy was my joy that the legend was finally proven to be true.

"So those adults who instructed me were not liars after all!" I cried out in relief; and I rose to embrace Perkins, which was an awkward thing to do in view of the fact he remained seated. I flung my arms about him nonetheless and gave him a mighty squeeze as I guffawed hugely.

I felt the prod of branches beneath his skin and one or two twigs broke off with an audible but muted snapping sound.

He winced a little. And then, "You appear exceptionally delighted by my curious condition," he remarked dryly.

"I am indeed! Tell me, Perkins, tell all of us, how it is that you managed to cultivate an orchard in your stomach? I tried for many years but success has always eluded me. What is your secret? Is the lining of your belly different in composition from that of normal humans?"

He frowned for a minute in serious contemplation.

"I think not," he finally averred, "but it may have something to do with the fact that the first fruit I ate was a miniature apple. It came from a miniature tree, a *bonsai*. The plants inside me are all very small; but the quantity of fruit they produce is still sufficient to glut me."

I know nearly nothing about the art of *bonsai* trees, so I did not raise an objection as he proceeded to describe how that first tiny pip grew into the first tree that produced fruit that fell and grew into other trees, until his stomach had at least thirty trees inside it, at a rough guess.

"I do not know for certain the precise number," he said.

"Have you never been examined?"

"By a doctor, you mean?" He was horrified. "What do they know about botany? And what would a botanist know about stomachs? No, it is best that my secret is revealed only to a handful of close friends such as yourselves. I do not wish to be experimented upon by bunglers!"

And we nodded sagely at his words, for many of us had graduated in the sciences and therefore did not trust scientists.

I had many questions to ask him. I wanted to know what he did when the trees were not fruiting and whether ordinary food caught on the branches of his internal forest; whether the rustling leaves produced nausea; if the roots tickled or not; and how he never grew tired of apples.

"But I *do* grow tired of them," he replied; and then with a sigh, "I wanted to join in with this feast, truly I did, so I made no sudden movements all day. As I was walking here at a sedate pace, I was startled by a man who lost control of his bicycle and veered towards me. I jumped."

"Which made the trees inside you shake off all their fruit?"

"Yes. My preparations were ruined."

"Another question. Is there is a sun in your belly?"

He shook his head and swirled his glass. "Wine is liquid sunshine, so they say, and it does seem to be true that a claret provides all the ultraviolet radiation my trees need in order to photosynthesise."

The elegance and simplicity of this solution thrilled me. We know that a vineyard is a solar reservoir, each grape on its stalk an ellipsoid filled with the juice of the sun, with celestial warmth, with the light kisses of that star around which our world must rotate in endless waltz.

"Perkins, dear fellow, I am touched by your tale and I insist that you take one spoonful of this excellent pudding to symbolically join with us in our feast. A small spoonful will not be unmanageable for you. A token gesture, that is all. I want you to be fully a part of our celebration."

He declined the suggestion with polite firmness, but emboldened by wine and brandy, the assembled company would not permit him to refuse; and after a great deal of raucous but fraternal goading, he assented to a single mouthful of plum pudding. A plum, after all, is not an apple.

My friends insist it was this spoonful that caused the regrettable incident that followed, and that the responsibility must be shared equally between us, but I am of the opinion they are endeavouring to protect me; that it was my embrace that caused the damage, that the fault was mine.

I believe that I fatally weakened the casing of his belly.

Perkins swallowed, clamped his mouth shut, turned red, then purple, then green, rolled his protruding eyes, gripped the edge of the table, opened his jaws again, poked out his tongue, gurgled, tried to rise from his seat and fell onto the table, climbed up on it and turned onto his back.

He had scattered dishes and glasses in doing so and I was mildly annoyed by the performance, which I assumed was his exaggerated protest at being made to sample the pudding. So I leaned forward to address some words to him. But I never had a chance to begin. He promptly burst.

It was not nearly as messy as you probably imagine...

Leaves swirled around the room and the scent of apples was strong. The breeze that had been allowed unimpeded access wafted this aroma around and then diluted it to almost nothing. Miniature squirrels leaped out onto the table. Tiny owls took flight and brushed our noses.

Having your nose wiped by the wing of an owl is not something that one accepts without arched eyebrows, even when the nose requires it. I sneezed and I was not the only one. Nobody said, "Bless you."

Where Perkins had sat there was now an orchard in his place. Because it was smaller in size than orchards usually are, we all had the impression that we were standing far away from it, on the brow of an arid hill, looking down on an idealised vista, a fertile valley in a barren land.

"It is what he would have wanted," I heard myself saying.

Pathetically, we avoided each other's eyes and none of us spoke another word. Too guilty to continue eating, my guests sloped off one by one, waving a solemn farewell and leaving me alone with the tiny orchard. I could not bear to live with the thing, nor did I wish to destroy it.

I simply went to bed; and the following morning I left my room forever and caught a train to my new life. Guilt might have remained with me until the end of my days, were it not for another strange incident that occurred a decade or so later when I was hiking in the mountains.

I do not feel it is sensible to reveal which range I was exploring. All I can state is that it happened in a country famous for the beauty of its women, which means it might be in any country on Earth, for beautiful women are everywhere, even when they themselves insist they are not.

I had stopped to rest under a gnarled tree and while eating my sandwiches I heard a voice issuing from inside the trunk. I soon learned the tree was hollow and that it contained a genuine living woman.

Her voice told me her story, how the tree had swallowed her one day and how she lived there now, and how she made babies and needed a man every so often to enter the tree too in order to ensure the babies kept coming, and would I be interested? I had to think deeply about this.

I decided that what the tree had done was less justifiable than what I had done and my conscience stopped bothering me.

The tree opened to let me in. If a man can swallow a pip and grow a tree inside him in order to procure fruit, why should trees not occasionally swallow women in order to obtain babies? It seems fair.

I stayed with the woman in the tree one night. Each time a child is born to her, a magnificent stork comes along to claim it, perching briefly on the highest branches before carrying it off to a new mother.

But let us not be too fanciful.

A stork is not strong enough for that.

It is a phoenix.

CHOPSTICKS

Burton had started dating a woman who impressed him more and more each time they met. He was filled with a desire to impress her in return. She was a Chinese student and he decided to take her to a restaurant he knew that was high quality but not expensive. He wanted to demonstrate that he knew how to use chopsticks. Indeed he was an expert.

The restaurant was long and narrow. There were paintings on the walls that depicted the mountains of China. The waitress was dressed in a cheongsam and wore flowers in her hair. It all seemed very authentic to Burton, but he kept a close eye on Hongyi to monitor her reaction. She seemed pleased if not overwhelmed. He ordered tea for them both while they studied the menu.

At the far end of the elongated room was an old piano. Perhaps this was an incongruous touch but what did that matter? There is no pure authenticity anywhere, unless it is faked. He was happy enough and Hongyi was smiling too, which made him even happier, and when the waitress came to take their order the combined happiness of the couple made her smile a little too.

They chatted while they waited for the food. Burton was an archivist in the university library and she was studying to be a translator in the same university. Neither was in a rush for romance but they enjoyed each other's company and wanted to see what might develop over time. Although generally introverted, Burton did have a theatrical streak inside him and the urge to express it.

The food arrived and the meal began. Hongyi picked up her chopsticks and started eating, but Burton turned the exercise into a flamboyant drama. He clicked the sticks together in a rhythm designed to catch her attention and then he wielded them with incredible dexterity. He used them to fling morsels of food into the air and catch them in mid flight. Hongyi blinked at him.

"Note the position of my wrist," he said, then before she could reply he summoned the waitress. "Bring me a longer pair please. These are too easy to use," he told her.

"A longer pair? Certainly."

She returned with chopsticks that were as long as his arm. Burton thanked her and proceeded to feed Hongyi from her own plate. She laughed as he did this, partly from amusement and partly from embarrassment. These chopsticks were too long for Burton to feed himself with, but this didn't matter at all. He wanted to feed her across the table. Then he stopped and called the waitress again.

"These are very good chopsticks," he explained, "but I would be very grateful if I could have an even longer pair."

The waitress brought him what he asked for. The new chopsticks were so long that Burton was able to feed the only other couple in the restaurant at that hour. They thought it a good joke and didn't resist. His skill really was amazing and not a speck of food was dropped. He worked the chopsticks as if they were an integral part of his anatomy. But his theatrical streak was even more ambitious.

"Do you happen to have an even longer pair?"

The waitress said that she did.

Hongyi was about to say something, maybe to gently protest at this escalation, but Burton was too carried away to halt the process and he placed his finger to his lips. Hongyi puffed out her cheeks in dismay at this curt gesture. The waitress returned with a pair of chopsticks so long that they had no end in sight. They vanished through an open window halfway down the length of the restaurant.

"Where do they go to?" he asked.

The waitress shrugged. "No one is really sure, but probably to some other district of the city. Shall I make enquiries?"

247

"No need," answered Burton. "They go where they go and that's good enough for me. Let's try them out..."

And he manipulated them precisely and intensely for several minutes. He was unable to see what he was doing and so had to work by touch alone. He screwed up his face in concentration and beads of sweat rolled over his forehead and combined into droplets as large as small radishes. He was no longer able to maintain a blasé expression. Working these monstrous chopsticks required real effort.

"Is it working?" Hongyi wondered.

"Yes, it seems so. I am feeding someone at a great distance. I don't know who they are but I'm sure they are enjoying it."

After another five minutes, he finished and wiped his mouth with a red napkin. "Bring me a longer pair!" he called to the waitress. She was surprised but ready for him and brought them. These vanished out of another window further down and when he picked them up his eyebrows rose and he whistled. "Quite heavy."

"Because they are so very long," she explained.

"How long exactly?"

"I am only able to give you an estimate. They reach from here into a neighbouring country. That's my guess."

"There's one way to find out," said Burton and he commenced operating them with all the strength and delicacy at his disposal. Hongyi watched him and a flicker of doubt crept into her expression. He was clearly a chopsticks genius but wasn't he overreaching himself now? He seemed to have forgotten all about her. He shut his eyes to avoid being distracted while he worked.

He was probing and feeling something with the distant tips of the immensely long chopsticks. He was like an artist painting miniatures and making very precise movements with a delicate brush. The strain revealed itself in the muscles of his face and neck, which began to swell and twitch. He was in his own world, a surgeon performing an operation in his dreams at a great distance. And then—

"I am feeding a family across the sea," he announced.

"Are you sure?" asked Hongyi.

248

"Certain. What else could it be?" Burton kept his eyes closed but he reclined in the chair. "No problems at all. Bring me a longer pair!" he called to the waitress, then he began humming a soft little melody on his satisfied lips. The waitress was gone for a very long time. Hongyi wondered if this meant there was no longer set of chopsticks. But she eventually came back and said gravely:

"These are very special. The owner of the restaurant was reluctant to let you have them. But I pointed out how skilled you are, so finally he agreed. Their length is fully adjustable."

"What do you mean?" cried Burton.

"They are controlled by the mind as well as the hands. If you desire them to grow longer, they will, provided you push them properly with your mind. It is a rare privilege that has been granted to you."

Burton opened his eyes to examine the chopsticks. They were black and unadorned and they drank light like petrified snakes drinking time. He took them and closed his eyes again. Then he squeezed his face and uttered a little sigh and felt the chopsticks growing. They passed through the window and into the town and into the countryside, then they crossed the sea into other lands and they kept going.

"I am feeding the occupants of a tavern in the mountains."

"Really?" said Hongyi quietly.

"Now I am venturing into the tropical zone. There are people on the beach of a remote island. I am feeding them."

"Good for you," commented Hongyi.

"Good for them," he corrected her and she winced a little. Sweat was tumbling from his face and filling his empty cup with the tea of vanity. He grimaced and used all his mental energies in the task of extending the chopsticks. Now they had reached a distant continent and were crossing the borders of many countries unopposed. The muscles in his right arm bulged and it was clear the chopsticks were unexpectedly heavy.

"I think birds are perching on them," he said.

He shook the chopsticks and smiled. "Yes, they have flown away now. That's better. There were thousands of them."

"When will you stop?" asked Hongyi.

"I will push them to the limit," he said with a cold determination in his voice that made her recoil. "Beyond China itself!"

She sat and watched him. She was tempted to get up and leave on her own, but she wanted to witness the outcome of his ambition. His eyes were still closed, his teeth clenched, his face almost scarlet from the effort he was putting into doing this deed. Then finally there came a gentle tapping on the glass door of the restaurant. She looked and saw the tips of a pair of chopsticks probing the obstruction.

It was obvious what had happened. The chopsticks were now so long they had gone right round the world and come back to the restaurant. They pushed the door open and entered. With his eyes closed, Burton was unaware they were approaching him. He worked them with his expert hand and for a moment they lingered over that hand as if they intended to snatch themselves away from his grasp. Only a moment.

They passed on. Hongyi followed their progress down the length of the interior of the restaurant. The tips occasionally touched a wall, a vase, a table leg, then continued with their journey. Finally they reached the piano. They hovered above the keyboard. Then they descended onto it and began playing a terrible tune. It was terrible in itself but also it was played badly, which made it even worse. Many wrong notes.

"What are you doing now?" Hongyi asked him.

"I am feeding an old man," he said.

He seemed oblivious of the music. He just kept working the chopsticks with his eyes tight shut while the tips of them continued to play that horrid melody over and over without variation. Hongyi realised that Burton believed his own words. He really thought he was feeding an old man with the chopsticks instead of playing a piano. He was deceiving himself rather than trying to deceive her. Then she said:

"The same way you fed all those people in other lands?"

"Exactly the same," he said.

She shook her head even though he couldn't see the gesture. Should she break the news to him or remain silent? Every time he thought he had been feeding mouths he was in fact playing this awful tune on a piano. The motions of his hand were identical in each case. He had no idea he had got it so badly wrong. She was thoroughly unimpressed. She rose from her seat, put on her coat and left.

Burton continued to play. It seemed he would never stop. He was the greatest chopsticks expert who ever lived. Hongyi closed the door behind her, shutting out the music. She walked down the street and saw that someone had hung his or her washing on one of the chopsticks to dry. There was a gentle breeze and the light was fading. On sundry parts of the globe, distant pianos cooled.

SILKY SALATHIEL

It turns out that reincarnation is true and that when we die we are reborn. I'm glad the mystery has been cleared up, but the consequences of rebirth aren't always nice. I'll tell you my own story as a demonstration of the fact. It started when I heard about a cat called Salathiel. He had his nine lives, of course, and he used them up one by one. That's what cats do and in this regard he was no different from any other feline, but a weird thing happened to his lost lives. They were all reincarnated separately. Usually the 'nine lives' of a cat are just a figure of speech but in his case they turned out to be real lives that started again from a new birth.

Each of the lives became a different animal, and one of those animals was a man, a human being. That man grew up filled with wanderlust and he developed an interest in philosophy and questions of life and death. He actually became a sort of dilettante of mysticism. One afternoon while wandering in a remote eastern region he chanced on a crumbling temple in a clearing in the jungle, and because there was a downpour of ferocious rain he decided to

251

take refuge inside. There were big holes in the ceiling that allowed water to pour in and flow out of the main entrance and cascade down the eroded steps, but it was still drier than outside.

He huddled in a corner of the main hall, but when he leaned against the wall the stones groaned and swung on a hinge. Here was a hidden doorway! It opened and as he peered into the gloom he perceived a gently sloping corridor that led to a chamber that was bathed in a fluctuating glow.

Curiosity and a hunger for novelty pushed him along the passage and into the secret room, which was perfectly circular and serenely illuminated by several lamps that hung from the ceiling on golden chains. But the one aspect of the chamber that really surprised him was a wooden perch in the very centre on which was balanced a large graceful parrot.

He couldn't help himself. He uttered an "oh!" when he caught sight of the lovely bird, but tilting its head on one side the parrot regarded his intrusion with equanimity and then said, "You are fleeing the monsoon and I don't blame you. I hate getting my feathers wet. You are welcome to wait here until the rain stops, which it surely will in half an hour. Make yourself at home until then."

"That's kind of you, thanks."

"I am a wise old bird and this temple is the place where I meditate. It's one of the few surviving ruins of a mysterious civilization that is generally ignored by historians of the region. There is magic here that seeped into the stones over many centuries and now the broken stones radiate it back out."

"How can you be so certain of when the rain will stop?"

"That's one the things I'm wise about."

"Parrots live to be very old. May I ask your age?"

"Only sixty and my name is Salathiel," said the parrot, "and I'm the reincarnation of the first life lost by a certain cat who was also called Salathiel. In fact the reason I am Salathiel too is because I named myself after him. My original name was Kwaark but I changed it when I moved into this temple and my inner eye was

252

opened by the residual magic of the place and then I suddenly remembered my former life. Most of us never recall our previous incarnations."

"That must certainly be true," said the man, "because all the books on mysticism that I've read say precisely the same thing."

"Well, it's an unnatural thing to do, and it wouldn't have happened to me if I had taken up residence somewhere else. I came inside here for the same reason you did, to escape the rain. Such a fateful decision!"

"Should we always name ourselves after our previous incarnations if we become abruptly aware of them?" inquired the man.

"It's not absolutely necessary," replied the parrot, "but it certainly makes it easier to know who was who. The truth is that I'm rather proud that I was once the first life of the cat Salathiel, because he was such a unique entity. Every living thing is unique, of course, but there was something about him that elevated him above most other cats. And even one who has gained wisdom, such as myself, can still take pleasure from an illustrious ancestry. Not that he was my ancestor in the conventional sense, because I am him in a different form, but you get my drift."

The sound of trumpeting came from somewhere outside.

"Ah!" said the parrot. "He is coming."

"The cat, you mean? I thought he was long dead."

"Another one of his reincarnations is coming, that's what I meant. This one is an elephant that is almost fifty years old. He's a reincarnation of the cat's lost third life. I don't know what his real name is, but when he gets here I will tell him who he is and I will give him a new name. Salathiel."

"What a coincidence he should be heading this way too! It is almost as if a strange force is compelling all the incarnations of the dead cat's lives to gather at the temple, drawn here by some mystic magnetism."

"You took the words right out of my beak," said the parrot.

"This is remarkable!" cried the man.

253

There was a growl from somewhere close and then a lumbering shape came down the sloping corridor. It was a black bear and now there was no need for the parrot to explain that this creature too was a reincarnation of Salathiel the cat, of his fourth lost life in fact. It was followed by a magnificent wolf, and also the elephant who barely fitted into the passage, and between their legs scampered a monkey. The chamber was already packed, but somehow there was enough room for a mongoose and a snake. A forest cat was last of all, sleek and long legged.

"I suppose I ought to explain that you are reborn aspects of the same being, all of you reincarnations of the individual lives of a most remarkable cat," said the parrot in a voice loud enough to echo in the chamber.

"Wait a moment!" objected the man. "There are only eight beasts here in total if we include you, so why not wait for the ninth to arrive before you begin your lecture? It must be on its way and should be here soon."

"Who do you think *you* are," laughed the parrot, "if not the reincarnation of the second lost life of Salathiel the cat? And now your name is Salathiel too! All nine of us are here now. It is a most pleasant reunion."

The man was shocked to hear this, but the shock quickly wore off and he accepted the fact that he had once been a cat and was now intimately connected with all these other animals, which were in a sense him too. And I was shocked by the man's shock, for the simple reason that this man was me.

Yes, I am Salathiel and I went to that temple in a spirit of curiosity and came away satisfied. But as I said at the beginning of the tale, the consequences of reincarnation aren't always nice. There was a bit of a crush when it was time to leave the chamber in the ruined temple. We all tried to depart at the same time. The elephant trod on my foot, the snake bit me, I tripped over the mongoose.

It was accidental, I know, but that didn't lessen the pain. The wolf breathed on me and made me choke with its horrid breath, the bear somehow managed to lick me all across my face with its raspy

254

tongue, the monkey pulled my ears. The parrot flapped over my head and ruffled my wet hair into an absurd hairstyle.

The only one that did nothing to me was the forest cat. Later it made up for the omission in an unexpected way. There's a certain symmetry to life, it seems.

I limped out of the jungle and recovered my health eventually. But an idea came to me that wouldn't leave me alone. I thought about the reincarnation of the ninth lost life, the one that was a forest cat. The original Salathiel was a cat and now one of his lost lives was a cat too. So what would happen to the nine lives of this forest cat? If they were all reincarnated separately and one of *them* ended up as a cat too, this could potentially be the start of a chain of immortality.

All that mattered was that at least one of the reincarnations was a cat. Maybe even an outcome that could be arranged beforehand?

The idea gave me sleepless nights and I understood that this was the injury the forest cat had caused me, a worse one than a crushed foot or pulled ears. I lay awake at night and imagined a sequence of reincarnated cats stretching back in time to the first cat ever, and forward in time to the very last cat in history, and all of them were called Salathiel, or Silky Salathiel if you want me to be more exact, the cat who did more than any other simply because he himself was more of everything, a cat of one trillion circumstances, the feline with the innumerable faces, all of them whiskered and furry, variations on the same purring theme.

His immortality would be a special kind, not guaranteed but reliant on the whims of chance or the workings of karma, whichever was really responsible in this cosmos of ours.

And then I thought about my own opportunities for immortality. I am merely a man, not a cat, not a parrot, simply a dilettante of mysticism. How can I increase a lifespan that has been limited to that of a standard human organism?

An answer came while I was recuperating from my wounds. I was swinging on a hammock suspended between two palm trees in a desert oasis. I had come out here for the silence and the freshness of the air, the opportunity for idleness.

I had brought some magazines with me to read. One of them carried a story about how lazing around in a hammock is bad for the health and a sure way of reducing a lifespan.

The solution was to exercise instead! Apparently one hour of running adds nine hours to a runner's life. I jumped out of the hammock immediately and began running around the oasis with long easy strides. I didn't run in a straight line because I didn't want to get lost in the desert. I just circled the oasis, sweat pouring from my forehead, from a brow that had once been a cat's.

An hour later I had earned my extra nine hours. But then it occurred to me that if I spent all nine of those bonus hours running I could actually increase my lifespan by another eighty-one hours. And so on. To be immortal I just had to keep running.

With immortality would come a release from the cycle of rebirth. I would remain a human being forever. I would never be an elephant, bear, wolf, monkey, snake, mongoose or parrot. I wouldn't even be a cat again. Just a man, myself, Silky Salathiel, running in a circle as enduring as the Rings of Saturn, and Saturn sounds like satin, which is also quite silky really. I just had to turn my back on rest.

If I ran fast enough I might see that back ahead of me, my own back, and catch it up and even overtake it. Why not? And if I accumulated enough bonus hours I might be tempted to share them out with other beings. That seemed the nicest thing to do, a gesture that a wise old parrot would approve of. My hairstyle still hadn't settled down. I doubted it ever would now, but it didn't bother me.

I kept running and my feet began to dig a trench in the sand, and the trench soon became a moat, and I went deeper and deeper into the ground. But I didn't stop. This was a race against time and I was determined to win.

Soon I was far beneath the desert, where it is cool and other ruined temples lurk that aren't a rendezvous for a cat's nine reborn lives.

All Your Belongings

As the train approached the station, an announcement was made that reverberated up all the carriages, and the words were clear and helpful. "We will soon be arriving in Fusk. If this is your stop, please remember to take all your belongings with you." And because it *was* Jasper's stop, he nodded once and then looked around him, pulling one of his bewildered and unnecessary faces.

The announcement had been too direct, too easily understood. Usually they were twisted into unhappy dissonance by warped gutturals, choked with static, heavy with bee swarm sounds, and they could be safely ignored. Not this one. Jasper considered his situation as he prepared to rise from his seat. The train was slowing down and the windows were full of passing buildings.

"But this coat isn't mine, I borrowed it," he told himself, and he promptly sat back down hard, as if an invisible hand had pushed him firmly and decisively. It was time to wriggle out of the coat, despite the fact it was a chilly day, and drape it over the top of the seat in front of him. He contorted himself on the seat in order to do this. For a moment he feared his arms were trapped.

But no, they came free, and the coat was off. He draped it and tried to stand again, but the rocking of the train thwarted this second effort. He was returned to his seat by gravity, much more gently this time because there was no astonishment to accompany the reversal. Then he considered his shoes. They were black and shiny, absolutely the right shoes to be worn at a job interview.

The announcement had been precise. He had to take his own belongings with him. This implied he was required to leave behind anything that wasn't his. It had felt right to divest himself of the coat in this manner, to remove not only the garment but all the responsibility of looking after it in the future. He had been happy to conform to rules and regulations in this particular instance.

But his shoes were also borrowed attire, the original property of a different friend, and they too had to come off before he might allow himself to walk the fustian streets of Fusk. With a jerk he twisted his

257

left leg in the aisle, then bent the knee and drew it up to his chin, at the same time unlacing the shoe and dropping it to the floor. It was harder to remove the right shoe in such a constricted space, but he managed it, despite the tightness of his trousers, which were elegant and uncomfortable. He was nothing if not flexible. Then he stood successfully.

The floor of the train felt cold through his socks. Jasper frowned. These socks had been a gift, hadn't they? He certainly hadn't bought them himself. Did this mean he owned them? Technically he supposed he did, but would the railway authorities see it that way? It might be the case that their rules were more stringent than those of plain honest people. He looked for a ticket inspect in order to make inquiries, to check on what exactly he was supposed to do next.

"It's really rather confusing," he said to himself, with clenched fists. It wasn't that he was angry or even annoyed but that he was miming with his hands the shape the socks would make after he pulled them off, scrunched them up and flung them onto one of the empty seats in the carriage. There were many empty seats. Few passengers went to Fusk, a town in terminal decline.

"Perhaps I ought to decline too," he continued in a low grumble. "Decline to take these socks off. Yet I can't risk disobeying the announcer's instructions. There might be unpleasant consequences if I do. Maybe I will be fined or detained in a little room. Better to be safe than sorry, so they say."

The thought of the little room made him shudder.

"Yes, yes indeed," he continued, "I was taught that lesson in school. My history teacher was an authentic sage. '*Whenever I offend people, I put on a suit of armour rather than apologise. That's because it's better to be safe than sorry.*' Those were his very words. I have never forgotten them."

The train was braking with a squeal and now it was crawling along, as if the track was cracked and had to be tiptoed over, but most trains don't have toes, so this careful slowness was more of a respectful gesture, an act of politeness, than an efficient way to move across the brittle metal bars. Wasn't it? Jasper shook his flustered head to clear such nonsense from it. He knew the real reason the train had slowed so much. It was to prevent passengers and their possessions from being flung about when they stopped. The squeal was the swinish price.

"My tie is also the property of somebody else, my brother in this case. I must take it off immediately. It is silk and he claimed it would make a better impression at the interview than no tie at all or a woollen tie would have done. I agreed with him on the matter and I still do. It must be removed..."

He flung it away and it swam through the curdled air of the carriage like a water snake in a pool, undulating its entire length.

"What else is borrowed attire? What else is not mine?"

He examined himself closely.

As he raised his head to digest what he had observed, he caught the eye of one of the few other passengers, a young man who was sitting halfway along the carriage. It was clear that this youngster resented the accidental eye contact. He lifted higher the book he was reading to shield his face from Jasper's gaze and also to proclaim to the world that he was a student and shouldn't be disturbed in his studies. But Jasper was far too desperate for answers at this stage.

"Excuse me, sir!" he blurted, "but can you assist me?"

The student shook his hairy head.

"Not with actions but with advice," clarified Jasper.

The student shook his head again.

But Jasper wasn't dismayed. He said. "It occurs to me that none of the clothes I'm wearing were bought by myself from a shop or market stall, and this is an appalling realisation to have at this stage and frankly I don't know if any scrap of material that I am wearing counts as my belongings."

The student snorted, then after a pause finally spoke.

"Property is theft," he said, and he waved the book he was reading as if to explain with its cover that his wisdom had been authenticated long ago and was in print, and that even if it turned out to be wrong it wasn't his fault because he was the messenger and nothing more, so don't shoot him or even bother him in any way, thank you very much. Jasper recoiled but remained standing.

"Is it really? I say, that's odd!"

The student refused to respond to this in any way.

Jasper abandoned him as a source of information and turned inwardly to himself, to his own experience and powers of speculation. "If property is theft, then only the items I have stolen are my rightful property. If I buy or borrow things, they aren't my belongings. This is quite a revelation."

He wanted to thank the student, but decided against it.

There simply wasn't enough time.

He undid his belt, whipped it out of the loops and allowed his trousers to puddle around his ankles like agitated crude oil. Then he unbuttoned his shirt, flapped it open like cut-price angel's wings, shrugged himself out. His underpants were next. Now he was nude, an artist's model without an easel anywhere to be seen, without a canvas or artist, without any aesthetic context.

"I am shorn," he said, then clarified, "but that's not my name, my name is Jasper, and I am denuded of my belongings."

He nodded savagely to himself, because he had obeyed the announcement in full, but then it occurred to him to wonder if this savage nod, or any type of nod at all, was rightfully his. Did he own his gestures?

Perhaps not. All his gestures were made by the outlying parts of his physical body but what was a physical body other than a temporary home for his true self? A shell for his soul. His soul was what he really was. That was Jasper as he properly was, not the pale and ephemeral flesh of his corporeal vehicle, his sweating module, the shape he travelled around in, sat around in, frowned around in. No, he was purer than that. Not perfect by any means, but a soul.

Yes, a soul, not a porous bag of knitted bones washed by gore. He loved, accepted and endorsed the old dualism, the assumption that we are spirits in meat, despite the alternative views he had occasionally heard. He was Jasper, a soul, and his body was only a borrowed item, not one of his genuine possessions at all. It was a body that lost its balance once again as the train came to a halt. He looked out of the window. Yes, they were next to a platform. Time to alight, to get out and walk the streets of Fusk to his house, but alone? Oh no, not alone.

He gazed at his wife, who was asleep in the seat by the window. She had come all the way to the distant city with him, had waited outside the office while he went into the room of ordeals for his interview, had accompanied him all the way back, and she had slept for most of the return journey.

The announcer spoke again, as clear as before but more urgent. "We have arrived at Fusk. If this is your stop, please remember to take all your belongings with you. All your belongings. This station is Fusk…"

He ought to shake his wife awake quickly, they only had a minute before the train set off again, but was she actually one of his belongings? No, she wasn't, that was the simple answer. She was an independent being, associated with him, yes, but her own woman, not a possession of his. He was required to take all his belongings with him, but she wasn't one of those. Thus there was no need to wake her. He didn't have the authority to do that, to flout the rules. He was responsible for himself, for removing his spirit from the train, but not her body.

Nor his own. Both must be left behind.

Now that he knew exactly how to proceed, he moved with great efficiency. First he stepped out of his flesh, detaching his soul from the frame that held it with a click as if unhooking it from the protrusions of his skeleton, allowing a deflating cadaver to gently sink back onto the seat. One of its lifeless arms drooped and the hand ended up resting on his wife's knee, but there was nothing sordid or proprietorial about this. His husk was without lust, without aggression, without even any assumptions about anything. Then he turned to hurry out.

He glided past the political student and saw the hairs on the fellow's arms stand up straight, but he had no time to wonder at this. Probably just an eldritch chill due to his passing. Or maybe there was

261

a political reason for it, something to do with the means of production and its control. Jasper didn't regard the question as a priority issue. He removed himself from the train, leaving through the door without needing to open it, floating a short distance away. They he hovered on the platform a few inches off the ground and rotated his wispy contours.

A whistle sounded and the train began to leave.

Jasper looked at his wife through the window. She was lolling agape against his discarded body, which had a wide smile on its face. He wondered what would happen to them now. Beyond Fusk were towns even more obscure, faded seaside resorts that hadn't been viable for the best part of a century. But the main thing was that he hadn't broken the rules. He had followed the instructions. Yes, he had taken his belongings with him, all of them, and nothing else.

The train was gone now, so he lifted his arms and allowed the evening breeze to waft him in roughly the right direction.

THE PARTIAL RAPTURE

Through the iron gates we hurry, in order to escape the streets. Unbearable out there, the shambles, the dismay. This route will take us along the back lanes. We seek the security of home. But first we must pass the church. There are broken statues here and it is impossible for us to know if they are part of the process or not. Rearing over the graves, headless. Some are toppled, the legless ones. Erosion or explosion, who can tell? Now look at this man, this remnant of a man. He wants to speak but he has no lungs. He is just a head. His lips move silently, his eyes rolling but going nowhere. We are inclined to stop, perhaps unwisely.

Can you lip-read? I know that I can't. I peer closer and see nothing but vibrations of a peculiarly disturbing kind, the two lips rippling. I confuse that urgency to express oneself with hunger. But yes, you nod, you believe you understand what he is trying to say,

262

what this disembodied head wishes to convey. We are kneeling before him, we ought to lift him, but his hair isn't long enough to entwine in my fingers and the idea of cradling him like a football under my arm is repellent. There is no blood. That isn't a factor. All wounds are sealed. A day of miracles, or one big miracle. The problem is that it didn't happen quite as it should have.

But we are only human beings, after all, and what we think is the right way for an overwhelming event to occur isn't necessarily the best way. In fact, this vanity of ours is surely what kept us whole, down here, among other sins. No part of us is missing, a relief that is also a horror. It means we weren't worthy, not even fractionally. The head cares nothing about us, concerned as it is with its own woes. "My head is wicked," it keeps repeating. We stand, because there is nothing more to learn here. That was once the priest. He had a good body and now it's in heaven. The crimes of his head I have no desire to learn. The algebra of hypocrisy.

"Shall we move him to a safer location?" you ask.

"I'm not touching," is my reply.

"We could nudge and roll him with our feet."

"Leave the thing there, please."

A little further on we have to step over an arm. Just an arm clutching flowers that writhes like a snake on the path. Someone came to visit a grave. They were Raptured up to heaven, but not their arm. The arm must have been dubious, perhaps evil. It has to remain down here, on this planet, with all the others who failed, with the rejected ones, or their various parts. Out through the smaller gate at the rear of the churchyard and we are in the narrow lanes. It is quieter here. The main street was a nightmare, a seething chaos of stumbling amputees and detached extremities, the walking headless treading on crawling hands and hopping feet.

I don't think that the statues have been partially Raptured too. How can dead stone be good or evil? There needs to be an element of choice or the exercise is worthless. Smoke drifts into the alley from a burning building. Vehicles have collided, drivers snapped out of existence, their hands no longer on the steering wheels but their feet perhaps still pressing on the accelerator pedals. Unattended stoves have set fire to the kitchens in which blind, deaf, helpless individuals are trapped by their incompetence, and the flames are spreading like angel wings.

But only if angels have wings the colour of rich wine and sultry lips. Could those twin sins have been responsible for our downfall, drink and lust? And by downfall, I mean our unchanged situation on this planet, which on the surface seems to be better than those of others, but actually is worse. The man without a body, the priest who is now just a head, has the consolation of knowing that the rest of him is in heaven. His body was pure, unsullied. Only his head was a rascal, a deviant. But as for us, every inch has been judged inadequate for paradise.

How exactly are we supposed to feel about this fact? There ought to be despair, of course, a falling onto our knees in beseeching prayer. Yet our reflex is to celebrate, to consider that we have escaped mutilation. That's natural enough. No one anticipated a Rapture like this. The general assumption, among the true believers I mean, was that the whole person would be whisked up, dematerialised in one piece, popped from this reality, inserted into a better one, into heaven itself. There was no consideration that a partial Rapture might be on the divine agenda.

It never occurred to anyone at all that some parts of us were good and other parts evil, that our legs would deserve a place with the angels but not our arms, our elbows but not our knees, that our buttocks were holy but not our hearts, that four fingers out of five had sinned, but the little finger and thumb were pious. Even if a wise man had considered such an outcome as an option, and spread the word, who among us could have guessed that the detached parts would have a life of their own, that a headless body would still be able to move around, that heads could be healthy while detached? It is a horror at odds with our spiritual outlook.

A partial Rapture is worse than no Rapture at all. The fact it happened so abruptly, without warning, is no problem. We all know that it was supposed to be a surprise, a shock, a wipe-out of the status quo. One instant, business as usual. The next, a slap across the cheeks of our souls. The good ones would vanish without warning, a little pop as air filled the vacuums where once they had been. And the spurned ones would remain on solid ground, chilled by the sudden understanding that they weren't good enough, that we aren't up to scratch, you and I.

A man with only one arm, one leg, one eye, one ear, with huge chunks absent in his torso, a man who had been exactly one half good and one half bad, undulates out at us from behind a pile of festering rubbish. He is like the uncompleted jigsaw of a snake. Probably he only wants to engage with us in philosophical speculation. But a panic has already established itself in our bones, all of which are in place, and our reaction is powered by instinct alone. You kick him and so do I. We tread on him as we flee, hand in hand, these attached hands of ours linked together by intertwined fingers, and we hear his single lung rasp in pain.

"We will soon be home."

"But how shall we carry on as normal?"

"We can't, that's the truth."

We slow our pace to a trot but keep going until the twisting sequence of lanes disgorge us into the quiet residential street where our apartment is located. Then it is with extreme relief that we unlock our front door and tumble into our home, a fortress for the foreseeable future. We draw the curtains, afraid of what might climb up to alarm us through the glass. Tongues like flatworms or intestines like roundworms of appalling size. The power is still on, though we have no doubt that soon enough it will fail. Civilisation itself surely has to come to an end in the next few days? How can mutilated workers maintain all the standards?

We are left with the uncomfortable realisation that the world now has the worst fraction of the human race left in it, and only the worst, and that we are part of that portion. Life has been difficult before, nasty, brutish, vicious. Without the modifying influence of the good people, or at least the good parts of certain people, what chance does it stand now? Very little or none at all. I pour myself a whisky but you are more cultured and sit at the piano and play a nocturne badly. You are more cultured than I, yes indeed, but you aren't especially skilled at piano music. Your notes jar my nerves, those nerves still inside me, namely all of them.

"Stop that," I beg, and you do.

But then you crease your brow into folds of speculation and say, "There must be hands out there, severed hands, homeless hands, that once belonged to musicians. We could adopt one. Then it could play the piano for us, this piano we bought but never properly use. It could play the piano and entertain us in the chaotic times that are to come." It is an outrageous idea and I support it.

"Let's find and raise a hand!"

"Only one hand? No, we need to adopt two. There are scherzos and etudes to be performed as well as the nocturnes."

I bellow, "Three!" with such mischievous delight that I spill half my whisky, and then I proceed to lick my damp shirt.

"Three hands on one piano? Splendid idea!" is your comment as you hurry off to fetch the laundry basket. When you return you set it down in the middle of the living room. It is empty, that basket. "They can live inside as if in a wicker house. We will have high quality renditions at last." And I want to jump up, embrace you and rush out to look for those hands, those three hands, that dexterous trio, but you calm down very quickly, shake your head, restrain me with the warning, "Let's not go back out until we are prepared for every eventuality..."

I know what you mean. Do we have any hatchets in the house? None. How about pitchforks? Zero. Flamethrowers? Ditto. In truth we aren't equipped for walks along the streets of hell, we never expected a situation remotely like this, a grotesque antic comedy. "You know something?" you say, and I wait to be told the very thing I never knew, and never even knew I didn't know, and you are gracious enough to provide me with the information. "We could do other acts of charity. Not just adopt a few hands. Think about it. There are bodies out there without heads, heads with no bodies. Legs

266

without the rest and the rest without legs. Arms without shoulders and shoulders that need arms. Loose eyeballs and gaping sockets."

"They are made for each other, those disparate parts?" I say.

"Mix and match!" you chortle.

It seems so obvious now. A great deed we can do. To make introductions, pair up fragments with each other, assemble new composite people from blocks of the old. It will surely help to modify the chaos, to settle down the world. If we begin and others join in, then the task can be completed within years or even months. Mosaic men and montage women. Patchwork people. The benefits will be profound, to us as well as to them. The world will be a better place than otherwise. It might even prove to be finer than if the partial Rapture had never occurred.

You join me in a drink at last. The taste is sour, yes, but our hearts feel lighter. We have a calling now, a purpose. We wince, making the faces that people unaccustomed to whisky feel they have to pull. Then we stop and gaze at each other. A thought has occurred to us, the same idea at the same time, and it has frozen our glee, frozen it so that it should tinkle like the ice we didn't include in our glasses, but of course it can't and doesn't. Then you turn our communal thought into words. You take my hands in your hands, how I love your touch, and you say:

"We are good people, clearly."

"Yes, we are. We have noble impulses."

"We plan to adopt severed hands and repair broken wholes."

"Our virtue is almost palpable."

"In that case, why weren't we Raptured too?"

"Maybe next time we will be."

"No, there won't be a next time. It's a singular event. It happens once only. We are left behind and we must face that fact. Face it with whole faces, missing no nose, eye or cheek. We are *good folks*, don't you understand? We should have been sucked into heaven. At least parts of us should be up there!"

"Has there been a mistake?"

"An administrative error, you mean? I don't know."

"But who is responsible?"

"It's not us, that's for sure. Not us at all."

"Perhaps intentions aren't enough. Maybe we never actually did anything to turn our potential virtue into kinetic merit."

"Or could it be that..."

You look at me, and I look at you. Then we nod. How do we really know that we weren't partially Raptured? Maybe we were. Nothing big is missing, nothing visible, but what about inside us? Organs might be absent now. Veins and arteries gone. Even if our hearts have been taken, we might not yet be aware. The rules seem to be that a partially Raptured human doesn't die. I check my pulse. So do you. No, our hearts are where they have always been. All the major organs are surely still in place. Why cling to a false hope? But not all body parts are important. Our hair falls out. We shed skin flakes naturally every hour of every day.

And we don't even feel that. We don't think about it. Yet how can we be sure that those hairs and flakes of skin weren't Raptured, that they aren't in heaven now? And on a microscopic level there's the question of individual molecules. We don't know if our bones, our skeletons, are exactly as they were before the miracle. They might be smaller by tiny amounts. Our flesh, our blood cells. There's no need for full despair just yet. We can still follow the plan we have devised. Rescue hands, conjoin broken people. We are together, the greater parts of us, down here, for sure, but maybe, just maybe, some crumbs of us dwell in paradise.

THE CHIMERA AT HOME

The Chimera is waiting for the next hero to come and try their luck. A vain or foolish fancy he is not. Most certainly a dreadful beast occupies a remote cave in Lycia.

The hours pass and when night finally falls the glare of the volcano on the other side of the valley drenches the landscape with a deep pulsation of colour.

The volcano never explodes. It is an open geological wound and the curdled blood rolls slowly down the slopes.

And the Chimera's cave is dimly illuminated by the distant glow. This cave on a colder mountain.

Even monsters can grow bored... The Chimera must seek a solution to the tedium of waiting. To share tales is one possibility. The lion head speaks first.

"Did I ever tell you who I was before I was joined with you two? I was a proud lion, captured one day by hunters and dragged in a net to the palace of Darius. I was kept in a room with other lions and our job was to eat condemned prisoners. One day a pious man was given to us but our jaws were locked by some spiritual force. We were unable to devour the mortal morsel. Later I learned that the man's name was Daniel. And so..."

"I was the serpent in Eden," interrupted the snake tail, who had reared high and now was swaying from side to side, "and I tempted the woman Eve with an apple and..."

"That's a boring story," growls the lion head.

"It is better than yours!"

At this point the goat calls for order, the goat head that is oddly positioned halfway along the body of the monster. Of the three constituent parts of the Chimera, the goat is the least imposing, the most domestic, the wisest.

"My friends! To argue amongst ourselves is futile. We are only one creature now. We must learn to harmonise."

"But what were *you*?" demands the lion.

"Before the accident. Before we were joined together," adds the snake, in case the goat has not understood, but the goat always understands. The goat is sagacious.

"Were you the Scapegoat that took on all the sins of a community and was expelled into the wilderness?" wonders the lion.

269

"Or the goat who was slaughtered so that Joseph's coat of many colours might be dipped in the blood?"

"My friends!" The goat is unable to look at the lion and the snake at the same time. He must constantly turn his head from one to the other. And the light pulses as the volcano dribbles lava down its own flank. "No!"

The lion and the snake fall silent.

"Then who were you?" they finally ask.

The goat sighs. Goats can sigh, it is true, but they rarely do. A sagacious sigh is softer than the exasperated kind. "The examples you have given all come from a religion and cultural tradition that is not ours. A religion and cultural tradition that are inapplicable to us. Our origins are in the ancient Classical myths and we should never lose sight of this simple fact. Daniel, Eve, Joseph: those are alien names, flights of fancy, references that have no bearing on our reality. We are the Chimera! If you wish to discuss your individual origins, please try again!"

There is a lengthy pause, a shifting of shadows.

Then the lion says, "I lived in the cave in a desert and one day I trod on a thorn. A man named Androcles sought refuge in that cave and when he saw how distressed I was, he plucked the thorn from my paw. Later I was netted by hunters and taken as a prisoner to Rome. My job was to eat condemned prisoners in the Circus Maximus. One day a victim was thrown to me and I recognised Androcles and refused to maul him. The audience was very impressed by this. And so..."

The lion head pauses for breath.

"I was one of the two serpents sent by Athena to strangle the priest Laocoön and his sons." The snake tail has taken advantage of the pause. "For he had warned the Trojans not to wheel the wooden horse inside the city walls and Athena was annoyed by this and when that goddess is angry she has a tendency..."

"...the life of Androcles was spared!" roars the lion.

"...to destroy the mortals who oppose her and so I went and crushed Laocoön."

The lion and the snake fall silent. They are waiting for the goat to rebuke them. The goat does so with an expression, not with words, and the stern but kindly face he makes is bathed in the unstable red light that turns the interior of the cave into a giant's mouth.

"And what were *you*?" the lion finally asks the goat.

"Before the accident," adds the snake.

"My friends!" The goat is smiling now, tolerant, more tolerant than it ought to be and amused by its own tolerance.

"What is our mistake this time?" he is asked.

The goat obliges with an answer. "The stories you have told me are fabrications, and I know this because they only exist for real in the future. Neither Troy nor the Circus Maximus will be built for at least another thousand years. The ancient Classical myths have a very clear chronology and we, the Chimera, are placed near the beginning of it. As for thorns and a wooden horse..."

"What about them?"

"It is a sword and a winged horse that ought to concern us more. We are waiting, always waiting, but the time is surely growing near when Bellerophon swoops down on Pegasus to slay us, to separate us from each other again."

"Ah yes, the appointed hero. Curse him!"

"Or bless him perhaps," muses the goat.

"Is life as a Chimera really so irksome?" asks the lion, but he already knows the answer. The snake flicks out its forked tongue. "Yes, it is. Of course it is!"

"We are an unnatural fusion," says the goat.

The other two nod their heads, but they are still not fully satisfied. "But what *were* you before the accident?"

The goat allows a tear to roll from the corner of its slitted eye and lose itself in the wool of his cheek. "You know the god Pan?"

"Half man and half goat," they reply.

"Well, once he was *all* goat but fate had other ideas and the top part of him was removed and transplanted. I am the head of Pan, my friends, and my lower half is off somewhere else, playing his pipes and cavorting with nymphs and so..."

Another lie. But can we blame the poor Chimera for taking refuge in fantasy? The truth is less mythical and more chemical. In the books of Servius Honoratus we read that in Lycia there was a volcano by the name of Mount Chimera. The base of this volcano swarmed with snakes, higher on its slopes were pastures where goats lived, and near the summit a pride of lions dwelled.

These creatures avoided the dribbles of lava successfully for many generations but one day a spurt more vigorous than usual discharged a quantity of molten rock at an unexpected velocity. One of the lions was swept away with the bubbling stream and carried down the flank of the mountain, where he collided with a stray goat, and this pair continued to descend to the zone of serpents.

A sleepy snake was caught up too and the intense heat fused the three beasts into one. It took the Chimera a long time to grow strong and competent. It was unsteady on its feet at first and found it difficult to control its fire-breathing abilities. Some of the lava must have got inside it. Unable to live at any level of Mount Chimera and be accepted there, it found a new home on a mountain across the valley. And that's a fact.

DOGEARS

He entered his hotel room and threw his bag in a corner and then gazed around and nodded once to himself without conviction but also without rancour. A typical cheap hotel room, not very spacious, quite clean, with an uninspiring view through the window of the street and the crumbling buildings of the district. Good enough for one night. He was on his way from one side of the continent to the other and this was the midpoint of the journey. Everything was middling.

We muddle through, he told himself pointlessly, all of us, as he removed his shoes and lay on the bed, stretching his cramped limbs, staring up at the ceiling. Later he would have a shower and go down to dinner but right now he wanted to ease his mind out of this reality and into another. The book he was reading was in the pocket of his jacket. He pulled it out and turned to the page he was on, marked by a fold, a dogear. He respected stories but not books. He always dogeared pages.

Other readers despise the habit. They use proper bookmarks or old train tickets, dried leaves, lengths of ribbon or string, even banknotes. He preferred to dispense with such extras. The book was capable of marking itself and he was there to take advantage of the fact. Back into the narrative went his focus, the words hurried his awareness along a journey unlike his own and yet oddly familiar. It was different in sensibility yet it had the same corners, turnings, reversals.

He shifted his position on the bed and frowned, snapped back into the bigger world, the prosaic hotel room. The pillow on which the back of his head rested was uncommonly hard. Or rather it had something beneath it with edges. But what? He groped with a hand and pulled out a book. Some former guest must have left it there accidentally, forgotten in the fuss of packing up and moving on. He examined the cover and a small gasp of surprise escaped his lips. Then he laughed.

It was exactly the same book that he was reading. But in a hardcover edition, larger and more expensive than his pocket sized paperback. How curious! Or was it really? The book was a popular one, doubtless bought by millions, and yet he felt a real connection to that unknown guest and it wasn't entirely a pleasant sensation. Almost as if he was intruding on a previously claimed experience. Be realistic, he warned himself, it is only a minor coincidence. Perhaps even a useful one.

He cast aside his paperback and claimed the hardback as his prize. He opened it and began searching for his page. Then a series of chills ran up his spine, even though his back was sunk in the mattress, as he discovered that this book too had been dogeared and precisely at the point where he had dogeared his copy. His predecessor had abandoned his reading on exactly the same page that he himself had paused on. What did this mean?

Probably nothing too significant. In fact his reaction ought to be pleasure rather than apprehension. He was in touch with a kindred soul but also leaving that soul behind, for every page he read beyond the fold of the dogear pushed him further into territory unknown to his predecessor. This earlier explorer of the book had reached a certain paragraph, yes, but he was forging deeper into the forest of words on a later expedition. His destination was the very end of the book and from there a simple step back into the real world. Success had eluded the other reader. The way ahead was clear.

But he felt tired and saw no need to rush onwards through the chapters. A shower and a meal before sleep were the wisest courses of action. He dogeared a new page, closed the book and slipped it under the pillow. Then he rose and made his way towards the bathroom. Only now did he notice the rug he walked on. A corner had been folded over. Someone had dogeared it. His predecessor! Certainly, but why? In order to remember the room, he concluded, this particular room among many in the hotel.

The full implications of this discovery were troubling to dwell on. Did the dogear in the rug signify that the return of that other guest was imminent? He would surely want his book back, unless he had forgotten it, which was more than likely. Books are tools of little importance to many people. I must enjoy my shower anyway, he told himself. And that is what he proceeded to do. The water pressure was high and the shower cubicle was narrow.

When he emerged, dripping, fifteen minutes later, he reached for the towel on the rail. His arm froze in an extended position as he saw the fold in the towel. His predecessor had used it too, had marked which towel it was, undoubtedly was planning to return to it, to complete the drying of a body that miraculously was still damp. It seemed sinister. Then the bright thought occurred to him that his predecessor might have been a woman. He felt less threatened but more embarrassed. With enormous effort he snatched the towel from the rail.

And wrapped it around himself. He left the bathroom and walked to the window to draw the curtains. He noticed the fold in one of them as he pulled them together and he recoiled. Was this dogear to help that mysterious woman remember the window or the view through it? He dressed himself and went down for dinner. It was a relief to be out of that room. I knew all along I was an intruder, he told himself, but he shrugged and took his place at a vacant table in the dining room.

He realised after a rather absurd pause that in fact all the tables were vacant. He was the only guest present. Then he saw the fold on the tablecloth but before he had a chance to move to a different table the waiter appeared from a little hatch in the wall to take his order. This might have been a comical scene in a fiction but the reality was unsettling. The waiter was a diminutive and agile fellow. He stood in anticipation and his eyebrows danced on his forehead like brackets in the flames of a burning text. No, that was too elaborate.

He studied the menu and ordered an omelette and the waiter went away with an amused snort, climbing back through the hatch and descending into the kitchen below. Then he realised that a man as small as the waiter, only half the average size, could plausibly be regarded as a folded person. Someone had dogeared his entire body. That was ruthless, possibly demented, and inspired little hope that events would become less strange in the near future. But he drank a glass of water and awaited his meal calmly enough. What happens must happen, he advised himself. Accept it.

There was the soft hum of a motor, the squeak of gears, and the waiter reappeared in the mouth of the hatch. He was riding the hydraulic lift mechanism in order to save his little legs. But save them from what? From more than the obvious, this much was clear. The omelette steamed on a large plate. It naturally had a fold in it. Someone had planned to return to it, had dogeared the exact point on the circumference of its flavour.

"Do you know who stayed in my room before me?" he asked the waiter, but it was a useless question. The waiter raised a finger to his lips to indicate that he would say nothing and he flicked a napkin at the dust motes in the air and turned to walk away. The napkin had a fold in it. He reached the hatch and the delights of the hydraulic mechanism within and disappeared. It was not at all apparent that he even knew the answer to the question.

The omelette was devoured, dogear and all, the glass of water was drunk and the meal was finished. He had planned to go to bed immediately after his repast but now he could not stomach the thought of returning to his room. I will enjoy a walk instead, he told himself. He stood and left the hotel and sauntered down the narrow street, a crevice between crumbling buildings that still had charm. He turned the corner and realised at the same instant that corners are dogears in city schemes. In the layout of an urban zone they are deliberate folds.

He glanced up at the sky. A few clouds drifted across the blue dome and one of them had a fold in it. Who on earth would want to remember a particular cloud and take it up again where they had left off? Perhaps no one on the earth but above it, an entity who enjoyed reading the sky. No, that was too fanciful. Better to keep walking and ignore those white masses of cool vapour. He passed several shops but went into none of them. He knew that it would be unbearable to make a purchase here at this time. He felt sure the banknotes in his wallet would all be folded.

This mysterious woman, if she really was a woman, was close now. Her invisible presence was a tangible absence, despite the contradiction inherent in that claim. Who was she? More to the point, who was he? He had forgotten his own name, he now realised. Forgotten too the reason for his journey from one side of the continent to the other. Forgotten even which continent it was. Why should this be?

Because he had no fold in his soul. That was the solution. He had neglected to dogear his identity, his purpose, his existence. Now he was bereft on a street with a steep gradient and sliding gently down towards the harbour. The sea sparkled but the sun was sinking. On the horizon a sailing vessel with a large square sail. There was a dogear in that sail, of course. He reached the harbour and sat on a low wall, dangling his legs into a very minor void. He opened his mouth to laugh but no sound emerged. Someone had folded his tongue. He was speechless, mirthless, dogeared.

The sail on the distant ship slowly grew larger. He was certain that the imaginary woman was on board. She was returning to reclaim and resume the things she had abandoned halfway, including himself. The sunset ended. He would wait forever if necessary. The hours passed, each one with a folded minute within it, and the moon came up. It was not quite a full disc. A flap of the dark side had been folded over the bright face. A dogeared moon. The ship was very near, the creaking of its timbers was audible. Another voyage almost over. He sighed but not with discouragement.

There are inevitable pauses in all our lives. He had always marked his with a fold. Others despise the habit. They use train tickets, wedding invitations, death certificates. The dogear was about to be smoothed out of the text of the story of his life. The shop was docking. He no longer expected the passenger to be a woman. His life was not like the book he had been reading. It was both more frustrating and stranger.

From the deck of the vessel and onto the harbour wall jumped a large dog. It landed next to him, sat facing him and panted in his eyes. In the book the unnamed narrator had set off on a long journey. Everybody and everything was moving somewhere else, it seemed. Had he finished reading the story he would have reached the point where the narrator leaps off a ship and onto a harbour wall to confront a man who is waiting for someone else. The author belongs to the reader. The reader belongs to the characters. The dog, he now saw with very little surprise, was missing an ear. One large and memorable ear.

RHYS HUGHES was born in 1966 in Wales but has lived in many countries. His first book, *Worming the Harpy*, was published in 1995 and since that time he has had more than fifty books and nine hundred short stories published in ten different languages. His most recent books include *Carrying Women Across Rivers, The Meandering Knight* and *Corybantic Fulgours*. He is currently working on a fantasy novel, *Unevensong*, a collection of science fiction tales, *A Spaceship in the Shape of a Woman*, a volume of short plays, *Trumpet Strudel Mineshafts*, and his first book of essays, *Bullshit with Footnotes*. He cites his main literary influences as Calvino, Barthelme and Vian, but reviewers prefer to compare his work to that of R.A. Lafferty, whom he has never read. A vegetarian most of his life, he delights in coconuts and tropical fruits. He has different coloured eyes and slightly crooked teeth. He enjoys climbing high mountains.

Made in the USA
Las Vegas, NV
13 May 2021

22943785R10154